Our Cast of Characters

Hyacinth Bridgerton: The youngest of the famed Bridgerton siblings, she's a little too smart, a little too outspoken, and certainly not your average romance heroine. She's also, much to her dismay, falling in love with . . .

Gareth St. Clair: There are some men in London with wicked reputations, and there are others who are handsome as sin. But Gareth is the only one who manages to combine the two with such devilish success. He'd be a complete rogue, if not for . . .

Lady Danbury: Grandmother to Gareth, mentor to Hyacinth, she has an opinion on everything, especially love and marriage. And she'd like nothing better than to see Gareth and Hyacinth joined in holy matrimony. Luckily, she's to have help from . . .

One meddling mother, one overprotective brother, one very bad string quartet, one (thankfully fictional) mad baron, and of course, let us not forget the shepherdess, the unicorn, and Henry the Eighth.

Join them all in the most memorable love story of the year . . .

It's In His Kiss by the incomparable Julia Quinn

By Julia Quinn

BECAUSE OF MISS BRIDGERTON

The Bridgerton Series
THE DUKE AND I
THE VISCOUNT WHO LOVED ME
AN OFFER FROM A GENTLEMAN
ROMANCING MR. BRIDGERTON
TO SIR PHILLIP, WITH LOVE
WHEN HE WAS WICKED
IT'S IN HIS KISS
ON THE WAY TO THE WEDDING
THE BRIDGERTONS: HAPPILY EVER AFTER

The Smythe-Smith Quartet
JUST LIKE HEAVEN
A NIGHT LIKE THIS
THE SUM OF ALL KISSES
THE SECRETS OF SIR RICHARD KENWORTHY

The Bevelstoke Series
THE SECRET DIARIES OF MISS MIRANDA CHEEVER
WHAT HAPPENS IN LONDON
TEN THINGS I LOVE ABOUT YOU

Julia Quinn

It's In His Kiss

AVONBOOKS

An Imprint of HarperCollinsPublishers

For Steve Axelrod, for a hundred different reasons.
(But especially the caviar!)

And also for Paul, even though he seems to think
I'm the sort of person who likes to share caviar.

This is a work of fiction. Names, characters, places, and incidents are products of the author's imagination or are used fictitiously and are not to be construed as real. Any resemblance to actual events, locales, organizations, or persons, living or dead, is entirely coincidental.

"It's in His Kiss: The 2nd Epilogue" was originally published as an e-book. "It's in His Kiss: The 2nd Epilogue" copyright © 2006 by Julie Cotler Pottinger.

Meet the Bridgerton family teaser excerpts copyright © 2000, 2001, 2002, 2003, 2004, 2005 by Julie Cotler Pottinger.

First Avon Books mass market printing: April 2017

ISBN 978-0-06-235379-5

Avon Trademark Reg. U.S. Pat. Off. and in Other Countries, Marca Registrada, Hecho en U.S.A.
Avon, Avon Books, and the Avon logo are trademarks of HarperCollins Publishers.
HarperCollins® is a registered trademark of HarperCollins Publishers.

17 18 19 20 21 QGM 10 9 8 7 6 5 4 3 2 1

Acknowledgments

The author wishes to thank
Eloisa James and Alessandro Vettori
for their expertise in all things Italian.

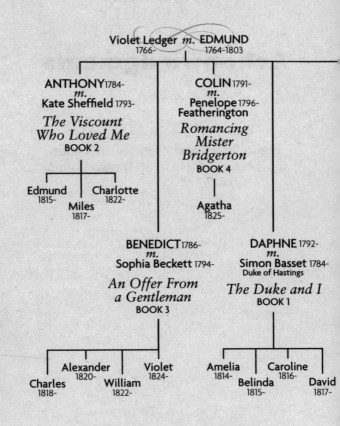

Violet Ledger *m.* EDMUND
1766-   1764-1803

ANTHONY 1784-
m.
Kate Sheffield 1793-

*The Viscount
Who Loved Me*
BOOK 2

Edmund   Charlotte
1815-   1822-
    Miles
    1817-

COLIN 1791-
m.
Penelope 1796-
Featherington

*Romancing
Mister
Bridgerton*
BOOK 4

Agatha
1825-

BENEDICT 1786-
m.
Sophia Beckett 1794-

*An Offer From
a Gentleman*
BOOK 3

Charles   Alexander   Violet
1818-   1820-   1824-
     William
     1822-

DAPHNE 1792-
m.
Simon Basset 1784-
Duke of Hastings

The Duke and I
BOOK 1

Amelia   Caroline
1814-   1816-
   Belinda   David
   1815-   1817-

Bridgerton
FAMILY
TREE

FRANCESCA 1797-
m.1
John Stirling
8th Earl of Kilmartin
1792-1820
m.2
Michael Stirling 1791-
9th Earl of Kilmartin

*When He
Was Wicked*
BOOK 6

HYACINTH
1803-

*It's In
His Kiss*
BOOK 7

featuring

Gareth St. Clair
1797-

ELOISE 1796-
m.2
Sir Phillip Crane 1794-
m.1
Marina Thompson
1794-1823

*To Sir Phillip,
With Love*
BOOK 5

GREGORY
1801-

Oliver
1816-

Amanda
1816-

Penelope
1825-

FOR MORE INFORMATION, PLEASE VISIT WWW.JULIAQUINN.COM

Prologue

1815, ten years before our story begins in earnest . . .

There were four principles governing Gareth St. Clair's relationship with his father that he relied upon to maintain his good humor and general sanity.

One: They did not converse unless absolutely necessary.

Two: All absolutely necessary conversations were to be kept as brief as possible.

Three: In the event that more than the simplest of salutations was to be spoken, it was always best to have a third party present.

And finally, four: For the purpose of achieving points one, two, and three, Gareth was to conduct himself in a manner so as to garner as many invitations as possible to spend school holidays with friends.

In other words, not at home.

In more precise words, away from his father.

All in all, Gareth thought, when he bothered to think about it, which wasn't often now that he had his avoidance tactics down to a science, these principles served him well.

And they served his father just as well, since Richard

St. Clair liked his younger son about as much as his younger son liked him. Which was why, Gareth thought with a frown, he'd been so surprised to be summoned home from school.

And with such force.

His father's missive had held little ambiguity. Gareth was to report to Clair Hall immediately.

It was dashed irritating, this. With only two months left at Eton, his life was in full swing at school, a heady mix of games and studies, and of course the occasional surreptitious foray to the local public house, always late at night, and always involving wine and women.

Gareth's life was exactly as a young man of eighteen years would wish it. And he'd been under the assumption that, as long as he managed to remain out of his father's line of sight, his life at nineteen would be similarly blessed. He was to attend Cambridge in the fall, along with all of his closest friends, where he had every intention of pursuing his studies and social life with equal fervor.

As he glanced around the foyer of Clair Hall, he let out a long sigh that was meant to sound impatient but came out more nervous than anything else. What on earth could the baron—as he had taken to calling his father—want with him? His father had long since announced that he had washed his hands of his younger son and that he was only paying for his education because it was expected of him.

Which everyone knew really meant: It would look bad to their friends and neighbors if Gareth wasn't sent to a proper school.

When Gareth and his father *did* cross paths, the baron

usually spent the entire time going on about what a disappointment the boy was.

Which only made Gareth wish to upset his father even more. Nothing like living down to expectations, after all.

Gareth tapped his foot, feeling rather like a stranger in his own home as he waited for the butler to alert his father as to his arrival. He'd spent so little time here in the last nine years it was difficult to feel much in the way of attachment. To him, it was nothing but a pile of stones that belonged to his father and would eventually go to his elder brother, George. Nothing of the house, and nothing of the St. Clair fortunes would come to Gareth, and he knew that his lot was to make his own way in the world. He supposed he would enter the military after Cambridge; the only other acceptable avenue of vocation was the clergy, and heaven knew he wasn't suited for *that*.

Gareth had few memories of his mother, who had died in an accident when he was five, but even he could recall her tousling his hair and laughing about how he was never serious.

"My little imp, you are," she used to say, followed by a whispered, "Don't lose that. Whatever you do, don't lose it."

He hadn't. And he rather doubted the Church of England would wish to welcome him into their ranks.

"Master Gareth."

Gareth looked up at the sound of the butler's voice. As always, Guilfoyle spoke in flat sentences, never queries.

"Your father will see you now," Guilfoyle intoned. "He is in his study."

Gareth nodded at the aging butler and made his way down the hall toward his father's study, always his least favorite room in the house. It was where his father delivered his lectures, where his father told him he would never amount to anything, where his father icily speculated that he should never have had a second son, that Gareth was nothing but a drain on the family finances and a stain on their honor.

No, Gareth thought as he knocked on the door, no happy memories here.

"Enter!"

Gareth pushed open the heavy oak door and stepped inside. His father was seated behind his desk, scribbling something on a sheet of paper. He looked well, Gareth thought idly. His father always looked well. It would have been easier had he turned into a ruddy caricature of a man, but no, Lord St. Clair was fit and strong and gave the appearance of a man two decades younger than his fifty-odd years.

He looked like the sort of man a boy like Gareth ought to respect.

And it made the pain of rejection all the more cruel.

Gareth waited patiently for his father to look up. When he didn't, he cleared his throat.

No response.

Gareth coughed.

Nothing.

Gareth felt his teeth grinding. This was his father's routine—ignoring him for just long enough to act as a reminder that he found him beneath notice.

Gareth considered saying, "Sir." He considered saying, "My lord." He even considered uttering the word, "Father," but in the end he just slouched against the doorjamb and started to whistle.

His father looked up immediately. "Cease," he snapped.

Gareth quirked a brow and silenced himself.

"And stand up straight. Good God," the baron said testily, "how many times have I told you that whistling is ill-bred?"

Gareth waited a second, then asked, "Am I meant to answer that, or was it a rhetorical question?"

His father's skin reddened.

Gareth swallowed. He shouldn't have said that. He'd known that his deliberately jocular tone would infuriate the baron, but sometimes it was so damned hard to keep his mouth shut. He'd spent years trying to win his father's favor, and he'd finally given in and given up.

And if he took some satisfaction in making the old man as miserable as the old man made him, well, so be it. One had to take one's pleasures where one could.

"I am surprised you're here," his father said.

Gareth blinked in confusion. "You asked me to come," he said. And the miserable truth was—he'd never defied his father. Not really. He poked, he prodded, he added a touch of insolence to his every statement and action, but he had never behaved with out-and-out defiance.

Miserable coward that he was.

In his dreams, he fought back. In his dreams, he told his father exactly what he thought of him, but in reality, his defiance was limited to whistles and sullen looks.

"So I did," his father said, leaning back slightly in his chair. "Nonetheless, I never issue an order with the expectation that you will follow it correctly. You so rarely do."

Gareth said nothing.

His father stood and walked to a nearby table, where

he kept a decanter of brandy. "I imagine you're wondering what this is all about," he said.

Gareth nodded, but his father didn't bother to look at him, so he added, "Yes, sir."

The baron took an appreciative sip of his brandy, leaving Gareth waiting while he visibly savored the amber liquid. Finally, he turned, and with a coolly assessing stare said, "I have finally discovered a way for you to be useful to the St. Clair family."

Gareth's head jerked in surprise. "You have? Sir?"

His father took another drink, then set his glass down. "Indeed." He turned to his son and looked at him directly for the first time during the interview. "You will be getting married."

"Sir?" Gareth said, nearly gagging on the word.

"This summer," Lord St. Clair confirmed.

Gareth grabbed the back of a chair to keep from swerving. He was eighteen, for God's sake. Far too young to marry. And what about Cambridge? Could he even attend as a married man? And where would he put his wife?

And, good God above, *whom* was he supposed to marry?

"It's an excellent match," the baron continued. "The dowry will restore our finances."

"Our finances, sir?" Gareth whispered.

Lord St. Clair's eyes clamped down on his son's. "We're mortgaged to the hilt," he said sharply. "Another year, and we will lose everything that isn't entailed."

"But . . . how?"

"Eton doesn't come cheap," the baron snapped.

No, but surely it wasn't enough to beggar the family, Gareth thought desperately. This couldn't be *all* his fault.

"Disappointment you may be," his father said, "but I

have not shirked my responsibilities to you. You have been educated as a gentleman. You have been given a horse, clothing, and a roof over your head. Now it is time you behaved like a man."

"Who?" Gareth whispered.

"Eh?"

"Who," he said a little louder. Whom was he meant to marry?

"Mary Winthrop," his father said in a matter-of-fact voice.

Gareth felt the blood leave his body. "Mary . . ."

"Wrotham's daughter," his father added.

As if Gareth didn't know that. "But Mary . . ."

"Will be an excellent wife," the baron continued. "Biddable, and you can dump her in the country should you wish to gad about town with your foolish friends."

"But Father, Mary—"

"I accepted on your behalf," his father stated. "It's done. The agreements have been signed."

Gareth fought for air. This couldn't be happening. Surely a man could not be forced into marriage. Not in this day and age.

"Wrotham would like to see it done in July," his father added. "I told him we have no objections."

"But . . . Mary . . ." Gareth gasped. "I can't marry Mary!"

One of his father's bushy brows inched toward his hairline. "You can, and you will."

"But Father, she's . . . she's . . ."

"Simple?" the baron finished for him. He chuckled. "Won't make a difference when she's under you in bed. And you don't have to have anything to do with her otherwise." He walked toward his son until they were uncomfortably close. "All you need to do is show up at the church. Do you understand?"

Gareth said nothing. He didn't *do* much of anything, either. It was all he could manage just to breathe.

He'd known Mary Winthrop his entire life. She was a year his elder, and their families' estates had bordered on one another's for over a century. They'd been playmates as young children, but it soon became apparent that Mary wasn't quite right in the head. Gareth had remained her champion whenever he was in the district; he'd bloodied more than one bully who had thought to call her names or take advantage of her sweet and unassuming nature.

But he couldn't *marry* her. She was like a child. It had to be a sin. And even if it wasn't, he could never stomach it. How could she possibly understand what was meant to transpire between them as man and wife?

He could never bed her. Never.

Gareth just stared at his father, words failing him. For the first time in his life, he had no easy reply, no flip retort.

There were no words. Simply no words for such a moment.

"I see we understand each other," the baron said, smiling at his son's silence.

"No!" Gareth burst out, the single syllable ripping itself from his throat. "No! I can't!"

His father's eyes narrowed. "You'll be there if I have to tie you up."

"No!" He felt like he was choking, but somehow he got the words out. "Father, Mary is . . . Well, she's a child. She'll never be more than a child. You know that. I can't marry her. It would be a sin."

The baron chuckled, breaking the tension as he turned swiftly away. "Are you trying to convince me that you, of all people, have suddenly found religion?"

"No, but—"

"There is nothing to discuss," his father cut in. "Wrotham has been extremely generous with the dowry. God knows he has to be, trying to unload an idiot."

"Don't speak of her that way," Gareth whispered. He might not want to marry Mary Winthrop, but he'd known her all his life, and she did not deserve such talk.

"It is the best you will ever do," Lord St. Clair said. "The best you will ever have. Wrotham's settlement is extraordinarily generous, and I will arrange for an allowance that will keep you comfortable for life."

"An allowance," Gareth echoed dully.

His father let out one short chuckle. "Don't think I would trust you with a lump sum," he said. "You?"

Gareth swallowed uncomfortably. "What about school?" he whispered.

"You can still attend," his father said. "In fact, you have your new bride to thank for that. Wouldn't have had the blunt to send you without the marriage settlement."

Gareth stood there, trying to force his breathing into something that felt remotely even and normal. His father knew how much it meant to him to attend Cambridge. It was the one thing upon which the two of them agreed: A gentleman needed a gentleman's education. It didn't matter that Gareth craved the entire experience, both social and academic, whereas Lord St. Clair saw it merely as something a man had to do to keep up appearances. It had been decided upon for years—Gareth would attend and receive his degree.

But now it seemed that Lord St. Clair had known that he could not pay for his younger son's education. When had he planned to tell him? As Gareth was packing his bags?

"It's done, Gareth," his father said sharply. "And it has to be you. George is the heir, and I can't have him sullying the bloodlines. Besides," he added with pursed lips, "I wouldn't subject him to this, anyway."

"But you would me?" Gareth whispered. Was this how much his father hated him? How little he thought of him? He looked up at his father, at the face that had brought him so much unhappiness. There had never been a smile, never an encouraging word. Never a—

"Why?" Gareth heard himself saying, the word sounding like a wounded animal, pathetic and plaintive. "Why?" he said again.

His father said nothing, just stood there, gripping the edge of his desk until his knuckles grew white. And Gareth could do nothing but stare, somehow transfixed by the ordinary sight of his father's hands. "I'm your son," he whispered, still unable to move his gaze from his father's hands to his face. "Your son. How could you do this to your own son?"

And then his father, who was the master of the cutting retort, whose anger always came dressed in ice rather than fire, exploded. His hands flew from the table, and his voice roared through the room like a demon.

"By God, how could you not have figured it out by now? You are not my son! You have never been my son! You are nothing but a by-blow, some mangy whelp your mother got off another man while I was away."

Rage poured forth like some hot, desperate thing, too long held captive and repressed. It hit Gareth like a wave, swirling around him, squeezing and choking until he could barely breathe. "No," he said, desperately shaking his head. It was nothing he hadn't considered, nothing he hadn't even hoped for, but it couldn't be true. He *looked* like his father. They had the same nose, didn't they? And—

"I have fed you," the baron said, his voice low and hard. "I have clothed you and presented you to the world as my son. I have supported you when another man would have tossed you into the street, and it is well past time that you returned the favor."

"No," Gareth said again. "It can't be. I look like you. I—"

For a moment Lord St. Clair remained silent. Then he said, bitterly, "An unhappy coincidence, I assure you."

"But—"

"I could have turned you out at your birth," Lord St. Clair cut in, "sent your mother packing, tossed you both into the street. But I did not." He closed the distance between them and put his face very close to Gareth's. "You have been acknowledged, and you are legitimate." And then, in a voice furious and low: "You owe me."

"No," Gareth said, his voice finally finding the conviction he was going to need to last him through the rest of his days. "No. I won't do it."

"I will cut you off," the baron warned. "You won't see another penny from me. You can forget your dreams of Cambridge, your—"

"No," Gareth said again, and he sounded different. He felt changed. This was the end, he realized. The end of his childhood, the end of his innocence, and the beginning of—

God only knew what it was the beginning of.

"I am through with you," his father—no, not his father—hissed. "Through."

"So be it," Gareth said.

And he walked away.

Chapter 1

Ten years have passed, and we meet our heroine, who, it must be said, has never been known as a shy and retiring flower. The scene is the annual Smythe-Smith musicale, about ten minutes before Mr. Mozart begins to rotate in his grave.

"Why do we do this to ourselves?" Hyacinth Bridgerton wondered aloud.

"Because we are good, kind people," her sister-in-law replied, sitting in—God help them—a front-row seat.

"One would think," Hyacinth persisted, regarding the empty chair next to Penelope with the same excitement she might show a sea urchin, "that we would have learned our lesson last year. Or perhaps the year before that. Or maybe even—"

"Hyacinth?" Penelope said.

Hyacinth swung her gaze to Penelope, lifting one brow in question.

"Sit."

Hyacinth sighed. But she sat.

The Smythe-Smith musicale. Thankfully, it came

around just once per year, because Hyacinth was quite certain it would take a full twelve months for her ears to recover.

Hyacinth let out another sigh, this one louder than the last. "I'm not entirely certain that I'm either good or kind."

"I'm not certain, either," Penelope said, "but I have decided to have faith in you nevertheless."

"Rather sporting of you," Hyacinth said.

"I thought so."

Hyacinth glanced at her sideways. "Of course you did not have any choice in the matter."

Penelope turned in her seat, her eyes narrowing. "Meaning?"

"Colin refused to accompany you, didn't he?" Hyacinth said with a sly look. Colin was Hyacinth's brother, and he'd married Penelope a year earlier.

Penelope clamped her mouth into a firm line.

"I do love it when I am right," Hyacinth said triumphantly. "Which is fortunate, since I so often am."

Penelope just looked at her. "You do know that you are insufferable."

"Of course." Hyacinth leaned toward Penelope with a devilish smile. "But you love me, anyway, admit it."

"I admit nothing until the end of the evening."

"After we have both gone deaf?"

"After we see if you behave yourself."

Hyacinth laughed. "You married into the family. You have to love me. It's a contractual obligation."

"Funny how I don't recall that in the wedding vows."

"Funny," Hyacinth returned, "I remember it perfectly."

Penelope looked at her and laughed. "I don't know

how you do it, Hyacinth," she said, "but exasperating as you are, you somehow always manage to be charming."

"It's my greatest gift," Hyacinth said demurely.

"Well, you do receive extra points for coming with me tonight," Penelope said, patting her on the hand.

"Of course," Hyacinth replied. "For all my insufferable ways, I am in truth the soul of kindness and amiability." And she'd have to be, she thought, as she watched the scene unfolding on the small, makeshift stage. Another year, another Smythe-Smith musicale. Another opportunity to learn just how many ways one could ruin a perfectly good piece of music. Every year Hyacinth swore she wouldn't attend, then every year she somehow found herself at the event, smiling encouragingly at the four girls on the stage.

"At least last year I got to sit in the back," Hyacinth said.

"Yes, you did," Penelope replied, turning on her with suspicious eyes. "How did you manage that? Felicity, Eloise, and I were all up front."

Hyacinth shrugged. "A well-timed visit to the ladies' retiring room. In fact—"

"Don't you dare try that tonight," Penelope warned. "If you leave me up here by myself . . ."

"Don't worry," Hyacinth said with a sigh. "I am here for the duration. But," she added, pointing her finger in what her mother would surely have termed a most unladylike manner, "I want my devotion to you to be duly noted."

"Why is it," Penelope asked, "that I am left with the feeling that you are keeping score of something, and when I least expect it, you will jump out in front of me, demanding a favor?"

Hyacinth looked at her and blinked. "Why would I need to jump?"

"Ah, look," Penelope said, after staring at her sister-in-law as if she were a lunatic, "here comes Lady Danbury."

"Mrs. Bridgerton," Lady Danbury said, or rather barked. "Miss Bridgerton."

"Good evening, Lady Danbury," Penelope said to the elderly countess. "We saved you a seat right in front."

Lady D narrowed her eyes and poked Penelope lightly in the ankle with her cane. "Always thinking of others, aren't you?"

"Of course," Penelope demurred. "I wouldn't dream of—"

"Ha," Lady Danbury said.

It was, Hyacinth reflected, the countess's favorite syllable. That and *hmmmph*.

"Move over, Hyacinth," Lady D ordered. "I'll sit between you."

Hyacinth obediently moved one chair to the left. "We were just pondering our reasons for attending," she said as Lady Danbury settled into her seat. "I for one have come up blank."

"I can't speak for you," Lady D said to Hyacinth, "but *she*"—at this she jerked her head toward Penelope—"is here for the same reason I am."

"For the music?" Hyacinth queried, perhaps a little too politely.

Lady Danbury turned back to Hyacinth, her face creasing into what might have been a smile. "I've always liked you, Hyacinth Bridgerton."

"I've always liked you, too," Hyacinth replied.

"I expect it is because you come and read to me from time to time," Lady Danbury said.

"Every week," Hyacinth reminded her.

"Time to time, every week . . . pfft." Lady Danbury's hand cut a dismissive wave through the air. "It's all the same if you're not making it a daily endeavor."

Hyacinth judged it best not to speak. Lady D would surely find some way to twist her words into a promise to visit every afternoon.

"And I might add," Lady D said with a sniff, "that you were most unkind last week, leaving off with poor Priscilla hanging from a cliff."

"What are you reading?" Penelope asked.

"*Miss Butterworth and the Mad Baron,*" Hyacinth replied. "And she wasn't hanging. Yet."

"Did you read ahead?" Lady D demanded.

"No," Hyacinth said with a roll of her eyes. "But it's not difficult to forecast. Miss Butterworth has already hung from a building and a tree."

"And she's still living?" Penelope asked.

"I said hung, not hanged," Hyacinth muttered. "More's the pity."

"Regardless," Lady Danbury cut in, "it was most unkind of you to leave *me* hanging."

"It's where the author ended the chapter," Hyacinth said unrepentantly, "and besides, isn't patience a virtue?"

"Absolutely not," Lady Danbury said emphatically, "and if you think so, you're less of a woman than I thought."

No one understood why Hyacinth visited Lady Danbury every Tuesday and read to her, but she enjoyed her afternoons with the countess. Lady Danbury was crotchety and honest to a fault, and Hyacinth adored her.

"The two of you together are a menace," Penelope remarked.

"My aim in life," Lady Danbury announced, "is to be a menace to as great a number of people as possible, so I shall take that as the highest of compliments, Mrs. Bridgerton."

"Why is it," Penelope wondered, "that you only call me Mrs. Bridgerton when you are opining in a grand fashion?"

"Sounds better that way," Lady D said, punctuating her remark with a loud thump of her cane.

Hyacinth grinned. When she was old, she wanted to be exactly like Lady Danbury. Truth be told, she liked the elderly countess better than most of the people she knew her own age. After three seasons on the marriage mart, Hyacinth was growing just a little bit weary of the same people day after day. What had once been exhilarating—the balls, the parties, the suitors—well, it was still enjoyable—that much she had to concede. Hyacinth certainly wasn't one of those girls who complained about all of the wealth and privilege she was forced to endure.

But it wasn't the same. She no longer held her breath each time she entered a ballroom. And a dance was now simply a dance, no longer the magical swirl of movement it had been in years gone past.

The excitement, she realized, was gone.

Unfortunately, every time she mentioned this to her mother, the reply was simply to find herself a husband. That, Violet Bridgerton took great pains to point out, would change everything.

Indeed.

Hyacinth's mother had long since given up any pretense of subtlety when it came to the unmarried state of her fourth and final daughter. It had, Hyacinth thought grimly, turned into a personal crusade.

Forget Joan of Arc. Her mother was Violet of Mayfair, and neither plague nor pestilence nor perfidious paramour would stop her in her quest to see all eight of her children happily married. There were only two remaining, Gregory and Hyacinth, but Gregory was still just twenty-four, which was (rather unfairly, in Hyacinth's opinion) considered a perfectly acceptable age for a gentleman to remain a bachelor.

But Hyacinth at twenty-two? The only thing staving off her mother's complete collapse was the fact that her elder sister Eloise had waited until the grand old age of twenty-eight before finally becoming a bride. By comparison, Hyacinth was practically in leading strings.

No one could say that Hyacinth was hopelessly on the shelf, but even she had to admit that she was edging toward that position. She had received a few proposals since her debut three years earlier, but not as many as one would think, given her looks—not the prettiest girl in town but certainly better than at least half—and her fortune—again, not the largest dowry on the market, but certainly enough to make a fortune hunter look twice.

And her connections were, of course, nothing short of impeccable. Her brother was, as their father had been before him, the Viscount Bridgerton, and while theirs might not have been the loftiest title in the land, the family was immensely popular and influential. And if that weren't enough, her sister Daphne was the Duchess of Hastings, and her sister Francesca was the Countess of Kilmartin.

If a man wanted to align himself with the most powerful families in Britain, he could do a lot worse than Hyacinth Bridgerton.

But if one took the time to reflect upon the timing of the proposals she had received, which Hyacinth didn't care to admit that she had, it was starting to look damning indeed.

Three proposals her first season.

Two her second.

One last year.

And none thus far this time around.

It could only be argued that she was growing less popular. Unless, of course, someone was foolish enough actually to *make* the argument, in which case Hyacinth would have to take the other side, facts and logic notwithstanding.

And she'd probably win the point, too. It was a rare man—or woman—who could outwit, outspeak, or outdebate Hyacinth Bridgerton.

This might, she'd thought in a rare moment of self-reflection, have something to do with why her rate of proposals was declining at such an alarming pace.

No matter, she thought, watching the Smythe-Smith girls mill about on the small dais that had been erected at the front of the room. It wasn't as if she should have accepted any of her six proposals. Three had been fortune hunters, two had been fools, and one had been quite terminally boring.

Better to remain unmarried than shackle herself to someone who'd bore her to tears. Even her mother, inveterate matchmaker that she was, couldn't argue that point.

And as for her current proposal-free season—well, if

the gentlemen of Britain couldn't appreciate the inherent value of an intelligent female who knew her own mind, that was their problem, not hers.

Lady Danbury thumped her cane against the floor, narrowly missing Hyacinth's right foot. "I say," she said, "have either of you caught sight of my grandson?"

"Which grandson?" Hyacinth asked.

"Which grandson," Lady D echoed impatiently. "Which grandson? The only one I like, that's which."

Hyacinth didn't even bother to hide her shock. "Mr. St. Clair is coming tonight?"

"I know, I know," Lady D cackled. "I can hardly believe it myself. I keep waiting for a shaft of heavenly light to burst through the ceiling."

Penelope's nose crinkled. "I think that might be blasphemous, but I'm not sure."

"It's not," Hyacinth said, without even looking at her. "And why is he coming?"

Lady Danbury smiled slowly. Like a snake. "Why are you so interested?"

"I'm *always* interested in gossip," Hyacinth said quite candidly. "About anyone. You should know that already."

"Very well," Lady D said, somewhat grumpily after having been thwarted. "He's coming because I blackmailed him."

Hyacinth and Penelope regarded her with identically arched brows.

"Very well," Lady Danbury conceded, "if not blackmail, then a heavy dose of guilt."

"Of course," Penelope murmured, at the exact time Hyacinth said, "*That* makes much more sense."

Lady D sighed. "I might have told him I wasn't feeling well."

Hyacinth was dubious. "*Might* have?"

"Did," Lady D admitted.

"You must have done a very good job of it to get him to come tonight," Hyacinth said admiringly. One had to appreciate Lady Danbury's sense of the dramatic, especially when it resulted in such impressive manipulation of the people around her. It was a talent Hyacinth cultivated as well.

"I don't think I have ever seen him at a musicale before," Penelope remarked.

"Hmmmph," Lady D grunted. "Not enough loose women for him, I'm sure."

From anyone else, it would have been a shocking statement. But this was Lady Danbury, and Hyacinth (and the rest of the *ton* for that matter) had long since grown used to her rather startling turns of phrase.

And besides, one did have to consider the man in question.

Lady Danbury's grandson was none other than the notorious Gareth St. Clair. Although it probably wasn't entirely his fault that he had gained such a wicked reputation, Hyacinth reflected. There were plenty of other men who behaved with equal lack of propriety, and more than a few who were as handsome as sin, but Gareth St. Clair was the only one who managed to combine the two to such success.

But his reputation was abominable.

He was certainly of marriageable age, but he'd never, not even once, called upon a proper young lady at her home. Hyacinth was quite sure of *that*; if he'd ever even hinted at courting someone, the rumor mills would have run rampant. And furthermore, Hyacinth would have heard it from Lady Danbury, who loved gossip even more than she did.

And then, of course, there was the matter of his father, Lord St. Clair. They were rather famously estranged, although no one knew why. Hyacinth personally thought it spoke well of Gareth that he did not air his familial travails in public—especially since she'd met his father and thought him a boor, which led her to believe that whatever the matter was, the younger St. Clair was not at fault.

But the entire affair lent an air of mystery to the already charismatic man, and in Hyacinth's opinion made him a bit of a challenge to the ladies of the *ton*. No one seemed quite certain how to view him. On the one hand, the matrons steered their daughters away; surely a connection with Gareth St. Clair could not enhance a girl's reputation. On the other hand, his brother had died tragically young, almost a year earlier, and now he was the heir to the barony. Which had only served to make him a more romantic—and eligible—figure. Last month Hyacinth had seen a girl swoon—or at least pretend to—when he had deigned to attend the Bevelstoke Ball.

It had been appalling.

Hyacinth had *tried* to tell the foolish chit that he was only there because his grandmother had forced him into it, and of course because his father was out of town. After all, everyone knew that he only consorted with opera singers and actresses, and certainly not any of the ladies he might meet at the Bevelstoke Ball. But the girl would not be swayed from her overemotional state, and eventually she had collapsed onto a nearby settee in a suspiciously graceful heap.

Hyacinth had been the first to locate a vinaigrette and shove it under her nose. Really, some behavior just couldn't be tolerated.

But as she stood there, reviving the foolish chit with the noxious fumes, she had caught sight of him staring at her in that vaguely mocking way of his, and she couldn't shake the feeling that he found her amusing.

Much in the same way she found small children and large dogs amusing.

Needless to say, she hadn't felt particularly complimented by his attention, fleeting though it was.

"Hmmph."

Hyacinth turned to face Lady Danbury, who was still searching the room for her grandson. "I don't think he's here yet," Hyacinth said, then added under her breath, "No one's fainted."

"Enh? What was that?"

"I said I don't think he's here yet."

Lady D narrowed her eyes. "I heard that part."

"It's all I said," Hyacinth fibbed.

"Liar."

Hyacinth looked past her to Penelope. "She treats me quite abominably, did you know that?"

Penelope shrugged. "Someone has to."

Lady Danbury's face broke out into a wide grin, and she turned to Penelope, and said, "Now then, I must ask—" She looked over at the stage, craning her neck as she squinted at the quartet. "Is it the same girl on cello this year?"

Penelope nodded sadly.

Hyacinth looked at them. "What are you talking about?"

"If you don't know," Lady Danbury said loftily, "then you haven't been paying attention, and shame on you for that."

Hyacinth's mouth fell open. "Well," she said, since the alternative was to say nothing, and she never liked to do *that*. There was nothing more irritating than being left out of a joke. Except, perhaps, being scolded for something one didn't even understand. She turned back to the stage, watching the cellist more closely. Seeing nothing out of the ordinary, she twisted again to face her companions and opened her mouth to speak, but they were already deep in a conversation that did not include her.

She hated when that happened.

"Hmmmph." Hyacinth sat back in her chair and did it again. "Hmmmph."

"You sound," came an amused voice from over her shoulder, "exactly like my grandmother."

Hyacinth looked up. There he was, Gareth St. Clair, inevitably at the moment of her greatest discomfiture. And, of course, the only empty seat was next to her.

"Doesn't she, though?" Lady Danbury asked, looking up at her grandson as she thumped her cane against the floor. "She's quickly replacing you as my pride and joy."

"Tell me, Miss Bridgerton," Mr. St. Clair asked, one corner of his lips curving into a mocking half smile, "is my grandmother remaking you in her image?"

Hyacinth had no ready retort, which she found profoundly irritating.

"Move over again, Hyacinth," Lady D barked. "I need to sit next to Gareth."

Hyacinth turned to say something, but Lady Danbury cut in with, "Someone needs to make sure he behaves."

Hyacinth let out a noisy exhale and moved over another seat.

"There you go, my boy," Lady D said, patting the empty chair with obvious glee. "Sit and enjoy."

He looked at her for a long moment before finally saying, "You owe me for this, Grandmother."

"Ha!" was her response. "Without me, you wouldn't exist."

"A difficult point to refute," Hyacinth murmured.

Mr. St. Clair turned to look at her, probably only because it enabled him to turn away from his grandmother. Hyacinth smiled at him blandly, pleased with herself for showing no reaction.

He'd always reminded her of a lion, fierce and predatory, filled with restless energy. His hair, too, was tawny, hovering in that curious state between light brown and dark blond, and he wore it rakishly, defying convention by keeping it just long enough to tie in a short queue at the back of his neck. He was tall, although not overly so, with an athlete's grace and strength and a face that was just imperfect enough to be handsome, rather than pretty.

And his eyes were blue. Really blue. Uncomfortably blue.

Uncomfortably blue? She gave her head a little shake. That had to be quite the most asinine thought that had ever entered her head. Her own eyes were blue, and there was certainly nothing uncomfortable about *that*.

"And what brings you here, Miss Bridgerton?" he asked. "I hadn't realized you were such a lover of music."

"If she loved music," Lady D said from behind him, "she'd have already fled to France."

"She does hate to be left out of a conversation, doesn't she?" he murmured, without turning around. "Ow!"

"Cane?" Hyacinth asked sweetly.

"She's a threat to society," he muttered.

Hyacinth watched with interest as he reached behind him, and without even turning his head, wrapped his hand around the cane and wrenched it from his grandmother's grasp. "Here," he said, handing it to her, "you will look after this, won't you? She won't need it while she's sitting down."

Hyacinth's mouth fell open. Even she had never dared to interfere with Lady Danbury's cane.

"I see that I have finally impressed you," he said, sitting back in his chair with the expression of one who is quite pleased with himself.

"Yes," Hyacinth said before she could stop herself. "I mean, no. I mean, don't be silly. I certainly haven't been *not* impressed by you."

"How gratifying," he murmured.

"What I meant," she said, grinding her teeth together, "was that I haven't really thought about it one way or the other."

He tapped his heart with his hand. "Wounded," he said flippantly. "And right through the heart."

Hyacinth gritted her teeth. The only thing worse than being made fun of was not being sure if one was being made fun of. Everyone else in London she could read like a book. But with Gareth St. Clair, she simply never knew. She glanced past him to see if Penelope was listening—

not that she was sure why that mattered one way or another—but Pen was busy placating Lady Danbury, who was still smarting over the loss of her cane.

Hyacinth fidgeted in her seat, feeling uncommonly closed-in. Lord Somershall—never the slenderest man in the room—was on her left, spilling onto her chair. Which only forced her to scoot a little to the right, which of course put her in even closer proximity to Gareth St. Clair, who was positively radiating heat.

Good God, had the man smothered himself in hot-water bottles before setting out for the evening?

Hyacinth picked up her program as discreetly as she was able and used it to fan herself.

"Is something amiss, Miss Bridgerton?" he inquired, tilting his head as he regarded her with curious amusement.

"Of course not," she answered. "It's merely a touch warm in here, don't you think?"

He eyed her for one second longer than she would have liked, then turned to Lady Danbury. "Are you overheated, Grandmother?" he asked solicitously.

"Not at all," came the brisk reply.

He turned back to Hyacinth with a tiny shrug. "It must be you," he murmured.

"It must," she ground out, facing determinedly forward. Maybe there still was time to escape to the ladies' retiring room. Penelope would want to have her drawn and quartered, but did it really count as abandonment when there were two people seated between them? Besides, she could surely use Lord Somershall as an excuse. Even now he was shifting in his seat, bumping up against her in a way that Hyacinth wasn't entirely certain was accidental.

Hyacinth shifted slightly to the right. Just an inch—not

even. The last thing she wanted was to be pressed up against Gareth St. Clair. Well, the second-to-last, anyway. Lord Somershall's portly frame was decidedly worse.

"Is something amiss, Miss Bridgerton?" Mr. St. Clair inquired.

She shook her head, getting ready to push herself up by planting the heels of her hands on the chair on either side of her lap. She couldn't—

Clap.

Clap clap clap.

Hyacinth nearly groaned. It was one of the Ladies Smythe-Smith, signaling that the concert was about to begin. She'd lost her moment of opportunity. There was no way she could depart politely now.

But at least she could take some solace in the fact that she wasn't the only miserable soul. Just as the Misses Smythe-Smith lifted their bows to strike their instruments, she heard Mr. St. Clair let out a very quiet groan, followed by a heartfelt, "God help us all."

Chapter 2

Thirty minutes later, and somewhere not too far away, a small dog is howling in agony. Unfortunately, no one can hear him over the din . . .

 There was only one person in the world for whom Gareth would sit politely and listen to really bad music, and Grandmother Danbury happened to be it.

"Never again," he whispered in her ear, as something that might have been Mozart assaulted his ears. This, after something that might have been Haydn, which had followed something that might have been Handel.

"You're not sitting politely," she whispered back.

"We could have sat in the back," he grumbled.

"And missed all the fun?"

How anyone could term a Smythe-Smith musicale fun was beyond him, but his grandmother had what could only be termed a morbid love for the annual affair.

As usual, four Smythe-Smith girls were seated on a small dais, two with violins, one with a cello, and one at a pianoforte, and the noise they were making was so discordant as to be almost impressive.

Almost.

"It's a good thing I love you," he said over his shoulder.

"Ha," came her reply, no less truculent for its whispered tone. "It's a good thing I love *you*."

And then—thank God—it was over, and the girls were nodding and making their curtsies, three of them looking quite pleased with themselves, and one—the one on the cello—looking as if she might like to hurl herself through a window.

Gareth turned when he heard his grandmother sigh. She was shaking her head and looking uncharacteristically sympathetic.

The Smythe-Smith girls were notorious in London, and each performance was somehow, inexplicably, worse than the last. Just when one thought there was no possible way to make a deeper mockery of Mozart, a new set of Smythe-Smith cousins appeared on the scene, and proved that yes, it could be done.

But they were nice girls, or so he'd been told, and his grandmother, in one of her rare fits of unabashed kindness, insisted that someone had to sit in the front row and clap, because, as she put it, "Three of them couldn't tell an elephant from a flute, but there's always one who is ready to melt in misery."

And apparently Grandmother Danbury, who thought nothing of telling a duke that he hadn't the sense of a gnat, found it vitally important to clap for the one Smythe-Smith girl in each generation whose ear wasn't made of tin.

They all stood to applaud, although he suspected his grandmother did so only to have an excuse to retrieve her cane, which Hyacinth Bridgerton had handed over with no protest whatsoever.

"Traitor," he'd murmured over his shoulder.

"They're your toes," she'd replied.

He cracked a smile, despite himself. He had never met anyone quite like Hyacinth Bridgerton. She was vaguely amusing, vaguely annoying, but one couldn't quite help but admire her wit.

Hyacinth Bridgerton, he reflected, had an interesting and unique reputation among London socialites. She was the youngest of the Bridgerton siblings, famously named in alphabetical order, A-H. And she was, in theory at least and for those who cared about such things, considered a rather good catch for matrimony. She had never been involved, even tangentially, in a scandal, and her family and connections were beyond compare. She was quite pretty, in wholesome, unexotic way, with thick, chestnut hair and blue eyes that did little to hide her shrewdness. And perhaps most importantly, Gareth thought with a touch of the cynic, it was whispered that her eldest brother, Lord Bridgerton, had increased her dowry last year, after Hyacinth had completed her third London season without an acceptable proposal of marriage.

But when he had inquired about her—not, of course because he was interested; rather he had wanted to learn more about this young lady who seemed to enjoy spending a great deal of time with his grandmother—his friends had all shuddered.

"Hyacinth Bridgerton?" one had echoed. "Surely not to marry? You must be mad."

Another had called her terrifying.

No one actually seemed to dislike her—there was a certain charm to her that kept her in everyone's good graces—but the consensus was that she was best in small doses. "Men don't like women who are more intelligent than they are," one of his shrewder friends had commented, "and Hyacinth Bridgerton isn't the sort to feign stupidity."

She was, Gareth had thought on more than one occasion, a younger version of his grandmother. And while there was no one in the world he adored more than Grandmother Danbury, as far as he was concerned, the world needed only one of her.

"Aren't you glad you came?" the elderly lady in question asked, her voice carrying quite well over the applause.

No one ever clapped as loudly as the Smythe-Smith audience. They were always so glad that it was over.

"Never again," Gareth said firmly.

"Of course not," his grandmother said, with just the right touch of condescension to show that she was lying through her teeth.

He turned and looked her squarely in the eye. "You will have to find someone else to accompany you next year."

"I wouldn't dream of asking you again," Grandmother Danbury said.

"You're lying."

"What a terrible thing to say to your beloved grandmother." She leaned slightly forward. "How did you know?"

He glanced at the cane, dormant in her hand. "You haven't waved that thing through the air once since you tricked Miss Bridgerton into returning it," he said.

"Nonsense," she said. "Miss Bridgerton is too sharp to be tricked, aren't you, Hyacinth?"

Hyacinth shifted forward so that she could see past him to the countess. "I beg your pardon?"

"Just say yes," Grandmother Danbury said. "It will vex him."

"Yes, of course, then," she said, smiling.

"And," his grandmother continued, as if that entire ridiculous exchange had not taken place, "I'll have you know that I am the soul of discretion when it comes to my cane."

Gareth gave her a look. "It's a wonder I still have my feet."

"It's a wonder you still have your ears, my dear boy," she said with lofty disdain.

"I will take that away again," he warned.

"No you won't," she replied with a cackle. "I'm leaving with Penelope to find a glass of lemonade. You keep Hyacinth company."

He watched her go, then turned back to Hyacinth, who was glancing about the room with slightly narrowed eyes.

"Who are you looking for?" he asked.

"No one in particular. Just examining the scene."

He looked at her curiously. "Do you always sound like a detective?"

"Only when it suits me," she said with a shrug. "I like to know what is going on."

"And is anything 'going on'?" he queried.

"No." Her eyes narrowed again as she watched two people in a heated discussion in the far corner. "But you never know."

He fought the urge to shake his head. She was the *strangest* woman. He glanced at the stage. "Are we safe?"

She finally turned back, her blue eyes meeting his with uncommon directness. "Do you mean is it over?"

"Yes."

Her brow furrowed, and in that moment Gareth realized that she had the lightest smattering of freckles on her nose. "I think so," she said. "I've never known them to hold an intermission before."

"Thank God," he said, with great feeling. "Why do they do it?"

"The Smythe-Smiths, you mean?"

"Yes."

For a moment she remained silent, then she just shook her head, and said, "I don't know. One would think . . ."

Whatever she'd been about to say, she thought the better of it. "Never mind," she said.

"Tell me," he urged, rather surprised by how curious he was.

"It was nothing," she said. "Just that one would think that someone would have told them by now. But actually . . ." She glanced around the room. "The audience has grown smaller in recent years. Only the kindhearted remain."

"And do you include yourself among those ranks, Miss Bridgerton?"

She looked up at him with those intensely blue eyes. "I wouldn't have thought to describe myself as such, but yes, I suppose I am. Your grandmother, too, although she would deny it to her dying breath."

Gareth felt himself laugh as he watched his grandmother poke the Duke of Ashbourne in the leg with her cane. "Yes, she would, wouldn't she?"

His maternal grandmother was, since the death of his brother George, the only person left in the world he truly loved. After his father had booted him out, he'd made his way to Danbury House in Surrey and told her what had transpired. Minus the bit about his bastardy, of course.

Gareth had always suspected that Lady Danbury would have stood up and cheered if she knew he wasn't really a St. Clair. She'd never liked her son-in-law, and in fact routinely referred to him as "that pompous idiot." But the truth would reveal his mother—Lady Danbury's youngest daughter—as an adulteress, and he hadn't wanted to dishonor her in that way.

And strangely enough, his father—funny how he still called him that, even after all these years—had never publicly denounced him. This had not surprised Gareth at first. Lord St. Clair was a proud man, and he certainly would not relish revealing himself as a cuckold. Plus, he probably still hoped that he might eventually rein Gareth in and bend him to his will. Maybe even get him to marry Mary Winthrop and restore the St. Clair family coffers.

But George had contracted some sort of wasting disease at the age of twenty-seven, and by thirty he was dead.

Without a son.

Which had made Gareth the St. Clair heir. And left him, quite simply, stuck. For the past eleven months, it seemed he had done nothing but wait. Sooner or later, his father was going to announce to all who would listen that Gareth wasn't really his son. Surely the baron, whose third-favorite pastime (after hunting and raising hounds) was tracing the St. Clair family tree back to the Plantagenets, would not countenance his title going to a bastard of uncertain blood.

Gareth was fairly certain that the only way the baron could remove him as his heir would be to haul him, and a pack of witnesses as well, before the Committee for Privileges in the House of Lords. It would be a messy, detestable affair, and it probably wouldn't work, either. The baron had been married to Gareth's mother when she had given birth, and that rendered Gareth legitimate in the eyes of the law, regardless of his bloodlines.

But it would cause a huge scandal and quite possibly ruin Gareth in the eyes of society. There were plenty of aristocrats running about who got their blood and their names from two different men, but the *ton* didn't like to talk about it. Not publicly, anyway.

But thus far, his father had said nothing.

Half the time Gareth wondered if the baron kept his silence just to torture him.

Gareth glanced across the room at his grandmother, who was accepting a glass of lemonade from Penelope Bridgerton, whom she'd somehow coerced into waiting on her hand and foot. Agatha, Lady Danbury, was most usually described as crotchety, and that was by the people who held her in some affection. She was a lioness among the *ton*, fearless in her words and willing to poke fun at the most august of personages, and even, occasionally, herself. But for all her acerbic ways, she was famously loyal to the ones she loved, and Gareth knew he ranked at the top of that list.

When he'd gone to her and told her that his father had turned him out, she had been livid, but she had never attempted to use her power as a countess to force Lord St. Clair to take back his son.

"Ha!" his grandmother had said. "I'd rather keep you myself."

And she had. She'd paid Gareth's expenses at Cambridge, and when he'd graduated (not with a first, but he had acquitted himself well), she had informed him that his mother had left him a small bequest. Gareth hadn't been aware that she'd had any money of her own, but Lady Danbury had just twisted her lips and said, "Do you really think I'd let that idiot have complete control of her money? I wrote the marriage settlement, you know."

Gareth didn't doubt it for an instant.

His inheritance gave him a small income, which funded a very small suite of apartments, and Gareth was able to support himself. Not lavishly, but well enough to make him feel he wasn't a complete wastrel, which, he was surprised to realize, mattered more to him than he would have thought.

This uncharacteristic sense of responsibility was probably a good thing, too, since when he did assume the St. Clair title, he was going to inherit a mountain of debt along with it. The baron had obviously been lying when he'd told Gareth that they would lose everything that wasn't entailed if he didn't marry Mary Winthrop, but still, it was clear that the St. Clair fortune was meager at best. Furthermore, Lord St. Clair didn't appear to be managing the family finances any better than he had when he'd tried to force Gareth into marriage. If anything, he seemed to be systematically running the estates into the ground.

It was the one thing that made Gareth wonder if perhaps the baron *didn't* intend to denounce him. Surely the ultimate revenge would be to leave his false son riddled with debt.

And Gareth knew—with every fiber of his being he knew—that the baron wished him no happiness. Gareth didn't bother with most *ton* functions, but London wasn't such a large city, socially speaking, and he couldn't always manage to avoid his father completely. And Lord St. Clair never made any effort to hide his enmity.

As for Gareth—well, he wasn't much better at keeping his feelings to himself. He always seemed to slip into his old ways, doing something deliberately provoking, just to make the baron angry. The last time they'd found themselves in each other's company, Gareth had laughed too loudly, then danced far too closely with a notoriously merry widow.

Lord St. Clair had turned very red in the face, then hissed something about Gareth being no better than he should be. Gareth hadn't been exactly certain to what his father had been referring, and the baron had been drunk, in any case. But it had left him with one powerful certainty—

Eventually, the other shoe was going to drop. When Gareth least expected it, or perhaps, now that he'd grown so suspicious, precisely when he most suspected it. But as soon as Gareth attempted to make a change in his life, to move forward, to move up . . .

That was when the baron would make his move. Gareth was sure of it.

And his world was going to come crashing down.

"Mr. St. Clair?"

Gareth blinked and turned to Hyacinth Bridgerton, whom, he realized somewhat sheepishly, he'd been ignoring in favor of his own thoughts. "So sorry," he murmured, giving her the slow and easy smile that seemed to work so well when he needed to placate a female. "I was woolgathering."

At her dubious expression, he added, "I *do* think from time to time."

She smiled, clearly despite herself, but he counted that as

a success. The day he couldn't make a woman smile was the day he ought to just give up on life and move to the Outer Hebrides.

"Under normal circumstances," he said, since the occasion seemed to call for polite conversation, "I would ask if you enjoyed the musicale, but somehow that seems cruel."

She shifted slightly in her seat, which was interesting, since most young ladies were trained from a very young age to hold themselves with perfect stillness. Gareth found himself liking her the better for her restless energy; he, too, was the sort to find himself drumming his fingers against a tabletop when he didn't realize it.

He watched her face, waiting for her to reply, but all she did was look vaguely uncomfortable. Finally, she leaned forward and whispered, "Mr. St. Clair?"

He leaned in as well, giving her a conspiratorial quirk of his brow. "Miss Bridgerton?"

"Would you mind terribly if we took a turn about the room?"

He waited just long enough to catch her motioning over her shoulder with the tiniest of nods. Lord Somershall was wiggling slightly in his chair, and his copious form was edged right up next to Hyacinth.

"Of course," Gareth said gallantly, rising to his feet and offering her his arm. "I need to save Lord Somershall, after all," he said, once they had moved several paces away.

Her eyes snapped to his face. "I beg your pardon?"

"If I were a betting man," he said, "I'd lay the odds four-to-one in your favor."

For about half a second she looked confused, and then her face slid into a satisfied smile. "You mean you're not a betting man?" she asked.

He laughed. "I haven't the blunt to be a betting man," he said quite honestly.

"That doesn't seem to stop most men," she said pertly.

"Or most women," he said, with a tilt of his head.

"*Touché*," she murmured, glancing about the room. "We are a gambling people, aren't we?"

"And what about you, Miss Bridgerton? Do you like to wager?"

"Of course," she said, surprising him with her candor. "But only when I know I will win."

He chuckled. "Strangely enough," he said, guiding her toward the refreshment table, "I believe you."

"Oh, you should," she said blithely. "Ask anyone who knows me."

"Wounded again," he said, offering her his most engaging smile. "I thought *I* knew you."

She opened her mouth, then looked shocked that she didn't have a reply. Gareth took pity on her and handed her a glass of lemonade. "Drink up," he murmured. "You look thirsty."

He chuckled as she glowered at him over the rim of her glass, which of course only made her redouble her efforts to incinerate him with her glare.

There was something very amusing about Hyacinth Bridgerton, he decided. She was smart—very smart—but she had a certain air about her, as if she was used to always being the most intelligent person in the room. It wasn't unattractive; she was quite charming in her own way, and he imagined that she would have to have learned to speak her own mind in order to be heard in her family—she was the youngest of eight, after all.

But it did mean that he rather enjoyed seeing her at a loss for words. It was *fun* to befuddle her. Gareth didn't know why he didn't make a point of doing it more often.

He watched as she set her glass down. "Tell me, Mr. St. Clair," she said, "what did your grandmother say to you to convince you to attend this evening?"

"You don't believe I came of my own free will?"

She lifted one brow. He was impressed. He'd never known a female who could do that.

"Very well," he said, "there was a great deal of hand fluttering, then something about a visit to her physician, and then I believe she sighed."

"Just once?"

He quirked a brow back at her. "I'm made of stronger stuff than that, Miss Bridgerton. It took a full half hour to break me."

She nodded. "You *are* good."

He leaned toward her and smiled. "At many things," he murmured.

She blushed, which pleased him mightily, but then she said, "I've been warned about men like you."

"I certainly hope so."

She laughed. "I don't think you're nearly as dangerous as you'd like to be thought."

He tilted his head to the side. "And why is that?"

She didn't answer right away, just caught her lower lip between her teeth as she pondered her words. "You're far too kind to your grandmother," she finally said.

"Some would say she's too kind to me."

"Oh, many people say that," Hyacinth said with a shrug.

He choked on his lemonade. "You haven't a coy bone in your body, do you?"

Hyacinth glanced across the room at Penelope and Lady Danbury before turning back to him. "I keep trying, but no, apparently not. I imagine it's why I am still unmarried."

He smiled. "Surely not."

"Oh, indeed," she said, even though it was clear he was funning her. "Men need to be trapped into marriage, whether they realize it or not. And I seem to be completely lacking in the ability."

He grinned. "You mean you're not underhanded and sly?"

"I'm both those things," she admitted, "just not subtle."

"No," he murmured, and she couldn't decide whether his agreement bothered her or not.

"But tell me," he continued, "for I'm most curious. Why do you think men must be trapped into marriage?"

"Would *you* go willingly to the altar?"

"No, but—"

"You see? I am affirmed." And somehow that made her feel a great deal better.

"Shame on you, Miss Bridgerton," he said. "It's not very sporting of you not to allow me to finish my statement."

She cocked her head. "Did you have anything interesting to say?"

He smiled, and Hyacinth felt it down to her toes. "I'm always interesting," he murmured.

"*Now* you're just trying to scare me." She didn't know where this was coming from, this crazy sense of daring.

Hyacinth wasn't shy, and she certainly wasn't as demure as she ought to have been, but nor was she foolhardy. And Gareth St. Clair was not the sort of man with whom one ought to trifle. She was playing with fire, and she knew it, but somehow she couldn't stop herself. It was as if each statement from his lips was a dare, and she had to use her every faculty just to keep up.

If this was a competition, she wanted to win.

And if any of her flaws was going to prove to be fatal, this was surely it.

"Miss Bridgerton," he said, "the devil himself couldn't scare you."

She forced her eyes to meet his. "That's not a compliment, is it?"

He lifted her hand to his lips, brushing a feather-light kiss across her knuckles. "You'll have to figure that out for yourself," he murmured.

To all who observed, he was the soul of propriety, but Hyacinth caught the daring gleam in his eye, and she felt the breath leave her body as tingles of electricity rushed across her skin. Her lips parted, but she had nothing to say, not a single word. There was nothing but air, and even that seemed in short supply.

And then he straightened as if nothing had happened and said, "Do let me know what you decide."

She just stared at him.

"About the compliment," he added. "I am sure you will wish to let me know how I feel about you."

Her mouth fell open.

He smiled. Broadly. "Speechless, even. I'm to be commended."

"You—"

"No. No," he said, lifting one hand in the air and pointing toward her as if what he really wanted to do was place his finger on her lips and shush her. "Don't ruin it. The moment is too rare."

And she could have said something. She should have said something. But all she could do was stand there like an idiot, or if not that, then like someone completely unlike herself.

"Until next time, Miss Bridgerton," he murmured.

And then he was gone.

Chapter 3

Three days later, and our hero learns that one can never really escape one's past.

 "There is a woman to see you, sir."

Gareth looked up from his desk, a huge mahogany behemoth that took up nearly half of his small study. "A woman, you say?"

His new valet nodded. "She said she is your brother's wife."

"Caroline?" Gareth's attention snapped into sharp focus. "Show her in. Immediately."

He rose to his feet, awaiting her arrival in his study. He hadn't seen Caroline in months, only once since George's funeral, truth be told. And Lord knew that hadn't been a joyful affair. Gareth had spent the entire time avoiding his father, which had added stress on top of his already crushing grief.

Lord St. Clair had ordered George to cease all brotherly relations with Gareth, but George had never cut him off. In all else, George had obeyed his father, but never that. And Gareth had loved him all the more for it. The baron hadn't wanted Gareth to attend the ceremony, but when Gareth had pushed his way into the church, even he hadn't been willing to make a scene and have him evicted.

"Gareth?"

He turned away from the window, unaware that he'd even been looking out. "Caroline," he said warmly, crossing the room to greet his sister-in-law. "How have you been?"

She gave a helpless little shrug. Hers had been a love match, and Gareth had never seen anything quite as devastating as Caroline's eyes at her husband's funeral.

"I know," Gareth said quietly. He missed George, too. They had been an unlikely pair—George, sober and serious, and Gareth, who had always run wild. But they had been friends as well as brothers, and Gareth liked to think that they had complemented each other. Lately Gareth had been thinking that he ought to try to lead a somewhat tamer life, and he had been looking to his brother's memory to guide his actions.

"I was going through his things," Caroline said. "I found something. I believe that it is yours."

Gareth watched curiously as she reached into her satchel and pulled out a small book. "I don't recognize it," he said.

"No," Caroline replied, handing it to him. "You wouldn't. It belonged to your father's mother."

Your father's mother. Gareth couldn't quite prevent his grimace. Caroline did not know that Gareth was not truly a St. Clair. Gareth had never been certain if George had known the truth, either. If he had, he'd never said anything.

The book was small, bound with brown leather. There was a little strap that reached from back to front, where it could be fastened with a button. Gareth carefully undid it and turned the book open, taking extra care with the aged paper. "It's a diary," he said with surprise. And then he had to smile. It was written in Italian. "What does it say?"

"I don't know," Caroline said. "I didn't even know it existed until I found it in George's desk earlier this week. He never mentioned it."

Gareth looked down at the diary, at the elegant hand-writing forming words he could not understand. His father's mother had been the daughter of a noble Italian house. It had always amused Gareth that his father was half-Italian; the baron was so insufferably proud of his St. Clair ancestry and liked to boast that they had been in England since the Norman Invasion. In fact, Gareth couldn't recall him ever making mention of his Italian roots.

"There was a note from George," Caroline said, "instructing me to give this to you."

Gareth glanced back down at the book, his heart heavy. Just one more indication that George had never known that they were not full brothers. Gareth bore no blood relationship to Isabella Marinzoli St. Clair, and he had no real right to her diary.

"You shall have to find someone to translate it," Caroline said with a small, wistful smile. "I'm curious as to what it says. George always spoke so warmly of your grandmother."

Gareth nodded. He remembered her fondly as well, though they hadn't spent very much time together. Lord St. Clair hadn't gotten on very well with his mother, so Isabella did not visit very often. But she had always doted upon her *due ragazzi*, as she liked to call her two grandsons, and Gareth recalled feeling quite crushed when, at the age of seven, he'd heard that she had died. If affection was anywhere near as important as blood, then he supposed the diary would find a better home in his hands than anyone else's.

"I'll see what I can do," Gareth said. "It can't be that difficult to find someone who can translate from the Italian."

"I wouldn't trust it to just anyone," Caroline said. "It is your grandmother's diary, after all. Her personal thoughts."

Gareth nodded. Caroline was right. He owed it to Isabella to find someone discreet to translate her memoirs. And he knew exactly where to start in his search.

"I'll take this to Grandmother Danbury," Gareth suddenly said, allowing his hand to bob up and down with the diary, almost as if he was testing its weight. "She'll know what to do."

And she would, he thought. Grandmother Danbury liked to say that she knew everything, and the annoying truth was, she was most often right.

"Do let me know what you find out," Caroline said, as she headed for the door.

"Of course," he murmured, even though she was already gone. He looked down at the book. *10 Settembre, 1793* . . .

Gareth shook his head and smiled. It figured his one bequest from the St. Clair family coffers would be a diary he couldn't even read.

Ah, irony.

Meanwhile, in a drawing room not so very far away . . .

"Enh?" Lady Danbury screeched. "You're not speaking loudly enough!"

Hyacinth allowed the book from which she was reading to fall closed, with just her index finger stuck inside to mark her place. Lady Danbury liked to feign deafness when it suited her, and it seemed to suit her every time Hyacinth got to the racy parts of the lurid novels that the countess enjoyed so well.

"I said," Hyacinth said, leveling her gaze onto Lady Danbury's face, "that our dear heroine was breathing hard, no, let me check, she was *breathy* and *short of breath*." She looked up. "Breathy *and* short of breath?"

"Pfft," Lady Danbury said, waving her hand dismissively.

Hyacinth glanced at the cover of the book. "I wonder if English is the author's first language?"

"Keep reading," Lady D ordered.

"Very well, let me see, *Miss Bumblehead ran like the wind as she saw Lord Savagewood coming toward her.*"

Lady Danbury narrowed her eyes. "Her name isn't Bumblehead."

"It ought to be," Hyacinth muttered.

"Well, that's true," Lady D agreed, "but we didn't write the story, did we?"

Hyacinth cleared her throat and once again found her place in the text. "*He was coming closer,*" she read, "*and Miss Bumbleshoot—*"

"Hyacinth!"

"Butterworth," Hyacinth grumbled. "Whatever her name is, she ran for the cliffs. End of chapter."

"The cliffs? Still? Wasn't she running at the end of the last chapter?"

"Perhaps it's a long way."

Lady Danbury narrowed her eyes. "I don't believe you."

Hyacinth shrugged. "It is certainly true that I would lie to you to get out of reading the next few paragraphs of Priscilla Butterworth's remarkably perilous life, but as it happens, I'm telling the truth." When Lady D didn't say anything, Hyacinth held out the book, and asked, "Would you like to check for yourself?"

"No, no," Lady Danbury said, with a great show of acceptance. "I believe you, if only because I have no choice."

Hyacinth gave her a pointed look. "Are you blind now, as well as deaf?"

"No." Lady D sighed, letting one hand flutter until it rested palm out on her forehead. "Just practicing my high drama."

Hyacinth laughed out loud.

"I do not jest," Lady Danbury said, her voice returning to its usual sharp tenor. "And I am thinking of making a change in life. I could do a better job on the stage than most of those fools who call themselves actresses."

"Sadly," Hyacinth said, "there doesn't seem to be much demand for aging countess roles."

"If anyone else said that to me," Lady D said, thumping her cane against the floor even though she was seated in a perfectly good chair, "I'd take it as an insult."

"But not from me?" Hyacinth queried, trying to sound disappointed.

Lady Danbury chuckled. "Do you know why I like you so well, Hyacinth Bridgerton?"

Hyacinth leaned forward. "I'm all agog."

Lady D's face spread into a creased smile. "Because you, dear girl, are exactly like me."

"Do you know, Lady Danbury," Hyacinth said, "if you said that to anyone else, she'd probably take it as an insult."

Lady D's thin body quivered with mirth. "But not you?"

Hyacinth shook her head. "Not me."

"Good." Lady Danbury gave her an uncharacteristically grandmotherly smile, then glanced up at the clock on the mantel. "We've time for another chapter, I think."

"We agreed, one chapter each Tuesday," Hyacinth said, mostly just to be vexing.

Lady D's mouth settled into a grumpy line. "Very well, then," she said, eyeing Hyacinth in a sly manner, "we'll talk about something else."

Oh, dear.

"Tell me, Hyacinth," Lady Danbury said, leaning forward, "how are your prospects these days?"

"You sound like my mother," Hyacinth said sweetly.

"A compliment of the highest order," Lady D tossed back. "I like your mother, and I hardly like anyone."

"I'll be sure to tell her."

"Bah. She knows that already, and you're avoiding the question."

"My prospects," Hyacinth replied, "as you so delicately put it, are the same as ever."

"Such is the problem. You, my dear girl, need a husband."

"Are you quite certain my mother isn't hiding behind the curtains, feeding you lines?"

"See?" Lady Danbury said with a wide smile. "I *would* be good on the stage."

Hyacinth just stared at her. "You have gone quite mad, did you know that?"

"Bah. I'm merely old enough to get away with speaking my mind. You'll enjoy it when you're my age, I promise."

"I enjoy it now," Hyacinth said.

"True," Lady Danbury conceded. "And it's probably why you're still unmarried."

"If there were an intelligent unattached man in London," Hyacinth said with a beleaguered sigh, "I assure you I would set my cap for him." She let her head cock to the side with a sarcastic tilt. "Surely you wouldn't see me married to a fool."

"Of course not, but—"

"And *stop* mentioning your grandson as if I weren't intelligent enough to figure out what you're up to."

Lady D gasped in full huff. "I didn't say a *word*."

"You were about to."

"Well, he's perfectly nice," Lady Danbury muttered, not even trying to deny it, "and more than handsome."

Hyacinth caught her lower lip between her teeth, trying not to remember how very strange she'd felt at the Smythe-Smith musicale with Mr. St. Clair at her side. That was the problem with him, she realized. She didn't feel like herself when he was near. And it was the most disconcerting thing.

"I see you don't disagree," Lady D said.

"About your grandson's handsome visage? Of course not," Hyacinth replied, since there was little point in debating it. There were some people for whom good looks were a fact, not an opinion.

"And," Lady Danbury continued in grand fashion, "I'm happy to say that he inherited his brain from *my* side of the family, which, I might regretfully add, isn't the case with all of my progeny."

Hyacinth glanced up at the ceiling in an attempt to avoid comment. Lady Danbury's eldest son had famously gotten his head stuck between the bars of the front gate of Windsor Castle.

"Oh, go ahead and say it," Lady D grumbled. "At least two of my children are half-wits, and heaven knows about *their* children. I flee in the opposite direction when they come to town."

"I would never—"

"Well, you were thinking it, and rightly you should. Serves me right for marrying Lord Danbury when I knew he hadn't two thoughts to bang together in his head. But Gareth *is* a prize, and you're a fool if you don't—"

"Your grandson," Hyacinth cut in, "isn't the least bit interested in me or any marriageable female, for that matter."

"Well, that *is* a problem," Lady Danbury agreed, "and for the life of me, I don't know why the boy shuns your sort."

"My *sort*?" Hyacinth echoed.

"Young, female, and someone he would actually have to marry if he dallied with."

Hyacinth felt her cheeks burn. Normally this would be exactly the sort of conversation she relished—it was far more fun to be improper than otherwise, within rea-son, of course—but this time it was all she could do to say, "I hardly think you should be discussing such things with me."

"Bah," Lady D said, gesturing dismissively with her hand. "Since when have you become so missish?"

Hyacinth opened her mouth, but thankfully, Lady Danbury didn't seem to desire an answer. "He's a rogue, it's true," the countess sailed on, "but it's nothing you can't overcome if you put your mind to it."

"I'm not going to—"

"Just yank your dress down a little when next you see him," Lady D cut in, waving her hand impatiently in front of her face. "Men lose all sense at the sight of a healthy bosom. You'll have him—"

"Lady Danbury!" Hyacinth crossed her arms. She did have her pride, and she wasn't about to go chasing after a rake who clearly had no interest in marriage. That sort of public humiliation she could do without.

And besides, it would require a great deal of imagination to describe her bosom as healthy. Hyacinth knew she wasn't built like a boy, thank goodness, but nor did she possess attributes that would cause any man to look twice in the area directly below her neck.

"Oh, very well," Lady Danbury said, sounding exceedingly grumpy, which, for her, was exceeding indeed. "I won't say another word."

"Ever?"

"Until," Lady D said firmly.

"Until when?" Hyacinth asked suspiciously.

"I don't know," Lady Danbury replied, in much the same tone.

Which Hyacinth had a feeling meant five minutes hence.

The countess was silent for a moment, but her lips were pursed, signaling that her mind was up to something that was probably devious in the extreme. "Do you know what I think?" she asked.

"Usually," Hyacinth replied.

Lady D scowled. "You are entirely too mouthy."

Hyacinth just smiled and ate another biscuit.

"I think," Lady Danbury said, apparently over her pique, "that we should write a book."

To Hyacinth's credit, she didn't choke on her food. "I beg your pardon?"

"I need a challenge," Lady D said. "Keeps the mind sharp. And surely we could do better than *Miss Butterworth and the Mealymouthed Baron*."

"*Mad Baron*," Hyacinth said automatically.

"Precisely," Lady D said. "Surely we can do better."

"I'm sure we could, but it does beg the question—why would we want to?"

"Because we *can*."

Hyacinth considered the prospect of a creative liaison with Lady Danbury, of spending hours upon hours—

"No," she said, quite firmly, "we can't."

"Of course we can," Lady D said, thumping her cane for what was only the second time during the interview—surely a new record of restraint. "I'll think up the ideas, and you can figure out how to word it all."

"It doesn't sound like an equitable division of labor," Hyacinth remarked.

"And why should it be?"

Hyacinth opened her mouth to reply, then decided there was really no point.

Lady Danbury frowned for a moment, then finally added, "Well, think about my proposal. We'd make an excellent team."

"I shudder to think," came a deep voice from the doorway, "what you might be attempting to browbeat poor Miss Bridgerton into now."

"Gareth!" Lady Danbury said with obvious pleasure. "How nice of you *finally* to come visit me."

Hyacinth turned. Gareth St. Clair had just stepped into the room, looking alarmingly handsome in his elegant afternoon clothing. A shaft of sunlight was streaming through the window, landing on his hair like burnished gold.

His presence was most surprising. Hyacinth had been visiting every Tuesday for a year now, and this was only the second time their paths had crossed. She had begun to think he might be purposefully avoiding her.

Which begged the question—why was he here now? Their conversation at the Smythe-Smith musicale was the first they had ever shared that went beyond the most basic of pleasantries, and suddenly he was here in his grandmother's drawing room, right in the middle of their weekly visit.

"Finally?" Mr. St. Clair echoed with amusement. "Surely you haven't forgotten my visit last Friday." He turned to Hyacinth, his face taking on a rather convincing expression of concern. "Do you think she might be beginning to lose her memory, Miss Bridgerton? She is, what can it be now, ninety—"

Lady D's cane came down squarely on his toes. "Not even close, my dear boy," she barked, "and if you value your appendages, you shan't blaspheme in such a manner again."

"The Gospel according to Agatha Danbury," Hyacinth murmured.

Mr. St. Clair flashed her a grin, which surprised her, first because she hadn't thought he would hear her remark, and second because it made him seem so boyish and innocent, when she knew for a fact that he was neither.

Although . . .

Hyacinth fought the urge to shake her head. There was always an *although*. Lady D's "finallys" aside, Gareth St. Clair *was* a frequent visitor at Danbury House. It made Hyacinth wonder if he was truly the rogue society made him out to be. No true devil would be so devoted to his grandmother. She'd said as much at the Smythe-Smith musicale, but he'd deftly changed the subject.

He was a puzzle. And Hyacinth hated puzzles.

Well, no, in truth she loved them.

Provided, of course, that she solved them.

The puzzle in question ambled across the room, leaning down to drop a kiss on his grandmother's cheek. Hyacinth found herself staring at the back of his neck, at the rakish queue of hair brushing up against the edge of his bottle green coat.

She knew he hadn't a great deal of money for tailors and such, and she knew he never asked his grandmother for anything, but lud, that coat fit him to perfection.

"Miss Bridgerton," he said, settling onto the sofa and allowing one ankle to rest rather lazily on the opposite knee. "It must be Tuesday."

"It must," Hyacinth agreed.

"How fares Priscilla Butterworth?"

Hyacinth lifted her brows, surprised that he knew which book they were reading. "She is running for the cliffs," she replied. "I fear for her safety, if you must know. Or rather, I would," she added, "if there were not eleven chapters still to be read."

"Pity," he remarked. "The book would take a far more interesting turn if she was killed off."

"Have you read it, then?" Hyacinth queried politely.

For a moment it seemed he would do nothing but give her a *Surely You Jest* look, but he punctuated the expression with, "My grandmother likes to recount the tale when I see her each Wednesday. Which I *always do*," he added, sending a heavy-lidded glance in Lady Danbury's direction. "And most Fridays and Sundays as well."

"Not last Sunday," Lady D said.

"I went to church," he deadpanned.

Hyacinth choked on her biscuit.

He turned to her. "Didn't you see the lightning strike the steeple?"

She recovered with a sip of tea, then smiled sweetly. "I was listening too devotedly to the sermon."

"Claptrap last week," Lady D announced. "I think the priest is getting old."

Gareth opened his mouth, but before he could say a word, his grandmother's cane swung around in a remarkably steady horizontal arc. "Don't," she warned, "make a comment beginning with the words, 'Coming from you . . . '"

"I wouldn't dream of it," he demurred.

"Of course you would," she stated. "You wouldn't be my grandson if you wouldn't." She turned to Hyacinth. "Don't you agree?"

To her credit, Hyacinth folded her hands in her lap and said, "Surely there is no right answer to that question."

"Smart girl," Lady D said approvingly.

"I learn from the master."

Lady Danbury beamed. "Insolence aside," she continued determinedly, gesturing toward Gareth as if he were some sort of zoological specimen, "he really is an exceptional grandson. Couldn't have asked for more."

Gareth watched with amusement as Hyacinth murmured something that was meant to convey her agreement without actually doing so.

"Of course," Grandmother Danbury added with a dismissive wave of her hand, "he hasn't much in the way of competition. The rest of them have only three brains to share among them."

Not the most ringing of endorsements, considering that she had twelve living grandchildren.

"I've heard some animals eat their young," Gareth murmured, to no one in particular.

"This being a *Tuesday*," his grandmother said, ignoring his comment completely, "what brings you by?"

Gareth wrapped his fingers around the book in his pocket. He'd been so intrigued by its existence since Caroline had handed it over that he had completely forgotten about his grandmother's weekly visit with Hyacinth Bridgerton. If he'd been thinking clearly, he would have waited until later in the afternoon, after she had departed.

But now he was here, and he had to give them some reason for his presence. Otherwise—God help him—his grandmother would assume he'd come *because* of Miss

Bridgerton, and it would take months to dissuade her of the notion.

"What is it, boy?" his grandmother asked, in her inimitable way. "Speak up."

Gareth turned to Hyacinth, slightly pleased when she squirmed a little under his intent stare. "Why do you visit my grandmother?" he asked.

She shrugged. "Because I like her."

And then she leaned forward and asked, "Why do *you* visit her?"

"Because she's my—" He stopped, caught himself. He didn't visit just because she was his grandmother. Lady Danbury was a number of things to him—trial, termagant, and bane of his existence sprang to mind—but never a duty. "I like her, too," he said slowly, his eyes never leaving Hyacinth's.

She didn't blink. "Good."

And then they just stared at each other, as if trapped in some sort of bizarre contest.

"Not that I have any complaints with this particular avenue of conversation," Lady Danbury said loudly, "but what the devil are the two of you talking about?"

Hyacinth sat back and looked at Lady Danbury as if nothing had happened. "I have no idea," she said blithely, and proceeded to sip at her tea. Setting the cup back in its saucer, she added, "He asked me a question."

Gareth watched her curiously. His grandmother wasn't the easiest person to befriend, and if Hyacinth Bridgerton happily sacrificed her Tuesday afternoons to be with her, that was certainly a point in her favor. Not to mention that Lady Danbury hardly liked anyone, and she raved about

Miss Bridgerton at every possible opportunity. It was, of course, partly because she was trying to pair the two of them up; his grandmother had never been known for her tact or subtlety.

But still, if Gareth had learned one thing over the years, it was that his grandmother was a shrewd judge of character. And besides, the diary was written in Italian. Even if it did contain some indiscreet secret, Miss Bridgerton would hardly know.

His decision made, he reached into his pocket and pulled out the book.

Chapter 4

At which point Hyacinth's life finally becomes almost as exciting as Priscilla Butterworth's. Minus the cliffs, of course . . .

 Hyacinth watched with interest as Mr. St. Clair appeared to hesitate. He glanced over at her, his clear blue eyes narrowing almost imperceptibly before he turned back to his grandmother. Hyacinth tried not to look too interested; he was obviously trying to decide if he should mention his business in her presence, and she suspected that any interference on her part would cause him to keep his counsel.

But apparently she passed muster, because after a brief moment of silence, he reached into his pocket and pulled out what appeared to be a small, leather-bound book.

"What is this?" Lady Danbury asked, taking it into her hands.

"Grandmother St. Clair's diary," he replied. "Caroline brought it over this afternoon. She found it among George's effects."

"It's in Italian," Lady D said.

"Yes, I was aware."

"I meant, why did you bring it to *me*?" she asked, somewhat impatiently.

Mr. St. Clair gave her a lazy half smile. "You are always telling me you know everything, or if not everything, then everyone."

"You said that to me earlier this afternoon," Hyacinth put in helpfully.

Mr. St. Clair turned to her with a vaguely patronizing, "Thank you," which arrived at precisely the same moment as Lady Danbury's glare.

Hyacinth squirmed. Not at Lady D's glare—she was quite impervious to those. But she hated this feeling that Mr. St. Clair thought her deserving of condescension.

"I was hoping," he said to his grandmother, "that you might know of a reputable translator."

"For Italian?"

"It would seem to be the required language."

"Hmmph." Lady D tap tap tapped her cane against the carpet, much the way a normal person would drum fingers atop a table. "Italian? Not nearly as ubiquitous as French, which of course any decent person would—"

"I can read Italian," Hyacinth interrupted.

Two identical pairs of blue eyes swung her direction.

"You're joking," Mr. St. Clair said, coming in a mere half second before his grandmother barked, "You can?"

"You don't know everything about me," Hyacinth said archly. To Lady Danbury, of course, since Mr. St. Clair could hardly make that claim.

"Well, yes, of course," Lady D blustered, "but Italian?"

"I had an Italian governess when I was small," Hyacinth said with a shrug. "It amused her to teach me. I'm not fluent," she allowed, "but given a page or two, I can make out the general meaning."

"This is quite more than a page or two," Mr. St. Clair said, tilting his head toward the diary, which still rested in his grandmother's hands.

"Clearly," Hyacinth replied peevishly. "But I'm not likely to read more than a page or two at a time. And she didn't write it in the style of the ancient Romans, did she?"

"That would be Latin," Mr. St. Clair drawled.

Hyacinth clamped her teeth together. "Nevertheless," she ground out.

"For the love of God, boy," Lady Danbury cut in, "give her the book."

Mr. St. Clair forbore to point out that she was still holding it, which Hyacinth thought showed remarkable restraint on his part. Instead, he rose to his feet, plucked the slim volume from his grandmother's hands, and turned toward Hyacinth. He hesitated then—just for a moment, and Hyacinth would have missed it had she been looking anywhere but directly at his face.

He brought the book to her then, holding it out with a softly murmured, "Miss Bridgerton."

Hyacinth accepted it, shivering against the odd feeling that she had just done something far more powerful than merely taking a book into her hands.

"Are you cold, Miss Bridgerton?" Mr. St. Clair murmured.

She shook her head, using the book as a means to avoid looking at him. "The pages are slightly brittle," she said, carefully turning one.

"What does it say?" Mr. St. Clair asked.

Hyacinth gritted her teeth. It was never fun to be forced to perform under pressure, and it was nigh near impossible with Gareth St. Clair breathing down her neck.

"Give her some room!" Lady D barked.

He moved, but not enough to make Hyacinth feel any more at ease.

"Well?" he demanded.

Hyacinth's head bobbed slightly back and forth as she worked out the meaning. "She's writing about her upcoming wedding," she said. "I think she's due to marry your grandfather in"—she bit her lip as she scanned down the page for the appropriate words—"three weeks. I gather the ceremony was in Italy."

Mr. St. Clair nodded once before prodding her with, "And?"

"And . . ." Hyacinth wrinkled her nose, as she always did when she was thinking hard. It wasn't a terribly attractive expression, but the alternative was simply not to think, which she didn't find appealing.

"What did she say?" Lady Danbury urged.

"*Orrendo orrendo . . . ,*" Hyacinth murmured. "Oh, right." She looked up. "She's not very happy about it."

"Who *would* be?" Lady D put in. "The man was a bear, apologies to those in the room sharing his blood."

Mr. St. Clair ignored her. "What else?"

"I told you I'm not fluent," Hyacinth finally snapped. "I need time to work it out."

"Take it home," Lady Danbury said. "You'll be seeing him tomorrow night, anyway."

"I am?" Hyacinth asked, at precisely the moment Mr. St. Clair said, "She will?"

"You're accompanying me to the Pleinsworth poetry reading," Lady D told her grandson. "Or have you forgotten?"

Hyacinth sat back, enjoying the sight of Gareth St. Clair's mouth opening and closing in obvious distress. He looked a bit like a fish, she decided. A fish with the features of a Greek god, but still, a fish.

"I really . . ." he said. "That is to say, I can't—"

"You can, and you will be there," Lady D said. "You promised."

He regarded her with a stern expression. "I cannot imagine—"

"Well, if you didn't promise, you should have done, and if you love me . . ."

Hyacinth coughed to cover her laugh, then tried not to smirk when Mr. St. Clair shot a dirty look in her direction.

"When I die," he said, "surely my epitaph will read, 'He loved his grandmother when no one else would.'"

"And what's wrong with that?" Lady Danbury asked.

"I'll be there," he sighed.

"Bring wool for your ears," Hyacinth advised.

He looked aghast. "It cannot possibly be worse than the musicale."

Hyacinth couldn't quite keep one corner of her mouth from tilting up. "Lady Pleinsworth used to *be* a Smythe-Smith."

Across the room, Lady Danbury chortled with glee.

"I had best be getting home," Hyacinth said, rising to her feet. "I shall try to translate the first entry before I see you tomorrow evening, Mr. St. Clair."

"You have my gratitude, Miss Bridgerton."

Hyacinth nodded and crossed the room, trying to ignore the strangely giddy sensation growing in her chest. It was just a book, for heaven's sake.

And he was just a man.

It was annoying, this strange compulsion she felt to impress him. She wanted to do something that would prove her intelligence and wit, something that would force him to look at her with an expression other than vague amusement.

"Allow me to walk you to the door," Mr. St. Clair said, falling into step beside her.

Hyacinth turned, then felt her breath stop short in surprise. She hadn't realized he was standing so close. "I . . . ah . . ."

It was his eyes, she realized. So blue and clear she ought to have felt she could read his thoughts, but instead she rather thought he could read hers.

"Yes?" he murmured, placing her hand on his elbow.

She shook her head. "It's nothing."

"Why, Miss Bridgerton," he said, guiding her into the hall. "I don't believe I've ever seen you at a loss for words. Except for the other night," he added, cocking his head ever so slightly to the side.

She looked at him, narrowing her eyes.

"At the musicale," he supplied helpfully. "It was lovely." He smiled, most annoyingly. "Wasn't it lovely?"

Hyacinth clamped her lips together. "You barely know me, Mr. St. Clair," she said.

"Your reputation precedes you."

"As does yours."

"*Touché*, Miss Bridgerton," he said, but she didn't particularly feel she'd won the point.

Hyacinth saw her maid waiting by the door, so she extricated her hand from Mr. St. Clair's elbow and crossed the foyer. "Until tomorrow, Mr. St. Clair," she said.

And as the door shut behind her, she could have sworn she heard him reply, "*Arrivederci*."

Hyacinth arrives home.
Her mother has been waiting for her.
This is not good.

"Charlotte Stokehurst," Violet Bridgerton announced, "is getting married."

"Today?" Hyacinth queried, taking off her gloves.

Her mother gave her a look. "She has become engaged. Her mother told me this morning."

Hyacinth looked around. "Were you waiting for me in the hall?"

"To the Earl of Renton," Violet added. "Renton."

"Have we any tea?" Hyacinth asked. "I walked all the way home, and I'm thirsty."

"Renton!" Violet exclaimed, looking about ready to throw up her hands in despair. "Did you hear me?"

"Renton," Hyacinth said obligingly. "He has fat ankles."

"He's—" Violet stopped short. "Why were you looking at his ankles?"

"I couldn't very well miss them," Hyacinth replied. She handed her reticule—which contained the Italian diary—to a maid. "Would you take this to my room, please?"

Violet waited until the maid scurried off. "I have tea in

the drawing room, and there is nothing wrong with Renton's ankles."

Hyacinth shrugged. "If you like the puffy sort."

"Hyacinth!"

Hyacinth sighed tiredly, following her mother into the drawing room. "Mother, you have six married children, and they all are quite happy with their choices. Why must you try to push *me* into an unsuitable alliance?"

Violet sat and prepared a cup of tea for Hyacinth. "I'm not," she said, "but Hyacinth, couldn't you even look?"

"Mother, I—"

"Or for my sake, pretend to?"

Hyacinth could not help but smile.

Violet held the cup out, then took it back and added another spoonful of sugar. Hyacinth was the only one in the family who took sugar in her tea, and she'd always liked it extra sweet.

"Thank you," Hyacinth said, tasting the brew. It wasn't quite as hot as she preferred, but she drank it anyway.

"Hyacinth," her mother said, in that tone of voice that always made Hyacinth feel a little guilty, even though she knew better, "you know I only wish to see you happy."

"I know," Hyacinth said. That was the problem. Her mother did only wish her to be happy. If Violet had been pushing her toward marriage for social glory or financial gain, it would have been much easier to ignore her. But no, her mother loved her and truly did want her to be happy, not just married, and so Hyacinth tried her best to maintain her good humor through all of her mother's sighs.

"I would never wish to see you married to someone whose company you did not enjoy," Violet continued.

"I know."

"And if you never met the right person, I would be perfectly happy to see you remain unwed."

Hyacinth eyed her dubiously.

"Very well," Violet amended, "not *perfectly* happy, but you know I would never pressure you to marry someone unsuitable."

"I know," Hyacinth said again.

"But darling, you'll never find anyone if you don't look."

"I look!" Hyacinth protested. "I have gone out almost every night this week. I even went to the Smythe-Smith musicale. Which," she said quite pointedly, "I might add *you* did not attend."

Violet coughed. "Bit of a cough, I'm afraid."

Hyacinth said nothing, but no one could have mistaken the look in her eyes.

"I heard you sat next to Gareth St. Clair," Violet said, after an appropriate silence.

"Do you have spies *every*where?" Hyacinth grumbled.

"Almost," Violet replied. "It makes life so much easier."

"For you, perhaps."

"Did you like him?" Violet persisted.

Like him? It seemed such an odd question. Did she like Gareth St. Clair? Did she like that it always felt as if he was silently laughing at her, even after she'd agreed to translate his grandmother's diary? Did she like that she could never tell what he was thinking, or that he left her feeling unsettled, and not quite herself?

"Well?" her mother asked.

"Somewhat," Hyacinth hedged.

Violet didn't say anything, but her eyes took on a gleam that terrified Hyacinth to her very core.

"*Don't*," Hyacinth warned.

"He would be an excellent match, Hyacinth."

Hyacinth stared at her mother as if she'd sprouted an extra head. "Have you gone mad? You know his reputation as well as I."

Violet brushed that aside instantly. "His reputation won't matter once you're married."

"It would if he continued to consort with opera singers and the like."

"He wouldn't," Violet said, waving her hand dismissively.

"How could you possibly know that?"

Violet paused for a moment. "I don't know," she said. "I suppose it's a feeling I have."

"Mother," Hyacinth said with a great show of solicitude, "you know I love you dearly—"

"Why is it," Violet pondered, "that I have come to expect nothing good when I hear a sentence beginning in that manner?"

"But," Hyacinth cut in, "you must forgive me if I decline to marry someone based upon a feeling you might or might not have."

Violet sipped her tea with rather impressive nonchalance. "It's the next best thing to a feeling *you* might have. And if I may say so myself, my feelings on these things tend to be right on the mark." At Hyacinth's dry expression, she added, "I haven't been wrong yet."

Well, that was true, Hyacinth had to acknowledge. To herself, of course. If she actually admitted as much out loud, her mother would take that as a *carte blanche* to pursue Mr. St. Clair until he ran screaming for the trees.

"Mother," Hyacinth said, pausing for slightly longer

than normal to steal a bit of time to organize her thoughts, "I am not going to chase after Mr. St. Clair. He's not at all the right sort of man for me."

"I'm not certain you'd know the right sort of man for you if he arrived on our doorstep riding an elephant."

"I would think the elephant would be a fairly good indication that I ought to look elsewhere."

"*Hyacinth.*"

"And besides that," Hyacinth added, thinking about the way Mr. St. Clair always seemed to look at her in that vaguely condescending manner of his, "I don't think he likes me very much."

"Nonsense," Violet said, with all the outrage of a mother hen. "Everyone likes you."

Hyacinth thought about that for a moment. "No," she said, "I don't think everyone does."

"Hyacinth, I am your mother, and I know—"

"Mother, you're the *last* person anyone would tell if they didn't like me."

"Nevertheless—"

"Mother," Hyacinth cut in, setting her teacup firmly in its saucer, "it is of no concern. I don't mind that I am not universally adored. If I wanted everyone to like me, I'd have to be kind and charming and bland and boring all the time, and what would be the fun in that?"

"You sound like Lady Danbury," Violet said.

"I like Lady Danbury."

"I like her, too, but that doesn't mean I want her as my daughter."

"Mother—"

"You won't set your cap for Mr. St. Clair because he scares you," Violet said.

Hyacinth actually gasped. "That is not true."

"Of course it is," Violet returned, looking vastly pleased with herself. "I don't know why it hasn't occurred to me sooner. And he isn't the only one."

"I don't know what you're talking about."

"Why have you not married yet?" Violet asked.

Hyacinth blinked at the abruptness of the question. "I beg your pardon."

"Why have you not married?" Violet repeated. "Do you even want to?"

"Of course I do." And she did. She wanted it more than she would ever admit, probably more than she'd ever realized until that very moment. She looked at her mother and she saw a matriarch, a woman who loved her family with a fierceness that brought tears to her eyes. And in that moment Hyacinth realized that she wanted to love with that fierceness. She wanted children. She wanted a family.

But that did not mean that she was willing to marry the first man who came along. Hyacinth was nothing if not pragmatic; she'd be happy to marry someone she didn't love, provided he suited her in almost every other respect. But good heavens, was it so much to ask for a gentleman with some modicum of intelligence?

"Mother," she said, softening her tone, since she knew that Violet meant well, "I do wish to marry. I swear to you that I do. And clearly I have been looking."

Violet lifted her brows. "Clearly?"

"I have had six proposals," Hyacinth said, perhaps a touch defensively. "It's not my fault that none was suitable."

"Indeed."

Hyacinth felt her lips part with surprise at her mother's tone. "What do you mean by that?"

"Of *course* none of those men was suitable. Half were after your fortune, and as for the other half—well, you would have reduced them to tears within a month."

"Such tenderness for your youngest child," Hyacinth muttered. "It quite undoes me."

Violet let out a ladylike snort. "Oh, *please*, Hyacinth, you know exactly what I mean, and you know that I am correct. None of those men was your match. You need someone who is your equal."

"That is exactly what I have been trying to tell you."

"But my question to you is—*why* are the wrong men asking for your hand?"

Hyacinth opened her mouth, but she had no answer.

"You say you wish to find a man who is your match," Violet said, "and I think you think you do, but the truth is, Hyacinth—every time you meet someone who can hold his own with you, you push him away."

"I don't," Hyacinth said, but not very convincingly.

"Well, you certainly don't encourage them," Violet said. She leaned forward, her eyes filled with equal parts concern and remonstration. "You know I love you dearly, Hyacinth, but you do like to have the upper hand in the conversation."

"Who doesn't?" Hyacinth muttered.

"Any man who is your equal is not going to allow you to manage him as you see fit."

"But that's not what I want," Hyacinth protested.

Violet sighed. But it was a nostalgic sound, full of warmth and love. "I wish I could explain to you how I felt the day you were born," she said.

"Mother?" Hyacinth asked softly. The change of subject was sudden, and somehow Hyacinth knew that whatever her mother said to her, it was going to matter more than anything she'd ever heard in her life.

"It was so soon after your father died. And I was so sad. I can't even begin to tell you how sad. There's a kind of grief that just eats one up. It weighs one down. And one can't—" Violet stopped, and her lips moved, the corners tightening in that way they did when a person was swallowing . . . and trying not to cry. "Well, one can't do anything. There's no way to explain it unless you've felt it yourself."

Hyacinth nodded, even though she knew she could never truly understand.

"That entire last month I just didn't know how to feel," Violet continued, her voice growing softer. "I didn't know how to feel about you. I'd had seven babies already; one would think I would be an expert. But suddenly everything was new. You wouldn't have a father, and I was so scared. I was going to have to be everything to you. I suppose I was going to have to be everything to your brothers and sisters as well, but somehow that was different. With you . . ."

Hyacinth just watched her, unable to take her eyes from her mother's face.

"I was scared," Violet said again, "terrified that I might fail you in some way."

"You didn't," Hyacinth whispered.

Violet smiled wistfully. "I know. Just look how well you turned out."

Hyacinth felt her mouth wobble, and she wasn't sure whether she was going to laugh or cry.

"But that's not what I'm trying to tell you," Violet said,

her eyes taking on a slightly determined expression. "What I'm trying to say is that when you were born, and they put you into my arms—it's strange, because for some reason I was so convinced you would look just like your father. I thought for certain I would look down and see his face, and it would be some sort of sign from heaven."

Hyacinth's breath caught as she watched her, and she wondered why her mother had never told her this story. And why she'd never asked.

"But you didn't," Violet continued. "You looked rather like me. And then—oh my, I remember this as if it were yesterday—you looked into my eyes, and you blinked. Twice."

"Twice?" Hyacinth echoed, wondering why this was important.

"Twice." Violet looked at her, her lips curving into a funny little smile. "I only remember it because you looked so *deliberate*. It was the strangest thing. You gave me a look as if to say, 'I know exactly what I'm doing.'"

A little burst of air rushed past Hyacinth's lips, and she realized it was a laugh. A small one, the kind that takes a body by surprise.

"And then you let out a *wail*," Violet said, shaking her head. "My heavens, I thought you were going to shake the paint right off the walls. And I smiled. It was the first time since your father died that I smiled."

Violet took a breath, then reached for her tea. Hyacinth watched as her mother composed herself, wanting desperately to ask her to continue, but somehow knowing the moment called for silence.

For a full minute Hyacinth waited, and then finally her mother said, softly, "And from that moment on, you were so dear to me. I love all my children, but you . . ." She looked up, her eyes catching Hyacinth's. "You saved me."

Something squeezed in Hyacinth's chest. She couldn't quite move, couldn't quite breathe. She could only watch her mother's face, listen to her words, and be so very, very grateful that she'd been lucky enough to be her child.

"In some ways I was a little too protective of you," Violet said, her lips forming the tiniest of smiles, "and at the same time too lenient. You were so exuberant, so completely sure of who you were and how you fit into the world around you. You were a force of nature, and I didn't want to clip your wings."

"Thank you," Hyacinth whispered, but the words were so soft, she wasn't even sure she'd said them aloud.

"But sometimes I wonder if this left you too unaware of the people around you."

Hyacinth suddenly felt awful.

"No, no," Violet said quickly, seeing the stricken expression on Hyacinth's face. "You are kind, and you're caring, and you are far more thoughtful than I think anyone realizes. But—oh dear, I don't know how to explain this." She took a breath, her nose wrinkling as she searched for the right words. "You are so used to being completely comfortable with yourself and what you say."

"What's wrong with that?" Hyacinth asked. Not defensively, just quietly.

"Nothing. I wish more people had that talent." Violet clasped her hands together, her left thumb rubbing against her right palm. It was a gesture Hyacinth had seen on her mother countless times, always when she was lost in thought.

"But what I think happens," Violet continued, "is that when you *don't* feel that way—when something happens to give you unease—well, you don't seem to know how to manage it. And you run. Or you decide it isn't worth it." She looked at her daughter, her eyes direct and perhaps just a little bit resigned. "And that," she finally said, "is why I'm afraid you will never find the right man. Or rather, you'll find him, but you won't know it. You won't let yourself know it."

Hyacinth stared at her mother, feeling very still, and very small, and very unsure of herself. How had this happened? How had she come in here, expecting the usual talk of husbands and weddings and the lack thereof, only to find herself laid bare and open until she wasn't quite certain who she was anymore.

"I'll think about that," she said to her mother.

"That's all I can ask."

And it was all she could promise.

Chapter 5

The next evening, in the drawing room of the estimable Lady Pleinsworth. For some strange reason, there are twigs attached to the piano. And a small girl has a horn on her head.

"People will think you're courting me," Hyacinth said, when Mr. St. Clair walked directly to her side without any pretense of glancing about the room first.

"Nonsense," he said, sitting down in the empty chair next to her. "Everyone knows I don't court respectable women, and besides, I should think it would only enhance your reputation."

"And here I thought modesty an overrated virtue."

He flashed her a bland smile. "Not that I wish to give you any ammunition, but the sad fact of it is—most men are sheep. Where one goes, the rest will follow. And didn't you say you wished to be married?"

"Not to someone who follows you as the lead sheep," she replied.

He grinned at that, a devilish smile that Hyacinth had a feeling he had used to seduce legions of women. Then he looked about, as if intending to engage in something surreptitious, and leaned in.

Hyacinth couldn't help it. She leaned in, too. "Yes?" she murmured.

"I am about *this* close to bleating."

Hyacinth tried to swallow her laugh, which was a mistake, since it came out as an exceedingly inelegant splutter.

"How fortunate that you weren't drinking a glass of milk," Gareth said, sitting back in his chair. He was still the picture of perfect composure, drat the man.

Hyacinth tried to glare at him, but she was fairly certain she wasn't able to wipe the humor out of her eyes.

"It would have come out your nose," he said with a shrug.

"Hasn't anyone ever told you that's not the sort of thing you say to impress a woman?" she asked, once she'd regained her voice.

"I'm not trying to impress you," he replied, glancing up at the front of the room. "Gads," he said, blinking in surprise. "What is *that*?"

Hyacinth followed his gaze. Several of the Pleinsworth progeny, one of whom appeared to be costumed as a shepherdess, were milling about.

"Now that's an interesting coincidence," Gareth murmured.

"It might be time to start bleating," she agreed.

"I thought this was meant to be a poetry recitation."

Hyacinth grimaced and shook her head. "An unexpected change to the program, I'm afraid."

"From iambic pentameter to Little Bo Peep?" he asked doubtfully. "It does seem a stretch."

Hyacinth gave him a rueful look. "I think there will still be iambic pentameter."

His mouth fell open. "From Peep?"

She nodded, holding up the program that had been resting in her lap. "It's an original composition," she said, as if that would explain everything. "By Harriet Pleinsworth. *The Shepherdess, the Unicorn, and Henry VIII.*"

"All of them? At once?"

"I'm not jesting," she said, shaking her head.

"Of course not. Even you couldn't have made this up."

Hyacinth decided to take that as a compliment.

"Why didn't I receive one of these?" he asked, taking the program from her.

"I believe it was decided not to hand them out to the gentlemen," Hyacinth said, glancing about the room. "One has to admire Lady Pleinsworth's foresight, actually. You'd surely flee if you knew what was in store for you."

Gareth twisted in his seat. "Have they locked the doors yet?"

"No, but your grandmother has already arrived."

Hyacinth wasn't sure, but it sounded very much like he groaned.

"She doesn't seem to be coming this way," Hyacinth added, watching as Lady Danbury took a seat on the aisle, several rows back.

"Of course not," Gareth muttered, and Hyacinth knew he was thinking the same thing she was.

Matchmaker.

Well, it wasn't as if Lady Danbury had ever been especially subtle about it.

Hyacinth started to turn back to the front, then halted when she caught sight of her mother, for whom she'd been holding an empty seat to her right. Violet pretended (rather badly, in Hyacinth's opinion) not to see her, and she sat down right next to Lady Danbury.

"Well," Hyacinth said under her breath. Her mother had never been known for her subtlety, either, but she would have thought that after their conversation the previous afternoon, Violet wouldn't have been *quite* so obvious.

A few days to reflect upon it all might have been nice.

As it was, Hyacinth had spent the entire past two days pondering her conversation with her mother. She tried to think about all the people she had met during her years on the Marriage Mart. For the most part, she had had a fine time. She'd said what she wished and made people laugh and had rather enjoyed being admired for her wit.

But there had been a few people with whom she had not felt completely comfortable. Not many, but a few. There had been a gentleman during her first season with whom she'd been positively tongue-tied. He had been intelligent and handsome, and when he'd looked at her, Hyacinth had thought her legs might give out. And then just a year ago her brother Gregory had introduced her to one of his school friends who, Hyacinth had to admit, had been dry and sarcastic and more than her match. She'd told herself she hadn't liked him, and then she'd told her mother that she thought he seemed the sort to be unkind to animals. But the truth was—

Well, she didn't know what the truth was. She didn't know everything, much as she tried to give the impression otherwise.

But she had avoided those men. She'd said she didn't like them, but maybe that wasn't it. Maybe she just hadn't liked herself when she was with them.

She looked up. Mr. St. Clair was leaning back in his seat, his face looking a little bit bored, a little bit amused—that sophisticated and urbane sort of expression men across London sought to emulate. Mr. St. Clair, she decided, did it better than most.

"You look rather serious for an evening of bovine pentameter," he remarked.

Hyacinth looked over at the stage in surprise. "Are we expecting cows as well?"

He handed the small leaflet back to her and sighed. "I'm preparing myself for the worst."

Hyacinth smiled. He really *was* funny. And intelligent. And very, very handsome, although that had certainly never been in doubt.

He was, she realized, everything she'd always told herself she was looking for in a husband.

Good *God*.

"Are you all right?" he asked, sitting up quite suddenly.

"Fine," she croaked. "Why?"

"You looked . . ." He cleared his throat. "Well, you looked . . . ah . . . I'm sorry. I can't say it to a woman."

"Even one you're not trying to impress?" Hyacinth quipped. But her voice sounded a little bit strained.

He stared at her for a moment, then said, "Very well. You looked rather like you were going to be sick."

"I'm never sick," she said, looking resolutely forward. Gareth St. Clair was *not* everything she'd ever wanted in a husband. He couldn't be. "And I don't swoon, either," she added. "Ever."

"*Now* you look angry," he murmured.

"I'm not," she said, and she was rather pleased with how positively sunny she sounded.

He had a terrible reputation, she reminded herself. Did she really wish to align herself with a man who'd had relations with so many women? And unlike most unmarried women, Hyacinth actually knew what "relations" entailed. Not firsthand, of course, but she'd managed to wrench the most basic of details from her older married sisters. And while Daphne, Eloise, and Francesca assured her it was all very enjoyable with the right sort of husband, it stood to reason that the right sort of husband was one who remained faithful to one's wife. Mr. St. Clair, in contrast, had had relations with *scores* of women.

Surely such behavior couldn't be healthy.

And even if "scores" was a bit of an exaggeration, and the true number was much more modest, how could she compete? She knew for a fact that his last mistress had been none other than Maria Bartolomeo, the Italian soprano as famed for her beauty as she was for her voice. Not even her own mother could claim that Hyacinth was anywhere near as beautiful as *that*.

How horrible that must be, to enter into one's wedding night, knowing that one would suffer by comparison.

"I think it's beginning." She heard Mr. St. Clair sigh.

Footmen were crisscrossing the room, snuffing candles to dim the light. Hyacinth turned, catching sight of Mr. St. Clair's profile. A candelabrum had been left alive over his shoulder, and in the flickering light his hair appeared almost streaked with gold. He was wearing his queue, she thought idly, the only man in the room to do so.

She liked that. She didn't know why, but she liked it.

"How bad would it be," she heard him whisper, "if I ran for the door?"

"Right now?" Hyacinth whispered back, trying to ignore the tingling feeling she got when he leaned in close. "Very bad."

He sat back with a sad sigh, then focused on the stage, giving every appearance of the polite, and only very slightly bored, gentleman.

But it was only one minute later when Hyacinth heard it. Soft, and for her ears only:

"Baaa.

"Baaaaaaaaa."

Ninety mind-numbing minutes later, and sadly, our hero was right about the cows.

"Do you drink port, Miss Bridgerton?" Gareth asked, keeping his eyes on the stage as he stood and applauded the Pleinsworth children.

"Of course not, but I've always wanted to taste it, why?"

"Because we both deserve a drink."

He heard her smother a laugh, then say, "Well, the unicorn was rather sweet."

He snorted. The unicorn couldn't have been more than ten years old. Which would have been fine, except that Henry VIII had insisted upon taking an unscripted ride. "I'm surprised they didn't have to call for a surgeon," he muttered.

Hyacinth winced. "She did seem to be limping a bit."

"It was all I could do not to whinny in pain on her behalf. Good God, who—Oh! Lady Pleinsworth," Gareth said, pasting a smile on his face with what he thought was admirable speed. "How nice to see you."

"Mr. St. Clair," Lady Pleinsworth said effusively. "I'm so delighted you could attend."

"I wouldn't have missed it."

"And Miss Bridgerton," Lady Pleinsworth said, clearly angling for a bit of gossip. "Do I have you to thank for Mr. St. Clair's appearance?"

"I'm afraid his grandmother is to blame," Hyacinth replied. "She threatened him with her cane."

Lady Pleinsworth didn't seem to know quite how to respond to this, so she turned back to Gareth, clearing her throat a few times before asking, "Have you met my daughters?"

Gareth managed not to grimace. This was exactly why he tried to avoid these things. "Er, no, I don't believe I've had the pleasure."

"The shepherdess," Lady Pleinsworth said helpfully.

Gareth nodded. "And the unicorn?" he asked with a smile.

"Yes," Lady Pleinsworth replied, blinking in confusion, and quite possibly distress, "but she's a bit young."

"I'm sure Mr. St. Clair would be delighted to meet Harriet," Hyacinth cut in before turning to Gareth with an explanatory, "The shepherdess."

"Of course," he said. "Yes, delighted."

Hyacinth turned back to Lady Pleinsworth with a smile that was far too innocent. "Mr. St. Clair is an expert on all things ovine."

"Where is *my* cane when I need it?" he murmured.

"I beg your pardon?" Lady Pleinsworth said, leaning forward.

"I would be honored to meet your daughter," he said, since it seemed the only acceptable statement at that point.

"Wonderful!" Lady Pleinsworth exclaimed, clapping her hands together. "I know she will be so excited to meet you." And then, saying something about needing to see to the rest of her guests, she was off.

"Don't look so upset," Hyacinth said, once it was just the two of them again. "You're quite a catch."

He looked at her assessingly. "Is one meant to say such things quite so directly?"

She shrugged. "Not to men one is trying to impress."

"*Touché*, Miss Bridgerton."

She sighed happily. "My three favorite words."

Of that, he had no doubt.

"Tell me, Miss Bridgerton," he said, "have you begun to read my grandmother's diary?"

She nodded. "I was surprised you didn't ask earlier."

"Distracted by the shepherdess," he said, "although please don't say as much to her mother. She'd surely take it the wrong way."

"Mothers always do," she agreed, glancing around the room.

"What are you *looking* for?" he asked.

"Hmmm? Oh, nothing. Just looking."

"For what?" he persisted.

She turned to him, her eyes wide, unblinking, and startlingly blue. "Nothing in particular. Don't you like to know everything that is going on?"

"Only as it pertains to me."

"Really?" She paused. "I like to know everything."

"So I'm gathering. And speaking of which, what have you learned of the diary?"

"Oh, yes," she said, brightening before his eyes. It seemed an odd sort of metaphor, but it was true. Hyacinth Bridgerton positively sparkled when she had the opportunity to speak with authority. And the strangest thing was, Gareth thought it rather charming.

"I have only read twelve pages, I'm afraid," she said. "My mother required my assistance with her correspondence this afternoon, and I did not have the time I would have wished to work on it. I didn't tell her about it, by the way. I wasn't sure if it was meant to be a secret."

Gareth thought of his father, who would probably want the diary, if only because Gareth had it in his possession. "It's a secret," he said. "At least until I deem otherwise."

She nodded. "It's probably best not to say anything until you know what she wrote."

"What did you find out?"

"Well . . ."

He watched her as she grimaced. "What is it?" he asked.

Both corners of her mouth stretched out and down in that expression one gets when one is trying not to deliver bad news. "There's really no polite way to say it, I'm afraid," she said.

"There rarely is, when it comes to my family."

She eyed him curiously, saying, "She didn't particularly wish to marry your grandfather."

"Yes, you said as much this afternoon."

"No, I mean she *really* didn't want to marry him."

"Smart woman," he muttered. "The men in my family are bullheaded idiots."

She smiled. Slightly. "Yourself included?"

He should have anticipated that. "You couldn't resist, could you?" he murmured.

"Could *you*?"

"I imagine not," he admitted. "What else did she say?"

"Not a great deal more," Hyacinth told him. "She was only seventeen at the beginning of the diary. Her parents forced the match, and she wrote three pages about how upset she was."

"Upset?"

She winced. "Well, a bit more than upset, I must say, but—"

"We'll leave it at 'upset.'"

"Yes," she agreed, "that's best."

"How did they meet?" he asked. "Did she say?"

Hyacinth shook her head. "No. She seems to have begun the journal after their introduction. Although she did make reference to a party at her uncle's house, so perhaps that was it."

Gareth nodded absently. "My grandfather took a grand tour," he said. "They met and married in Italy, but that's all I've been told."

"Well, I don't think he compromised her, if that's what you wish to know," Hyacinth said. "I would think she'd mention *that* in her diary."

He couldn't resist a little verbal poke. "Would *you*?"

"I beg your pardon?"

"Would you write about it in your diary if someone compromised you?"

She blushed, which delighted him. "I don't keep a diary," she said.

Oh, he was loving this. "But if you did . . ."

"But I *don't*," she ground out.

"Coward," he said softly.

"Would you write all of your secrets down in a diary?" she countered.

"Of course not," he said. "If someone found it, that would hardly be fair to the people I've mentioned."

"People?" she dared.

He flashed her a grin. "Women."

She blushed again, but it was softer this time, and he rather doubted she even knew she'd done it. It tinged her pink, played with the light sprinkling of freckles across her nose. At this point, most women would have expressed their outrage, or at least pretended to, but not Hyacinth. He watched as her lips pursed slightly—maybe to hide her embarrassed expression, maybe to bite off a retort, he wasn't sure which.

And he realized that he was enjoying himself. It was hard to believe, since he was standing next to a piano covered with twigs, and he was well aware that he was going to have to spend the rest of the evening avoiding a shepherdess and her ambitious mother, but he was enjoying himself.

"Are you really as bad as they say?" Hyacinth asked.

He started in surprise. He hadn't expected that. "No," he admitted, "but don't tell anyone."

"I didn't think so," she said thoughtfully.

Something about her tone scared him. He didn't want Hyacinth Bridgerton thinking so hard about him. Because he had the oddest feeling that if she did, she might see right through him.

And he wasn't sure what she'd find.

"Your grandmother is coming this way," she said.

"So she is," he said, glad for the distraction. "Shall we attempt an escape?"

"It's far too late for that," Hyacinth said, her lips twisting slightly. "She's got my mother in tow."

"Gareth!" came his grandmother's strident voice.

"Grandmother," he said, gallantly kissing her hand when she reached his side. "It is always a pleasure to see you."

"Of course it is," she replied pertly.

Gareth turned to face an older, slightly fairer, version of Hyacinth. "Lady Bridgerton."

"Mr. St. Clair," said Lady Bridgerton warmly. "It has been an age."

"I don't often attend such recitations," he said.

"Yes," Lady Bridgerton said frankly, "your grandmother told me she was forced to twist your arm to attend."

He turned to his grandmother with raised brows. "You are going to ruin my reputation."

"You've done that all on your own, m'dear boy," Lady D said.

"I think what he means," Hyacinth put in, "is that he's not likely to be thought dashing and dangerous if the world knows how well he dotes upon you."

A slightly awkward silence fell over the group as Hyacinth realized that they had all understood his remark. Gareth found himself taking pity on her, so he filled the gap by saying, "I do have another engagement this evening, however, so I'm afraid I must take my leave."

Lady Bridgerton smiled. "We will see you Tuesday evening, however, yes?"

"Tuesday?" he queried, realizing that Lady Bridgerton's smile was nowhere near as innocent as it looked.

"My son and his wife are hosting a large ball. I'm sure you received an invitation."

Gareth was sure he had, too, but half the time he tossed them aside without looking at them.

"I promise you," Lady Bridgerton continued, "there will be no unicorns."

Trapped. And by a master, too. "In that case," he said politely, "how could I refuse?"

"Excellent. I'm sure Hyacinth will be delighted to see you."

"I am quite beside myself with glee," Hyacinth murmured.

"Hyacinth!" Lady Bridgerton said. She turned to Gareth. "She doesn't mean that."

He turned to Hyacinth. "I'm crushed."

"Because I'm beside myself, or because I'm not?" she queried.

"Whichever you prefer." Gareth turned to the group at large. "Ladies," he murmured.

"Don't forget the shepherdess," Hyacinth said, her smile sweet and just a little bit wicked. "You *did* promise her mother."

Damn. He'd forgotten. He glanced across the room. Little Bo Peep had begun to point her crook in his direction, and Gareth had the unsettling feeling that if he got close enough, she might loop it round and reel him in.

"Aren't the two of you friends?" he asked Hyacinth.

"Oh, no," she said. "I hardly know her."

"Wouldn't you like to *meet* her?" he ground out.

She tapped her finger against her jaw. "I . . . No." She smiled blandly. "But I will watch you from afar."

"Traitor," he murmured, brushing past her on the way to the shepherdess.

And for the rest of the night, he couldn't quite forget the smell of her perfume.

Or maybe it was the soft sound of her chuckle.

Or maybe it was neither of those things. Maybe it was just her.

Chapter 6

The following Tuesday, in the ballroom at Bridgerton House. The candles are lit, music fills the air, and the night seems made for romance

But not, however, for Hyacinth, who is learning that friends can be just as vexing as family

Sometimes more so.

"Do you know whom I think you should marry? I think you should marry Gareth St. Clair."

Hyacinth looked at Felicity Albansdale, her closest friend, with an expression that hovered somewhere between disbelief and alarm. She absolutely, positively, was not prepared to say that she should marry Gareth St. Clair, but on the other hand, she had begun to wonder if perhaps she ought to give it just a touch of consideration.

But still, was she so transparent?

"You're mad," she said, since she wasn't about to tell anyone that she might be developing a bit of a *tendre* for the man. She didn't like to do anything if she didn't do it well, and she had a sinking feeling that she did not know how to pursue a man with anything resembling grace or dignity.

"Not at all," Felicity said, eyeing the gentleman in question from across the ballroom. "He would be perfect for you."

As Hyacinth had spent the last several days thinking of nothing but Gareth, his grandmother, and his other grandmother's diary, she had no choice but to say, "Nonsense. I hardly know the man."

"No one does," Felicity said. "He's an enigma."

"Well, I wouldn't say *that*," Hyacinth muttered. *Enigma* sounded far too romantic, and—

"Of course he is," Felicity said, cutting into her thoughts. "What do we know about him? Nothing. Ergo—"

"Ergo nothing," Hyacinth said. "And I'm certainly not going to marry him."

"Well, you have to marry somebody," Felicity said.

"This is what happens when people get married," Hyacinth said disgustedly. "All they want is to see everyone else married."

Felicity, who had wed Geoffrey Albansdale six months earlier, just shrugged. "It's a noble goal."

Hyacinth glanced back at Gareth, who was dancing with the very lovely, very blond, and very petite Jane Hotchkiss. He appeared to be hanging on her every word.

"I am *not*," she said, turning to Felicity with renewed determination, "setting my cap for Gareth St. Clair."

"Methinks the lady doth protest too much," Felicity said airily.

Hyacinth gritted her teeth. "The lady protested *twice*."

"If you stop to think about it—"

"Which I won't do," Hyacinth interjected.

"—you'll see that he is a perfect match."

"And how is that?" Hyacinth asked, even though she knew it would only encourage Felicity.

Felicity turned to her friend and looked her squarely in the eye. "He is the only person I can think of who you wouldn't—or rather, couldn't—run into the ground."

Hyacinth looked at her for a long moment, feeling unaccountably stung. "I am unsure of whether to be complimented by that."

"Hyacinth!" Felicity exclaimed. "You know I meant no insult. For heaven's sake, what is the matter with you?"

"It's nothing," Hyacinth mumbled. But between this conversation and the one the previous week with her mother, she was beginning to wonder how, exactly, the world saw her.

Because she wasn't so certain it corresponded with how she saw herself.

"I wasn't saying that I want you to change," Felicity said, taking Hyacinth's hand in a gesture of friendship. "Goodness, no. Just that you need someone who can keep up with you. Even you must confess that most people can't."

"I'm sorry," Hyacinth said, giving her head a little shake. "I overreacted. I just . . . I haven't felt quite like myself the last few days."

And it was true. She hid it well, or at least she thought she did, but inside, she was in a bit of a turmoil. It was that talk with her mother. No, it was that talk with Mr. St. Clair.

No, it was everything. Everything all at once. And she was left feeling as if she wasn't quite sure who she was anymore, which was almost impossible to bear.

"It's probably a sniffle," Felicity said, looking back out

at the ballroom floor. "Everyone seems to have one this week."

Hyacinth didn't contradict her. It would have been nice if it was just a sniffle.

"I know you are friendly with him," Felicity continued. "I heard you sat together at both the Smythe-Smith musicale and the Pleinsworth poetry recitation."

"It was a play," Hyacinth said absently. "They changed it at the last moment."

"Even worse. I would have thought you'd have managed to get out of attending at least one."

"They weren't so awful."

"Because you were sitting next to Mr. St. Clair," Felicity said with a sly smile.

"You are terrible," Hyacinth said, refusing to look at her. If she did, Felicity was sure to see the truth in her eyes. Hyacinth was a good liar, but not that good, and not with Felicity.

And the worst of it was—she could hear herself in Felicity's words. How many times had she teased Felicity in the very same way before Felicity had married? A dozen? More?

"You should dance with him," Felicity said.

Hyacinth kept her eyes on the ballroom floor. "I can't do anything if he does not ask."

"Of course he'll ask. You have only to stand on the other side of the room, where he is more likely to see you."

"I'm not going to *chase* him."

Felicity's smile spread across her face. "You do like him! Oh, this is lovely! I have never seen—"

"I don't like him," Hyacinth cut in. And then, because

she realized how juvenile that sounded, and that Felicity would never believe her, she added, "I merely think that perhaps I ought to see if I *might* like him."

"Well, that's more than you've ever said about any other gentleman," Felicity pointed out. "And you have no need to chase him. He wouldn't dare ignore you. You are the sister of his host, and besides, wouldn't his grandmother take him to task if he didn't ask you to dance?"

"Thank you for making me feel like such a prize."

Felicity chuckled. "I have never seen you like this, and I must say, I'm enjoying it tremendously."

"I'm glad one of us is," Hyacinth grumbled, but her words were lost under the sharp sound of Felicity's gasp.

"What is it?" Hyacinth asked.

Felicity tilted her head slightly to the left, motioning across the room. "His father," she said in a low voice.

Hyacinth turned around sharply, not even trying to conceal her interest. Good heavens, Lord St. Clair was here. All of London knew that father and son did not speak, but invitations to parties were still issued to both. The St. Clair men seemed to have a remarkable talent for not appearing where the other might be, and so hostesses were generally spared the embarrassment of having them attend the same function.

But obviously, something had gone wrong this evening. Did Gareth know his father was there? Hyacinth looked quickly back to the dance floor. He was laughing at something Miss Hotchkiss was saying. No, he didn't know. Hyacinth had witnessed him with his father once. It had been from across the room, but there had been no mistaking the strained expression on his face.

Or the way both had stormed off to separate exits.

Hyacinth watched as Lord St. Clair glanced around the room. His eyes settled on his son, and his entire face hardened.

"What are you going to do?" Felicity whispered.

Do? Hyacinth's lips parted as she glanced from Gareth to his father. Lord St. Clair, still unaware of her regard, turned on his heel and walked out, possibly in the direction of the card room.

But there was no guarantee he wouldn't be back.

"You're going to do something, aren't you?" Felicity pressed. "You have to."

Hyacinth was fairly certain *that* wasn't true. She had never done anything before. But now it was different. Gareth was . . . Well, she supposed he was her friend, in a strange, unsettling sort of way. And she did need to speak with him. She'd spent the entire morning and most of the afternoon in her room, translating his grandmother's diary. Surely he would wish to know what she had learned.

And if she managed to prevent an altercation in the process . . . Well, she was always happy to be the heroine of the day, even if no one but Felicity would be aware of it.

"I will ask him to dance," Hyacinth announced.

"You will?" Felicity asked, eyes bugging out. Hyacinth was certainly known as An Original, but even she had never dared to ask a gentleman to dance.

"I shan't make a big scene about it," Hyacinth said. "No one will know but Mr. St. Clair. And you."

"And whoever happens to be standing next to him. And whomever *they* tell, and whoever—"

"Do you know what is nice about friendships as long-standing as ours?" Hyacinth interrupted.

Felicity shook her head.

"You won't take permanent offense when I turn my back and walk away."

And then Hyacinth did just that.

But the drama of her exit was considerably diminished when she heard Felicity chuckle and say, "Good luck!"

Thirty seconds later. It doesn't take very long to cross a ballroom, after all.

Gareth had always liked Jane Hotchkiss. Her sister was married to his cousin, and as a result they saw each other from time to time at Grandmother Danbury's house. More importantly, he knew he could ask her to dance without her wondering if there was some sort of ulterior matrimonial purpose.

But on the other hand—she knew him well. Or at least well enough to know when he was acting out of character.

"What are you looking for?" she asked, as their quadrille was drawing to a close.

"Nothing," he answered.

"Very well," she said, her pale blond brows coming together in a slightly exasperated expression. "*Who* are you looking for, then? And don't say no one, because you have been craning your neck throughout the dance."

He swung his head around so that his gaze was firmly

fixed on her face. "Jane," he said, "your imagination knows no bounds."

"Now I know you're lying."

She was right, of course. He'd been looking for Hyacinth Bridgerton since he had walked through the door twenty minutes earlier. He'd thought he caught sight of her before he'd stumbled upon Jane, but it had turned out to be one of her numerous sisters. All the Bridgertons looked devilishly alike. From across the room, they were practically indistinguishable.

As the orchestra played the last notes of their dance, Gareth took Jane's arm and led her to the side of the room. "I would never lie to you, Jane," he said, giving her a jaunty half smile.

"Of course you would," she returned. "And anyway, it's as obvious as day. Your eyes give you away. The only time they ever look serious is when you're lying."

"That can't be—"

"It's true," she said. "Trust me. Oh, good evening, Miss Bridgerton."

Gareth turned sharply to see Hyacinth, standing before them like a vision in blue silk. She looked especially lovely this evening. She'd done something different with her hair. He wasn't sure what; he was rarely observant enough to notice such minutiae. But it was altered somehow. It must have framed her face differently, because something about her didn't look quite the same.

Maybe it was her eyes. They looked determined, even for Hyacinth.

"Miss Hotchkiss," Hyacinth said with a polite nod. "How lovely to see you again."

Jane smiled warmly. "Lady Bridgerton always hosts such lovely parties. Please convey my regards."

"I shall. Kate is just over there by the champagne," Hyacinth said, referring to her sister-in-law, the current Lady Bridgerton. "In case you wished to tell her yourself."

Gareth felt his eyebrows rise. Whatever Hyacinth was up to, she wanted to speak with him alone.

"I see," Jane murmured. "I had best go speak with her, then. I wish you both a pleasant evening."

"Smart girl," Hyacinth said, once they were alone.

"You weren't exactly subtle," Gareth said.

"No," she replied, "but then, I rarely am. It's a skill one must be born with, I'm afraid."

He smiled. "Now that you have me all to yourself, what do you wish to do with me?"

"Don't you wish to hear about your grandmother's diary?"

"Of course," he said.

"Shall we dance?" she suggested.

"You're asking *me*?" He rather liked this.

She scowled at him.

"Ah, there is the real Miss Bridgerton," he teased. "Shining through like a surly—"

"Would you care to dance with me?" she ground out, and he realized with surprise that this wasn't easy for her. Hyacinth Bridgerton, who almost never gave the impression of being at odds with anything she did, was scared to ask him to dance.

How fun.

"I'd be delighted," he said immediately. "May I guide

you onto the floor, or is that a privilege reserved for the one doing the asking?"

"You may lead," she said, with all the hauteur of a queen.

But when they reached the floor, she seemed a little less sure of herself. And though she hid it quite well, her eyes were flicking around the room.

"Who are you looking for?" Gareth asked, letting out an amused snuff of air as he realized he was echoing Jane's exact words to him.

"No one," Hyacinth said quickly. She snapped her gaze back to his with a suddenness that almost made him dizzy. "What is so amusing?"

"Nothing," he countered, "and you were most certainly looking for someone, although I will compliment you on your ability to make it seem like you weren't."

"That's because I wasn't," she said, dipping into an elegant curtsy as the orchestra began the first strains of a waltz.

"You're a good liar, Hyacinth Bridgerton," he murmured, taking her into his arms, "but not quite as good as you think you are."

Music began to float through the air, a soft, delicate tune in three-four time. Gareth had always enjoyed dancing, particularly with an attractive partner, but it became apparent with the first—no, one must be fair, probably not until the sixth—step that this would be no ordinary waltz.

Hyacinth Bridgerton, he was quite amused to note, was a clumsy dancer.

Gareth couldn't help but smile.

He didn't know why he found this so entertaining. Maybe it was because she was so capable in everything else she did; he'd heard that she'd recently challenged a young man to a horse race in Hyde Park and won. And he was quite certain that if she ever found someone willing to teach her to fence, she'd soon be skewering her opponents through the heart.

But when it came to dancing . . .

He should have known she'd try to lead.

"Tell me, Miss Bridgerton," he said, hoping that a spot of conversation might distract her, since it always seemed that one danced with more grace when one wasn't thinking quite so hard about it. "How far along are you with the diary?"

"I've only managed ten pages since we last spoke," she said. "It might not seem like much—"

"It seems like quite a lot," he said, exerting a bit more pressure on the small of her back. A little more, and maybe he could force . . . her . . . to turn . . .

Left.

Phew.

It was quite the most exerting waltz he'd ever danced.

"Well, I'm not fluent," she said. "As I told you. So it's taking me much longer than if I could just sit down and read it like a book."

"You don't need to make excuses," he said, wrenching her to the right.

She stepped on his toe, which he ordinarily would have taken as retaliation, but under the present circumstances, he rather thought it was accidental.

"Sorry," she muttered, her cheeks turning pink. "I'm not usually so clumsy."

He bit his lip. He couldn't possibly laugh at her. It would break her heart. Hyacinth Bridgerton, he was coming to realize, didn't like to do anything if she didn't do it well. And he suspected that she had no idea that she was such an abysmal dancer, not if she took the toe-stomping as such an aberration.

It also explained why she felt the need to continually remind him that she wasn't fluent in Italian. She couldn't possibly bear for him to think she was slow without a good reason.

"I've had to make a list of words I don't know," she said. "I'm going to send them by post to my former governess. She still resides in Kent, and I'm sure she'll be happy to translate them for me. But even so—"

She grunted slightly as he swung her to the left, somewhat against her will.

"Even so," she continued doggedly, "I'm able to work out most of the meaning. It's remarkable what you can deduce with only three-quarters of the total."

"I'm sure," he commented, mostly because some sort of agreement seemed to be required. Then he asked, "Why don't you purchase an Italian dictionary? I will assume the expense."

"I have one," she said, "but I don't think it's very good. Half the words are missing."

"Half?"

"Well, some," she amended. "But truly, that's not the problem."

He blinked, waiting for her to continue.

She did. Of course. "I don't think Italian is the author's native tongue," she said.

"The author of the dictionary?" he queried.

"Yes. It's not terribly idiomatic." She paused, apparently deep in whatever odd thoughts were racing through her mind. Then she gave a little shrug—which caused her to miss a step in the waltz, not that she noticed—and continued with, "It's really of no matter. I'm making fair progress, even if it is a bit slow. I'm already up to her arrival in England."

"In just ten pages?"

"Twenty-two in total," Hyacinth corrected, "but she doesn't make entries every day. In fact, she often skips several weeks at a time. She only devoted one paragraph to the sea crossing—just enough to express her delight that your grandfather was afflicted by seasickness."

"One must take one's happiness where one can," Gareth murmured.

Hyacinth nodded. "And also, she, ah, declined to mention her wedding night."

"I believe we may consider that a small blessing," Gareth said. The only wedding night he wanted to hear about less than Grandmother St. Clair's would have to be Grandmother Danbury's.

Good God, that would send him right over the edge.

"What has you looking so pained?" Hyacinth asked.

He just shook his head. "There are some things one should never know about one's grandparents."

Hyacinth grinned at that.

Gareth's breath caught for a moment, then he found himself grinning back. There was something infectious about Hyacinth's smiles, something that forced her companions to stop what they were doing, even what they were thinking, and just smile back.

When Hyacinth smiled—when she really smiled, not one of those faux half smiles she did when she was trying to be clever—it transformed her face. Her eyes lit, her cheeks seemed to glow, and—

And she was beautiful.

Funny how he'd never noticed it before. Funny how no one had noticed it. Gareth had been out and about in London since she'd made her nod several years earlier, and while he'd never heard anyone speak of her looks in an uncomplimentary manner, nor had he heard anyone call her beautiful.

He wondered if perhaps everyone was so busy trying to keep up with whatever it was she was saying to stop and actually look at her face.

"Mr. St. Clair? Mr. St. Clair?"

He glanced down. She was looking up at him with an impatient expression, and he wondered how many times she'd uttered his name.

"Under the circumstances," he said, "you might as well use my given name."

She nodded approvingly. "A fine idea. You may of course use mine as well."

"Hyacinth," he said. "It suits you."

"It was my father's favorite flower," she explained. "Grape hyacinths. They bloom like mad in spring near our home in Kent. The first to show color every year."

"And the exact color of your eyes," Gareth said.

"A happy coincidence," she admitted.

"He must have been delighted."

"He never knew," she said, looking away. "He died before my birth."

"I'm sorry," Gareth said quietly. He did not know the Bridgertons well, but unlike the St. Clairs, they seemed to actually like each other. "I knew he had passed on some time ago, but I was not aware that you never knew him."

"It shouldn't matter," she said softly. "I shouldn't miss what I never had, but sometimes . . . I must confess . . . I do."

He chose his words carefully. "It's difficult . . . I think, not to know one's father."

She nodded, looking down, then over his shoulder. It was odd, he thought, but still somewhat endearing that she didn't wish to look at him during such a moment. Thus far their conversations had been all sly jokes and gossip. This was the first time they had ever said anything of substance, anything that truly revealed the person beneath the ready wit and easy smile.

She kept her eyes fixed on something behind him, even after he'd expertly twirled her to the left. He couldn't help but smile. She was a much better dancer now that she was distracted.

And then she turned back, her gaze settling on his face with considerable force and determination. She was ready for a change of subject. It was clear.

"Would you like to hear the remainder of what I've translated?" she inquired.

"Of course," he said.

"I believe the dance is ending," she said. "But it looks as if there is a bit of room over there." Hyacinth motioned with her head to the far corner of the ballroom, where several chairs had been set up for those with weary feet. "I am sure we could manage a few moments of privacy without anyone intruding."

The waltz drew to a close, and Gareth took a step back

and gave her a small bow. "Shall we?" he murmured, holding out his arm so that she might settle her hand in the crook of his elbow.

She nodded, and this time, he let *her* lead.

Chapter 7

Ten minutes later, and our scene has moved to the hall.

 Gareth generally had little use for large balls; they were hot and crowded, and much as he enjoyed dancing, he'd found that he usually spent the bulk of his time making idle conversation with people in whom he wasn't particularly interested. But, he thought as he made his way into the side hall of Bridgerton House, he was having a fine time this evening.

After his dance with Hyacinth, they had moved to the corner of the ballroom, where she'd informed him of her work with the diary. Despite her excuses, she had made good progress, and had in fact just reached the point of Isabella's arrival in England. It had not been auspicious. His grandmother had slipped while exiting the small dinghy that had carried her to shore, and thus her first connection with British soil had been her bottom against the wet sludge of the Dover shore.

Her new husband, of course, hadn't lifted a hand to help her.

Gareth shook his head. It was a wonder she hadn't

turned tail and run back to Italy right then. Of course, according to Hyacinth, there wasn't much waiting for her there, either. Isabella had repeatedly begged her parents not to make her marry an Englishman, but they had insisted, and it did not sound as if they would have been particularly welcoming if she had run back home.

But there was only so long he could spend in a somewhat secluded corner of the ballroom with an unmarried lady without causing talk, and so once Hyacinth had finished the tale, he had bid her farewell and handed her off to the next gentleman on her dance card.

His objectives for the evening accomplished (greeting his hostess, dancing with Hyacinth, discerning her progress with the diary), he decided he might as well leave altogether. The night was still reasonably young; there was no reason he couldn't go to his club or a gambling hell.

Or, he thought with a bit more anticipation, he hadn't seen his mistress in some time. Well, not a mistress, exactly. Gareth hadn't enough money to keep a woman like Maria in the style to which she was accustomed, but luckily one of her previous gentlemen had given her a neat little house in Bloomsbury, eliminating the need for Gareth to do the same. Since he wasn't paying her bills, she felt no need to remain faithful, but that hardly signified, since he didn't, either.

And it had been a while. It seemed the only woman he'd spent any time with lately was Hyacinth, and the Lord knew he couldn't dally there.

Gareth murmured his farewells to a few acquaintances near the ballroom door, then slipped out into the hall. It was surprisingly empty, given the number of people attending the party. He started to walk toward the front of the house, but then stopped. It was a long way to Blooms-bury, especially in a hired hack, which was what he was going to need to use, since he'd gained a ride over with his grandmother. The Bridgertons had set aside a room in the back for gentlemen to see to their needs. Gareth de-cided to make use of it.

He turned around and retraced his steps, then by-passed the ballroom door and headed farther down the hall. A couple of laughing gentlemen stepped out as he reached the door, and Gareth nodded his greetings be-fore entering.

It was one of those two-room chambers, with a small waiting area outside an inner sanctum to afford a bit more privacy. The door to the second room was closed, so Gareth whistled softly to himself as he waited his turn.

He loved to whistle.

My bonnie lies over the ocean . . .

He always sang the words to himself as he whistled.

My bonnie lies over the sea. . . .

Half the songs he whistled had words he couldn't very well sing aloud, anyway.

My bonnie lies over the ocean . . .

"I should have known it was you."

Gareth froze, finding himself face-to-face with his fa-ther, who, he realized, had been the person for whom he had been waiting so patiently to relieve himself.

"So bring back my bonnie to me," Gareth sang out loudly, giving the final word a nice, dramatic flourish.

He watched his father's jaw set into an uncomfortable line. The baron hated singing even more than he did whistling.

"I'm surprised they let you in," Lord St. Clair said, his voice deceptively placid.

Gareth shrugged insolently. "Funny how one's blood remains so conveniently hidden inside, even when it's not quite blue." He gave the older man a game smile. "All of the world thinks I am yours. Is that not just the most—"

"Stop," the baron hissed. "Good God, it's enough just to look at you. Listening makes me ill."

"Strangely enough, I remain unbothered."

But inside, Gareth could feel himself beginning to change. His heart was beating faster, and his chest had taken on a strange, shaky feeling. He felt unfocused, restless, and it took all of his self-control to hold his arms still at his sides.

One would think he'd have grown used to this, but every time, it took him by surprise. He always told himself that this would be the time he would see his father and it just wouldn't matter, but no . . .

It always did.

And Lord St. Clair wasn't even really his father. That was the true rub. The man had the ability to turn him into an immature idiot, and he wasn't even really his father. Gareth had told himself, time and again, that it didn't matter. *He* didn't matter. They weren't related by blood, and the baron should not mean any more to him than a stranger on the street.

But he did. Gareth didn't want his approval; he'd long since given up on that, and besides, why would he want approbation from a man he didn't even respect?

It was something else. Something much harder to define. He saw the baron and he suddenly had to assert himself, to make his presence known.

To make his presence felt.

He had to *bother* the man. Because the Lord knew, the man bothered him.

He felt this way whenever he saw him. Or at least when they were forced into conversation. And Gareth knew that he had to end the contact now, before he did something he might regret.

Because he always did. Every time he swore to himself that he would learn, that he'd be more mature, but then it happened again. He saw his father, and he was fifteen again, all smirky smiles and bad behavior.

But this time he was going to try. He was in Bridgerton House, for God's sake, and the least he could do was try to avoid a scene.

"If you'll excuse me," he said, trying to brush past him.

But Lord St. Clair stepped to the side, forcing their shoulders to collide. "She won't have you, you know," he said, chuckling under the words.

Gareth held himself very still. "What are you talking about?"

"The Bridgerton chit. I saw you panting after her."

For a moment Gareth didn't move. He hadn't even realized his father had been in the ballroom. Which bothered him. Not that it should have done. Hell, he should have been whooping with joy that he'd finally managed to enjoy an event without being needled by Lord St. Clair's presence.

But instead he just felt somehow deceived. As if the baron had been hiding from him.

Spying on him.

"Nothing to say?" the baron taunted.

Gareth just lifted a brow as he looked through the open door to the chamber pot. "Not unless you wish me to aim from here," he drawled.

The baron turned, saw what he meant, then said disgustedly, "You would do it, too."

"You know, I believe I would," Gareth said. Hadn't really occurred to him until that moment—his comment had been more of a threat than anything else—but he might be willing to engage in a bit of crude behavior if it meant watching his father's veins nearly burst with fury.

"You are revolting."

"You raised me."

A direct hit. The baron seethed visibly before he shot back with, "Not because I wanted to. And I certainly never dreamed I would have to pass the title on to you."

Gareth held his tongue. He would say a lot of things to anger his father, but he would not make light of his brother's death. Ever.

"George must be spinning in his grave," Lord St. Clair said in a low voice.

And Gareth snapped. One moment he was standing in the middle of the small room, his arms hanging stiffly at his sides, and the next he had his father pinned up against the wall, one hand on his shoulder, the other at his throat.

"He was my brother," Gareth hissed.

The baron spit in his face. "He was my son."

Gareth's lungs were beginning to shake. It felt as if he couldn't get enough air. "He was my brother," he repeated, putting every ounce of his will into keeping his voice even. "Maybe not through you, but through our mother. And I loved him."

And somehow the loss felt all the more severe. He had mourned George since the day he'd died, but right now it felt like a big, gaping hole was yawning within him, and Gareth didn't know how to fill it.

He was down to one person now. Just his grandmother. Just one person he could honestly say he loved.

And loved him in return.

He hadn't realized this before. Maybe he hadn't wanted to. But now, standing here with the man he'd always called Father, even after he'd learned the truth, he realized just how alone he was.

And he was disgusted with himself. With his behavior, with what he became in the baron's presence.

Abruptly, he let go, backing up as he watched the baron catch his breath.

Gareth's own breathing wasn't so steady, either.

He should go. He needed to get out, away, be anywhere but here.

"You'll never have her, you know," came his father's mocking voice.

Gareth had taken a step toward the door. He hadn't even realized he'd moved until the baron's words caused him to freeze.

"Miss Bridgerton," his father clarified.

"I don't want Miss Bridgerton," Gareth said carefully.

This made the baron laugh. "Of course you do. She is everything you're not. Everything you could never hope to be."

Gareth forced himself to relax, or at least give the appearance of it. "Well, for one thing," he said with the cocky little smile he knew his father hated, "she's female."

His father sneered at his feeble attempt at humor. "She will never marry you."

"I don't recall asking her."

"Bah. You've been lapping at her heels all week. Everyone's been commenting on it."

Gareth knew that his uncharacteristic attention paid to a proper young lady had raised a few eyebrows, but he also knew that the gossip wasn't anywhere near what his father intimated.

Still, it gave him a sick sort of satisfaction to know that his father was as obsessed with him and his doings as the other way around.

"Miss Bridgerton is a good friend of my grandmother's," Gareth said lightly, enjoying the slight curl of his father's lip at the mention of Lady Danbury. They had always hated each other, and when they'd still spoken, Lady D had never ceded the upper hand. She was the wife of an earl, and Lord St. Clair a mere baron, and she never allowed him to forget it.

"Of course she's a friend of the countess," the baron said, recovering quickly. "I'm sure it's why she tolerates your attentions."

"You would have to ask Miss Bridgerton," Gareth said lightly, trying to brush off the topic as inconsequential. He certainly wasn't about to reveal that Hyacinth was translating Isabella's diary. Lord St. Clair would probably demand that he hand it over, and that was one thing Gareth absolutely did not intend to do.

And it wasn't just because it meant that he possessed

something his father might desire. Gareth truly wanted to know what secrets lay in the delicate handwritten pages. Or maybe there were no secrets, just the daily monotony of a noblewoman married to a man she did not love.

Either way, he wanted to hear what she'd had to say.

So he held his tongue.

"You can try," Lord St. Clair said softly, "but they will never have you. Blood runs true. It always does."

"What do you mean by that?" Gareth asked, his tone carefully even. It was always difficult to tell whether his father was threatening him or just expounding upon his most favorite of subjects—bloodlines and nobility.

Lord St. Clair crossed his arms. "The Bridgertons," he said. "They will never allow her to marry you, even if she is foolish enough to fancy herself in love with you."

"She doesn't—"

"You're uncouth," the baron burst out. "You're stupid—"

It shot out of his mouth before he could stop himself: "I am *not*—"

"You behave stupidly," the baron cut in, "and you're certainly not good enough for a Bridgerton girl. They'll see through you soon enough."

Gareth forced himself to get his breathing under control. The baron loved to provoke him, loved to say things that would make Gareth protest like a child.

"In some ways," Lord St. Clair continued, a slow, self-satisfied smile spreading across his face, "it's an interesting question."

Gareth just stared at him, too angry to give him the satisfaction of asking what he meant.

"Who, pray tell," the baron mused, "is your father?"

Gareth caught his breath. It was the first time the baron had ever come out and asked it so directly. He'd called Gareth a by-blow, he'd called him a mongrel and a mangy whelp. And he had called Gareth's mother plenty of other, even less flattering things. But he'd never actually come out and pondered the question of Gareth's paternity.

And it made him wonder—had he learned the truth?

"You'd know better than I," Gareth said softly.

The moment was electric, with silence rocking the air. Gareth didn't breathe, would have stopped his heart from beating if he could have done, but in the end all Lord St. Clair said was, "Your mother wouldn't say."

Gareth eyed him warily. His father's voice was still laced with bitterness, but there was something else there, too, a certain probing, testing quality. Gareth realized that the baron was feeling him out, trying to see if Gareth had learned something of his paternity.

"It's eating you alive," Gareth said, unable to keep from smiling. "She wanted someone else more than you, and it's killing you, even after all these years."

For a moment he thought the baron might strike him, but at the last minute, Lord St. Clair stepped back, his arms stiff at his sides. "I didn't love your mother," he said.

"I never thought you had," Gareth replied. It had never been about love. It had been about pride. With the baron, it was always about pride.

"I want to know," Lord St. Clair said in a low voice. "I want to know who it was, and I will give you the satisfaction of admitting to that desire. I have never forgiven her for her sins. But you . . . you . . ." He laughed, and the sound shivered right into Gareth's soul.

"You *are* her sins," the baron said. He laughed again, the sound growing more chilling by the second. "You'll never know. You will never know whose blood passes through your veins. And you'll never know who didn't love you well enough to claim you."

Gareth's heart stopped.

The baron smiled. "Think about that the next time you ask Miss Bridgerton to dance. You're probably nothing more than the son of a chimney sweep." He shrugged, the motion purposefully disdainful. "Maybe a footman. We always did have strapping young footmen at Clair Hall."

Gareth almost slapped him. He wanted to. By God, he itched to, and it took more restraint than he'd ever known he possessed not to do it, but somehow he managed to remain still.

"You're nothing but a mongrel," Lord St. Clair said, walking to the door. "That's all you'll ever be."

"Yes, but I'm *your* mongrel," Gareth said, smiling cruelly. "Born in wedlock, even if not by your seed." He stepped forward, until they were nearly nose to nose. "I'm yours."

The baron swore and moved away, grasping the doorknob with shaking fingers.

"Doesn't it just slay you?"

"Don't attempt to be better than you are," the baron hissed. "It's too painful to watch you try."

And then, before Gareth could get in the last word, the baron stormed out of the room.

For several seconds Gareth didn't move. It was as if something in his body recognized the need for absolute stillness, as if a single motion might cause him to shatter.

And then—

His arms pumped madly through the air, his fingers curling into furious claws. He clamped his teeth together to keep from screaming, but sounds emerged all the same, low and guttural.

Wounded.

He hated this. Dear God, why?

Why why why?

Why did the baron still have this sort of power over him? He wasn't his father. He'd never been his father, and damn it all, Gareth should have been glad for that.

And he was. When he was in his right mind, when he could think clearly, he was.

But when they were face-to-face, and the baron was whispering all of Gareth's secret fears, it didn't matter.

There was nothing but pain. Nothing but the little boy inside, trying and trying and trying, always wondering why he was never quite good enough.

"I need to leave," Gareth muttered, crashing through the door into the hall. He needed to leave, to get away, to not be with people.

He wasn't fit company. Not for any of the reasons his father said, but still, he was likely to—

"Mr. St. Clair!"

He looked up.

Hyacinth.

She was standing in the hall, alone. The light from the candles seemed to leap against her hair, bringing out rich red undertones. She looked lovely, and she somehow looked . . . complete.

Her life was full, he realized. She might not have been married, but she had her family.

She knew who she was. She knew where she belonged.

And he had never felt more jealous of another human being than he did in that moment.

"Are you all right?" she asked.

He didn't say anything, but that never stopped Hyacinth. "I saw your father," she said softly. "Down the hall. He looked angry, and then he saw me, and he laughed."

Gareth's fingernails bit into his palms.

"Why would he laugh?" Hyacinth asked. "I hardly know the man, and—"

He had been staring at a spot past her shoulder, but her silence made his eyes snap back to her face.

"Mr. St. Clair?" she asked softly. "Are you sure there is nothing wrong?" Her brow was crinkled with concern, the kind one couldn't fake, then she added, more softly, "Did he say something to upset you?"

His father was right about one thing. Hyacinth Bridgerton was good. She may have been vexing, managing, and often annoying as hell, but inside, where it counted, she was good.

And he heard his father's voice.

You'll never have her.

You're not good enough for her.

You'll never—

Mongrel. Mongrel. Mongrel.

He looked at her, really looked at her, his eyes sweeping from her face to her shoulders, laid bare by the seductive décolletage of her dress. Her breasts weren't large, but they'd been pushed up, surely by some contraption meant to tease and entice, and he could see the barest hint of her cleavage, peeking out at the edge of the midnight blue silk.

"Gareth?" she whispered.

She'd never called him by his given name before. He'd told her she could, but she hadn't yet done so. He was quite certain of that.

He wanted to touch her.

No, he wanted to consume her.

He wanted to use her, to prove to himself that he was every bit as good and worthy as she was, and maybe just to show his father that he *did* belong, that he wouldn't corrupt every soul he touched.

But more than that, he just plain wanted her.

Her eyes widened as he took a step toward her, halving the distance between them.

She didn't move away. Her lips parted, and he could hear the soft rush of her breath, but she didn't move.

She might not have said yes, but she didn't say no.

He reached out, snaking his arm around her back, and in an instant she was pressed against him. He wanted her. God, how he wanted her. He needed her, for more than just his body.

And he needed her now.

His lips found hers, and he was none of the things one should be the first time. He wasn't gentle, and he wasn't sweet. He did no seductive dance, idly teasing her until she couldn't say no.

He just kissed her. With everything he had, with every ounce of desperation coursing through his veins.

His tongue parted her lips, swooped inside, tasting her, seeking her warmth. He felt her hands at the back of his neck, holding on for all she was worth, and he felt her heart racing against chest.

She wanted him. She might not understand it, she

might not know what to do with it, but she wanted him.

And it made him feel like a king.

His heart pounded harder, and his body began to tighten. Somehow they were against a wall, and he could barely breathe as his hand crept up and around, skimming over her ribs until he reached the soft fullness of her breast. He squeezed—softly, so as not to scare her, but with just enough strength to memorize the shape of her, the feel, the weight in his hand.

It was perfect, and he could feel her reaction through her dress.

He wanted to take her into his mouth, to peel the dress from her body and do a hundred wicked things to her.

He felt the resistance slip from her body, heard her sigh against his mouth. She'd never been kissed before; he was quite certain of that. But she was eager, and she was aroused. He could feel it in the way her body pressed against his, the way her fingers clutched desperately at his shoulders.

"Kiss me back," he murmured, nibbling at her lips.

"I *am*," came her muffled reply.

He drew back, just an inch. "You need a lesson or two," he said with a smile. "But don't worry, we'll get you good at this."

He leaned in to kiss her once more—dear God, he was enjoying this—but she wriggled away.

"Hyacinth," he said huskily, catching her hand in his. He tugged, intending to pull her back against him, but she yanked her hand free.

Gareth raised his brows, waiting for her to say something.

This was Hyacinth, after all. Surely she'd say something.

But she just looked stricken, sick with herself.

And then she did the one thing he never would have thought she'd do.

She ran away.

Chapter 8

The next morning. Our heroine is sitting on her bed, perched against her pillows. The Italian diary is at her side, but she has not picked it up.

She has relived the kiss in her mind approximately forty-two times.

In fact, she is reliving it right now:

 Hyacinth would have liked to think that she would be the sort of woman who could kiss with aplomb, then carry on for the rest of the evening as if nothing had happened. She'd have liked to think when the time came to treat a gentleman with well-deserved disdain, that butter wouldn't melt in her mouth, her eyes would be perfect chips of ice, and she would manage a cut direct with style and flair.

And in her imagination, she did all of that and more.

Reality, however, had not been so sweet.

Because when Gareth had said her name and tried to tug her back to him for another kiss, the only thing she could think to do was run.

Which was not, she had assured herself, for what had

to be the forty-third time since his lips had touched hers, in keeping with her character.

It couldn't be. She couldn't let it be. She was Hyacinth Bridgerton.

Hyacinth.

Bridgerton.

Surely that had to mean something. One kiss could not turn her into a senseless ninny.

And besides, it wasn't the kiss. The kiss hadn't bothered her. The kiss had, in fact, been rather nice. And, to be honest, long overdue.

One would think, in her world, among her society, that she would have taken pride in her untouched, never-been-kissed status. After all, the mere hint of impropriety was enough to ruin a woman's reputation.

But one did not reach the age of two-and-twenty, or one's fourth London season, without feeling the littlest bit rejected that no one had thus far attempted a kiss.

And no one had. Hyacinth wasn't asking to be *ravished*, for heaven's sake, but no one had even leaned in, or dropped a heavy gaze to her lips, as if he was thinking about it.

Not until last night. Not until Gareth St. Clair.

Her first instinct had been to jump with surprise. For all Gareth's rakish ways, he hadn't shown any interest in extending his reputation as a rogue in her direction. The man had an opera singer tucked away in Bloomsbury, after all. What on earth would he need with *her*?

But then . . .

Well, good heavens, she still didn't know how it had all come about. One moment she was asking him if he was unwell—he'd looked very odd, after all, and it was obvious he'd had some sort of altercation with his father, despite her efforts to separate the two—and then the next he was staring at her with an intensity that had made her shiver. He'd looked possessed, consumed.

He'd looked as if he wanted to consume *her*.

And yet Hyacinth couldn't shake the feeling that he hadn't really meant to kiss her. That maybe any woman happening across him in the hall would have done just as well.

Especially after he'd laughingly told her that she needed improvement.

She didn't think he had meant to be cruel, but still, his words had stung.

"Kiss me back," she said to herself, her voice a whiny mimic of his. "Kiss me back."

She flopped back against her pillows. "I *did*." Good heavens, what did it say about her if a man couldn't even tell when she was trying to kiss him back?

And even if she hadn't been doing such a good job of it—and Hyacinth wasn't quite ready to admit to *that*—it seemed the sort of thing that ought to come naturally, and certainly the sort of thing that ought to have come naturally to *her*. Well, still, what on earth was she expected to do? Wield her tongue like a sword? She'd put her hands on his shoulders. She hadn't struggled in his arms. What else was she supposed to have done to indicate that she was enjoying herself?

It seemed a wretchedly unfair conundrum to her. Men wanted their women chaste and untouched, then they mocked them for their lack of experience.

It was just . . . it was just . . .

Hyacinth chewed on her lip, horrified by how close to tears she was.

It was just that she'd thought her first kiss would be magical. And she'd *thought* that the gentleman in question would emerge from the encounter if not impressed then at least a little bit pleased by her performance.

But Gareth St. Clair had been his usual mocking self, and Hyacinth hated that she'd allowed him to make her feel small.

"It's just a kiss," she whispered, her words floating through the empty room. "Just a kiss. It doesn't mean a thing."

But she knew, even as she tried so hard to lie to herself about it, that it had been more than a kiss.

Much, much more.

At least that was how it had been for her. She closed her eyes in agony. Dear God, while she'd been lying on her bed thinking and thinking, then rethinking and thinking again, he was probably sleeping like a baby. The man had kissed—

Well, she didn't care to speculate on how many women he had kissed, but it certainly had to have been enough to make her seem the greenest girl in London.

How was she going to face him? And she was going to have to face him. She was translating his grandmother's diary, for heaven's sake. If she tried to avoid him, it would seem so obvious.

And the last thing she wanted to do was allow him to see how upset he had made her. There were quite a few things in life a woman needed a great deal more than pride, but Hyacinth figured that as long as dignity was still an option, she might as well hang on to it.

And in the meantime . . .

She picked up his grandmother's diary. She hadn't done any work on it for a full day. She was only twenty-two pages in; there were at least a hundred more to go.

She looked down at the book, lying unopened on her lap. She supposed she could send it back. In fact, she probably *should* send it back. It would serve him right to be forced to find another translator after his behavior the night before.

But she was enjoying the diary. Life didn't toss very many challenges in the direction of well-bred young ladies. Frankly, it would be nice to be able to say she had translated an entire book from the Italian. And it would probably be nice to actually do it, too.

Hyacinth fingered the small bookmark she'd used to hold her place and opened the book. Isabella had just arrived in England in the middle of the season, and after a mere week in the country, her new husband had dragged her off to London, where she was expected—without the benefit of fluent English—to socialize and entertain as befitted her station.

To make matters worse, Lord St. Clair's mother was in residence at Clair House and was clearly unhappy about having to give up her position as lady of the house.

Hyacinth frowned as she read on, stopping every now and then to look up an unfamiliar word. The dowager baroness was interfering with the servants, countermanding Isabella's orders and making it uncomfortable for those who accepted the new baroness as the woman in charge.

It certainly didn't make marriage look terribly appealing. Hyacinth made a mental note to try to marry a man without a mother.

"Chin up, Isabella," she muttered, wincing as she read about the latest altercation—something about an addition of mussels to the menu, despite the fact that shellfish made Isabella develop hives.

"You need to make it clear who's in charge," Hyacinth said to the book. "You—"

She frowned, looking down at the latest entry. This didn't make sense. Why was Isabella talking about her *bambino?*

Hyacinth read the words three times before thinking to glance back up at the date at top. *24 Ottobre, 1766.*

1766? Wait a minute . . .

She flipped back one page.

1764.

Isabella had skipped two years. Why would she do that?

Hyacinth looked quickly through the next twenty or so pages. *1766 . . . 1769 . . . 1769 . . . 1770 . . . 1774 . . .*

"You're not a very dedicated diarist," Hyacinth murmured. No wonder Isabella had managed to fit decades into one slim volume; she frequently went years between entries.

Hyacinth turned back to the passage about the *bambino,* continuing her laborious translation. Isabella was back in London, this time without her husband, which didn't seem to bother her one bit. And she seemed to have gained a bit of self-confidence, although that might have been merely the result of the death of the dowager, which Hyacinth surmised had happened a year earlier.

I found the perfect spot, Hyacinth translated, jotting the words down on paper. *He will never . . .* She frowned. She didn't know the rest of the sentence, so she put some dashes down on her paper to indicate an untranslated phrase and moved on. *He does not think I am intelligent enough*, she read. *And so he won't suspect . . .*

"Oh, my goodness," Hyacinth said, sitting up straight. She flipped the page of the diary, reading it as quickly as she could, her attempts at a written translation all but forgotten.

"Isabella," she said with admiration. "You sly fox."

*An hour or so later, an instant before Gareth knocks
on Hyacinth's door.*

Gareth sucked in a deep breath, summoning the courage to wrap his fingers around the heavy brass knocker that sat on the front door of Number Five, Bruton Street, the elegant little house Hyacinth's mother had purchased after her eldest son had married and taken over Bridgerton House.

Then he tried not to feel completely disgusted with himself for feeling he needed the courage in the first place. And it wasn't really courage he needed. For God's sake, he wasn't *afraid*. It was . . . well, no, it wasn't quite dread. It was—

He groaned. In every life, there were moments a person would do just about anything to put off. And if it meant he was less of a man because he *really* didn't feel like dealing with Hyacinth Bridgerton . . . well, he was perfectly willing to call himself a juvenile fool.

Frankly, he didn't know anyone who'd want to deal with Hyacinth Bridgerton at a moment like this.

He rolled his eyes, thoroughly impatient with himself. This shouldn't be difficult. He shouldn't feel strained. Hell, it wasn't as if he had never kissed a female before and had to face her the next day.

Except . . .

Except he'd never kissed a female like Hyacinth, one who A) hadn't been kissed before and B) had every reason to expect that a kiss might mean something more.

Not to mention C) was Hyacinth.

Because one really couldn't discount the magnitude of that. If there was one thing he had learned in this past week, it was that Hyacinth was quite unlike any other woman he'd ever known.

At any rate, he'd sat at home all morning, waiting for the package that would surely arrive, escorted by a liveried footman, returning his grandmother's diary. Hyacinth couldn't possibly wish to translate it now, not after he had insulted her so grievously the night before.

Not, he thought, only a little bit defensively, that he'd meant to insult her. In truth, he hadn't meant anything one way or another. He certainly hadn't meant to kiss her. The thought hadn't even occurred to him, and in fact he rather thought it *wouldn't* have occurred to him except that he had been so off-balance, and then she'd somehow been there, right in the hallway, almost as if summoned by magic.

Right after his father had taunted him about her.

What the hell else was he expected to do?

And it hadn't meant anything. It was enjoyable—

certainly more enjoyable than he would have imagined, but it hadn't meant a thing.

But women tended to view these things badly, and her expression when she broke it off had not been terribly inviting.

If anything, she had looked horrified.

Which had made him feel a fool. He'd never disgusted a woman with his kiss before.

And it had all been magnified later that night, when he'd overheard someone asking her about him, and she had brushed it off with a laugh, saying that she couldn't possibly have refused to dance with him; she was far too good friends with his grandmother.

Which was true, and he certainly understood that she was attempting to save face, even if she hadn't known that he could hear, but all the same, it was too close an echo of his father's words for him not to feel it.

He let out a sigh. There was no putting it off any longer. He lifted his hand, intending to grasp the knocker—

And then quite nearly lost his balance when the door flew open.

"For heaven's sake," Hyacinth said, looking at him through impatient eyes, "were you ever going to knock?"

"Were you watching for me?"

"Of course I was. My bedroom is right above. I can see everyone."

Why, he wondered, did this not surprise him?

"And I did send you a note," she added. She stood aside, motioning for him to come in. "Recent behavior notwithstanding," she continued, "you do seem to possess manners enough not to refuse a direct written request from a lady."

"Er . . . yes," he said. It was all he could seem to think of, faced as he was by the whirlwind of energy and activity standing across from him.

Why wasn't she angry with him? Wasn't she *supposed* to be angry?

"We need to talk," Hyacinth said.

"Of course," he murmured. "I must apologize—"

"Not about that," she said dismissively, "although . . ." She looked up, her expression somewhere between thoughtful and peeved. "You certainly *should* apologize."

"Yes, of course, I—"

"But that's not why I summoned you," she cut in.

If it had been polite, he would have crossed his arms. "Do you wish for me to apologize or not?"

Hyacinth glanced up and down the hall, placing one finger to her lips with a soft, "Shhh."

"Have I suddenly been transported into a volume of *Miss Butterworth and the Mad Baron*?" Gareth wondered aloud.

Hyacinth scowled at him, a look that he was coming to realize was quintessentially her. It was a frown, yes, but with a hint—no, make that three hints—of impatience. It was the look of a woman who had spent her life waiting for people to keep up with her.

"In here," she said, motioning toward an open doorway.

"As you wish, my lady," he murmured. Far be it for him to complain about not having to apologize.

He followed her into what turned out to be a drawing room, tastefully decorated in shades of rose and cream. It was very delicate and very feminine, and Gareth half wondered if it had been designed for the sole purpose of making men feel overlarge and ill at ease.

Hyacinth waved him over to a sitting area, so he went, watching her curiously as she carefully maneuvered the door until it was shut most of the way. Gareth eyed the four-inch opening with amusement. Funny how such a small space could mean the difference between propriety and disaster.

"I don't want to be overheard," Hyacinth said.

Gareth just lifted his brows in question, waiting for her to seat herself on the sofa. When he was satisfied that she wasn't going to jump up and check behind the drapes for an eavesdropper, he sat in a Hepplewhite armchair that was catercorner to the sofa.

"I need to tell you about the diary," she said, her eyes alight with excitement.

He blinked with surprise. "You're not going to return it, then?"

"Of course not. You don't think I—" She stopped, and he noticed that her fingers were twisting spirals in the soft green fabric of her skirt. For some reason this pleased him. He was rather relieved that she was not furious with him for kissing her—like any man, he'd go to great lengths to avoid any sort of hysterical feminine scene. But at the same time, he didn't wish for her to be completely unaffected.

Good God, he was a better kisser than *that*.

"I *should* return the diary," she said, sounding rather like herself again. "Truly, I should force you to find someone else to translate it. You deserve no less."

"Absolutely," he demurred.

She gave him a look, saying that she didn't appreciate such perfunctory agreement. *"However,"* she said, as only she could say it.

Gareth leaned forward. It seemed expected.

"However," she said again, "I rather like reading your grandmother's diary, and I see no reason to deprive myself of an enjoyable challenge simply because you have behaved recklessly."

Gareth held silent, since his last attempt at agreement had been so ill received. It soon became apparent, however, that this time he was expected to make a comment, so he quickly chimed in with, "Of course not."

Hyacinth nodded approvingly, then added, "And besides"—and here she leaned forward, her bright blue eyes sparkling with excitement—*"it just got interesting."*

Something turned over in Gareth's stomach. Had Hyacinth discovered the secret of his birth? It hadn't even occurred to him that Isabella might have known the truth; she'd had very little contact with her son, after all, and rarely visited.

But if she did know, she very well might've written it down.

"What do you mean?" he asked carefully.

Hyacinth picked up the diary, which had been sitting on a nearby end table. "Your grandmother," she said, her entire bearing radiating excitement, "had a secret." She opened the book—she'd marked a page with an elegant little bookmark—and held it out, pointing with her index finger to a sentence in the middle of the page as she said, *"Diamanti. Diamanti."* She looked up, unable to contain an exhilarated grin. "Do you know what that means?"

He shook his head. "I'm afraid not."

"Diamonds, Gareth. It means diamonds."

He found himself looking at the page, even though he couldn't possibly understand the words. "I beg your pardon?"

"Your grandmother had jewels, Gareth. And she never told your grandfather about them."

His lips parted. "What are you saying?"

"*Her* grandmother came to visit shortly after your father was born. And she brought with her a set of jewels. Rings, I think. And a bracelet. And Isabella never told anyone."

"What did she do with them?"

"She hid them." Hyacinth was practically bouncing off the sofa now. "She hid them in Clair House, right here in London. She wrote that your grandfather didn't much like London, so there would be less chance he'd discover them here."

Finally, some of Hyacinth's enthusiasm began to seep into him. Not much—he wasn't going to allow himself to get too excited by what was probably going to turn out to be a wild-goose chase. But her fervor was infectious, and before he realized it, he was leaning forward, his heart beginning to beat just a little bit faster. "What are you saying?" he asked.

"I'm saying," she said, as if she was repeating something she'd uttered five times already, in every possible permutation, "that those jewels are probably still there. Oh!" She stopped short, her eyes meeting his with an almost disconcerting suddenness. "Unless you already know about them. Does your father already have them in his possession?"

"No," Gareth said thoughtfully. "I don't think so. At least, not that I've ever been told."

"You see? We can—"

"But I'm rarely told of anything," he cut in. "My father has never considered me his closest confidant."

For a moment her eyes took on a sympathetic air, but that was quickly trampled by her almost piratical zeal. "Then they're still there," she said excitedly. "Or at least there is a very good chance that they are. We have to go get them."

"What—*We?*" Oh, no.

But Hyacinth was too lost in her own excitement to have noticed his emphasis. "Just think, Gareth," she said, clearly now perfectly comfortable with the use of his given name, "this could be the answer to all of your financial problems."

He drew back. "What makes you think I have financial problems?"

"Oh, please," she scoffed. "Everyone knows you have financial problems. Or if you don't, you will. Your father has run up debts from here to Nottinghamshire and back." She paused, possibly for air, then said, "Clair Hall is in Nottinghamshire, isn't it?"

"Yes, of course, but—"

"Right. Well. You're going to inherit those debts, you know."

"I'm aware."

"Then what better way to ensure your solvency than to secure your grandmother's jewels before Lord St. Clair finds them? Because we both know that he will only sell them and spend the proceeds."

"You seem to know a great deal about my father," Gareth said in a quiet voice.

"Nonsense," she said briskly. "I know nothing about him except that he detests you."

Gareth cracked a smile, which surprised him. It wasn't a topic about which he usually possessed a great deal of humor. But then again, no one had ever dared broach it with such frankness before.

"I could not speak on your behalf," Hyacinth continued with a shrug, "but if *I* detested someone, you can be sure I would go out of my way to make certain he didn't get a treasure's worth of jewels."

"How positively Christian of you," Gareth murmured.

She lifted a brow. "I never said I was a model of goodness and light."

"No," Gareth said, feeling his lips twitch. "No, you certainly did not."

Hyacinth clapped her hands together, then set them both palms down on her lap. She looked at him expectantly. "Well, then," she said, once it was apparent that he had no further comment, "when shall we go?"

"Go?" he echoed.

"To look for the diamonds," she said impatiently. "Haven't you been listening to anything I've said?"

Gareth suddenly had a terrifying vision of what it must be like inside her mind. She was dressed in black, clearly, and—good God—almost certainly in men's clothing as well. She'd probably insist upon lowering herself out her bedroom window on knotted sheets, too.

"*We* are not going anywhere," he said firmly.

"Of course we are," she said. "You must get those jewels. You can't let your father have them."

"*I* will go."

"You're not leaving *me* behind." It was a statement, not

a question. Not that Gareth would have expected otherwise from her.

"*If* I attempt to break into Clair House," Gareth said, "and that is a rather large *if,* I will have to do so in the dead of night."

"Well, of course."

Good God, did the woman *never* cease talking? He paused, waiting to make sure that she was done. Finally, with a great show of exaggerated patience, he finished with, "I am not dragging you around town at midnight. Forget, for one moment, about the danger, of which I assure you there is plenty. If we were caught, I would be required to marry you, and I can only assume your desire for that outcome evenly matches mine."

It was an overblown speech, and his tone had been rather pompous and stuffy, but it had the desired effect, forcing her to close her mouth for long enough to sort through the convoluted structure of his sentences.

But then she opened it again, and said, "Well, you won't have to drag me."

Gareth thought his head might explode. "Good God, woman, have you been listening to anything I've said?"

"Of course I have. I have four older brothers. I can recognize a supercilious, pontificating male when I see one."

"Oh, for the love of—"

"You, Mr. St. Clair, aren't thinking clearly." She leaned forward, lifting one of her brows in an almost disconcertingly confident manner. "You need me."

"Like I need a festering abscess," he muttered.

"I am going to pretend I didn't hear that," Hyacinth said. Between her teeth. "Because if I did otherwise, I would not be inclined to aid you in your endeavors. And if I did not aid you—"

"Do you have a *point?*"

She eyed him coolly. "You are not nearly as sensible a person as I thought you."

"Strangely enough, you are *exactly* as sensible as I thought you."

"I will pretend I didn't hear *that* as well," she said, jabbing her index finger in his direction in a most unladylike manner. "You seem to forget that of the two of us, I am the only one who reads Italian. And I don't see how you are going find the jewels without my aid."

His lips parted, and when he spoke, it was in a low, almost terrifyingly even voice. "You would withhold the information from me?"

"Of course not," Hyacinth said, since she couldn't bring herself to lie to him, even if he did deserve it. "I do have *some* honor. I was merely trying to explain that you will need me *there*, in the house. My knowledge of the language isn't perfect. There are some words that could be open to interpretation, and I might need to see the actual room before I can tell exactly what she was talking about."

His eyes narrowed.

"It's the truth, I swear!" She quickly grabbed the book, flipping a page, then another, then going back to the original. "It's right here, see? *Armadio*. It could mean cabinet. Or it could mean wardrobe. Or—" She stopped, swallowing. She hated to admit that she wasn't quite sure what she was talking about, even if that deficiency was the only thing that was going to secure her a place by his side when he went to look for the jewels. "If you must know," she said, unable to keep her irritation out of her voice, "I'm not precisely certain what it means. Precisely, that is," she added, because the truth was, she *did* have a fairly good idea. And it just wasn't in her character to admit to faults she didn't have.

Good gracious, she had a difficult enough time with faults she did possess.

"Why don't you look it up in your Italian dictionary?"

"It's not listed," she lied. It wasn't really *such* an egregious fib. The dictionary had listed several possible translations, certainly enough for Hyacinth to truthfully claim an imprecise understanding.

She waited for him to speak—probably not as long as she should have done, but it seemed like an eternity. And she *just* couldn't keep quiet. "I could, if you wish, write to my former governess and ask for a more exact definition, but she's not the most reliable of correspondents—"

"Meaning?"

"Meaning I haven't written to her in three years," Hyacinth admitted, "although I'm quite certain she would come to my aid now. It's just that I have no idea how busy she is or when she might find the time to reply—the last I'd heard she'd given birth to twins—"

"Why does this not surprise me?"

"It's true, and heaven only knows how long it will take her to respond. Twins are an uncommon amount of work, or so I'm told, and . . ." Her voice lost some of its volume as it became apparent he wasn't listening to her. She stole a glance at his face and finished, anyway, mostly because she'd already thought of the words, and there wasn't much point in *not* saying them. "Well, I don't think she has the means for a baby nurse," she said, but her voice had trailed off by the end of it.

Gareth held silent for what seemed an interminably long time before finally saying, "If what you say is correct, and the jewels are still hidden—and that is no certainty, given that she hid them"—his eyes floated briefly up as he did the math—"over sixty years ago, then surely they will remain in place until we can get an accurate translation from your governess."

"You could wait?" Hyacinth asked, feeling her entire head move forward and down with disbelief. "You could actually *wait*?"

"Why not?"

"Because they're *there*. Because—" She cut herself off, unable to do anything other than stare at him as if he were mad. She knew that people's minds did not work the same way. And she'd long since learned that hardly anyone's mind worked the way hers did. But she couldn't imagine that *any*one could wait when faced with *this*.

Good heavens, if it were up to her, they'd be scaling the wall of Clair House that night.

"Think about this," Hyacinth said, leaning forward. "If he finds those jewels between now and whenever you find the time to go look for them, you are never going to forgive yourself."

He said nothing, but she could tell that she'd finally got through to him.

"Not to mention," she continued, "that *I* would never forgive you were that to happen."

She stole a glance at him. He seemed unmoved by that particular argument.

Hyacinth waited quietly while he thought about what

to do. The silence was horrible. While she'd been going on about the diary, she'd been able to forget that he'd kissed her, that she'd enjoyed it, and that he apparently hadn't. She'd thought that their next meeting would be awkward and uncomfortable, but with a goal and a mission, she'd felt restored to her usual self, and even if he didn't take her along to find the diamonds, she supposed she still owed Isabella thanks for that.

But all the same, she rather thought she'd die if he left her behind. Either that or kill him.

She gripped her hands together, hiding them in the folds of her skirt. It was a nervous gesture, and the mere fact that she was doing it set her even more on edge. She hated that she was nervous, hated that he made her nervous, hated that she had to sit there and not say a word while he pondered her options. But contrary to popular belief, she did occasionally know when to keep her mouth shut, and it was clear that there was nothing more she could say that would sway him one way or the other. Except maybe . . .

No, even she wasn't crazy enough to threaten to go by herself.

"What were you going to say?" Gareth asked.

"I beg your pardon?"

He leaned forward, his blue eyes sharp and unwavering. "What were you going to say?"

"What makes you think I was going to say something?"

"I could see it in your face."

She cocked her head to the side. "You know me that well?"

"Frightening though it may seem, apparently I do."

She watched as he sat back in his seat. He reminded

her of her brothers as he shifted in the too-small chair; they were forever complaining that her mother's sitting room was decorated for tiny females. But that was where the resemblance ended. None of her brothers had ever possessed the daring to wear his hair back in such a rakish queue, and none of them ever looked at her with that blue-eyed intensity that made her forget her own name.

He seemed to be searching her face for something. Or maybe he was just trying to stare her down, waiting for her to crack under the pressure.

Hyacinth caught her lower lip between her teeth—she wasn't strong enough to maintain the perfect picture of composure. But she did manage to keep her back straight, and her chin high, and perhaps most importantly, her mouth shut as he pondered his options.

A full minute went by. Very well, it was probably no more than ten seconds, but it felt like a minute. And then finally, because she could stand it no longer, she said (but very softly), "You need me."

His gaze fell to the carpet for a moment before turning back to her face. "If I take you—"

"Oh, thank you!" she exclaimed, just barely resisting the urge to jump to her feet.

"I said *if* I take you," he said, his voice uncommonly stern.

Hyacinth silenced herself immediately, looking at him with an appropriately dutiful expression.

"If I take you," he repeated, his eyes boring into hers, "I expect you to follow my orders."

"Of course."

"We will proceed as I see fit."

She hesitated.

"Hyacinth."

"Of course," she said quickly, since she had a feeling that if she didn't, he would call it off right then and there. "But if I have a good idea . . ."

"Hyacinth."

"As pertains to the fact that I understand Italian and you don't," she added quickly.

The look he gave her was as exhausted as it was austere.

"You don't have to do what I ask," she finally said, "just listen."

"Very well," he said with a sigh. "We will go Monday night."

Hyacinth's eyes widened with surprise. After all the fuss he'd made, she hadn't expected him to elect to go so soon. But she wasn't about to complain. "Monday night," she agreed.

She could hardly wait.

Chapter 9

Monday night. Our hero, who has spent much of his life in reckless abandon, is discovering the rather odd sensation of being the more sensible member of a duo.

There were a number of reasons, Gareth decided as he stole around to the back of Hyacinth's house, why he should question his sanity.

One: It was after midnight.

Two: They would be quite alone.

Three: They were going to the baron's house to:

Four: Commit larceny.

As far as bad ideas went, this stole the prize.

But no, somehow she had talked him into it, and so here he was, against all better judgment, ready to lead a proper young miss out of her house, into the night, and quite possibly into danger.

Not to mention that if anyone caught wind of this, the Bridgertons would have him standing up before a priest before he could catch his breath, and they'd be shackled to each other for life.

He shivered. The thought of Hyacinth Bridgerton as

his lifelong companion . . . He stopped for a moment, blinking in surprise. Well, it wasn't horrible, actually, but at the same time, it did leave a man feeling very, very uneasy.

He knew she thought she'd talked him into doing this, and maybe she had contributed in some degree to his decision, but the truth was, a man in Gareth's financial position couldn't afford to turn his nose up when faced with an opportunity such as this. He'd been a little startled at Hyacinth's frank assessment of his financial situation. Forget for a moment that such matters were not considered polite conversation (he wouldn't have expected her to adhere to such normal notions of propriety in any case). But he'd had no idea that his state of affairs was such common knowledge.

It was disconcerting, that.

But what was even more compelling, and what was really egging him on to look for the jewels now, as opposed to waiting until Hyacinth could obtain a better translation of the diary, was the delicious thought that he might actually snatch the diamonds right from under his father's nose.

It was difficult to pass up an opportunity like *that*.

Gareth edged along the back of Hyacinth's house to the servants' entrance, located in the rear, across from the mews. They had agreed to meet there at precisely half one, and he had no doubt that she would be ready and waiting for him, dressed as he had instructed, all in black.

And sure enough, there she was, holding the back door an inch ajar, peeking out through the crack.

"You're right on time," she said, slipping outside.

He stared at her in disbelief. She'd taken his order to heart and was dressed head to toe in unrelenting black. Except that no skirt swirled about her feet. Instead, she wore breeches and a waistcoat.

He'd *known* she was going to do this. He'd known it, and yet still, he couldn't contain his surprise.

"It seemed more sensible than a dress," Hyacinth said, correctly interpreting his silence. "And besides, I don't own anything in pure black. Haven't ever been in mourning, thank goodness."

Gareth just stared. There was a reason, he was coming to realize, why women didn't wear breeches. He didn't know where she'd acquired her costume—it had probably belonged to one of her brothers in his youth. It hugged her body in a most scandalous fashion, outlining her curves in a manner Gareth would really rather not have seen.

He didn't want to know that Hyacinth Bridgerton had a delectable figure. He didn't want to know that her legs were quite long for her somewhat petite height or that her hips were gently rounded and that they twitched in the most mesmerizing fashion when they weren't hidden beneath the silky folds of a skirt.

It was bad enough that he'd kissed her. He didn't need to want to do it again.

"I can't believe I'm doing this," he muttered, shaking his head. Good God, he sounded like a stick, like all those sensible friends he'd dragged into mischief as a youth.

He was beginning to think they'd actually known what they were talking about.

Hyacinth looked at him with accusing eyes. "You cannot back out now."

"I wouldn't dream of it," he said with a sigh. The woman would probably chase him down with a club if he did. "Come along, let's be off before someone catches us right here."

She nodded, then followed his lead down Barlow Place. Clair House was located less than a quarter mile away, and so Gareth had plotted a route for them to travel on foot, sticking, whenever they could, to the quiet side streets where they'd be less likely to be spotted by a member of the *ton*, traveling home via carriage from a party.

"How did you know your father wouldn't be home this evening?" Hyacinth whispered as they approached the corner.

"I'm sorry?" He peered around the corner, making sure the coast was clear.

"How did you know your father wouldn't be home?" she said again. "I was surprised that you would have knowledge of such a thing. I can't imagine he makes you privy to his schedule."

Gareth gritted his teeth, surprised by the bubble of irritation her question brought up inside of him. "I don't know," he muttered. "I just do." It was damned annoying, actually, that he was always so aware of his father's movements, but at least he could take some satisfaction in knowing that the baron was similarly afflicted.

"Oh," Hyacinth said. And it was all she said. Which was nice. Out of character, but nice.

Gareth motioned for her to follow as they made their way the short distance up Hay Hill, and then finally they were on Dover Street, which led to the alleyway behind Clair House.

"When was the last time you were here?" Hyacinth whispered as they crept up to the back wall.

"On the inside?" he asked brusquely. "Ten years. But if we're lucky, that window"—he pointed to a ground-floor aperture, only a little out of their reach—"will still have a broken latch."

She nodded appreciatively. "I was wondering how we were going to get in."

They both held silent for a moment, looking up at the window.

"Higher than you remembered?" asked Hyacinth. But then, of course, she didn't wait for an answer before adding, "It's a good thing you brought me along. You can boost me up."

Gareth looked from her to the window and back. It somehow seemed wrong to send her into the house first. He hadn't considered this, though, when planning his entry.

"I'm not going to boost *you* up," Hyacinth said impatiently. "So unless you've a crate hidden away somewhere, or perhaps a small ladder—"

"Just go," Gareth practically growled, making a step for her with his hands. He had done this before, plenty of times. But it was a far different thing with Hyacinth Bridgerton brushing alongside his body than one of his school-chums.

"Can you reach?" he asked, hoisting her up.

"Mmm-hmm," was the reply.

Gareth looked up. Right at her bottom. He decided to

enjoy the view as long as she had no idea she was providing it.

"I just need to get my fingers under the edge," she whispered.

"Go right ahead," he said, smiling for the first time all night.

She twisted immediately around. "Why do you suddenly sound so equable?" she asked suspiciously.

"Just appreciating your usefulness."

"I—" She pursed her lips together. "Do you know, I don't think I trust you."

"Absolutely you shouldn't," he agreed.

He watched as she jiggled the window, then slid it up and open.

"Did it!" she said, sounding triumphant even through her whisper.

He gave her an appreciative nod. She was fairly insufferable, but it seemed only fair to give credit where credit was due. "I'm going to push you up," he said. "You should be able to—"

But she was already in. Gareth couldn't help but stand back in admiration. Hyacinth Bridgerton was clearly a born athlete.

Either that or a cat burglar.

Her face appeared in the open window. "I don't think anyone heard," she whispered. "Can you get up by yourself?"

He nodded. "As long as the window is already open, it's no trouble." He'd done this before, several times, when he'd been a schoolboy, home on holiday. The exterior wall was made of stone, and there were a few rough spots, with outcroppings just long enough to wedge his foot. Add that to the one knobby bit he could grasp with his hand . . .

He was inside in under twenty seconds.

"I'm impressed," Hyacinth said, peering back out the window.

"You're impressed by strange things," he said, brushing himself off.

"Anyone can bring flowers," she said with a shrug.

"Are you saying all a man needs to do to win your heart is scale a building?"

She looked back out the window. "Well, he'd have to do a bit more than this. Two stories, at the very least."

He shook his head, but he couldn't help but smile. "You said that the diary mentioned a room decorated in shades of green?"

She nodded. "I wasn't entirely certain of the meaning. It could have been a drawing room. Or maybe a study. But she did mention a small, round window."

"The baroness's office," he decided. "It's on the second floor, right off the bedroom."

"Of course!" She was whispering, but her excitement still rang through. "That would make perfect sense. Especially if she wanted to keep it from her husband. She wrote that he never visited her rooms."

"We'll go up the main stairs," Gareth said quietly. "We'll be less likely to be heard. The back ones are too close to the servants' quarters."

She nodded her agreement, and together they crept through the house. It was quiet, just as Gareth would have expected. The baron lived alone, and when he was out, the servants retired early.

Except one. Gareth stopped short, needing a moment

to reassess. The butler would be awake; he never went to bed when Lord St. Clair was still expected back and might require assistance.

"This way," Gareth mouthed to Hyacinth, doubling back to take a different route. They would still take the main stairs, but they would go the long way around to get there.

Hyacinth followed his lead, and a minute later they were creeping up the stairs. Gareth pulled her to the side; the steps had always creaked in the center, and he rather doubted his father possessed the funds to have them repaired.

Once in the upstairs hall, he led Hyacinth to the baroness's office. It was a funny little room, rectangular with one window and three doors, one to the hall, one to the baroness's bedroom, and the last to a small dressing room that was more frequently used for storage since there was a much more comfortable dressing area directly off the bedchamber.

Gareth motioned Hyacinth inside, then stepped in behind her, closing the door carefully, his hand tight on the doorknob as it turned.

It shut without a click. He let out a breath.

"Tell me exactly what she wrote," he whispered, pulling back the drapes to allow in a bit of moonlight.

"She said it was in the *armadio*," Hyacinth whispered back. "Which is probably a cabinet. Or maybe a set of drawers. Or—" Her eyes fell on a tall but narrow curio cabinet. It was triangular in shape, tucked into one of the rear corners. The wood was a dark, rich hue, and it stood on three spindly legs, leaving about two feet of space under its base. "This is it," Hyacinth whispered excitedly. "It has to be."

She was across the room before Gareth even had a chance to move, and by the time he joined her, she had one of the drawers open and was searching through.

"Empty," she said, frowning. She knelt and pulled open the bottom drawer. Also empty. She looked up at Gareth and said, "Do you think someone removed her belongings after she passed away?"

"I have no idea," he said. He gave the cabinet door a gentle tug and pulled it open. Also empty.

Hyacinth stood, planting her hands on her hips as she regarded the cabinet. "I can't imagine what else . . ." Her words trailed off as she ran her fingers over the decorative carvings near the top edge.

"Maybe the desk," Gareth suggested, crossing the distance to the desk in two strides.

But Hyacinth was shaking her head. "I don't think so," she said. "She wouldn't have called a desk an *armadio*. It would have been a *scrivania*."

"It still has drawers," Gareth muttered, pulling them open to inspect the contents.

"There's something about this piece," Hyacinth murmured. "It looks rather Mediterranean, don't you think?"

Gareth looked up. "It does," he said slowly, coming to his feet.

"If she brought this from Italy," Hyacinth said, her head tilting slightly to the side as she eyed the cabinet assessingly, "or if her grandmother brought it on her visit . . ."

"It would stand to reason that she would know if there was a secret compartment," Gareth finished for her.

"And," Hyacinth said, her eyes alight with excitement, "her husband *wouldn't*."

Gareth quickly set the desk to rights and returned to the curio cabinet. "Stand back," he instructed, wrapping his fingers around the lower lip so that he could pull it away from the wall. It was heavy, though, much heavier than it looked, and he was only able to move it a few inches, just far enough so that he could run his hand along the back.

"Do you feel anything?" Hyacinth whispered.

He shook his head. He couldn't reach very far in, so he dropped to his knees and tried feeling the back panel from underneath.

"Anything there?" Hyacinth asked.

He shook his head again. "Nothing. I just need to—" He froze as his fingers ran across a small, rectangular outcropping of wood.

"What is it?" she asked, trying to peer around the back.

"I'm not certain," he said, stretching his arm a half inch farther. "It's a knob of some sort, maybe a lever."

"Can you move it?"

"I'm trying," he nearly gasped. The knob was almost out of his reach, and he had to contort and twist just to catch it between his fingers. The lower front edge of the cabinet was digging painfully into the muscles of his upper arm, and his head was twisted awkwardly to the side, his cheek pressing up against the cabinet door.

All in all, not the most graceful of positions.

"What if I do this?" Hyacinth wedged herself next to the cabinet and slid her arm around back. Her fingers found the knob easily.

Gareth immediately let go and pulled his arm out from under the cabinet.

"Don't worry," she said, somewhat sympathetically, "you couldn't have fit your arm back here. There isn't much room."

"I don't care which of us can reach the knob," he said.

"You don't? Oh." She shrugged. "Well, I would."

"I know," he said.

"Not that it really matters, of course, but—"

"Do you feel anything?" he cut in.

She shook her head. "It doesn't seem to be moving. I've tried it up and down, and side to side."

"Push it in."

"That doesn't do it, either. Unless I—" Her breath caught.

"What?" Gareth asked urgently.

She looked up at him, her eyes shining, even in the dim light of the moon. "It twisted. And I felt something click."

"Is there a drawer? Can you pull it out?"

Hyacinth shook her head, her mouth scrunching into an expression of concentration as she moved her hand along the back panel of the cabinet. She couldn't find any cracks or cutouts. Slowly, she slid down, bending at the knees until her hand reached the lower edge. And then she looked down. A small piece of paper lay on the floor.

"Was this here before?" she asked. But the words were mere reflex; she knew it hadn't been.

Gareth dropped to his knees beside her. "What is it?"

"This," she said, unfolding the small piece of paper with trembling hands. "I think it fell from somewhere when I twisted the knob." Still on hands and knees, she moved about two feet so that the paper caught the narrow shaft of moonlight flowing through the window. Gareth crouched beside her, his body warm and hard and overwhelmingly close as she smoothed the brittle sheet open.

"What does it say?" he asked, his breath dancing across her neck as he leaned in.

"I-I'm not sure." She blinked, forcing her eyes to focus on the words. The handwriting was clearly Isabella's, but the paper had been folded and refolded several times, making it difficult to read. "It's in Italian. I think it might be another clue."

Gareth shook his head. "Trust Isabella to turn this into a fancy hunt."

"Was she very crafty, then?"

"No, but inordinately fond of games." He turned back to the cabinet. "I'm not surprised she would have a piece like this, with a secret compartment."

Hyacinth watched as he ran his hand along the underside of the cabinet. "There it is," he said appreciatively.

"Where?" she asked, moving beside him.

He took her hand and guided it to a spot toward the back. A piece of wood seemed to have rotated slightly, just enough to allow a scrap of paper to slide through and float to the ground.

"Do you feel it?" he murmured.

She nodded, and she couldn't be sure whether she was referring to the wood, or the heat of his hand over hers. His skin was warm, and slightly rough, as if he'd been out and about without his gloves. But mostly his hand was large, covering hers completely.

Hyacinth felt enveloped, swallowed whole.

And dear God, it was just his hand.

"We should put this back," she said quickly, eager for anything that forced her mind to focus on something else. Pulling her hand from his, she reached out and turned the wood back into place. It seemed unlikely that anyone would notice the change in the underside of the cabinet, especially considering that the secret compartment had gone undetected for over sixty years, but all the same, it seemed prudent to leave the scene as they had found it.

Gareth nodded his agreement, then motioned for her to move aside as he pushed the cabinet back against the wall. "Did you find anything useful in the note?" he asked.

"The note? Oh, the note," she said, feeling like the veriest fool. "Not yet. I can hardly read a thing with only the moonlight to see by. Do you think it would be safe to light a—"

She stopped. She had to. Gareth had clamped his hand unrelentingly over her mouth.

Eyes wide, she looked up at his face. He was holding one finger to his lips and motioning with his head toward the door.

And then Hyacinth heard it. Movement in the hall. "Your father?" she mouthed, once he had removed his hand. But he wasn't looking at her.

Gareth stood, and on careful and silent feet moved to the door. He placed his ear against the wood, and then, barely a second later, stepped quickly back, jerking his head to the left.

Hyacinth was at his side in an instant, and before she knew what was happening, he'd pulled her through a door into what seemed to be a large closet filled with clothes. The air was black as pitch, and there was little room to move about. Hyacinth was backed up against what felt like a brocaded gown, and Gareth was backed up against her.

She wasn't sure she knew how to breathe.

His lips found her ear, and she felt more than she heard, "Don't say a word."

The door connecting the office to the hall clicked open, and heavy footsteps thudded across the floor.

Hyacinth held her breath. Was it Gareth's father?

"That's odd," she heard a male voice say. It sounded like it was coming from the direction of the window, and—

Oh, *no.* They'd left the drapes pulled back.

Hyacinth grabbed Gareth's hand and squeezed hard, as if that might somehow impart this knowledge to him.

Whoever was in the room took a few steps, then stopped. Terrified at the prospect of being caught, Hyacinth reached carefully behind her with her hand, trying to gauge how far back the closet went. Her hand didn't touch another wall, so she wiggled between two of the gowns and positioned herself behind them, giving Gareth's hand a little tug before letting go so that he could do the same. Her feet were undoubtedly still visible, peeking out from under the hems of the dresses, but at least now, if someone opened the closet door, her face wouldn't be right there at eye level.

Hyacinth heard a door opening and closing, but then the footsteps moved across the carpet again. The man in the room had obviously just peered into the baroness's bedchamber, which Gareth had told her was connected to the small office.

Hyacinth gulped. If he'd taken the time to inspect the bedchamber, then the closet had to be next. She burrowed farther back, scooting herself until her shoulder connected with the wall. Gareth was right there next to her, and then he was pulling her against him, moving her to the corner before covering her body with his.

He was protecting her. Shielding her so that if the closet door was opened, his would be the only body seen.

Hyacinth heard the footsteps approach. The doorknob was loose and rattly, and it clattered when a hand landed on it.

She grabbed on to Gareth, clutching his coat along the side darts. He was close, scandalously close, with his back pressed up against her so tightly she could feel the entire length of him, from her knees to her shoulders.

And everything in between.

She forced herself to breathe evenly and quietly. There was something about her position, mixed with something about her circumstance—it was a combination of fear and awareness, and the hot proximity of his body. She felt strange, queer, almost as if she were somehow suspended in time, ready to lift off her toes and float away.

She had the strangest urge to press closer, to tip her hips forward and cradle him. She was in a closet—a stranger's closet in the dead of night—and yet even as she froze with terror, she couldn't help but feel something else . . . something more powerful than fright. It was excitement, a thrill, something heady and new that set her heart racing and her blood pounding, and . . .

And something else as well. Something she wasn't quite ready to analyze or name.

Hyacinth caught her lip between her teeth.

The doorknob turned.

Her lips parted.

The door opened.

And then, amazingly, it closed again. Hyacinth felt herself sag against the back wall, felt Gareth sag against her. She wasn't sure how it was they hadn't been detected; probably Gareth had been better shielded by the clothing than she'd thought. Or maybe the light was too dim, or the man hadn't thought to look down for feet peeking out from behind the gowns. Or maybe he'd had bad eyesight, or maybe . . .

Or maybe they were just damned lucky.

They waited in silence until it was clear that the man had left the baroness's office, and then they waited for a good five minutes more, just to be sure. But finally, Gareth moved away from her, pushing through the clothes to the closet door. Hyacinth waited in back until she heard his whispered, "Let's go."

She followed him in silence, creeping through the house until they reached the window with the broken latch. Gareth leapt down ahead of her, then held out his hands so that she could balance against the wall and pull the window shut before hopping down to the ground.

"Follow me," Gareth said, taking her hand and pulling her behind him as he ran through the streets of Mayfair. Hyacinth tripped along behind him, and with each step a sliver of the fear that had gripped her back in the closet was replaced by excitement.

Exhilaration.

By the time they reached Hay Hill, Hyacinth felt as if she was almost ready to bubble over with laughter, and finally, she had to dig in her heels and say, "Stop! I can't breathe."

Gareth stopped, but he turned with stern eyes. "I need to get you home," he said.

"I know, I know, I—"

His eyes widened. "Are you laughing?"

"No! Yes. I mean"—she smiled helplessly—"I might."

"You're a madwoman."

She nodded, still grinning like a fool. "I think so."

He turned on her, hands on hips. "Have you no sense? We could have been caught back there. That was my father's butler, and trust me, he has never been in possession of a sense of humor. If he had discovered us, my father would have thrown us in gaol, and your brother would have hauled us straight to a church."

"I know," Hyacinth said, trying to appear suitably solemn.

She failed.

Miserably.

Finally, she gave up and said, "But wasn't it fun?"

For a moment she didn't think he would respond. For a moment it seemed all he was capable of was a dull, stupefied stare. But then, she heard his voice, low and disbelieving. "Fun?"

She nodded. "A little bit, at least." She pressed her lips together, working hard to turn them down at the corners.

Anything to keep from bursting out with laughter.

"You're mad," he said, looking stern and shocked and—God help her—sweet, all at the same time. "You are stark, raving mad," he said. "Everyone told me, but I didn't quite believe—"

"Someone told you I was mad?" Hyacinth cut in.

"Eccentric."

"Oh." She pursed her lips together. "Well, that's true, I suppose."

"Far too much work for any sane man to take on."

"Is that what they say?" she asked, starting to feel slightly less than complimented.

"All that and more," he confirmed.

Hyacinth thought about that for a moment, then just shrugged. "Well, they haven't a lick of sense, any one of them."

"Good God," Gareth muttered. "You sound precisely like my grandmother."

"So you've mentioned," Hyacinth said. And then she couldn't resist. She just had to ask. "But tell me," she said, leaning in just a bit. "Truthfully. Weren't you just a tiny bit excited? Once the fear of discovery had worn off and you knew we would be undetected? Wasn't it," she asked, her words coming out on a sigh, "just a little bit wonderful?"

He looked down at her, and maybe it was the moonlight, or maybe just her wishful imagination, but she thought she saw something flash in his eyes. Something soft, something just a little bit indulgent.

"A little bit," he said. "But just a little bit."

Hyacinth smiled. "I knew you weren't a stick."

He looked down at her, with what had to be palpable irritation. No one had ever accused him of being stodgy before. "A stick?" he said disgustedly.

"In the mud."

"I knew what you meant."

"They why did you ask?"

"Because you, Miss Bridgerton . . ."

And so it went, the rest of the way home.

Chapter 10

*The next morning. Hyacinth is still in an excellent
mood. Unfortunately, her mother commented upon
this so many times at breakfast that Hyacinth was
finally forced to flee and barricade herself in her
bedchamber.*

*Violet Bridgerton is an exceptionally canny
woman, after all, and if anyone is going to guess
that Hyacinth is falling in love, it would be her.*

Probably before Hyacinth, even.

Hyacinth hummed to herself as she sat at the
small desk in her bedchamber, tapping her fingers against
the blotter. She had translated and retranslated the note
they'd found the night before in the small green office,
and she still wasn't satisfied with her results, but even that
could not dampen her spirits.

She'd been a little disappointed, of course, that they
had not found the diamonds the night before, but the note
in the curio cabinet seemed to indicate that the jewels
might still be theirs for the taking. At the very least, no

one else had reached any success with the trail of clues Isabella had left behind.

Hyacinth was never happier than when she had a task, a goal, some sort of quest. She loved the challenge of solving a puzzle, analyzing a clue. And Isabella Marinzoli St. Clair had turned what would surely have been a dull and ordinary season into the most exciting spring of Hyacinth's life.

She looked down at the note, twisting her mouth to the side as she forced her mind back to the task at hand. Her translation was still only about seventy percent complete, in Hyacinth's optimistic estimation, but she rather thought she'd managed enough of a translation to justify another attempt. The next clue—or the actual diamonds, if they were lucky—was almost certainly in the library.

"In a book, I imagine," she murmured, gazing sightlessly out the window. She thought of the Bridgerton library, tucked away at her brother's Grosvenor Square home. The room itself wasn't terribly large, but the shelves lined the walls from floor to ceiling.

And books filled the shelves. Every last inch of them.

"Maybe the St. Clairs aren't much for reading," she said to herself, turning her attention once again to Isabella's note. Surely there had to be something in the cryptic words to indicate which book she had chosen as her hiding spot. Something scientific, she was fairly sure. Isabella had underlined part of her note, which led Hyacinth to think that perhaps she was referring to a book title, since it didn't seem to make sense in context that she'd have been underlining for emphasis. And the part she'd underlined had mentioned water and "things that move," which sounded a bit like physics, not that Hyacinth had ever studied it. But she'd four brothers who had attended university, and she'd overheard enough of their studies to have a vague knowledge of, if not the subject, at least what the subject meant.

Still, she wasn't nearly as certain as she'd have liked about her translation, or what it meant. Maybe if she went to Gareth with what she'd translated thus far, he could read something into it that she didn't see. After all, he was more familiar with the house and its contents than she was. He might know of an odd or interesting book, something unique or out of the ordinary.

Gareth.

She smiled to herself, a loopy, silly grin that she would have died before allowing anyone else to see.

Something had happened the night before. Something special.

Something important.

He liked her. He really liked her. They had laughed and chattered the entire way home. And when he had dropped her off at the servants' entrance to Number Five, he had looked at her in that heavy-lidded, just a little bit intense way of his. He had smiled, too, one corner of his mouth lifting as if he had a secret.

She'd shivered. She'd actually forgotten how to speak. And she'd wondered if he might kiss her again, which of course he hadn't done, but maybe . . .

Maybe soon.

She had no doubt that she still drove him a little bit mad. But she seemed to drive everyone a little bit mad, so she decided not to attach too much importance to that.

But he liked her. And he respected her intelligence as well. And if he was occasionally reluctant to demonstrate this as often as she would like ... well, she had four brothers. She had long since learned that it took a fully formed miracle to get them to admit that a woman might be smarter than a man about anything other than fabrics, perfumed soaps, and tea.

She turned her head to look at the clock, which sat on the mantel over her small fireplace. It was already past noon. Gareth had promised that he would call on her this afternoon to see how she was faring with the note. That probably didn't mean before two, but technically it was the afternoon, and—

Her ears perked up. Was that someone at the door? Her room was at the front of the house, so she could generally hear when someone was entering or exiting. Hyacinth got up and went to the window, peeking out from behind the curtains to see if she could see anyone on the front step.

Nothing.

She went to the door and opened it just enough to listen. Nothing.

She stepped into the hall, her heart pounding with anticipation. Truly, there was no reason to be nervous, but she hadn't been able to stop thinking about Gareth, and the diamonds, and—

"Eh, Hyacinth, what're you doing?"

She nearly jumped out of her skin.

"Sorry," said her brother Gregory, not sounding sorry at all. He was standing behind her, or rather he had been, before she'd whirled around in surprise. He looked slightly disheveled, his reddish brown hair windblown and cut just a touch too long.

"Don't *do* that," she said, placing her hand over her heart, as if that might possibly calm it down.

He just crossed his arms and leaned one shoulder against the wall. "It's what I do best," he said with a grin.

"Not something *I'd* brag about," Hyacinth returned.

He ignored the insult, instead brushing an imaginary piece of lint off the sleeve of his riding coat. "What has you skulking about?"

"I'm not skulking."

"Of course you are. It's what you do best."

She scowled at him, even though she ought to have known better. Gregory was two and a half years her elder, and he lived to vex her. He always had. The two of them were a bit cut off from the rest of the family, in terms of age. Gregory was almost four years younger than Francesca, and a full ten from Colin, the next youngest son. As a result, he and Hyacinth had always been a bit on their own, a bit of a duo.

A bickering, poking, frog-in-the-bed sort of duo, but a duo nonetheless, and even though they had outgrown the worst of their pranks, neither seemed able to resist needling the other.

"I thought I heard someone come in," Hyacinth said.

He smiled blandly. "It was me."

"I realize that *now*." She placed her hand on the doorknob and pulled. "If you will excuse me."

"*You're* in a snit today."

"I'm not in a snit."

"Of course you are. It's—"

"*Not* what I do best." Hyacinth ground out.

He grinned. "You're definitely in a snit."

"I'm—" She clamped her teeth together. She was not

going to descend to the behavior of a three-year-old. "I am going back into my room now. I have a book to read."

But before she could make her escape, she heard him say, "I saw you with Gareth St. Clair the other night."

Hyacinth froze. Surely he couldn't have known . . . No one had seen them. She was sure of that.

"At Bridgerton House," Gregory continued. "Off in the corner of the ballroom."

Hyacinth let out a long, quiet breath before turning back around.

Gregory was looking at her with a casual, offhand smile, but Hyacinth could tell that there was something more to his expression, a certain shrewd look in his eye.

Most of his behavior to the contrary, her brother was not stupid. And he seemed to think it was his role in life to watch over his younger sister. Probably because he was the second youngest, and she was the only one with whom he could try to assume a superior role. The rest certainly would not have stood for it.

"I'm friends with his grandmother," Hyacinth said, since it seemed nicely neutral and dull. "You know that."

He shrugged. It was a gesture they shared, and sometimes Hyacinth felt she was looking in a mirror, which seemed mad, since he was a full foot taller than she was.

"You certainly looked to be in deep conversation about something," he said.

"It was nothing in which you'd be interested."

One of his brows arched annoyingly up. "I might surprise you."

"You rarely do."

"Are you setting your cap for him?"

"That's none of your business," she said tartly.

Gregory looked triumphant. "Then you *are*."

Hyacinth lifted her chin, looking her brother squarely in the eye. "I don't know," she said, since despite their constant bickering, he probably knew her better than anyone else in the world. And he'd know it for certain if she were lying.

Either that, or he would torture her until the truth slipped out, anyway.

Gregory's brows disappeared under the fringe of his hair, which, admittedly, was too long and constantly falling in his eyes. "Really?" he asked. "Well, *that* is news."

"For your ears only," Hyacinth warned, "and it's not really news. I haven't decided yet."

"Still."

"I mean this, Gregory," Hyacinth said. "Don't make me regret confiding in you."

"Ye of little faith."

He sounded far too flip for her comfort. Hands on hips, she said, "I only told you this because very occasionally you're not a complete idiot and despite all common sense, I do love you."

His face sobered, and she was reminded that despite her brother's asinine (in her opinion) attempts to appear the jaunty wastrel, he was actually quite intelligent and in possession of a heart of gold.

A *devious* heart of gold.

"And don't forget," Hyacinth felt it was necessary to add, "that I said *maybe*."

His brows came together. "Did you?"

"If I didn't, then I meant to."

He motioned magnanimously with his hand. "If there's anything I can do."

"Nothing," she said firmly, horrifying visions of Gregory's meddling floating through her mind. "Absolutely nothing. *Please*."

"Surely a waste of my talents."

"Gregory!"

"Well," he said with an affected sigh, "you have my approval, at least."

"Why?" Hyacinth asked suspiciously.

"It would be an excellent match," he continued. "If nothing else, think of the children."

She knew she'd regret it, but still she had to ask. "What children?"

He grinned. "The lovely lithping children you could have together. Garethhhh and Hyathinthhhh. Hyathinth and Gareth. And the thublime Thinclair tots."

Hyacinth stared at him like he was an idiot.

Which he was, she was quite certain of it.

She shook her head. "How on earth Mother managed to give birth to seven perfectly normal children and one freak is beyond me."

"Thith way to the nurthery." Gregory laughed as she headed back into the room. "With the thcrumptious little Tharah and Thamuel Thinclair. Oh, yeth, and don't forget wee little Thuthannah!"

Hyacinth shut the door in his face, but the wood wasn't thick enough to block his parting shot.

"You're such an easy mark, Hy." And then: "Don't forget to come down for tea."

One hour later. Gareth is about to learn what it means to belong to a large family.
  For better or for worthe.

"Miss Bridgerton is taking tea," said the butler, once he'd allowed Gareth admittance to the front hall of Number Five.

Gareth followed the butler down the hall to same rose-and-cream sitting room in which he'd met Hyacinth the week before.

Good God, was it just one week? It felt a lifetime ago.

Ah, well. Skulking about, breaking the law, and very nearly ruining the reputation of a proper young lady did tend to age a man before his time.

The butler stepped into the room, intoned Gareth's name, and moved to the side so that he could walk in.

"Mr. St. Clair!"

Gareth turned with surprise to face Hyacinth's mother, who was sitting on a striped sofa, setting her teacup down in its saucer. He didn't know *why* he was surprised to see Violet Bridgerton; it certainly stood to reason that she would be home at this time in the afternoon. But for whatever reason, he had only pictured Hyacinth on the way over.

"Lady Bridgerton," he said, turning to her with a polite bow. "How lovely to see you."

"Have you met my son?" she asked.

Son? Gareth hadn't even realized anyone else was in the room.

"My brother Gregory," came Hyacinth's voice. She was sitting across from her mother, on a matching sofa. She tilted her head toward the window, where Gregory

Bridgerton stood, assessing him with a scary little half smile.

The smirk of an older brother, Gareth realized. It was probably exactly how he would look if he'd had a younger sister to torture and protect.

"We've met," Gregory said.

Gareth nodded. They had crossed paths from time to time about town and had, in fact, been students at Eton at the same time. But Gareth was several years older, so they had never known each other well. "Bridgerton," Gareth murmured, giving the younger man a nod.

Gregory moved across the room and plopped himself down next to his sister. "It's good to see you," he said, directing his words at Gareth. "Hyacinth says you're her special friend."

"Gregory!" Hyacinth exclaimed. She turned quickly to Gareth. "I said no such thing."

"I'm heartbroken," Gareth said.

Hyacinth looked at him with a slightly peeved expression, then turned to her brother with a hissed, "Stop it."

"Won't you have tea, Mr. St. Clair?" Lady Bridgerton asked, glossing right over her children's squabbling as if it wasn't occurring right across from her. "It is a special blend of which I am particularly fond."

"I would be delighted." Gareth sat in the same chair he had chosen last time, mostly because it put the most room between him and Gregory, although in truth, he didn't know which Bridgerton was most likely to accidentally spill scalding tea on his lap.

But it was an odd position. He was at the short end of the low, center table, and with all the Bridgertons on the sofas, it almost felt as if he were seated at its head.

"Milk?" Lady Bridgerton asked.

"Thank you," Gareth replied. "No sugar, if you please."

"Hyacinth takes hers with three," Gregory said, reaching for a piece of shortbread.

"Why," Hyacinth ground out, "would he care?"

"Well," Gregory replied, taking a bite and chewing, "he *is* your special friend."

"He's not—" She turned to Gareth. "Ignore him."

There was something rather annoying about being condescended to by a man of lesser years, but at the same time Gregory seemed to be doing an excellent job of vexing Hyacinth, an endeavor of which Gareth could only approve.

So he decided to stay out of it and instead turned back to Lady Bridgerton, who was, as it happened, the closest person to him, anyway. "And how are you this afternoon?" he asked.

Lady Bridgerton gave him a very small smile as she handed him his cup of tea. "Smart man," she murmured.

"It's self-preservation, really," he said noncommittally.

"Don't say that. They wouldn't hurt you."

"No, but I'm sure to be injured in the cross fire."

Gareth heard a little gasp. When he looked over at Hyacinth, she was glaring daggers in his direction. Her brother was grinning.

"Sorry," he said, mostly because he thought he should. He certainly didn't mean it.

"You don't come from a large family, do you, Mr. St. Clair?" Lady Bridgerton asked.

"No," he said smoothly, taking a sip of his tea, which was of excellent quality. "Just myself and my brother." He stopped, blinking against the rush of sadness that washed over him every time he thought of George, then finished with: "He passed on late last year."

"Oh," Lady Bridgerton said, her hand coming to her mouth. "I'm so sorry. I'd forgotten completely. Please forgive me. And accept my deepest sympathies."

Her apology was so artless, and her condolences so sincere, that Gareth almost felt the need to comfort her. He looked at her, right into her eyes, and he realized that she understood.

Most people hadn't. His friends had all patted him awkwardly on the back and said they were sorry, but they hadn't understood. Grandmother Danbury had, perhaps— she'd grieved for George, too. But that was somehow different, probably because he and his grandmother were so close. Lady Bridgerton was almost a stranger, and yet, she cared.

It was touching, and almost disconcerting. Gareth couldn't remember the last time anyone had said something to him and meant it.

Except for Hyacinth, of course. She always meant what she said. But at the same time, she never laid herself bare, never made herself vulnerable.

He glanced over at her. She was sitting up straight, her hands folded neatly in her lap, watching him with a curious expression.

He couldn't fault her, he supposed. He was the exact same way.

"Thank you," he said, turning back to Lady Bridgerton. "George was an exceptional brother, and the world is poorer for his loss."

Lady Bridgerton was silent for a moment, and then, as if she could read his mind, she smiled and said, "But you do not wish to dwell on this now. We shall speak of something else."

Gareth looked at Hyacinth. She was holding herself still, but he could see her chest rise and fall in a long, impatient breath. She had worked on the translation, of that he had no doubt, and she surely wished to tell him what she'd learned.

Gareth carefully suppressed a smile. He was quite certain that Hyacinth would have feigned death if that would somehow have gotten them an interview alone.

"Lady Danbury speaks very highly of you," Lady Bridgerton said.

Gareth turned back to her. "I am fortunate to be her grandson."

"I have always liked your grandmother," Lady Bridgerton said, sipping at her tea. "I know she scares half of London—"

"Oh, more than that," Gareth said genially.

Lady Bridgerton chuckled. "So she would hope."

"Indeed."

"I, however, have always found her to be quite charming," Lady Bridgerton said. "A breath of fresh air, really. And, of course, a very shrewd and sound judge of character."

"I shall pass along your regards."

"She speaks very highly of you," Lady Bridgerton said.

She'd repeated herself. Gareth wasn't sure if it was accidental or deliberate, but either way, she couldn't have been more clear if she had taken him aside and offered him money to propose to her daughter.

Of course, she did not know that his father was not actually Lord St. Clair, or that he did not in fact know who his father was. As lovely and generous as Hyacinth's mother was, Gareth rather doubted that she'd be working so hard to bring him up to scratch if she knew that he most probably carried the blood of a footman.

"My grandmother speaks highly of you as well," Gareth said to Lady Bridgerton. "Which is quite a compliment, as she rarely speaks highly of anyone."

"Except for Hyacinth," Gregory Bridgerton put in.

Gareth turned. He'd almost forgotten the younger man was there. "Of course," he said smoothly. "My grandmother adores your sister."

Gregory turned to Hyacinth. "Do you still read to her each Wednesday?"

"Tuesday," Hyacinth corrected.

"Oh. Thorry."

Gareth blinked. Did Hyacinth's brother have a lisp?

"Mr. St. Clair," Hyacinth said, after what Gareth was quite certain was an elbow in her brother's ribs.

"Yes?" he murmured, mostly just to be kind. She'd paused in her speech, and he had a feeling she'd uttered his name without first thinking of something to ask him.

"I understand that you are an accomplished swordsman," she finally said.

He eyed her curiously. Where was she going with this? "I like to fence, yes," he replied.

"I have always wanted to learn."

"Good God," Gregory grunted.

"I would be quite good at it," she protested.

"I'm sure you would," her brother replied, "which is why you should never be allowed within thirty feet of a sword." He turned to Gareth. "She's quite diabolical."

"Yes, I'd noticed," Gareth murmured, deciding that maybe there might be a bit more to Hyacinth's brother than he had thought.

Gregory shrugged, reaching for a piece of shortbread. "It's probably why we can't seem to get her married off."

"Gregory!" This came from Hyacinth, but that was only because Lady Bridgerton had excused herself and followed one of the footmen into the hall.

"It's a compliment!" Gregory protested. "Haven't you waited your entire life for me to agree that you're smarter than any of the poor fools who have attempted to court you?"

"You might find it difficult to believe," Hyacinth shot back, "but I haven't been going to bed each night thinking to myself—*Oh, I do wish my brother would offer me something that passes for a compliment in his twisted mind.*"

Gareth choked on his tea.

Gregory turned to Gareth. "Do you see why I call her diabolical?"

"I refuse to comment," Gareth said.

"Look who is here!" came Lady Bridgerton's voice. And just in time, Gareth thought. Ten more seconds, and Hyacinth would have quite cheerfully murdered her brother.

Gareth turned to the doorway and immediately rose to his feet. Behind Lady Bridgerton stood one of Hyacinth's older sisters, the one who had married a duke. Or at least he thought that was the one. They all looked vexingly alike, and he couldn't be sure.

"Daphne!" Hyacinth said. "Come sit by me."

"There's no room next to you," Daphne said, blinking in confusion.

"There will be," Hyacinth said with cheerful venom, "as soon as Gregory gets up."

Gregory made a great show of offering his seat to his older sister.

"Children," Lady Bridgerton said with a sigh as she re-took her seat. "I am never quite certain if I'm glad I had them."

But no one could ever have mistaken the humor in her voice for anything other than love. Gareth found himself rather charmed. Hyacinth's brother was a bit of a pest, or at least he was when Hyacinth was in the vicinity, and the few times he'd heard more than two Bridgertons in the same conversation, they had talked all over each other and rarely resisted the impulse to trade sly jibes.

But they loved each other. Beneath the noise, it was startlingly clear.

"It is good to see you, your grace," Gareth said to the young duchess, once she'd seated herself next to Hyacinth.

"Please, call me Daphne," she said with a sunny smile. "There is no need to be so formal if you are a friend of Hyacinth's. Besides," she said, taking a cup and pouring herself some tea, "I cannot feel like a duchess in my mother's sitting room."

"What do you feel like, then?"

"Hmmm." She took a sip of her tea. "Just Daphne Bridgerton, I suppose. It's difficult to shed the surname in this clan. In spirit, that is."

"I hope that is a compliment," Lady Bridgerton re-marked.

Daphne just smiled at her mother. "I shall never escape you, I'm afraid." She turned to Gareth. "There is nothing like one's family to make one feel like one has never grown up."

Gareth thought about his recent encounter with the baron and said, with perhaps more feeling than he ought to make verbal, "I know precisely what you mean."

"Yes," the duchess said, "I expect you do."

Gareth said nothing. His estrangement from the baron was certainly common enough knowledge, even if the reason for it was not.

"How are the children, Daphne?" Lady Bridgerton asked.

"Mischievous as always. David wants a puppy, preferably one that will grow to the size of a small pony, and Caroline is desperate to return to Benedict's." She sipped at her tea and turned to Gareth. "My daughter spent three weeks with my brother and his family last month. He has been giving her drawing lessons."

"He is an accomplished artist, is he not?"

"Two paintings in the National Gallery," Lady Bridgerton said, beaming with pride.

"He rarely comes to town, though," Hyacinth said.

"He and his wife prefer the quiet of the country," her mother said. But there was a very faint edge to her voice. A firmness meant to indicate that she did not wish to discuss the matter any further.

At least not in front of Gareth.

Gareth tried to recall if he had ever heard some sort of scandal attached to Benedict Bridgerton. He didn't think so, but then again, Gareth was at least a decade his junior, and if there was something untoward in his past, it would probably have occurred before Gareth had moved to town.

He glanced over at Hyacinth to see her reaction to her

mother's words. It hadn't been a scolding, not exactly, but it was clear that she'd wanted to stop Hyacinth from speaking further.

But if Hyacinth took offense, she wasn't showing it. She turned her attention to the window and was staring out, her brows pulled slightly together as she blinked.

"Is it warm out of doors?" she asked, turning to her sister. "It looks sunny."

"It is quite," Daphne said, sipping her tea. "I walked over from Hastings House."

"I should love to go for a walk," Hyacinth announced.

It took Gareth only a second to recognize his cue. "I would be delighted to escort you, Miss Bridgerton."

"Would you?" Hyacinth said with a dazzling smile.

"I was out this morning," Lady Bridgerton said. "The crocuses are in bloom in the park. A bit past the Guard House."

Gareth almost smiled. The Guard House was at the far end of Hyde Park. It would take half the afternoon to get there and back.

He rose to his feet and offered her his arm. "Shall we see the crocuses then?"

"That would be delightful." Hyacinth stood. "I just need to fetch my maid to accompany us."

Gregory pushed himself off the windowsill, upon which he'd been leaning. "Perhaps I'll come along, too," he said.

Hyacinth threw him a glare.

"Or perhaps I won't," he murmured.

"I need you here, in any case," Lady Bridgerton said.

"Really?" Gregory smiled innocently. "Why?"

"Because I do," she ground out.

Gareth turned to Gregory. "Your sister will be safe with me," he said. "I give you my vow."

"Oh, I have no worries on that score," Gregory said with a bland smile. "The real question is—will you be safe with her?"

It was a good thing, Gareth later reflected, that Hyacinth had already quit the room to fetch her coat and her maid. She probably would have killed her brother on the spot.

Chapter 11

A quarter of an hour later. Hyacinth is completely unaware that her life is about to change.

"Your maid is discreet?" Gareth asked, just as soon as he and Hyacinth were standing on the pavement outside of Number Five.

"Oh, don't worry about Frances," Hyacinth said, adjusting her gloves. "She and I have an understanding."

He lifted his brows in an expression of lazy humor. "Why do those words, coming from your lips, strike terror in my soul?"

"I'm sure I don't know," Hyacinth said blithely, "but I can assure you that she won't come within twenty feet of us while we're strolling. We have only to stop and get her a tin of peppermints."

"Peppermints?"

"She's easily bribed," Hyacinth explained, looking back at Frances, who had already assumed the requisite distance to the couple and was now looking quite bored. "All the best maids are."

"I wouldn't know," Gareth murmured.

"*That* I find difficult to believe," Hyacinth said. He

had probably bribed maids all across London. Hyacinth couldn't imagine that he could have made it to his age, with his reputation, and not have had an affair with a woman who wanted it kept secret.

He smiled inscrutably. "A gentleman never tells."

Hyacinth decided not to pursue the topic any further. Not, of course, because she wasn't curious, but rather because she thought he'd meant what he'd said, and he wasn't going to spill any secrets, delicious though they might be.

And really, why waste one's energy if one was going to get nowhere?

"I thought we would never escape," she said, once they'd reached the end of her street. "I have much to tell you."

He turned to her with obvious interest. "Were you able to translate the note?"

Hyacinth glanced behind her. She knew she'd said Frances would remain far in back, but it was always good to check, especially as Gregory was no stranger to the concept of bribery, either.

"Yes," she said, once she was satisfied that they would not be overheard. "Well, most of it, at least. Enough to know that we need to focus our search in the library."

Gareth chuckled.

"Why is that funny?"

"Isabella was a great deal sharper than she let on. If she'd wanted to pick a room that her husband was not likely to enter, she could not have done better than the library. Except for the bedroom, I suppose, but"—he turned and gazed down at her with an annoyingly paternalistic glance—"that's not a topic for your ears."

"Stuffy man," she muttered.

"Not an accusation that is often flung my way," he said with a slightly amused smile, "but clearly you bring out the best in me."

He was so patently sarcastic that Hyacinth could do nothing but scowl.

"The library, you say," Gareth mused, after taking a moment to enjoy Hyacinth's distress. "It makes perfect sense. My father's father was no intellectual."

"I hope that means he didn't possess very many books," Hyacinth said with a frown. "I suspect that she left another clue tucked into one."

"No such luck," Gareth said with a grimace. "My grandfather might not have been fond of books, but he did care a great deal about appearances, and no self-respecting baron would have a house without a library, or a library without books."

Hyacinth let out a groan. "It will take all night to go through an entire library of books."

He gave her a sympathetic smile, and something fluttered in her stomach. She opened her mouth to speak, but all she did was inhale, and she couldn't shake the oddest feeling that she was surprised.

But by what, she had no idea.

"Perhaps, once you see what's there, something will suddenly make sense," Gareth said. He did a little one-shouldered shrug as he steered them around the corner and onto Park Lane. "That sort of thing happens to me all the time. Usually when I least expect it."

Hyacinth nodded in agreement, still a little unsettled by the strange, light-headed sensation that had just washed over her. "That's exactly what I've been hoping might happen," she said, forcing herself to reaffix her focus onto the matter at hand. "But Isabella was rather cryptic, I'm afraid. Or . . . I don't know . . . perhaps she wasn't deliberately cryptic, and it's just because I can't translate all the words. But I do think that we may assume that we will find not the diamonds but instead another clue."

"Why is that?"

She nodded thoughtfully as she spoke. "I'm almost certain that we must look in the library, specifically in a book. And I don't see how she would have fit diamonds between the pages."

"She could have hollowed the book out. Created a hiding spot."

Her breath caught. "I never thought of that," she said, her eyes widening with excitement. "We will need to redouble our efforts. I think—although I'm not certain—that the book will be one of a scientific topic."

He nodded. "That will narrow things down. It's been some time since I was in the library at Clair House, but I don't recall there being much in the way of scientific treatises."

Hyacinth screwed up her mouth a little as she tried to recall the precise words in the clue. "It was something having to do with water. But I don't think it was biological."

"Excellent work," he said, "and if I haven't said so, thank you."

Hyacinth almost stumbled, so unexpected was his compliment. "You're welcome," she replied, once she'd gotten over her initial surprise. "I'm happy to do it. To be honest, I don't know what I will do with myself when this is all over. The diary is truly a lovely distraction."

"What is it you need to be distracted from?" he asked.

Hyacinth thought about that for a moment. "I don't know," she finally said. She looked up at him, feeling her brows come together as her eyes found his. "Isn't that sad?"

He shook his head, and this time when he smiled, it wasn't condescending, and it wasn't even dry. It was just a smile. "I suspect it's rather normal," he said.

But she wasn't so convinced. Until the excitement over the diary and the search for the jewels had entered her life, she hadn't noticed how very much her days had been pressed into a mold. The same things, the same people, the same food, the same sights.

She hadn't even realized how desperately she wanted a change.

Maybe that was another curse to lay at the feet of Isabella Marinzoli St. Clair. Maybe she hadn't even wanted a change before she'd begun translating the diary. Maybe she hadn't known to want one.

But now . . . After this . . .

She had a feeling that nothing would ever be the same.

"When shall we return to Clair House?" she asked, eager to change the subject.

He sighed. Or maybe it was a groan. "I don't suppose you'd take it well if I said I was going alone."

"Very badly," she confirmed.

"I suspected as much." He gave her a sideways glance. "Is everyone in your family as obstinate as you?"

"No," she said quite freely, "although they do come close. My sister Eloise, especially. You haven't met her. And Gregory." She rolled her eyes. "He's a beast."

"Why do I suspect that whatever he's done to you, you've returned in kind, and then in tenfold?"

She cocked her head to the side, trying to look terribly dry and sophisticated. "Are you saying you don't believe I can turn the other cheek?"

"Not for a second."

"Very well, it's true," she said with a shrug. She wasn't going to be able to carry on that ruse for very long, anyway. "I can't sit still in a sermon, either."

He grinned. "Neither can I."

"Liar," she accused. "You don't even try. I have it on the best authority that you never go to church."

"The best authorities are watching out for me?" He smiled faintly. "How reassuring."

"Your grandmother."

"Ah," he said. "That explains it. Would you believe that my soul is already well past redemption?"

"Absolutely," she said, "but that's no reason to make the rest of us suffer."

He looked at her with a wicked glint in his eye. "Is it that deep a torture to be at church without my calming presence?"

"You *know* what I meant," she said. "It's not fair that I should have to attend when you do not."

"Since when are we such a pair that it's tit for tat for us?" he queried.

That stopped her short. Verbally, at least.

And he obviously couldn't resist teasing her further, because he said, "Your family certainly wasn't very subtle about it."

"Oh," she said, barely resisting a groan. "That."

"That?"

"*Them.*"

"They're not so bad," he said.

"No," she agreed. "But they *are* an acquired taste. I suppose I should apologize."

"No need," he murmured, but she suspected it was just an automatic platitude.

Hyacinth sighed. She was rather used to her family's often desperate attempts to get her married off, but she could see where it might be a bit unsettling for the poor man in question. "If it makes you feel better," she said, giving him a sympathetic glance, "you're hardly the first gentleman they've tried to foist me upon."

"How charmingly put."

"Although if you think about it," she said, "it is actually to our advantage if they do think we might make a match of it."

"How is that?"

She thought furiously. She still wasn't sure if she wished to set her cap for him, but she *was* sure that she didn't want him to *think* that she had. Because if he did, and then he rejected her . . . well, nothing could be more brutal.

Or heartbreaking.

"Well," she said, making it up as she went along, "we are going to need to spend a great deal of time in each other's company, at least until we finish with the diary. If my family thinks there might be a church at the end of the journey, they are far less likely to quibble."

He appeared to consider that. To Hyacinth's surprise, however, he didn't speak, which meant that she had to.

"The truth is," she said, trying to sound very offhand and unconcerned, "they're mad to get me off their hands."

"I don't think you're being fair to your family," he said softly.

Hyacinth's lips parted with astonishment. There was an edge to his voice, something serious and unexpected. "Oh," she said, blinking as she tried to come up with a suitable comment. "Well . . ."

He turned, and there was a strange, intense light in his eyes as he said, "You're quite lucky to have them."

She felt suddenly uncomfortable. Gareth was looking at her with such intensity—it was as if the world were dropping away around them, and they were only in Hyde Park for heaven's sake, talking about her family . . .

"Well, yes," she finally said.

When Gareth spoke, his tone was sharp. "They only love you and want what's best for you."

"Are you saying you're what's best for me?" Hyacinth teased. Because she had to tease. She didn't know how else to react to his strange mood. Anything else would reveal too much.

And maybe her joke would force him to reveal something instead.

"That's not what I meant, and you know it," he said hotly.

Hyacinth stepped back. "I'm sorry," she said, bewildered by his reaction.

But he wasn't done. He looked at her squarely, his eyes flashing with something she'd never seen there before. "You should count your blessings that you come from a large and loving family."

"I do. I—"

"Do you have any idea how many people I have in this world?" he cut in. He moved forward, closing in on her until he was uncomfortably close. "Do you?" he demanded.

"One. Just one," he said, not waiting for her reply. "My grandmother. And I would lay down my life for her."

Hyacinth had never seen this sort of passion in him, hadn't even dreamed he possessed it. He was normally so calm, so unflappable. Even that night at Bridgerton House, when he'd been upset by his encounter with his father, there had still been a certain air of levity about him. And then she realized what it was about him, what had set him apart . . . He was never quite serious.

Until now.

She couldn't tear her eyes from his face, even as he turned away, leaving her only his profile. He was staring at some distant spot on the horizon, some tree or some bush that he probably couldn't even identify.

"Do you know what it means to be alone?" he asked softly, still not looking at her. "Not for an hour, not for an evening, but just to know, to absolutely know that in a few years, you will have no one."

She opened her mouth to say no, of course not, but then she realized that there had been no question mark at the end of his statement.

She waited, because she did not know what to say. And then because she recognized that if she said something, if she tried to imply that she did understand, the moment would be lost, and she would never know what he'd been thinking.

And as she stood there, staring at his face as he lost himself in his thoughts, she realized that she *desperately* wanted to know what he was thinking.

"Mr. St. Clair?" she finally whispered, after a full minute had ticked away. "Gareth?"

She saw his lips move before she heard his voice. One

corner tilted up in a mocking smile, and she had the strangest sense that he'd accepted his own bad luck, that he was ready to embrace it and revel in it, because if he tried to smash it, he was simply going to have his heart broken.

"I would give the world to have one more person for whom I would lay down my life," he said.

And then Hyacinth realized that some things did come in a flash. And there were some things one simply knew without possessing the ability to explain them.

Because in that moment she knew that she was going to marry this man.

No one else would do.

Gareth St. Clair knew what was important. He was funny, he was dry, he could be arrogantly mocking, but he knew what was important.

And Hyacinth had never realized before just how important that was to *her*.

Her lips parted as she watched him. She wanted to say something, to do something. She'd finally realized just what it was she wanted in life, and it felt like she ought to leap in with both feet, work toward her goal and make sure she got it.

But she was frozen, speechless as she gazed at his profile. There was something in the way he was holding his jaw. He looked bleak, haunted. And Hyacinth had the most overpowering impulse to reach out and touch him, to let her fingers brush against his cheek, to smooth his hair where the dark blond strands of his queue rested against the collar of his coat.

But she didn't. She wasn't that courageous.

He turned suddenly, his eyes meeting hers with enough force and clarity to take her breath away. And she had the oddest sense that she was only just now seeing the man beneath the surface.

"Shall we return?" he asked, and his voice was light and disappointingly back to normal.

Whatever had happened between them, it had passed.

"Of course," Hyacinth said. Now wasn't the time to press him. "When do you wish to return to Clair . . ." Her words trailed off. Gareth had stiffened, and his eyes were focused sharply over her shoulder.

Hyacinth turned around to see what had grabbed his attention.

Her breath caught. His father was walking down the path, coming straight toward them.

She looked quickly around. They were on the less fashionable side of the park, and as such, it wasn't terribly crowded. She could see a few members of the *ton* across the clearing, but none was close enough to overhear a conversation, provided that Gareth and his father were able to remain civil.

Hyacinth looked again from one St. Clair gentleman to the other, and she realized that she had never seen them together before.

Half of her wanted to pull Gareth to the side and avoid a scene, and half was dying of curiosity. If they stayed put, and she was finally able to witness their interaction, she might finally learn the cause of their estrangement.

But it wasn't up to her. It had to be Gareth's decision. "Do you want to go?" she asked him, keeping her voice low.

His lips parted slowly as his chin rose a fraction of an inch. "No," he said, his voice strangely contemplative. "It's a public park."

Hyacinth looked from Gareth to his father and back, her head bobbing, she was sure, like a badly wielded tennis ball. "Are you certain?" she asked, but he didn't hear her. She didn't think he would have heard a cannon going off right by his ear, so focused was he on the man ambling too casually toward them.

"Father," Gareth said, giving him an oily smile. "How pleasant to see you."

A look of revulsion passed across Lord St. Clair's face before he suppressed it. "Gareth," he said, his voice even, correct, and in Hyacinth's opinion, utterly bloodless. "How . . . odd . . . to see you here with Miss Bridgerton."

Hyacinth's head jerked with surprise. He had said her name too deliberately. She hadn't expected to be drawn into their war, but it seemed that somehow it had already happened.

"Have you met my father?" Gareth drawled, directing the question to her even as his eyes did not leave the baron's face.

"We have been introduced," Hyacinth replied.

"Indeed," Lord St. Clair said, taking her hand and bending over to kiss her gloved knuckles. "You are always charming, Miss Bridgerton."

Which was enough to prove to Hyacinth that they were definitely talking about something else, because she *knew* she wasn't always charming.

"Do you enjoy my son's company?" Lord St. Clair asked her, and Hyacinth noticed that once again, someone was asking her a question without actually looking at her.

"Of course," she said, her eyes flitting back and forth between the two men. "He is a most entertaining companion." And then, because she couldn't resist, she added, "You must be very proud of him."

That got the baron's attention, and he turned to her, his eyes dancing with something that wasn't quite humor. "Proud," he murmured, his lips curving into a half smile that she thought was rather like Gareth's. "It's an interesting adjective."

"Rather straightforward, I would think," Hyacinth said coolly.

"Nothing is ever straightforward with my father," Gareth said.

The baron's eyes went hard. "What my son means to say is that I am able to see the nuance in a situation . . . when one exists." He turned to Hyacinth. "Sometimes, my dear Miss Bridgerton, the matters at hand are quite clearly black and white."

Her lips parted as she glanced to Gareth and then back at his father. What the devil were they *talking* about?

Gareth's hand on her arm tightened, but when he spoke, his voice was light and casual. Too casual. "For once my father and I are in complete agreement. Very often one *can* view the world with complete clarity."

"Right now, perhaps?" the baron murmured.

Well, no, Hyacinth wanted to blurt out. As far as she was concerned, this was the most abstract and muddied conversation of her life. But she held her tongue. Partly because it really wasn't her place to speak, but also partly because she didn't want to do anything to halt the unfolding scene.

She turned to Gareth. He was smiling, but his eyes were cold. "I do believe my opinions right now are clear," he said softly.

And then quite suddenly the baron shifted his attention to Hyacinth. "What about you, Miss Bridgerton?" he asked. "Do you see things in black and white, or is your world painted in shades of gray?"

"It depends," she replied, lifting her chin until she was able to look him evenly in the eye. Lord St. Clair was tall, as tall as Gareth, and he looked to be healthy and fit. His face was pleasing and surprisingly youthful, with blue eyes and high, wide cheekbones.

But Hyacinth disliked him on sight. There was something angry about him, something underhanded and cruel.

And she didn't like how he made Gareth feel.

Not that Gareth had said anything to her, but it was clear as day on his face, in his voice, even in the way he held his chin.

"A very politic answer, Miss Bridgerton," the baron said, giving her a little nod of salute.

"How funny," she replied. "I'm not often politic."

"No, you're not, are you?" he murmured. "You do have a rather . . . *candid* reputation."

Hyacinth's eyes narrowed. "It is well deserved."

The baron chuckled. "Just make certain you are in possession of all of your information before you form your opinions, Miss Bridgerton. Or"—his head moved slightly, causing his gaze to angle onto her face in strange, sly manner—"before you make any decisions."

Hyacinth opened her mouth to give him a stinging retort—one that she hoped she'd be able to make up as she went along, since she still had no idea just what he was warning her about. But before she could speak, Gareth's grip on her forearm grew painful.

"It's time to go," he said. "Your family will be expecting you."

"Do offer them my regards," Lord St. Clair said, executing a smart little bow. "They are good *ton*, your family. I'm certain they want what's best for you."

Hyacinth just stared at him. She had no idea what the subtext was in this conversation, but clearly she did not have all the facts. And she *hated* being left in the dark.

Gareth yanked on her arm, hard, and she realized that he'd already started walking away. Hyacinth tripped over a bump in the path as she fell into place at his side. "What was *that* all about?" she asked, breathless from trying to keep up with him. He was striding through the park with a speed her shorter legs simply could not match.

"Nothing," he bit off.

"It wasn't *nothing*." She glanced over her shoulder to see if Lord St. Clair was still behind them. He wasn't, and the motion set her off-balance, in any case. She stumbled, falling against Gareth, who didn't seem inclined to treat her with any exceptional tenderness and solicitude. He did stop, though, just long enough for her to regain her footing.

"It was nothing," he said, and his voice was sharp and curt and a hundred other things she'd never thought it could be.

She shouldn't have said anything else. She knew she shouldn't have said anything else, but she wasn't always cautious enough to heed her own warnings, and as he pulled her along beside him, practically dragging her east toward Mayfair, she asked, "What are we going to do?"

He stopped, so suddenly that she nearly crashed into him. "Do?" he echoed. "We?"

"We," she confirmed, although her voice didn't come out quite as firmly as she'd intended.

"*We* are not going to do anything," he said, his voice sharpening as he spoke. "*We* are going to walk back to your house, where we are going to deposit you on your doorstep, and then *we* are going to return to my small, cramped apartments and have a drink."

"Why do you hate him so much?" Hyacinth asked. Her voice was soft, but it was direct.

He didn't answer. He didn't answer, and then it became clear that he wasn't going to answer. It wasn't her business, but oh, how she wished it were.

"Shall I return you, or do you wish to walk with your maid?" he finally asked.

Hyacinth looked over her shoulder. Frances was still behind her, standing near a large elm tree. She didn't look the least bit bored.

Hyacinth sighed. She was going to need a lot of peppermints this time.

Chapter 12

Twenty minutes later, after a long and silent walk.

 It was remarkable, Gareth thought with more than a little self-loathing, how one encounter with the baron could ruin a perfectly good day.

And it wasn't even so much the baron. He couldn't stand the man, that was true, but that wasn't what bothered him, what kept him up at night, mentally smacking himself for his stupidity.

He hated what his father did to him, how one conversation could turn him into a stranger. Or if not a stranger, then an astonishingly good facsimile of Gareth William St. Clair . . . at the age of fifteen. For the love of God, he was an adult now, a man of twenty-eight. He'd left home and, one hoped, grown up. He should be able to behave like an adult when in an interview with the baron. He shouldn't feel this way.

He should feel nothing. Nothing.

But it happened every time. He got angry. And snappish. And he said things just for the sake of being provoking. It was rude, and it was immature, and he didn't know how to stop it.

And this time, it had happened in front of Hyacinth.

He had walked her home in silence. He could tell she wanted to speak. Hell, even if he hadn't seen it on her face, he would have known she wanted to speak. Hyacinth always wanted to speak. But apparently she did occasionally know when to leave well enough alone, because she'd held silent throughout the long walk through Hyde Park and Mayfair. And now here they were, in front of her house, Frances the maid still trailing them by twenty feet.

"I am sorry for the scene in the park," he said swiftly, since some kind of apology was in order.

"I don't think anyone saw," she replied. "Or at the very least, I don't think anyone heard. And it wasn't your fault."

He felt himself smile. Wryly, since that was the only sort he could manage. It *was* his fault. Maybe his father had provoked him, but it was long past time that Gareth learned to ignore it.

"Will you come in?" Hyacinth asked.

He shook his head. "I'd best not."

She looked up at him, her eyes uncommonly serious. "I would like you to come in," she said.

It was a simple statement, so bare and plain that he knew he could not refuse. He gave her a nod, and together they walked up the steps. The rest of the Bridgertons had dispersed, so they entered the now-empty rose-and-cream drawing room. Hyacinth waited near the door until he reached the seating area, and then she shut it. All the way.

Gareth lifted his brows in question. In some circles, a closed door was enough to demand marriage.

"I used to think," Hyacinth said after a moment, "that the only thing that would have made my life better was a father."

He said nothing.

"Whenever I was angry with my mother," she continued, still standing by the door, "or with one of my brothers or sisters, I used to think—*If only I had a father. Everything would be perfect, and he would surely take my side.*" She looked up, and her lips were curved in an endearingly lopsided smile. "He wouldn't have done, of course, since I'm sure that most of the time I was in the wrong, but it gave me great comfort to think it."

Gareth still said nothing. All he could do was stand there and imagine himself a Bridgerton. Picture himself with all those siblings, all that laughter. And he couldn't respond, because it was too painful to think that she'd had all that and still wanted more.

"I've always been jealous of people with fathers," she said, "but no longer."

He turned sharply, his eyes snapping to hers. She returned his gaze with equal directness, and he realized he couldn't look away. Not shouldn't—couldn't.

"It's better to have no father at all than to have one such as yours, Gareth," she said quietly. "I'm so sorry."

And that was his undoing. Here was this girl who had everything—at least everything *he* thought he'd ever wanted—and somehow she still understood.

"I have memories, at least," she continued, smiling wistfully. "Or at least the memories others have told to me. I know who my father was, and I know he was a good man. He would have loved me if he'd lived. He would have loved me without reservations and without conditions."

Her lips wobbled into an expression he had never seen on her before. A little bit quirky, an awful lot self-deprecating. It was entirely unlike Hyacinth, and for that reason completely mesmerizing.

"And I know," she said, letting out a short, staccato breath, the sort one did when one couldn't quite believe what one was saying, "that it's often rather hard work to love me."

And suddenly Gareth realized that some things did come in a flash. And there were some things one simply knew without being able to explain them. Because as he stood there watching her, all he could think was—*No*.

No.

It would be rather easy to love Hyacinth Bridgerton.

He didn't know where the thought had come from, or what strange corner of his brain had come to that conclusion, because he was quite certain it would be nearly impossible to *live* with her, but somehow he knew that it wouldn't be at all difficult to love her.

"I talk too much," she said.

He'd been lost in his own thoughts. What was she saying?

"And I'm very opinionated."

That was true, but what was—

"And I can be an absolute pill when I do not get my way, although I would like to think that most of the time I'm reasonably reasonable . . ."

Gareth started to laugh. Good God, she was cataloguing all the reasons why she was difficult to love. She was right, of course, about all of them, but none of it seemed to matter. At least not right then.

"What?" she asked suspiciously.

"Be quiet," he said, crossing the distance between them.

"Why?"

"Just be quiet."

"But—"

He placed a finger on her lips. "Grant me one favor," he said softly, "and don't say a word."

Amazingly, she complied.

For a moment he did nothing but look at her. It was so rare that she was still, that something on her face wasn't moving or speaking or expressing an opinion with nothing more than a scrunch of her nose. He just looked at her, memorizing the way her eyebrows arched into delicate wings and her eyes grew wide under the strain of keeping quiet. He savored the hot rush of her breath across his finger, and the funny little sound she made at the back of her throat without realizing it.

And then he couldn't help it. He kissed her.

He took her face in his hands, and he lowered his mouth to hers. The last time he'd been angry, and he'd seen her as little more than a piece of forbidden fruit, the one girl his father thought he couldn't have.

But this time he was going to do it right. *This* would be their first kiss.

And it would be one to remember.

His lips were soft, gentle. He waited for her to sigh, for her body to soften against his. He wouldn't take until she made it clear she was ready to give.

And then he would offer himself in return.

He brushed his mouth against hers, with just enough friction to feel the texture of her lips, to sense the heat of her body. He tickled her with his tongue, tender and sweet, until her lips parted.

And then he tasted her. She was sweet, and she was warm, and she was returning his kiss with the most devilish mix of innocence and experience he could ever have imagined. Innocence, because it was quite clear she didn't know what she was doing. And experience, because despite all that, she drove him wild.

He deepened the kiss, his hands sliding down the length of her back until one rested on the curve of her bottom and the other at the small of her back. He pulled her against him, against the rising evidence of his desire. This was insane. It was mad. They were standing in her mother's drawing room, three feet from a door that could be opened at any moment, by a brother who certainly would feel no compunction at tearing Gareth apart limb from limb.

And yet he couldn't stop.

He wanted her. He wanted all of her.

God help him, he wanted her now.

"Do you like this?" he murmured, his lips moving to her ear.

He felt her nod, heard her gasp as he took her lobe between his teeth. It emboldened him, fired him.

"Do you like this?" he whispered, taking one hand and bringing it around to the swell of her breast.

She nodded again, this time gasping a tiny little, "Yes!"

He couldn't help but smile, nor could he do anything but

slide his hand inside the folds of her coat, so that the only thing between his hand and her body was the thin fabric of her dress.

"You'll like this even better," he said wickedly, skimming his palm over her until he felt her nipple harden.

She let out a moan, and he allowed himself even greater liberties, catching the nub between his fingers, rolling it just a touch, tweaking it until she moaned again, and her fingers clutched frantically at his shoulders.

She would be good in bed, he realized with a primitive satisfaction. She wouldn't know what she was doing, but it wouldn't matter. She'd learn soon enough, and he would have the time of his life teaching her.

And she would be his.

His.

And then, as his lips found hers again, as his tongue slid into her mouth and claimed her as his own, he thought—

Why not?

Why not marry her? Why n—

He pulled back, still holding her face in his hands. Some things needed to be considered with a clear mind, and the Lord knew that his head wasn't clear when he was kissing Hyacinth.

"Did I do something wrong?" she whispered.

He shook his head, unable to do anything but look at her.

"Then wh—"

He quieted her with a firm finger to her lips.

Why not marry her? Everybody seemed to want them to. His grandmother had been hinting about it for over a year, and her family was about as subtle as a sledgehammer. Furthermore, he actually rather *liked* Hyacinth,

which was more than he could say for most of the
women he'd met during his years as a bachelor. Certainly
she drove him mad half the time, but even with that, he
liked her.

Plus, it was becoming increasingly apparent that he
would not be able to keep his hands off her for very much
longer. Another afternoon like this, and he'd ruin her.

He could picture it, see it in his mind. Not just the two
of them, but all of the people in their lives—her family,
his grandmother.

His father.

Gareth almost laughed aloud. What a boon. He could
marry Hyacinth, which was shaping up in his mind to be
an extremely pleasant endeavor, and at the same time
completely show up the baron.

It would kill him. Absolutely kill him.

But, he thought, letting his fingers trail along the line of
her jaw as he pulled away, he needed to do this right. He
hadn't always lived his life on the correct side of propriety,
but there were some things a man had to do as a gentleman.

Hyacinth deserved no less.

"I have to go," he murmured, taking one of her hands
and lifting it to his mouth in a courtly gesture of farewell.

"Where?" she blurted out, her eyes still dazed with
passion.

He liked that. He liked that he befuddled her, left her
without her famous self-possession.

"There are a few things I need to think about," he said,
"and a few things I need to do."

"But . . . what?"

He smiled down at her. "You'll find out soon enough."

"When?"

He walked to the door. "You're a bundle of questions this afternoon, aren't you?"

"I wouldn't have to be," she retorted, clearly regaining her wits, "if you'd actually say something of substance."

"Until next time, Miss Bridgerton," he murmured, slipping out into the hall.

"But *when*?" came her exasperated voice.

He laughed all the way out.

One hour later, in the foyer of Bridgerton House. Our hero, apparently, doesn't waste any time.

"The viscount will see you now, Mr. St. Clair."

Gareth followed Lord Bridgerton's butler down the hall to a private section of the house, one which he had never seen during the handful of times he had been a guest at Bridgerton House.

"He is in his study," the butler explained.

Gareth nodded. It seemed the right place for such an interview. Lord Bridgerton would wish to appear in command, in control, and this would be emphasized by their meeting in his private sanctuary.

When Gareth had knocked upon the front door of Bridgerton House five minutes earlier, he had not given the butler any indication as to his purpose there that day, but he had no doubt that Hyacinth's brother, the almost infamously powerful Viscount Bridgerton, knew his intentions exactly.

Why else would Gareth come calling? He had never

had any cause before. And after becoming acquainted with Hyacinth's family—some of them, at least—he had no doubt that her mother had already met with her brother and discussed the possibility of their making a match.

"Mr. St. Clair," the viscount said, rising from behind his desk as Gareth entered the room. That was promising. Etiquette did not demand that the viscount come to his feet, and it was a show of respect that he did.

"Lord Bridgerton," Gareth said, nodding. Hyacinth's brother possessed the same deep chestnut hair as his sister, although his was just starting to gray at the temples. The faint sign of age did nothing to diminish him, however. He was a tall man, and probably a dozen years Gareth's senior, but he was still superbly fit and powerful. Gareth would not have wanted to meet him in a boxing ring. Or a dueling field.

The viscount motioned to a large leather chair, positioned opposite to his desk. "Sit," he said, "please."

Gareth did so, working fairly hard to hold himself still and keep his fingers from drumming nervously against the arm of the chair. He had never done this before, and damned if it wasn't the most unsettling thing. He needed to appear calm, his thoughts organized and collected. He didn't think his suit would be refused, but he'd like to come through the experience with a modicum of dignity. If he did marry Hyacinth, he was going to be seeing the viscount for the rest of his life, and he didn't need the head of the Bridgerton family thinking him a fool.

"I imagine you know why I am here," Gareth said.

The viscount, who had resumed his seat behind his large mahogany desk, tilted his head very slightly to the side. He was tapping his fingertips together, his hands making a hollow triangle. "Perhaps," he said, "to save both of us from possible embarrassment, you could state your intentions clearly."

Gareth sucked in a breath. Hyacinth's brother wasn't going to make this easy on him. But that didn't matter. He had vowed to do this right, and he would not be cowed.

He looked up, meeting the viscount's dark eyes with steady purpose. "I would like to marry Hyacinth," he said. And then, because the viscount did not say anything, because he didn't even move, Gareth added, "Er, if she'll have me."

And then about eight things happened at once. Or perhaps there were merely two or three, and it just seemed like eight, because it was all so unexpected.

First, the viscount exhaled, although that did seem to understate the case. It was more of a sigh, actually—a huge, tired, heartfelt sigh that made the man positively deflate in front of Gareth. Which was astonishing. Gareth had seen the viscount on many occasions and was quite familiar with his reputation. This was not a man who sagged or groaned.

His lips seemed to move through the whole thing, too, and if Gareth were a more suspicious man, he would have *thought* that the viscount had said, "Thank you, Lord."

Combined with the heavenward tilt of the viscount's eyes, it did seem the most likely translation.

And then, just as Gareth was taking all of this in, Lord

Bridgerton let the palms of his hands fall against the desk with surprising force, and he looked Gareth squarely in the eye as he said, "Oh, she'll have you. She will definitely have you."

It wasn't quite what Gareth had expected. "I beg your pardon," he said, since truly, he could think of nothing else.

"I need a drink," the viscount said, rising to his feet. "A celebration is in order, don't you think?"

"Er . . . yes?"

Lord Bridgerton crossed the room to a recessed bookcase and plucked a cut-glass decanter off one of the shelves. "No," he said to himself, putting it haphazardly back into place, "the good stuff, I think." He turned to Gareth, his eyes taking on a strange, almost giddy light. "The good stuff, wouldn't you agree?"

"Ehhhh . . ." Gareth wasn't quite sure what to make of this.

"The good stuff," the viscount said firmly. He moved some books to the side and reached behind to pull out what looked to be a very old bottle of cognac. "Have to keep it hidden," he explained, pouring it liberally into two glasses.

"Servants?" Gareth asked.

"Brothers." He handed Gareth a glass. "Welcome to the family."

Gareth accepted the offering, almost disconcerted by how easy this had turned out to be. He wouldn't have been surprised if the viscount had somehow managed to produce a special license and a vicar right then and there. "Thank you, Lord Bridgerton, I—"

"You should call me Anthony," the viscount cut in. "We're to be brothers, after all."

"Anthony," Gareth repeated. "I just wanted . . ."

"This is a wonderful day," Anthony was muttering to himself. "A wonderful day." He looked up sharply at Gareth. "You don't have sisters, do you?"

"None," Gareth confirmed.

"I am in possession of four," Anthony said, tossing back at least a third of the contents of his glass. "Four. And now they're all off my hands. I'm done," he said, looking as if he might break into a jig at any moment. "I'm free."

"You've daughters, don't you?" Gareth could not resist reminding him.

"Just one, and she's only three. I have years before I have to go through this again. If I'm lucky, she'll convert to Catholicism and become a nun."

Gareth choked on his drink.

"It's good, isn't it?" Anthony said, looking at the bottle. "Aged twenty-four years."

"I don't believe I've ever ingested anything quite so ancient," Gareth murmured.

"Now then," Anthony said, leaning against the edge of his desk, "you'll want to discuss the settlements, I'm sure."

The truth was, Gareth hadn't even thought about the settlements, strange as that seemed for a man in possession of very few funds. He'd been so surprised by his sudden decision to marry Hyacinth that his mind hadn't even touched upon the practical aspects of such a union.

"It is common knowledge that I increased her dowry last year," Anthony said, his face growing more serious. "I will stand by that, although I would hope that it is not your primary reason for marrying her."

"Of course not," Gareth replied, bristling.

"I didn't think so," Anthony said, "but one has to ask."

"I would hardly think a man would admit it to you if it were," Gareth said.

Anthony looked up sharply. "I would like to think I can read a man's face well enough to know if he is lying."

"Of course," Gareth said, sitting back down.

But it didn't appear that the viscount had taken offense. "Now then," he said, "her portion stands at . . ."

Gareth watched with a touch of confusion as Anthony just shook his head and allowed his words to trail off. "My lord?" he murmured.

"My apologies," Anthony said, snapping back to attention. "I'm a bit unlike myself just now, I must assure you."

"Of course," Gareth murmured, since agreement was really the only acceptable course of action at that point.

"I never thought this day would come," the viscount said. "We've had offers, of course, but none I was willing to entertain, and none recently." He let out a long breath. "I had begun to despair that anyone of merit would wish to marry her."

"You seem to hold your sister in an unbecomingly low regard," Gareth said coolly.

Anthony looked up and actually smiled. Sort of. "Not at all," he said. "But nor am I blind to her . . . ah . . . unique qualities." He stood, and Gareth realized instantly that Lord Bridgerton was using his height to intimidate. He also realized that he should not misinterpret the viscount's initial display of levity and relief. This was a dangerous man, or at least he could be when he so chose, and Gareth would do well not to forget it.

"My sister Hyacinth," the viscount said slowly, walking

toward the window, "is a prize. You should remember that, and if you value your skin, you will treat her as the treasure she is."

Gareth held his tongue. It didn't seem the correct time to chime in.

"But while Hyacinth may be a prize," Anthony said, turning around with the slow, deliberate steps of a man who is well familiar with his power, "she isn't easy. I will be the first one to admit to this. There aren't many men who can match wits with her, and if she is trapped into marriage with someone who does not appreciate her . . . singular personality, she will be miserable."

Still, Gareth did not speak. But he did not remove his eyes from the viscount's face.

And Anthony returned the gesture. "I will give you my permission to marry her," he said. "But you should think long and hard before you ask her yourself."

"What are you saying?" Gareth asked suspiciously, rising to his feet.

"I will not mention this interview to her. It is up to you to decide if you wish to take the final step. And if you do not . . ." The viscount shrugged, his shoulders rising and falling in an oddly Gallic gesture. "In that case," he said, sounding almost disturbingly calm, "she will never know."

How many men had the viscount scared off in this manner, Gareth wondered. Good God, was this why Hyacinth had gone unmarried for so long? He supposed he should be grateful, since it had left her free to marry him, but still, did she realize her eldest brother was a *madman?*

"If you don't make my sister happy," Anthony Bridgerton continued, his eyes just intense enough to confirm Gareth's suspicions about his sanity, "then *you* will not be happy. I will see to it myself."

Gareth opened his mouth to offer the viscount a scathing retort—to hell with treating him with kid gloves and tiptoeing around his high and mightiness. But then, just when he was about to insult his future brother-in-law, probably irreversibly, something else popped out of his mouth instead.

"You love her, don't you?"

Anthony snorted impatiently. "Of course I love her. She's my sister."

"I loved my brother," Gareth said quietly. "Besides my grandmother, he was the only person I had in this world."

"You do not intend to mend your rift with your father, then," Anthony said.

"No."

Anthony did not ask questions; he just nodded and said, "If you marry my sister, you will have all of us."

Gareth tried to speak, but he had no voice. He had no words. There were no words for what was rushing through him.

"For better or for worse," the viscount continued, with a light, self-mocking chuckle. "And I assure you, you will very often wish that Hyacinth were a foundling, left on a doorstep with not a relation to her name."

"No," Gareth said with soft resolve. "I would not wish that on anyone."

The room held silent for a moment, and then the viscount asked, "Is there anything you wish to share with me about him?"

Unease began to seep through Gareth's blood. "Who?"

"Your father."

"No."

Anthony appeared to consider this, then he asked, "Will he make trouble?"

"For me?"

"For Hyacinth."

Gareth couldn't lie. "He might."

And that was the worst of it. That was what would keep him up at night. Gareth had no idea what the baron might do. Or what he might say.

Or how the Bridgertons might feel if they learned the truth.

And in that moment, Gareth realized that he needed to do two things. First, he had to marry Hyacinth as soon as possible. She—and her mother—would probably wish for one of those absurdly elaborate weddings that took months to plan, but he would need to put his foot down and insist that they wed quickly.

And second, as a sort of insurance, he was going to have to do something to make it impossible for her to back out, even if his father came forward with proof of Gareth's parentage.

He was going to have to compromise her. As soon as possible. There was still the matter of Isabella's diary. She might have known the truth, and if she'd written about it, Hyacinth would learn his secrets even without the intervention of the baron.

And while Gareth didn't much mind Hyacinth learning the true facts of his birth, it was vital that it not happen until after the wedding.

Or after he'd secured its eventuality with seduction.

Gareth didn't much like being backed into a corner. Nor was he especially fond of having to *have* to do anything.

But this . . .

This, he decided, would be pure pleasure.

Chapter 13

Only one hour later. As we have noted, when our hero puts his mind to something . . .

And did we mention that it's a Tuesday?

"Enh?" Lady Danbury screeched. "You're not speaking loudly enough!"

Hyacinth allowed the book from which she was reading to fall closed, with just her index finger stuck inside to mark her place. "Why," she wondered aloud, "does it feel like I have heard this before?"

"You have," Lady D declared. "You never speak loudly enough."

"Funny, but my mother never makes that complaint."

"Your mother's ears aren't of the same vintage as mine," Lady Danbury said with a snort. "And where's my cane?"

Ever since she'd seen Gareth in action, Hyacinth had felt emboldened when it came to encounters with Lady Danbury's cane. "I hid it," she said with an evil smile.

Lady Danbury drew back. "Hyacinth Bridgerton, you sly cat."

"Cat?"

"I don't like dogs," Lady D said with a dismissive wave of her hand. "Or foxes, for that matter."

Hyacinth decided to take it as a compliment—always the best course of action when Lady Danbury was making no sense—and she turned back to *Miss Butterworth and the Mad Baron*, chapter seventeen. "Let's see," she murmured, "where were we . . ."

"Where did you hide it?"

"It wouldn't be hidden if I told you, now would it?" Hyacinth said, not even looking up.

"I'm trapped in this chair without it," Lady D said. "You wouldn't wish to deprive an old lady of her only means of transport, would you?"

"I would," Hyacinth said, still looking down at the book. "I absolutely would."

"You've been spending too much time with my grandson," the countess muttered.

Hyacinth kept her attention diligently on the book, but she knew she wasn't managing a completely straight face. She sucked in her lips, then pursed them, as she always did when she was trying not to look at someone, and if the temperature of her cheeks was any indication, she was blushing.

Dear God.

Lesson Number One in dealings with Lady Danbury: Never show weakness.

Lesson Number Two being, of course: When in doubt, refer to Lesson Number One.

"Hyacinth Bridgerton," Lady Danbury said, too slowly for her to be up to anything but the most devious sort of mischief, "are your cheeks pink?"

Hyacinth looked up with her blankest expression. "I can't see my cheeks."

"They *are* pink."

"If you say so." Hyacinth flipped a page with a bit more purpose than was necessary, then looked down in dismay at the small rip near the binding. Oh dear. Well, nothing she could do about it now, and Priscilla Butterworth had certainly survived worse.

"Why are you blushing?" Lady D asked.

"I'm not blushing."

"I do believe you are."

"I'm n—" Hyacinth caught herself before they started bickering like a pair of children. "I'm warm," she said, with what she felt was an admirable display of dignity and decorum.

"It's perfectly pleasant in this room," Lady Danbury said immediately. "Why are you blushing?"

Hyacinth glared at her. "Do you wish for me to read this book or not?"

"Not," Lady D said definitively. "I would much rather learn why you are blushing."

"I'm not blushing!" Hyacinth fairly yelled.

Lady Danbury smiled, an expression that on anyone else might have been pleasant but on her was diabolical. "Well, you are now," she said.

"If my cheeks are pink," Hyacinth ground out, "it is from anger."

"At me?" Lady D inquired, placing one, oh-so-innocent hand over her heart.

"I'm going to read the book now," Hyacinth announced.

"If you must," Lady D said with a sigh. She waited

about a second before adding, "I believe Miss Butterworth was scrambling up the hillside."

Hyacinth turned her attention resolutely to the book in her hands.

"Well?" Lady Danbury demanded.

"I have to find my place," Hyacinth muttered. She scanned the page, trying to find Miss Butterworth and the correct hillside (there were more than one, and she'd scrambled up them all), but the words swam before her eyes, and all she saw was Gareth.

Gareth, with those rakish eyes and perfect lips. Gareth, with a dimple she was sure he'd deny if she ever pointed it out to him. Gareth . . .

Who was making her sound as foolish as Miss Butterworth. Why would he deny a dimple?

In fact . . .

Hyacinth flipped back a few pages. Yes, indeed, there it was, right in the middle of chapter sixteen:

> His eyes were rakish and his lips perfectly molded. And he possessed a dimple, right above the left corner of his mouth, that he would surely deny if she were ever brave enough to point it out to him.

"Good God," Hyacinth muttered. She didn't think Gareth even *had* a dimple.

"We're not that lost, are we?" Lady D demanded. "You've gone back three chapters, at least."

"I'm looking, I'm looking," Hyacinth said. She was going mad. That had to be it. She'd clearly lost her wits if she was now unconsciously quoting from *Miss Butterworth.*

But then again . . .

He'd kissed her.

He'd really kissed her. The first time, back in the hall at Bridgerton House—that had been something else entirely. Their lips had touched, and in truth quite a few other things had touched as well, but it hadn't been a kiss.

Not like this one.

Hyacinth sighed.

"*What* are you huffing about?" Lady Danbury demanded.

"Nothing."

Lady D's mouth clamped into a firm line. "You are not yourself this afternoon, Miss Bridgerton. Not yourself at all."

Not a point Hyacinth wished to argue. "*Miss Butterworth,*" she read with more force than was necessary, "*scrambled up the hillside, her fingers digging deeper into the dirt with each step.*"

"Can fingers step?" Lady D asked.

"They can in this book." Hyacinth cleared her throat and continued: "*She could hear him behind her. He was closing the distance between them, and soon she would be caught. But for what purpose? Good or evil?*"

"Evil, I hope. It'll keep things interesting."

"I am in complete agreement," Hyacinth said. "*How would she know?*" she read on. "*How would she know? How WOULD she know?*" She looked up. "Emphasis mine."

"Allowed," Lady D said graciously.

"*And then she recalled the advice given to her by her mother, before the blessed lady had gone to her reward, pecked to death by pigeons—*"

"This can't be real!"

"Of course it can't. It's a novel. But I swear to you, it's right here on page 193."

"Let me see that!"

Hyacinth's eyes widened. Lady Danbury frequently accused Hyacinth of embellishment, but this was the first time she had actually demanded verification. She got up and showed the book to the countess, pointing to the paragraph in question.

"Well, I'll be," Lady Danbury said. "The poor lady did get done in by pigeons." She shook her head. "It's not how I'd like to go."

"You probably don't need to worry on that score," Hyacinth said, resuming her seat.

Lady D reached for her cane, then scowled when she realized it was gone. "Continue," she barked.

"Right," Hyacinth said to herself, looking back down at the book. "Let me see. Ah, yes . . . *gone to her reward, pecked to death by pigeons.*" She looked up, spluttering. "I'm sorry. I can't read that without laughing."

"Just read!"

Hyacinth cleared her throat several times before resuming. "*She had been only twelve, far too young for such a conversation, but perhaps her mother had anticipated her early demise.* I'm sorry," she cut in again, "but how on earth could someone anticipate something like that?"

"As you said," Lady D said dryly, "it's a novel."

Hyacinth took a breath and read on: "*Her mother had clutched her hand, and with sad, lonely eyes had said, 'Dearest, dearest Priscilla. There is nothing in this world more precious than love.'*"

Hyacinth stole a peek at Lady Danbury, who she fully expected to be snorting with disgust. But to her great surprise, the countess was rapt, hanging on her every word.

Quickly returning her attention to the book, Hyacinth read, "*'But there are deceivers, darling Priscilla, and there are men who will attempt to take advantage of you without a true meeting of the hearts.'*"

"It's true," Lady Danbury said.

Hyacinth looked up, and it was immediately apparent that Lady Danbury had not realized that she'd spoken aloud.

"Well, it is," Lady D said defensively, when she realized that Hyacinth was looking at her.

Not wishing to embarrass the countess any further, Hyacinth turned back to the book without speaking. Clearing her throat, she continued: "*'You will need to trust your instincts, dearest Priscilla, but I will give you one piece of advice. Hold it to your heart and remember it always, for I vow it is true.'*"

Hyacinth turned the page, a little embarrassed to realize that she was as captured by the book as she'd ever been.

"*Priscilla leaned forward, touching her mother's pale cheek. 'What is it, Mama?' she asked.*

"*'If you want to know if a gentleman loves you,'* her mother said, *'there is only one true way to be sure.'*"

Lady Danbury leaned forward. Even Hyacinth leaned forward, and she was holding the book.

"*'It's in his kiss,'* her mother whispered. *'It's all there, in his kiss.'*"

Hyacinth's lips parted, and one hand come up to touch them, without her even realizing it.

"Well," Lady Danbury declared. "That wasn't what I was expecting."

It's in his kiss. Could it be true?

"I would think," Lady D continued officiously, "that it's in his actions or his deeds, but I suppose that wouldn't have sounded romantic enough for Miss Butterworth."

"And the Mad Baron," Hyacinth murmured.

"Exactly! Who in her right mind would want a madman?"

"It's in his kiss," Hyacinth whispered to herself.

"Enh?" Lady Danbury screeched. "I can't hear you."

"It's nothing," Hyacinth said quickly, giving her head a little shake as she forced her attention back to the countess. "I was merely woolgathering."

"Pondering the intellectual dogmas laid out by Mother Butterworth?"

"Of course not." She coughed. "Shall we read some more?"

"We'd better," Lady D grumbled. "The sooner we finish this one, the sooner we can move on to another."

"We don't *need* to finish this one," Hyacinth said, although if they didn't, she was going to have to sneak it home and finish it herself.

"Don't be silly. We can't *not* finish it. I paid good money for that nonsense. And besides"—Lady D looked as sheepish as she was able when she said this, which, admittedly, wasn't very sheepish—"I wish to know how it ends."

Hyacinth smiled at her. It was as close to an expression of softheartedness as Lady Danbury was likely to display, and Hyacinth rather thought it should be encouraged. "Very well," she said. "If you will allow me to find my place again . . ."

"Lady Danbury," came the deep, even voice of the butler, who had entered the drawing room on silent feet, "Mr. St. Clair would like an audience."

"And he's asking for it?" Lady D inquired. "He usually just barges right in."

The butler lifted an eyebrow, more expression than Hyacinth had ever seen on a butler's face. "He has requested an audience with Miss Bridgerton," he said.

"Me?" Hyacinth squeaked.

Lady Danbury's jaw dropped. "Hyacinth!" she spluttered. "In *my* drawing room?"

"That is what he said, my lady."

"Well," Lady D declared, looking around the room even though there was no one present save Hyacinth and the butler. "Well."

"Shall I escort him in?" the butler inquired.

"Of course," Lady Danbury replied, "but I'm not going anywhere. Anything he has to say to Miss Bridgerton, he can say in front of me."

"What?" Hyacinth demanded, finally tearing her eyes off the butler and turning toward Lady Danbury. "I hardly think—"

"It's my drawing room," Lady D said, "and he's my grandson. And you're—" She clamped her mouth together as she regarded Hyacinth, her diatribe momentarily halted. "Well, you're you," she finally finished. "Hmmph."

"Miss Bridgerton," Gareth said, appearing in the doorway and filling it, to wax Butterworthian, with his marvelous presence. He turned to Lady Danbury. "Grandmother."

"Anything you have to say to Miss Bridgerton, you can say in front of me," she told him.

"I'm almost tempted to test that theory," he murmured.

"Is something amiss?" Hyacinth asked, perching at the front of her chair. After all, they'd parted ways barely two hours earlier.

"Not at all," Gareth replied. He crossed the room until he was at her side, or at least as close to it as the furniture would allow. His grandmother was staring at him with unconcealed interest, and he was beginning to doubt the wisdom of coming straight here from Bridgerton House.

But he had stepped out onto the pavement and realized that it was Tuesday. And somehow that had seemed auspicious. This had all started on a Tuesday, good heavens, was it just two weeks earlier?

Tuesdays were when Hyacinth read to his grandmother. Every Tuesday, without fail, at the same time, in the same place. Gareth had realized, as he walked down the street, pondering the new direction of his life, that he knew exactly where Hyacinth was in that moment. And if he wanted to ask her to marry him, he had only to walk the brief distance across Mayfair to Danbury House.

He probably should have waited. He probably should have picked a far more romantic time and place, something that would sweep her off her feet and leave her breathless for more. But he'd made his decision, and he didn't want to wait, and besides, after all his grandmother had done for him over the years, she deserved to be the first to know.

He hadn't, however, expected to have to make his proposal in the old lady's presence.

He glanced over at her.

"What is it?" she barked.

He should ask her to leave. He really should, although . . .

Oh, hell. She wouldn't quit the room if he got down on his knees and begged her. Not to mention that Hyacinth would have an extremely difficult time refusing him with Lady Danbury in attendance.

Not that he thought she'd say no, but it really did make sense to stack the deck in his favor.

"Gareth?" Hyacinth said softly.

He turned to her, wondering how long he'd been standing there, pondering his options. "Hyacinth," he said.

She looked at him expectantly.

"Hyacinth," he said again, this time with a bit more certitude. He smiled, letting his eyes melt into hers. "Hyacinth."

"We *know* her name," came his grandmother's voice.

Gareth ignored her and pushed a table aside so that he could drop to one knee. "Hyacinth," he said, relishing her gasp as he took her hand in his, "would you do me the very great honor of becoming my wife?"

Her eyes widened, then misted, and her lips, which he'd been kissing so deliciously mere hours earlier, began to quiver. "I . . . I . . ."

It was unlike her to be so without words, and he was enjoying it, especially the show of emotion on her face.

"I . . . I . . ."

"Yes!" his grandmother finally yelled. "Yes! She'll marry you!"

"She can speak for herself," he said.

"No," Lady D said, "she can't. Quite obviously."

"Yes," Hyacinth said, nodding through her sniffles. "Yes, I'll marry you."

He lifted her hand to his lips. "Good."

"Well," his grandmother declared. "Well." Then she muttered, "I need my cane."

"It's behind the clock," Hyacinth said, never taking her eyes off Gareth's.

Lady Danbury blinked with surprise, then actually got up and retrieved it.

"Why?" Hyacinth asked.

Gareth smiled. "Why what?"

"Why did you ask me to marry you?"

"I should think that was clear."

"Tell her!" Lady D bellowed, thumping her cane against the carpet. She gazed down at the stick with obvious affection. "That's much better," she murmured.

Gareth and Hyacinth both turned to her, Hyacinth somewhat impatiently and Gareth with that blank stare of his that hinted of condescension without actually rubbing the recipient's face in it.

"Oh very well," Lady Danbury grumbled. "I suppose you'd like a bit of privacy."

Neither Gareth nor Hyacinth said a word.

"I'm leaving, I'm leaving," Lady D said, hobbling to the door with suspiciously less agility than she'd displayed when she'd crossed the room to retrieve the cane just moments earlier. "But don't you think," she said, pausing in the doorway, "that I'm leaving you for long. I know *you*," she said, jabbing her cane in the air toward Gareth, "and if you think I trust you with her virtue . . ."

"I'm your grandson."

"Doesn't make you a saint," she announced, then slipped out of the room, shutting the door behind her.

Gareth regarded this with a quizzical air. "I rather think she wants me to compromise you," he murmured. "She'd never have closed it all the way, otherwise."

"Don't be silly," Hyacinth said, trying for a touch of bravado under her blush, which she could feel spreading across her cheeks.

"No, I think she does," he said, taking both her hands in his and raising them to his lips. "She wants you for a granddaughter, probably more than she wants me for a grandson, and she's just underhanded enough to facilitate your ruin to ensure the outcome."

"I wouldn't back out," Hyacinth mumbled, disconcerted by his nearness. "I gave you my word."

He took one of her fingers and placed the tip between his lips. "You did, didn't you?" he murmured.

She nodded, transfixed by the sight of her finger against his mouth. "You didn't answer my question," she whispered.

His tongue found the delicate crease beneath her fingertip and flicked back and forth. "Did you ask me one?"

She nodded. It was hard to think while he was seducing her, and amazing to think that he could reduce her to such a breathless state with just one finger to his lips.

He moved, sitting beside her on the sofa, never once releasing her hand. "So lovely," he murmured. "And soon to be mine." He took her hand and turned it over, so that her palm was facing up. Hyacinth watched him watching her, watched him as he leaned over her and touched his lips to the inside of her wrist. Her breath seemed overloud in the silent room, and she wondered what it was that was most responsible for her heightened state: the feel of his mouth on her skin or the sight of him, seducing her with only a kiss.

"I like your arms," he said, holding one as if it were a precious treasure, in need of examination as much as safekeeping. "The skin first, I think," he continued, letting his fingers slide lightly along the sensitive skin above her wrist. It had been a warm day, and she'd worn a summer frock under her pelisse. The sleeves were mere caps, and—she sucked in her breath—if he continued his exploration all the way up to her shoulder, she thought she might melt right there on the sofa.

"But I like the shape of them as well," he said, gazing down at it as if it were an object of wonder. "Slim, but with just a hint of roundness and strength." He looked up, lazy humor in his eyes. "You're a bit of a sportswoman, aren't you?"

She nodded.

He curved his lips into a half smile. "I can see it in the way you walk, the way you move. Even"—he stroked her arm one last time, his fingers coming to rest near her wrist—"the shape of your arm."

He leaned in, until his face was near hers, and she felt kissed by his breath as he spoke. "You move differently than other women," he said softly. "It makes me wonder."

"What?" she whispered.

His hand was somehow on her hip, then on her leg, resting on the curve of her thigh, not quite caressing her, just reminding her of its presence with the heat and weight of it. "I think you know," he murmured.

Hyacinth felt her body flush with heat as unbidden images filled her mind. She knew what went on between a man and a woman; she'd long since badgered the truth out of her older sisters. And she'd once found a scandalous book of erotic images in Gregory's room, filled with illustrations from the East that had made her feel very strange inside.

But nothing had prepared her for the rush of desire that she felt upon Gareth's murmured words. She couldn't help but picture him—stroking her, kissing her.

It made her weak.

It made her want him.

"Don't you wonder?" he whispered, the words hot against her ear.

She nodded. She couldn't lie. She felt bare in the moment, her very soul laid open to his gentle onslaught.

"What do you think?" he pressed.

She swallowed, trying not to notice the way her breath seemed to fill her chest differently. "I couldn't say," she finally managed.

"No, you couldn't," he said, smiling knowingly, "could you? But that's of no matter." He leaned in and kissed her, once, slowly, on the lips. "You will soon."

He rose to his feet. "I fear I must leave before my grandmother attempts to spy on us from the house across the way."

Hyacinth's eyes flew to the window in horror.

"Don't worry," Gareth said with a chuckle. "Her eyes aren't that good."

"She owns a telescope," Hyacinth said, still regarding the window with suspicion.

"Why does that not surprise me?" Gareth murmured, walking to the door.

Hyacinth watched him as he crossed the room. He had always reminded her of a lion. He still did, only now he was hers to tame.

"I shall call upon you tomorrow," Gareth said, honoring her with a small bow.

She nodded, watching as he took his leave. Then, when he was gone, she untwisted her torso so that she was once again facing front.

"Oh. My—"

"What did he say?" Lady Danbury demanded, reentering the room a scant thirty seconds after Gareth's departure.

Hyacinth just looked at her blankly.

"You asked him why he asked you to marry him," Lady D reminded her. "What did he say?"

Hyacinth opened her mouth to reply, and it was only then that she realized he had never answered her question.

"He said he couldn't not marry me," she lied. It was what she wished he'd said; it might as well be what Lady Danbury thought had transpired.

"Oh!" Lady D sighed, clasping a hand to her chest. "How lovely."

Hyacinth regarded her with a new appreciation. "You're a romantic," she said.

"Always," Lady D replied, with a secret smile that Hyacinth knew she didn't often share. "Always."

Chapter 14

Two weeks have passed. All of London now knows that Hyacinth is to become Mrs. St. Clair. Gareth is enjoying his new status as an honorary Bridgerton, but still, he can't help but wait for it all to fall apart.

The time is midnight. The place, directly below Hyacinth's bedroom window.

 He had planned for everything, plotted every last detail. He'd played it out in his mind, everything but the words he'd say, since those, he knew, would come in the heat of the moment.

It would be a thing of beauty.

It would be a thing of passion.

It would be that night.

Tonight, thought Gareth, with a strange mix of calculation and delight, he would seduce Hyacinth.

He had a few vague pangs about the degree to which he was plotting her downfall, but these were quickly dismissed. It wasn't as if he was going to ruin her and leave her to the wolves. He was planning to marry the girl, for heaven's sake.

And no one would know. No one but him and Hyacinth.

And her conscience, which would never allow her to pull out of a betrothal once she'd given herself to her fiancé.

They had made plans to search Clair House that night. Hyacinth had wanted to go the week before, but Gareth had put her off. It was too soon to set his plan in motion, so he had made up a story about his father having guests. Common sense dictated that they would wish to search the emptiest house possible, after all.

Hyacinth, being the practical girl she was, had agreed immediately.

But tonight would be perfect. His father would almost certainly be at the Mottram Ball, on the off chance that they actually made it to Clair House to conduct their search. And more importantly, Hyacinth was ready.

He'd made sure she was ready.

The past two weeks had been surprisingly delightful. He'd been forced to attend an astounding number of parties and balls. He had been to the opera and the theatre. But he had done it all with Hyacinth at his side, and if he'd had any doubts about the wisdom of marrying her, they were gone now. She was sometimes vexing, occasionally infuriating, but always entertaining.

She would make a fine wife. Not for most men, but for him, and that was all that mattered.

But first he had to make sure she could not back out. He had to make their agreement permanent.

He'd begun her seduction slowly, tempting her with glances, touches, and stolen kisses. He'd teased her, always leaving a hint of what might transpire next. He'd left her breathless; hell, he'd left himself breathless.

He'd started this two weeks earlier, when he had asked her to marry him, knowing all the while that theirs would need to be a hasty engagement. He'd started it with a kiss. Just a kiss. Just one little kiss.

Tonight he would show her just what a kiss could be.

All in all, Hyacinth thought as she hurried up the stairs to her bedroom, it had gone rather well.

She would have preferred to stay home that night—all the more time to prepare for her outing to Clair House, but Gareth had pointed out that if he was going to send his regrets to the Mottrams, she had best attend. Otherwise, there might be speculation as to both of their whereabouts. But after spending three hours talking and laughing and dancing, Hyacinth had located her mother and pleaded a headache. Violet was having a fine time, as Hyacinth had known she would be, and did not wish to depart, so instead she'd sent Hyacinth home in the carriage by herself.

Perfect, perfect. Everything was perfect. The carriage had not encountered any traffic on the way home, so it had to be just about midnight, which meant that Hyacinth had fifteen minutes to change her clothing and creep down to the back stairs to await Gareth.

She could hardly wait.

She wasn't certain if they would find the jewels that night. She wouldn't be surprised if Isabella had instead left more clues. But they would be one step closer to their goal.

And it would be an adventure.

Had she always possessed this reckless streak, Hyacinth wondered. Had she always thrilled to danger? Had she only been waiting for the opportunity to be wild?

She moved quietly down the upper hall to her bedroom door. The house was silent, and she certainly didn't wish to rouse any of the servants. She reached out and turned the well-oiled doorknob, then pushed the door open and slipped inside.

At last.

Now all she had to do was—

"Hyacinth."

She almost shrieked.

"Gareth?" she gasped, her eyes nearly bugging out. Good God, the man was lounging on her bed.

He smiled. "I've been waiting for you."

She looked quickly around the room. How had he got inside? "What are you doing here?" she whispered frantically.

"I arrived early," he said in a lazy voice. But his eyes were sharp and intense. "I thought I'd wait for you."

"*Here?*"

He shrugged, smiled. "It was cold outside."

Except it wasn't. It was unseasonably warm. Everyone had been remarking on it.

"How did you get in?" Good God, did the servants know? Had someone *seen* him?

"Scaled the wall."

"You scaled the—You what?" She ran to the window, peering out and down. "How did you—"

But he had risen from the bed and crept up behind her. His arms encircled her, and he murmured, low and close to her ear, "I'm very, very clever."

She let out a nervous laugh. "Or part cat."

She felt him smile. "That, too," he murmured. And then, after a pause: "I missed you."

"I—" She wanted to say that she'd missed him, too, but he was too close, and she was too warm, and her voice escaped her.

He leaned down, his lips finding the soft spot just below her ear. He touched her, so softly she wasn't even sure it was a kiss, then murmured, "Did you enjoy yourself this evening?"

"Yes. No. I was too . . ." She swallowed, unable to withstand the touch of his lips without making a reaction. ". . . anxious."

He took her hands, kissing each in turn. "Anxious? Whyever?"

"The jewels," she reminded him. Good heavens, did every woman have this much trouble breathing when standing so close to a handsome man?

"Ah, yes." His hand found her waist, and she felt herself being pulled toward him. "The jewels."

"Don't you want—"

"Oh, I do," he murmured, holding her scandalously close. "I want. Very much."

"Gareth," she gasped. His hands were on her bottom, and his lips on her neck.

And she wasn't sure how much longer she could remain standing.

He did things to her. He made her feel things she didn't recognize. He made her gasp and moan, and all she knew was that she wanted more.

"I think about you every night," he whispered against her skin.

"You do?"

"Mmm-hmm." His voice, almost a purr, rumbled against her throat. "I lie in bed, wishing you were there beside me."

It took every ounce of her strength just to breathe. And yet some little part of her, some wicked and very wanton corner of her soul, made her say, "What do you think about?"

He chuckled, clearly pleased with her question. "I think about doing *this*," he murmured, and his hand, already cupping her bottom, tightened until she was pressed against the evidence of his desire.

She made a noise. It might have been his name.

"And I think a *lot* about doing this," he said, his expert fingers flicking open one of the buttons on the back of her gown.

Hyacinth gulped. Then she gulped again when she realized he'd undone three more in the time it took her to draw one breath.

"But most of all," he said, his voice low and smooth. "I think about doing *this*."

He swept her into his arms, her skirt swirling around her legs even as the bodice of her dress slid down, resting precariously at the top of her breasts. She clutched at his shoulders, her fingers barely making a dent in his muscles, and she wanted to say something—anything that might make her seem more sophisticated than she actually was, but all she managed was a startled little, "Oh!" as she became weightless, seemingly floating through the air until he laid her down on her bed.

He lay down next to her, perched on his side, one hand

idly stroking the bare skin covering her breastbone. "So pretty," he murmured. "So soft."

"What are you doing?" she whispered.

He smiled. Slowly, like a cat. "To you?"

She nodded.

"That depends," he said, leaning down and letting his tongue tease where his fingers had just been. "How does it make you feel?"

"I don't know," she admitted.

He laughed, the sound low and soft, and strangely heartwarming. "That's a good thing," he said, his fingers finding the loosened bodice of her gown. "A very good thing."

He tugged, and Hyacinth sucked in her breath as she was bared, to the air, to the night.

To him.

"So pretty," he whispered, smiling down at her, and she wondered if his touch could possibly leave her as breathless as his gaze. He did nothing but look at her, and she was taut and tense.

Eager.

"You are so beautiful," he murmured, and then he touched her, his hand skimming along the tip of her breast so lightly he might have been the wind.

Oh, yes, his touch did quite a bit more than his gaze.

She felt it in her belly, she felt it between her legs. She felt it to the tips of her toes, and she couldn't help but arch up, reaching for more, for something closer, firmer.

"I thought you'd be perfect," he said, taking his torture to her other breast. "I didn't realize. I just didn't realize."

"What?" she whispered.

His eyes locked with hers. "That you're better," he said. "Better than perfect."

"Th-that's not possible," she said, "you can't—oh!" He'd done something else, something even more wicked, and if this was a battle for her wits, she was losing desperately.

"What can't I do?" he asked innocently, his fingers rolling over her nipple, feeling it harden into an impossibly taut little nub.

"Can't make something—can't make something—"

"I can't?" He smiled deviously, trying his tricks on the other side. "I think I can. I think I just did."

"No," she gasped. "You can't make something better than perfect. It's not proper English."

And then he stilled. Completely, which took her by surprise. But his gaze still smoldered, and as his eyes swept over her, she *felt* him. She couldn't explain it; she just knew that she did.

"That's what I thought," he murmured. "Perfection is absolute, is it not? One can't be slightly unique, and one can't be more than perfect. But somehow . . . you are."

"Slightly unique?"

His smile spread slowly across his face. "Better than perfect."

She reached up, touched his cheek, then brushed a lock of his hair back and tucked it behind his ear. The moonlight glinted off the strands, making them seem more golden than usual.

She didn't know what to say, didn't know what to do. All she knew was that she loved this man.

She wasn't sure when it had happened. It hadn't been like her decision to marry him, which had been sudden and clear in an instant. This . . . this love . . . it had crept up on her, rolling along, gaining in momentum until one day it was *there*.

It was there, and it was true, and she knew it would be with her always.

And now, lying on her bed, in the secret stillness of the night, she wanted to give herself to him. She wanted to love him in every way a woman could love a man, and she wanted him to take everything she could give. It didn't matter if they weren't married; they would be soon enough.

Tonight, she couldn't wait.

"Kiss me," she whispered.

He smiled, and it was in his eyes even more than his lips. "I thought you'd never ask." He leaned down, but his lips skimmed hers for barely a second. Instead they veered downward, breathing heat across her until they found her breast. And then he—

"Ohhhh!" she moaned. He couldn't do that. Could he?

He could. And he did.

Pure pleasure shot through her, tickling to every corner of her body. She clutched his head, her hands sinking into his thick, straight hair, and she didn't know if she was pulling or pushing. She didn't think she could stand any more, and yet she didn't want him to stop.

"Gareth," she gasped. "I . . . You . . ."

His hands seemed to be everywhere, touching her, caressing her, pushing her dress down, down . . . until it was pooled around her hips, just an inch from revealing the very core of her womanhood.

Panic began to rise in Hyacinth's chest. She wanted this. She knew she wanted this, and yet she was suddenly terrified.

"I don't know what to do," she said.

"That's all right." He straightened, yanking his shirt off with enough force it was amazing buttons didn't fly. "I do."

"I know, but—"

He touched her lips with his finger. "Shhh. Let me show you." He smiled down at her, his eyes dancing with mischief. "Do I dare?" he wondered aloud. "Should I . . . Well . . . maybe . . ."

He lifted his finger from her mouth.

She spoke instantly. "But I'm afraid I will—"

He put his finger back. "I knew that would happen."

She glared at him. Or rather, she tried to. Gareth had an uncanny ability to make her laugh at herself. And she could feel her lips twitching, even as he pressed them shut.

"Will you be quiet?" he asked, smiling down at her.

She nodded.

He pretended to think about it. "I don't believe you."

She planted her hands on her hips, which had to be a ludicrous position, naked as she was from the waist up.

"All right," he acceded, "but the only words I'll allow from your mouth are, 'Oh, Gareth,' and 'Yes, Gareth.' "

He lifted his finger.

"What about 'More, Gareth?' "

He almost kept a straight face. "That will be acceptable."

She felt laughter bubbling up within her. She didn't actually make a noise, but she felt it all the same—that silly, giddy feeling that tingled and danced in one's belly. And she marveled at it. She was so nervous—or rather, she had been.

He'd taken it away.

And she somehow knew that it would be all right. Maybe he'd done this before. Maybe he'd done this a hundred times before, with women a hundred times more beautiful than she.

It didn't matter. He was her first, and she was his last.

He lay down beside her, pulling her onto her side and against him for a kiss. His hands sank into her hair, pulling it free from its coils until it fell in silky waves down her back. She felt free, untamed.

Daring.

She took one hand and pressed it against his chest, exploring his skin, testing the contours of the muscles beneath. She'd never touched him, she realized. Not like this. She trailed her fingers down his side to his hip, tracing a line at the edge of his breeches.

And she could feel his reaction. His muscles leapt wherever she touched, and when she moved to his belly, to that spot between his navel and the last of his clothing, he sucked in his breath.

She smiled, feeling powerful, and so, so womanly.

She curved her fingers so that her nails would scrape his skin, lightly, softly, just enough to tickle and tease. His belly was flat, with a light dusting of hair that formed a line and disappeared below his breeches.

"Do you like this?" she whispered, taking her index finger and making a circle around his navel.

"Mmm-hmm." His voice was smooth, but she could hear his breathing growing ragged.

"What about this?" Her finger found the line of hair and slid slowly down.

He didn't say anything, but his eyes said yes.

"What about—"

"Undo the buttons," he grunted.

Her hand stilled. "Me?" Somehow it hadn't occurred to her that she might aid in their disrobing. It seemed the job of the seducer.

His hand took hers and led it to the buttons.

With trembling fingers, Hyacinth slid each disc free, but she did not pull back the fabric. That was something she was not quite ready to do.

Gareth seemed to understand her reluctance, and he hopped from the bed, for just long enough to pull off the rest of his clothing. Hyacinth averted her eyes . . . at first.

"Dear G—"

"Don't worry," he said, resuming his spot next to her. His hands found the edge of her dress and tugged it the rest of the way down. "Never"—he kissed her belly—"ever"—he kissed her hip—"worry."

Hyacinth wanted to say that she wouldn't, that she trusted him, but just then his fingers slid between her legs, and it was all she could do simply to breathe.

"Shhhh," he crooned, coaxing her apart. "Relax."

"I am," she gasped.

"No," he said, smiling down at her, "you're not."

"I *am*," she insisted.

He leaned down, dropping an indulgent kiss on her nose. "Trust me," he murmured. "Just for this moment, trust me." ·

And she tried to relax. She really did. But it was near impossible when he was teasing her body into such an inferno. One moment his fingers were on the inside of her thigh, and the next they'd parted her, and he was touching her where she'd never been touched before.

"Oh, m— Oh!" Her hips arched, and she didn't know what to do. She didn't know what to say.

She didn't know what to feel.

"You're perfect," he said, pressing his lips to her ear. "Perfect."

"Gareth," she gasped. "What are you—"

"Making love to you," he said. "I'm making love to you."

Her heart leapt in her chest. It wasn't quite *I love you*, but it was awfully close.

And in that moment, in that last moment of her brain actually functioning, he slid one finger inside her.

"Gareth!" She grabbed his shoulders. Hard.

"Shhhh." He did something utterly wicked. "The servants."

"I don't care," she gasped.

He gazed down at her in a most amused manner, then . . . whatever he'd done . . . did it again. "I think you do."

"No, I don't. I don't. I—"

He did something else, something on the outside, and her entire body felt it. "You're so ready," he said. "I can't believe it."

He moved, positioning himself above her. His fingers were still delivering their torture, but his face was over hers, and she was lost in the clear blue depths of his eyes.

"Gareth," she whispered, and she had no idea what she meant by it. It wasn't a question, or a plea, or really, anything but his name. But it had to be said, because it was him.

It was *him*, here with her.

And it was sacred.

His thighs settled between hers, and she felt him at her opening, large and demanding. His fingers were still between them, holding her open, readying her for his manhood.

"Please," she moaned, and this time it *was* a plea. She wanted this. She needed him.

"Please," she said again.

Slowly, he entered her, and she sucked in her breath, so startled was she by the size and feel of him.

"Relax," he said, only he didn't sound relaxed. She looked up at him. His face was strained, and his breathing was quick and shallow.

He held very still, giving her time to adjust to him, then pushed forward, just a little, but it was enough to make her gasp.

"Relax," he said again.

"I'm *trying*," she ground out.

Gareth almost smiled. There was something so quintessentially Hyacinth about the statement, and also something almost reassuring. Even now, in what had to be one of the most startling and strange experiences of her life, she was . . . the same.

She was herself.

Not many people were, he was coming to realize.

He pushed forward again, and he could feel her easing, stretching to accommodate him. The last thing he wanted was to hurt her, and he had a feeling he wouldn't be able to eliminate the pain completely, but by God, he would make this as perfect for her as he could. And if that meant nearly killing himself to go slowly, he would.

She was as stiff as a board beneath him, her teeth gritted as she anticipated his invasion. Gareth nearly groaned; he'd had her so close, so ready, and now she was trying so hard *not* to be nervous that she was about as relaxed as a wrought-iron fence.

He touched her leg. It was as rigid as a stick.

"Hyacinth," he murmured in her ear, trying not to sound amused, "I think you were enjoying yourself a bit more just a minute earlier."

There was a beat of silence, and she said, "That might be true."

He bit his lip to keep from laughing. "Do you think you might see your way to enjoying yourself again?"

Her lips pursed into that expression of hers—the one she made when she knew she was being teased and wished to return in kind. "I would like to, yes."

He had to admire her. It was a rare woman who could keep her composure in such a situation.

He flicked his tongue behind her ear, distracting her as his hand found its way between her legs. "I might be able to help you with that."

"With what?" she gasped, and he knew from the way her hips jerked that she was on her way back to oblivion.

"Oh, with that feeling," he said, stroking her almost offhandedly as he pushed farther within. "The *Oh, Gareth, Yes, Gareth, More Gareth* feeling."

"Oh," she said, letting out a high-pitched moan as his finger began to move in a delicate circle. "That feeling."

"It's a good feeling," he confirmed.

"It's going to . . . Oh!" She clenched her teeth and groaned against the sensations he was striking within her.

"It's going to what?" he asked, and now he was almost all the way in. He was going to earn a medal for this, he decided. He had to. Surely no man had ever exercised such restraint.

"Get me into trouble," she gasped.

"I certainly hope so," he said, and then he pushed forward, breaching her last barrier until he was fully sheathed. He shuddered as he felt her quiver around him. Every muscle in his body was screaming at him, demanding action, but he held still. He had to hold still. If he didn't give her time to adjust, he would hurt her, and there was no way Gareth was going to allow his bride to look back on her first intimacy with pain.

Good God, it could scar her for life.

But if Hyacinth was hurting, even she didn't know it, because her hips were starting to move beneath him, pressing up, grinding in circles, and when he looked at her face, he saw nothing but passion.

And the last strings of his control snapped.

He began to move, his body falling into its rhythm of need. His desire spiraled, until he was quite certain he could not bear it any longer, and then she would make a tiny little sound, nothing more than a moan, really, and he wanted her even more.

It seemed impossible.

It was magical.

His fingers grasped her shoulders with a force that was surely too intense, but he could not loose his hold. He was seized by an overwhelming urge to claim her, to mark her in some way as his.

"Gareth," she moaned. "Oh, Gareth."

And the sound was too much. It was all too much—the sight, the smell of her, and he felt himself shuddering toward completion.

He gritted his teeth. Not yet. Not when she was so close.

"Gareth!" she gasped.

He slid his hand between their bodies again. He found her, swollen and wet, and he pressed, probably with less finesse than he ought but certainly with as much as he was able.

And he never looked away from her face. Her eyes seemed to darken, the color turning almost marine. Her lips parted, desperately seeking breath, and her body was arching, pressing, pushing.

"Oh!" she cried out, and he quickly kissed her to swallow the sound. She was tense, she was quivering, and then she spasmed around him. Her hands grabbed at his shoulders, his neck, her fingers biting his skin.

But he didn't care. He couldn't feel it. There was nothing but the exquisite pressure of her, grabbing him, sucking him in until he quite literally exploded.

And he had to kiss her again, this time to tamp down his own cries of passion.

It had never been like this. He hadn't known it could.

"Oh, my," Hyacinth breathed, once he'd rolled off her and onto his back.

He nodded, still too spent to speak. But he took her hand in his. He wanted to touch her still. He needed the contact.

"I didn't know," she said.

"Neither did I," he somehow managed.

"Is it always—"

He squeezed her hand, and when he heard her turn to him, he shook his head.

"Oh." There was a moment of silence, then she said, "Well, it's a good thing we're getting married, then."

Gareth started to shake with laughter.

"What is it?" she demanded.

He couldn't speak. All he could do was lie there, his body shaking the entire bed.

"What's so funny?"

He caught his breath, turned and rolled until he was back on top of her, nose to nose. "You," he said.

She started to frown, but then melted into a smile.

A wicked smile.

Good Lord, but he was going to *enjoy* being married to this woman.

"I think we might need to move up the wedding date," she said.

"I'm willing to drag you off to Scotland tomorrow." And he was serious.

"I can't," she said, but he could tell she half wished she could.

"It would be an adventure," he said, sliding one hand along her hip to sweeten the deal.

"I'll talk to my mother," she promised. "If I'm sufficiently annoying, I'm sure I can get the engagement period cut in half."

"It makes me wonder," he said. "As your future husband, should I be concerned by your use of the phrase *if I'm sufficiently annoying*?"

"Not if you accede to all of my wishes."

"A sentence that concerns me even more," he murmured.

She did nothing but smile.

And then, just when he was starting to feel quite comfortable in every way, she let out an, "Oh!" and wriggled out from beneath him.

"What is it?" he asked, the question muffled by his inelegant landing in the pillows.

"The jewels," she said, clutching the sheet to her chest as she sat up. "I completely forgot about them. Good heavens, what time is it? We have to get going."

"You can *move?*"

She blinked. "You can't?"

"If I didn't have to vacate this bed before morning, I'd be quite content to snore until noon."

"But the jewels! Our plans!"

He closed his eyes. "We can go tomorrow."

"No," she said, batting him on the shoulder with the heel of her hand, "we can't."

"Why not?"

"Because I already have plans for tomorrow, and my mother will grow suspicious if I keep pleading headaches. And besides, we planned on this evening."

He opened one eye. "It's not as if anyone's expecting us."

"Well, I'm going," she stated, pulling the bedsheet around her body as she climbed from the bed.

Gareth's brows rose as he pondered his naked form. He looked at Hyacinth with a masculine smile, which spread even farther when she blushed and turned away.

"I . . . ah . . . just need to wash myself," she mumbled, scooting away to her dressing room.

With a great show of reluctance (even though Hyacinth had her back to him) Gareth began to pull on his clothing. He couldn't believe she would even ponder heading out that evening. Weren't virgins supposed to be stiff and sore after their first time?

She stuck her head out of the dressing room door. "I

purchased better shoes," she said in a stage whisper, "in case we have to run."

He shook his head. She was no ordinary virgin.

"Are you certain you wish to do this tonight?" he asked, once she reemerged in her black men's clothing.

"Absolutely," she said, pulling her hair into a queue at her neck. She looked up, her eyes shining with excitement. "Don't you?"

"I'm exhausted."

"Really?" She looked at him with open curiosity. "I feel quite the opposite. Energized, really."

"You *will* be the death of me, you do realize that."

She grinned. "Better me than someone else."

He sighed and headed for the window.

"Would you like me to wait for you at the bottom," she asked politely, "or would you prefer to go down the back stairs with me?"

Gareth paused, one foot on the windowsill. "Ah, the back stairs will be quite acceptable," he said.

And he followed her out.

Chapter 15

Inside the Clair House library. There is little reason to chronicle the journey across Mayfair, other than to make note of Hyacinth's wellspring of energy and enthusiasm, and Gareth's lack thereof.

"Do you see anything?" Hyacinth whispered.

"Only books."

She gave him a frustrated glare but decided not to chastise him for his lack of enthusiasm. Such an argument would only distract them from the task at hand. "Do you see," she said, with as much patience as she could muster, "any sections which seem to be composed of scientific titles?" She glanced at the shelf in front of her, which contained three novels, two works of philosophy, a three-volume history of ancient Greece, and *The Care and Feeding of Swine*. "Or are they in any order at all?" she sighed.

"Somewhat," came the reply from above. Gareth was standing on a stool, investigating the upper shelves. "Not really."

Hyacinth twisted her neck, glancing up until she had a fairly good view of the underside of his chin. "What do you see?"

"Quite a bit on the topic of early Britain. But look what I found, tucked away on the end." He plucked a small book from the shelf and tossed it down.

Hyacinth caught it easily, then turned it in her hands until the title was right side up. "No!" she said.

"Hard to believe, isn't it?"

She looked back down again. Right there, in gold lettering: *Miss Davenport and the Dark Marquis*. "I don't believe it," she said.

"Perhaps you should take it home to my grandmother. No one will miss it here."

Hyacinth opened to the title page. "It was written by the same author as *Miss Butterworth*."

"It would have to be," Gareth commented, bending his knees to better inspect the next shelf down.

"We didn't know about this one," Hyacinth said. "We've read *Miss Sainsbury and the Mysterious Colonel*, of course."

"A military tale?"

"Set in Portugal." Hyacinth resumed her inspection of the shelf in front of her. "It didn't seem terribly authentic, however. Not, of course, that I've ever been to Portugal."

He nodded, then stepped off his stool and moved it in front of the next set of shelves. Hyacinth watched as he climbed back up and began his work anew, on the highest shelf.

"Remind me," he said. "What, precisely, are we looking for?"

Hyacinth pulled the oft-folded note from her pocket. *"Discorso Intorno alle Cose che stanno in sù l'acqua."*

He stared at her for a moment. "Which means . . . ?"

"Discussion of inside things that are in water?" She hadn't meant to say it as a question.

He looked dubious. "Inside things?"

"That are in water. Or that move," she added. *"Ò che in quella si muovono.* That's the last part of it."

"And someone would wish to read that because . . . ?"

"I have no idea," she said, shaking her head. "You're the Cantabridgian."

He cleared his throat. "Yes, well, I wasn't much for the sciences."

Hyacinth decided not to comment and turned back to the shelf in front of her, which contained a seven-volume set on the topic of English botany, two works of Shakespeare, and a rather fat book titled, simply, *Wildflowers.* "I think," she said, chewing on her lower lip for a moment as she glanced back at several of the shelves she'd already cataloged, "that perhaps these books had been in order at some point. There does seem to be *some* organization to it. If you look right here"—she motioned to one of the first shelves she'd inspected—"it's almost completely works of poetry. But then right in the middle one finds something by Plato, and over on the end, *An Illustrated History of Denmark.*"

"Right," Gareth said, sounding a bit like he was grimacing. "Right."

"Right?" she echoed, looking up.

"Right." Now he sounded embarrassed. "That might have been my fault."

She blinked. "I beg your pardon?"

"It was one of my less mature moments," he admitted. "I was angry."

"You were . . . angry?"

"I rearranged the shelves."

"You *what*?" She'd have liked to yell, and frankly, she was rather proud of herself for not doing so.

He shrugged sheepishly. "It seemed impressively underhanded at the time."

Hyacinth found herself staring blankly at the shelf in front of her. "Who could have guessed it would come back to haunt you?"

"Who indeed." He moved to another shelf, tilting his head as he read the titles on the spines. "The worst of it was, it turned out to be a tad *too* underhanded. Didn't bother my father one bit."

"It would have driven me insane."

"Yes, but you read. My father never even noticed there was anything amiss."

"But someone must have been here since your little effort at reorganization." Hyacinth looked down at the book by her side. "I don't think *Miss Davenport* is more than a few years old."

Gareth shook his head. "Perhaps someone left it here. It could have been my brother's wife. I imagine one of the servants just tucked it on whichever shelf possessed the most room."

Hyacinth let out a long exhale, trying to figure out how best to proceed. "Can you remember anything about the organization of the titles?" she asked. "Anything at all? Were they grouped by author? By subject?"

Gareth shook his head. "I was in a bit of a rush. I just grabbed books at random and swapped their places." He stopped, exhaling as he planted his hands on his hips and surveyed the room. "I do recall that there was quite a bit on the topic of hounds. And over there there was . . ."

His words trailed off. Hyacinth looked up sharply and saw that he was staring at a shelf by the door. "What is it?" she asked urgently, coming to her feet.

"A section in Italian," he said, turning and striding to the opposite side of the room.

Hyacinth was right on his heels. "They must be your grandmother's books."

"And the last ones any of the St. Clairs might think to open," Gareth murmured.

"Do you see them?"

Gareth shook his head as he ran his finger along the spines of the books, searching for the ones in Italian.

"I don't suppose you thought to leave the set intact," Hyacinth murmured, crouching below him to inspect the lower shelves.

"I don't recall," he admitted. "But surely most will still be where they belong. I grew too bored of the prank to do a really good job of it. I left most in place. And in fact—" He suddenly straightened. "Here they are."

Hyacinth immediately stood up. "Are there many?"

"Only two shelves," he said. "I would imagine it was rather expensive to import books from Italy."

The books were right on a level with Hyacinth's face, so she had Gareth hold their candle while she scanned the titles for something that sounded like what Isabella had written in her note. Several did not have the entire title printed on the spine, and these she had to pull out to read the words on the front. Every time she did so, she could hear Gareth's sharply indrawn breath, followed by a disappointed exhale when she replaced the book on the shelf.

She reached the end of the lower shelf and then stood on her tiptoes to investigate the upper. Gareth was right behind her, standing so close that she could feel the heat of his body rippling through the air.

"Do you see anything?" he asked, his words low and warm by her ear. She didn't think he was purposefully trying to unsettle her with his nearness, but it was the end result all the same.

"Not yet," she said, shaking her head. Most of Isabella's books were poetry. A few seemed to be English poets, translated into Italian. As Hyacinth reached the midpoint of the shelf, however, the books turned to nonfiction. History, philosophy, history, history . . .

Hyacinth's breath caught.

"What is it?" Gareth demanded.

With trembling hands she pulled out a slim volume and turned it over until the front cover was visible to them both.

Galileo Galilei
Discorso intorno alle cose che stanno,
in sù l'acqua, ò che in quella si muovono

"Exactly what she wrote in the clue," Hyacinth whispered, hastily adding, "Except for the bit about Mr. Galilei. It would have been a great deal easier to find the book if we'd known the author."

Gareth waved aside her excuses and motioned to the text in her hands.

Slowly, carefully, Hyacinth opened the book to look for

the telltale slip of paper. There was nothing tucked right inside, so she turned a page, then another, then another . . .

Until Gareth yanked the book from her hands. "Do you want to be here until next week?" he whispered impatiently. With no delicacy whatsoever, he grasped both the front and back covers of the book and held it open, spine-side up so that the pages formed an upside-down fan.

"Gareth, you—"

"Shush." He shook the book, bent down and peered up and inside, then shook it again, harder. And sure enough, a slip of paper came free and fell to the carpet.

"Give that to me," Hyacinth demanded, after Gareth had grabbed it. "You won't be able to read it in any case."

Obviously swayed by her logic, he handed the clue over, but he remained close, leaning over her shoulder with the candle as she opened the single fold in the paper.

"What does it say?" he asked.

She shook her head. "I don't know."

"What do you mean, you don't—"

"I don't know," she snapped, *hating* that she had to admit defeat. "I don't recognize anything. I'm not even certain this is Italian. Do you know if she spoke another language?"

"I have no idea."

Hyacinth clamped her teeth together, thoroughly discouraged by the turn of events. She hadn't necessarily thought they would find the jewels that evening, but it had never occurred to her that the next clue might lead them straight into a brick wall.

"May I see?" Gareth asked.

She handed him the note, watching as he shook his head. "I don't know what that is, but it's not Italian."

"Nor anything related to it," Hyacinth said.

Gareth swore under his breath, something that Hyacinth was fairly certain she was not meant to hear.

"With your permission," she said, using that even tone of voice she'd long since learned was required when dealing with a truculent male, "I could show it to my brother Colin. He has traveled quite extensively, and he might recognize the language, even if he lacks the ability to translate it."

Gareth appeared to hesitate, so she added, "We can trust him. I promise you."

He gave her a nod. "We'd best leave. There's nothing more we can do this night, anyway."

There was little cleaning up to be done; they had put the books back on the shelves almost as soon as they'd removed them. Hyacinth moved a stool back in place against the wall, and Gareth did the same with a chair. The drapes had remained in place this time; there was little moonlight to see by, anyway.

"Are you ready?" he asked.

She grabbed *Miss Davenport and the Dark Marquis.* "Are you certain no one will miss this?"

He tucked Isabella's clue between the pages for safe-keeping. "Quite."

Hyacinth watched as he pressed his ear to the door. No one had been about when they had sneaked in a half hour earlier, but Gareth had explained that the butler never retired before the baron. And with the baron still out at the Mottram Ball, that left one man up and possibly about, and another who could return at any time.

Gareth placed one finger on his lips and motioned for her to follow him as he carefully turned the doorknob.

He opened the door an inch—just enough to peer out the crack and make sure that it was safe to proceed. Together they crept into the hall, moving swiftly to the stairs that led down to the ground floor. It was dark, but Hyacinth's eyes had adjusted well enough to see where she was going, and in under a minute they were back in the drawing room—the one with the faulty window latch.

As he had the time before, Gareth climbed out first, then formed a step with his hands for Hyacinth to balance upon as she reached up and shut the window. He lowered her down, dropped a quick kiss on her nose, and said, "You need to get home."

She couldn't help but smile. "I'm already hopelessly compromised."

"Yes, but I'm the only one who knows."

Hyacinth thought it rather charming of him to be so concerned for her reputation. After all, it didn't truly matter if anyone caught them or not; she had lain with him, and she must marry him. A woman of her birth could do no less. Good heavens, there could be a baby, and even if not, she was no longer a virgin.

But she had known what she was doing when she had given herself to him. She knew the ramifications.

Together they crept down the alley to Dover Street. It was imperative, Hyacinth realized, that they move quickly. The Mottram Ball was notorious for running into the wee hours of the morning, but they'd got a late start on their search, and surely everyone would be heading home soon. There would be carriages on the streets of Mayfair, which meant that she and Gareth needed to render themselves as invisible as possible.

Hyacinth's joking aside, she didn't wish to be caught out in the middle of the night. It was true that their marriage was now an inevitability, but all the same, she didn't particularly relish the thought of being the subject of scurrilous gossip.

"Wait here," Gareth said, barring her from moving forward with his arm. Hyacinth remained in the shadows as he stepped onto Dover Street, edging as close to the corner as she dared while he made sure there was no one about. After a few seconds she saw Gareth's hand, reaching back and making a scooping, "come along" gesture.

She stepped out onto Dover Street, but she was there barely a second before she heard Gareth's sharply indrawn breath and felt herself being shoved back into the shadows.

Flattening herself against the back wall of the corner building, she clutched *Miss Davenport*—and within it, Isabella's clue—to her chest as she waited for Gareth to appear by her side.

And then she heard it.

Just one word. In his father's voice.

"*You.*"

Gareth had barely a second to react. He didn't know how it had happened, didn't know where the baron had suddenly appeared from, but somehow he managed to push Hyacinth back into the alley in the very second before he was caught.

"Greetings," he said, in his jauntiest voice, stepping forward so as to put as much distance between him and the alley as possible.

His father was already striding over, his face visibly

angry, even in the dim light of the night. "What are you doing here?" he demanded.

Gareth shrugged, the same expression that had infuriated his father so many times before. Except this time he wasn't trying to provoke, he was just trying to keep the baron's attention firmly fixed. "Just making my way home," he said, with deliberate nonchalance.

His father's eyes were suspicious. "You're a bit far afield."

"I like to stop by and inspect my inheritance every now and then," Gareth said, his smile terribly bland. "Just to make sure you haven't burned the place down."

"Don't think I haven't thought about it."

"Oh, I'm sure you have."

The baron held silent for a moment, then said, "You weren't at the ball tonight."

Gareth wasn't sure how best to respond, so he just lifted his brows ever so slightly and kept his expression even.

"Miss Bridgerton wasn't there, either."

"Wasn't she?" Gareth asked mildly, hoping the lady in question possessed sufficient self-restraint not to leap out from the alley, yelling, "Yes, I was!"

"Just at the beginning," the baron admitted. "She left rather early."

Gareth shrugged again. "It's a woman's prerogative."

"To change her mind?" The baron's lips formed the tiniest of curves, and his eyes were mocking. "You had better hope she's a bit more steadfast than that."

Gareth gave him a cold stare. Somehow, amazingly, he still felt in control. Or at the very least, like the adult he liked to think that he was. He felt no childish desire to lash out, or to say something for the sole purpose of infuriating him. He'd spent half his life trying to impress the man, and the other half trying to aggravate him. But now . . . finally . . . all he wanted was to be rid of him.

He didn't quite feel the nothing he had wished for, but it was damned close.

Maybe, just maybe, it was because he'd finally found someone else to fill the void.

"You certainly didn't waste any time with her," the baron said, his voice snide.

"A gentleman must marry," Gareth said. It wasn't exactly the statement he wished to say in front of Hyacinth, but it was far more important to keep up the ruse with his father than it was to feed whatever need she might feel for romantic speech.

"Yes," the baron murmured. "A *gentleman* must."

Gareth's skin began to prickle. He knew what his father was hinting at, and even though he'd already compromised Hyacinth, he'd rather she didn't learn the truth of his birth until after the wedding. It would simply be easier that way, and maybe . . .

Well, maybe she'd never learn the truth at all. It seemed unlikely, between his father's venom and Isabella's diary, but stranger things had happened.

He needed to leave. Now. "I have to go," he said brusquely.

The baron's mouth curved into an unpleasant smile. "Yes, yes," he said mockingly. "You'll need to tidy yourself up before you go off to lick Miss Bridgerton's feet tomorrow."

Gareth spoke between his teeth. "Get out of my way."

But the baron wasn't done. "What I wonder is . . . how did you get her to say yes?"

A red haze began to wash over Gareth's eyes. "I said—"

"Did you seduce her?" his father laughingly asked. "Make sure she couldn't say no, even if—"

Gareth hadn't meant to do it. He'd meant to maintain his calm, and he would have managed it if the baron had kept his insults to him. But when he mentioned Hyacinth . . .

His fury took over, and the next thing he knew, he had his father pinned against the wall. "Do not," he warned, barely recognizing his own voice, "speak to me of her again."

"You would make the mistake of attempting to kill me here, on a public street?" The baron was gasping, but even so, his voice maintained an impressive degree of hatred.

"It's tempting."

"Ah, but you'd lose the title. And then where would you be? Oh yes," he said, practically choking on his words now, "at the end of a hangman's rope."

Gareth loosened his grip. Not because of his father's words, but because he was finally regaining his hold on his emotions. Hyacinth was listening, he reminded himself. She was right around the corner. He could not do something he might later regret.

"I knew you'd do it," his father said, just when Gareth had let go and turned to leave.

Damn. He always knew what to say, exactly which button to push to keep Gareth from doing the right thing.

"Do what?" Gareth asked, frozen in his tracks.

"Ask her to marry you."

Gareth turned slowly around. His father was grinning, supremely pleased with himself. It was a sight that made Gareth's blood run cold.

"You're so predictable," the baron said, cocking his head just an inch or so to the side. It was a gesture Gareth had seen a hundred times before, maybe a thousand. It was patronizing and it was contemptuous, and it always managed to make Gareth feel like he was a boy again, working so hard for his father's approval.

And failing every time.

"One word from me," the baron said, chuckling to himself. "Just one word from me."

Gareth chose his words very carefully. He had an audience. He had to remember that. And so, when he spoke, all he said was, "I have no idea what you're talking about."

And his father erupted with laughter. He threw back his head and roared, showing a degree of mirth that shocked Gareth into silence.

"Oh, come now," he said, wiping his eyes. "I told you you couldn't win her, and look what you did."

Gareth's chest began to feel very, very tight. What was his father saying? That he'd *wanted* him to marry Hyacinth?

"You went right out and asked her to marry you," the baron continued. "How long did that take? A day? Two? No more than a week, I'm sure."

"My proposal to Miss Bridgerton had nothing to do with you," Gareth said icily.

"Oh, please," the baron said, with utter disdain. "Everything you do is because of me. Haven't you figured that out by now?"

Gareth stared at him in horror. Was it true? Was it even a little bit true?

"Well, I do believe I shall take myself off to bed," the

baron said, with an affected sigh. "It's been . . . entertaining, don't you think?"

Gareth didn't know what to think.

"Oh, and before you marry Miss Bridgerton," the baron said, tossing the remark over his shoulder as he placed his foot on the first step up to Clair House's front door, "you might want to see about clearing up your other betrothal."

"*What?*"

The baron smiled silkily. "Didn't you know? You're still betrothed to poor little Mary Winthrop. She never did marry anyone else."

"That can't be legal."

"Oh, I assure you it is." The baron leaned slightly forward. "I made sure of it."

Gareth just stood there, his mouth slack, his arms hanging limply at his sides. If his father had yanked down the moon and clocked him on the head with it he couldn't have been more stunned.

"I'll see you at the wedding," the baron called out. "Oh, silly me. Which wedding?" He laughed, taking a few more steps up toward the front door. "Do let me know, once you sort it all out." He gave a little wave, obviously pleased with himself, and slipped inside the house.

"Dear God," Gareth said to himself. And then again, because never in his life had the moment more called for blasphemy: "Dear God."

What sort of mess was he in now? A man couldn't offer marriage to more than one woman at once. And while *he* might not have offered it to Mary Winthrop, the baron had done so in his name, and had signed documents to that effect. Gareth had no idea what this meant to his plans with Hyacinth, but it couldn't be good.

Oh, bloody . . . Hyacinth.

Dear God, indeed. She'd heard every word.

Gareth started to run for the corner, then stopped himself, glancing up at the house to make sure that his father wasn't watching for him. The windows were still dark, but that didn't mean . . .

Oh, hell. Who cared?

He ran around the corner, skidding to a halt in front of the alley, where he'd left her.

She was gone.

Chapter 16

Still in the alley. Gareth is staring at the spot where Hyacinth should have been standing.

He never wants to feel like this again.

Gareth's heart stopped.

Where the hell was Hyacinth?

Was she in danger? It was late, and even though they were in one of the most expensive and exclusive areas of London, thieves and cutthroats might still be about, and—

No, she couldn't have fallen prey to foul play. Not here. He would have heard something. A scuffle. A shout. Hyacinth would never be taken without a fight.

A very loud fight.

Which could only mean . . .

She must have heard his father talking about Mary Winthrop and run off. Damn the woman. She should have had more sense than that.

Gareth let out an aggravated grunt as he planted his hands on his hips and scanned the area. She could have dashed home any one of eight different ways, probably more if one counted all the alleys and mews, which he hoped she was sensible enough to avoid.

He decided to try the most direct route. It would take her right on Berkeley Street, which was a busy enough thoroughfare that there might be carriages rolling home from the Mottram Ball, but Hyacinth was probably just angry enough that her primary aim would have been to get home as quickly as possible.

Which was just fine with Gareth. He would much rather see her caught by a gossip on the main road than by a thief on a side street.

Gareth took off at a run toward Berkeley Square, slowing down at each intersection to glance up and down the cross streets.

Nothing.

Where the hell had she gone? He knew she was uncommonly athletic for a female, but good God, how fast could she run?

He dashed past Charles Street, onto the square proper. A carriage rolled by, but Gareth paid it no mind. Tomorrow's gossip would probably be filled with tales of his crazed middle-of-the-night run through the streets of Mayfair, but it was nothing his reputation couldn't withstand.

He ran along the edge of the square, and then finally he was on Bruton Street passing by Number Sixteen, Twelve, Seven . . .

There she was, running like the wind, heading around the corner so that she could enter the house from the back.

His body propelled by a strange, furious energy, Gareth took off even faster. His arms were pumping, and his legs were burning, and his shirt would surely be forever soiled with sweat, but he didn't care. He was going to catch that bloody woman before she entered her house, and when he did . . .

Hell, he didn't know what he was going to do with her, but it wasn't going to be pretty.

Hyacinth skidded around the last corner, slowing down just enough to glance over her shoulder. Her mouth opened as she spied him, and then, her entire body tensed with determination, she took off for the servants' entrance in the back.

Gareth's eyes narrowed with satisfaction. She was going to have to fumble for the key. She'd never make it now. He slowed a bit, just enough to attempt to catch his breath, then eased his gait into a stalk.

She was in for it now.

But instead of reaching behind a brick for a key, Hyacinth just opened the door.

Bloody hell. They hadn't locked the door behind them when they left.

Gareth vaulted into another sprint, and he almost made it.

Almost.

He reached the door just as she shut it in his face.

And his hand landed on the knob just in time to hear the lock click into place.

Gareth's hand formed a fist, and he itched to pound it against the door. More than anything he wanted to bellow her name, propriety be damned. All it would do was force their wedding to be held even sooner, which was his aim, anyway.

But he supposed some things were far too ingrained in

a man, and he was, apparently, too much of a gentleman to destroy her reputation in such a public manner.

"Oh, no," he muttered to himself, striding back to the front of the house, "all destruction shall be strictly in private."

He planted his hands on his hips and glared up at her bedroom window. He'd got himself in once; he could do it again.

A quick glance up and down the street assured him that no one was coming, and he quickly scaled the wall, his ascent much easier this time, now that he knew exactly where to place his hands and feet. The window was still slightly open, just as he'd left it the last time—not that he'd thought he was going to have to climb in again.

He jammed it up, tumbled through, and landed with a thud on the carpet just as Hyacinth entered through the door.

"You," he growled, coming to his feet like a cat, "have some explaining to do."

"Me?" Hyacinth returned. "Me? I hardly think—" Her lips parted as she belatedly assessed the situation. "And get out of my room!"

He quirked a brow. "Shall I take the front stairs?"

"You'll go back out the window, you miserable cur."

Gareth realized that he'd never seen Hyacinth angry. Irritated, yes; annoyed, certainly. But this . . .

This was something else entirely.

"How dare you!" she fumed. "How *dare* you." And then, before he could even begin to reply, she stormed to his side and smacked him with the heels of both of her hands. "Get out!" she snarled. "Now!"

"Not until you"—he punctuated this with a pointed finger, right against her breastbone—"promise me that you will never do anything as foolish as what you did tonight."

"Unh! Unh!" She let out a choking sort of noise, the kind one makes when one cannot manage even a single intelligible syllable. And then finally, after a few more gasps of fury, she said, her voice dangerously low, "You are in no position to demand anything of me."

"No?" He lifted one of his brows and looked down at her with an arrogant half smile. "As your future husband—"

"Do not even mention that to me right now."

Gareth felt something squeeze and turn over in his chest. "Do you plan to cry off?"

"No," she said, looking at him with a furious expression, "but you took care of that this evening, didn't you? Was that your purpose? To force my hand by rendering me unmarriageable for any other man?"

It had been exactly his purpose, and for that reason Gareth didn't say anything. Not a word.

"You'll rue this," Hyacinth hissed. "You will rue the day. Trust me."

"Oh, really?"

"As your future wife," she said, her eyes flashing dangerously, "I can make your life hell on earth."

Of that, Gareth had no doubt, but he decided to deal with that problem when he came to it. "This is not about what happened between us earlier," he said, "and it is not about anything you may or may not have heard the baron say. What this is about—"

"Oh, for the love of—" Hyacinth cut herself off in the nick of time. "Who do you think you are?"

He jammed his face next to hers. "The man who is going to marry you. And you, Hyacinth Bridgerton soon-to-be St. Clair, will never *ever* wander the streets of London without a chaperone, at any time of day."

For a moment she said nothing, and he almost let himself think that she was touched by his concern for her safety. But then, she just stepped back and said, "It's a rather convenient time to develop a sense of propriety."

He resisted the urge to grab her by the shoulders and shake—barely. "Do you have any idea how I felt when I came back around the corner, and you were gone? Did you even stop to think about what might have happened to you before you ran off on your own?"

One of her brows lifted into a perfectly arrogant arch. "Nothing more than what happened to me right here."

As strikes went, it was perfectly aimed, and Gareth nearly flinched. But he held on to his temper, and his voice was cool as he said, "You don't mean that. You might think you mean it, but you don't, and I'll forgive you for it."

She stood still, utterly and completely still save for the rise and fall of her chest. Her hands were fists at her sides, and her face was growing redder and redder.

"Don't you ever," she finally said, her voice low and clipped and terribly controlled, "speak to me in that tone of voice again. And don't you ever presume to know my mind."

"Don't worry, it's a claim I'm seldom likely to make."

Hyacinth swallowed—her only show of nerves before saying, "I want you to leave."

"Not until I have your promise."

"I don't owe you anything, Mr. St. Clair. And you certainly are not in a position to make demands."

"Your promise," he repeated.

Hyacinth just stared at him. How dare he come in here and try to make this about her? *She* was the injured party. He was the one who—He—

Good God, she couldn't even *think* in full sentences.

"I want you to leave," she said again.

His reply came practically on top of her last syllable. "And I want your promise."

She clamped her mouth shut. It would have been an easy promise to make; she certainly didn't plan on any more middle-of-the-night jaunts. But a promise would have been akin to an apology, and she would not give him that satisfaction.

Call her foolish, call her juvenile, but she would not do it. Not after what he'd done to her.

"Good God," he muttered, "you're stubborn."

She gave him a sickly smile. "It is going to be a joy to be married to me."

"Hyacinth," he said, or rather, half sighed. "In the name of all that is—" He raked his hand through his hair, and he seemed to look all around the room before finally turning back to her. "I understand that you're angry . . ."

"Do not speak to me as if I were a child."

"I wasn't."

She looked at him coolly. "You were."

He gritted his teeth together and continued. "What my father said about Mary Winthrop . . ."

Her mouth fell open. "Is *that* what you think this is about?"

He stared at her, blinking twice before saying, "Isn't it?"

"Of course not," she sputtered. "Good heavens, do you take me for a fool?"

"I . . . er . . . no?"

"I hope I know you well enough to know that you would not offer marriage to two women. At least not purposefully."

"Right," he said, looking a little confused. "Then what—"

"Do you know why you asked me to marry you?" she demanded.

"What the devil are you talking about?"

"Do you know?" she repeated. She'd asked him once before, and he had not answered.

"Of course I know. It's because—" But he cut himself off, and he obviously didn't know what to say.

She shook her head, blinking back tears. "I don't want to see you right now."

"What is *wrong* with you?"

"There is nothing wrong with me," she cried out, as loudly as she dared. "I at least know why I accepted your proposal. But you—You have no idea why you rendered it."

"Then tell me," he burst out. "Tell me what it is you think is so damned important. You always seem to know what is best for everything and everyone, and now you clearly know everyone's mind as well. So tell me. Tell me, Hyacinth—"

She flinched from the venom in his voice.

"—tell me."

She swallowed. She would not back down. She might be shaking, she might be as close to tears as she had ever been in her life, but she would not back down. "You did this," she said, her voice low, to keep the tremors at bay, "you asked me . . . because of *him*."

He just stared at her, making a *please elaborate* motion with his head.

"Your father." She would have yelled it, if it hadn't been the middle of the night.

"Oh, for God's sake," he swore. "Is that what you think? This has nothing to do with him."

Hyacinth gave him a pitying look.

"I don't do anything because of him," Gareth hissed, furious that she would even suggest it. "He means nothing to me."

She shook her head. "You are deluding yourself, Gareth. Everything you do, you do because of him. I didn't realize it until he said it, but it's true."

"You'd take his word over mine?"

"This isn't about someone's *word*," she said, sounding tired, and frustrated, and maybe just a little bit bleak. "It's just about the way things are. And you . . . you asked me to marry you because you wanted to show him you could. It had *nothing* to do with me."

Gareth held himself very still. "That is not true."

"Isn't it?" She smiled, but her face looked sad, almost resigned. "I know that you wouldn't ask me to marry you if you believed yourself promised to another woman, but I also know that you would do anything to show up your father. Including marrying me."

Gareth gave his head a slow shake. "You have it all wrong," he said, but inside, his certitude was beginning to slip. He had thought, more than once and with an unbecoming gleefulness, that his father must be livid over Gareth's marital success. And he'd enjoyed it. He'd enjoyed knowing that in the chess game that was his relationship with Lord St. Clair, he had finally delivered the killing move.

Checkmate.

It had been exquisite.

But it wasn't *why* he had asked Hyacinth to marry him. He'd asked her because—Well, there had been a hundred different reasons. It had been complicated.

He liked her. Wasn't that important? He even liked her family. And she liked his grandmother. He couldn't possibly marry a woman who couldn't deal well with Lady Danbury.

And he'd wanted her. He'd wanted her with an intensity that had taken his breath away.

It had made sense to marry Hyacinth. It still made sense.

That was it. That was what he needed to articulate. He just needed to make her understand. And she would. She was no foolish girl. She was Hyacinth.

It was why he liked her so well.

He opened his mouth, motioning with his hand before any words actually emerged. He had to get this right. Or if not right, then at least not completely wrong. "If you look at this sensibly," he began.

"I am looking at it sensibly," she shot back, cutting him off before he could complete the thought. "Good heavens, if I weren't so bloody *sensible*, I would have cried off." Her jaw went rigid, and she swallowed.

And he thought to himself—*My God, she's going to cry*.

"I knew what I was doing earlier this evening," she said, her voice painfully quiet. "I knew what it meant, and I knew that it was irrevocable." Her lower lip quivered, and she looked away as she said, "I just never expected to regret it."

It was like a punch to the gut. He'd hurt her. He'd really hurt her. He hadn't meant to, and he wasn't certain that she wasn't overreacting, but he'd hurt her.

And he was stunned to realize how much that hurt *him*.

For a moment they did nothing, just stood there, warily watching the other.

Gareth wanted to say something, thought perhaps that he should say something, but he had no idea. The words just weren't there.

"Do you know how it feels to be someone's pawn?" Hyacinth asked.

"Yes," he whispered.

The corners of her mouth tightened. She didn't look angry, just . . . sad. "Then you will understand why I'm asking you to leave."

There was something primal within him that cried out to stay, something primitive that wanted to grab her and make her understand. He could use his words or he could use his body. It didn't really matter. He just wanted to make her understand.

But there was something else within him—something sad and something lonely that knew what it was to hurt. And somehow he knew that if he stayed, if he tried to force her to understand, he would not succeed. Not this night.

And he'd lose her.

So he nodded. "We will discuss this later," he said.

She said nothing.

He walked back to the window. It seemed a bit ludicrous and anticlimactic, making his exit that way, but really, who the hell cared?

"This Mary person," Hyacinth said to his back, "whatever the problem is with her, I am certain it can be resolved. My family will pay hers, if necessary."

She was trying to gain control of herself, to tamp down her pain by focusing on practicalities. Gareth recognized this tactic; he had employed it himself, countless times.

He turned around, meeting her gaze directly. "She is the daughter of the Earl of Wrotham."

"Oh." She paused. "Well, that does change things, but I'm sure if it was a long time ago . . ."

"It was."

She swallowed before asking, "Is it the cause of your estrangement? The betrothal?"

"You're asking a rather lot of questions for someone who has demanded that I leave."

"I'm going to marry you," she said. "I will learn eventually."

"Yes, you will," he said. "But not tonight."

And with that, he swung himself through the window.

He looked up when he reached the ground, desperate for one last glimpse of her. Anything would have been nice, a silhouette, perhaps, or even just her shadowy form, moving behind the curtains.

But there was nothing.

She was gone.

Chapter 17

Teatime at Number Five. Hyacinth is alone in the drawing room with her mother, always a dangerous proposition when one is in possession of a secret.

"Is Mr. St. Clair out of town?"

Hyacinth looked up from her rather sloppy embroidery for just long enough to say, "I don't believe so, why?"

Her mother's lips tightened fleetingly before she said, "He hasn't called in several days."

Hyacinth affixed a bland expression onto her face as she said, "I believe he is busy with something or other relating to his property in Wiltshire."

It was a lie, of course. Hyacinth didn't think he possessed any property, in Wiltshire or anywhere else. But with any luck, her mother would be distracted by some other matter before she got around to inquiring about Gareth's nonexistent estates.

"I see," Violet murmured.

Hyacinth stabbed her needle into the fabric with perhaps a touch more vigor than was necessary, then looked down at her handiwork with a bit of a snarl. She was an

abysmal needlewoman. She'd never had the patience or
the eye for detail that it required, but she always kept an
embroidery hoop going in the drawing room. One never
knew when one would need it to provide an acceptable
distraction from conversation.

The ruse had worked quite well for years. But now that
Hyacinth was the only Bridgerton daughter living at
home, teatime often consisted of just her and her mother.
And unfortunately, the needlework that had kept her so
neatly out of three- and four-way conversations didn't
seem to do the trick so well with only two.

"Is anything amiss?" Violet asked.

"Of course not." Hyacinth didn't want to look up, but
avoiding eye contact would surely make her mother suspicious, so she set her needle down and lifted her chin. In
for a penny, in for a pound, she decided. If she was going
to lie, she might as well make it convincing. "He's merely
busy, that is all. I rather admire him for it. You wouldn't
wish for me to marry a wastrel, would you?"

"No, of course not," Violet murmured, "but still, it does
seem odd. You're so recently affianced."

On any other day, Hyacinth would have just turned to
her mother and said, "If you have a question, just ask it."

Except then her mother would ask a question.

And Hyacinth most certainly did not wish to answer.

It had been three days since she had learned the truth
about Gareth. It sounded so dramatic, melodramatic
even—"learned the truth." It sounded like she'd discovered some terrible secret, uncovered some dastardly
skeleton in the St. Clair family closet.

But there was no secret. Nothing dark or dangerous, or

even mildly embarrassing. Just a simple truth that had been staring her in the face all along.

And she had been too blind to see it. Love did that to a woman, she supposed.

And she had most certainly fallen in love with him. That much was clear. Sometime between the moment she had agreed to marry him and the night they had made love, she'd fallen in love with him.

But she hadn't known him. Or had she? Could she really say that she'd known him, truly known the measure of the man, when she hadn't even understood the most basic element of his character?

He'd used her.

That's what it was. He had used her to win his neverending battle with his father.

And it hurt far more than she would ever have dreamed.

She kept telling herself she was being silly, that she was splitting hairs. Shouldn't it count that he liked her, that he thought she was clever and funny and even occasionally wise? Shouldn't it count that she knew he would protect her and honor her and, despite his somewhat spotted past, be a good and faithful husband?

Why did it *matter* why he'd asked her to marry him? Shouldn't it only matter that he had?

But it did matter. She'd felt used, unimportant, as if she were just a chess piece on a much larger game board.

And the worst part of it was—she didn't even understand the game.

"That's a rather heartfelt sigh."

Hyacinth blinked her mother's face into focus. Good

heavens, how long had she been sitting there, staring into space?

"Is there something you wish to tell me?" Violet asked gently.

Hyacinth shook her head. How did one share something such as this with one's mother?

—*Oh, yes, by the by and in case you're interested, it has recently come to my attention that my affianced husband asked me to marry him because he wished to infuriate his father.*

—*Oh, and did I mention that I am no longer a virgin? No getting out of it now!*

No, that wasn't going to work.

"I suspect," Violet said, taking a little sip of her tea, "that you have had your first lovers' quarrel."

Hyacinth tried *very* hard not to blush. Lovers, indeed.

"It is nothing to be ashamed about," Violet said.

"I'm not ashamed," Hyacinth said quickly.

Violet raised her brows, and Hyacinth wanted to kick herself for falling so neatly into her mother's trap.

"It's nothing," she muttered, poking at her embroidery until the yellow flower she'd been working on looked like a fuzzy little chick.

Hyacinth shrugged and pulled out some orange thread. Might as well give it some feet and a beak.

"I know that it is considered unseemly to display one's emotions," Violet said, "and certainly I would not suggest that you engage in anything that might be termed histrionic, but sometimes it does help to simply tell someone how you feel."

Hyacinth looked up, meeting her mother's gaze directly. "I rarely have difficulty telling people how I feel."

"Well, that much is true," Violet said, looking slightly disgruntled at having her theory shot to pieces.

Hyacinth turned back to her embroidery, frowning as she realized that she'd put the beak too high. Oh, very well, it was a chick in a party hat.

"Perhaps," her mother persisted, "Mr. St. Clair is the one who finds it difficult to—"

"I know how he feels," Hyacinth cut in.

"Ah." Violet pursed her lips and let out a short little exhale through her nose. "Perhaps he is not sure how to proceed. How he ought to go about approaching you."

"He knows where I live."

Violet sighed audibly. "You're not making this easy for me."

"I'm *trying* to embroider." Hyacinth held up her handiwork as proof.

"You're trying to avoid—" Her mother stopped, blinking. "I say, why does that flower have an ear?"

"It's not an ear." Hyacinth looked down. "And it's not a flower."

"Wasn't it a flower yesterday?"

"I have a very creative mind," Hyacinth ground out, giving the blasted flower another ear.

"That," Violet said, "has never been in any doubt."

Hyacinth looked down at the mess on the fabric. "It's a tabby cat," she announced. "I just need to give it a tail."

Violet held silent for a moment, then said, "You can be very hard on people."

Hyacinth's head snapped up. "I'm your daughter!" she cried out.

"Of course," Violet replied, looking somewhat shocked by the force of Hyacinth's reaction. "But—"

"Why must you assume that whatever is the matter, it must be my fault?"

"I didn't!"

"You did." And Hyacinth thought of countless spats between the Bridgerton siblings. "You always do."

Violet responded with a horrified gasp. "That is not true, Hyacinth. It's just that I know you better than I do Mr. St. Clair, and—"

"—and therefore you know all of my faults?"

"Well . . . yes." Violet appeared to be surprised by her own answer and hastened to add, "That is not to say that Mr. St. Clair is not in possession of foibles and faults of his own. It's just that . . . Well, I'm just not acquainted with them."

"They are large," Hyacinth said bitterly, "and quite possibly insurmountable."

"Oh, Hyacinth," her mother said, and there was such concern in her voice that Hyacinth very nearly burst into tears right then and there. "Whatever can be the matter?"

Hyacinth looked away. She shouldn't have said anything. Now her mother would be beside herself with worry, and Hyacinth would have to sit there, feeling terrible, wanting desperately to throw herself into her arms and be a child again.

When she was small, she had been convinced that her mother could solve any problem, make anything better with a soft word and a kiss on the forehead.

But she wasn't a child any longer, and these weren't a child's problems.

And she couldn't share them with her mother.

"Do you wish to cry off?" Violet asked, softly and very carefully.

Hyacinth gave her head a shake. She *couldn't* back out of the marriage. But . . .

She looked away, surprised by the direction of her thoughts. Did she even *want* to back out of the marriage? If she had not given herself to Gareth, if they hadn't made love, and there was nothing forcing her to remain in the betrothal, what would she do?

She had spent the last three days obsessing about that night, about that horrible moment when she'd heard Gareth's father laughingly talk about how he had manipulated him into offering for her. She'd gone over every sentence in her head, every word she could remember, and yet she was only just now asking herself what had to be the most important question. The only question that mattered, really. And she realized—

She would stay.

She repeated it in her mind, needing time for the words to sink in.

She would stay.

She loved him. Was it really as simple as that?

"I don't wish to cry off," she said, even though she'd already shaken her head. Some things needed to be said aloud.

"Then you will have to help him," Violet said. "With whatever it is that troubles him, it will be up to you to help him."

Hyacinth nodded slowly, too lost in her thoughts to offer a more meaningful reply. Could she help him? Was it possible? She had known him barely a month; he'd had a lifetime to build this hatred with his father.

He might not want help, or perhaps more likely—he might not realize that he needed it. Men never did.

"I believe he cares for you," her mother said. "I truly believe that he does."

"I know he does," Hyacinth said sadly. But not as much as he hated his father.

And when he'd gone down on one knee and asked her to spend the rest of her life with him, to take his name and bear him children, it hadn't been because of *her*.

What did that say about *him?*

She sighed, feeling very weary.

"This isn't like you," her mother said.

Hyacinth looked up.

"To be so quiet," Violet clarified, "to wait."

"To wait?" Hyacinth echoed.

"For him. I assume that is what you're doing, waiting for him to call upon you and beg your forgiveness for whatever it is he has done."

"I—" She stopped. That was exactly what she'd been doing. She hadn't even realized it. And it was probably part of the reason she was feeling so miserable. She'd placed her fate and her happiness in the hands of another, and she hated it.

"Why don't you send him a letter?" Violet suggested. "Request that he pay you a visit. He is a gentleman, and you are his fiancée. He would never refuse."

"No," Hyacinth murmured, "he wouldn't. But"—she looked up, her eyes begging for advice—"what would I say?"

It was a silly question. Violet didn't even know what the problem was, so how could she know the solution? And yet, somehow, as always, she managed to say exactly the right thing.

"Say whatever is in your heart," Violet said. Her lips twisted wryly. "And if that doesn't work, I suggest that you take a book and knock him over the head with it."

Hyacinth blinked, then blinked again. "I beg your pardon."

"I didn't say that," Violet said quickly.

Hyacinth felt herself smile. "I'm rather certain you did."

"Do you think?" Violet murmured, concealing her own smile with her teacup.

"A large book," Hyacinth queried, "or small?"

"Large, I think, don't you?"

Hyacinth nodded. "Have we *The Complete Works of Shakespeare* in the library?"

Violet's lips twitched. "I believe that we do."

Something began to bubble in Hyacinth's chest. Something very close to laughter. And it felt so good to feel it again.

"I love you, Mother," she said, suddenly consumed by the need to say it aloud. "I just wanted you to know that."

"I know, darling," Violet said, and her eyes were shining brightly. "I love you, too."

Hyacinth nodded. She'd never stopped to think how precious that was—to have the love of a parent. It was something Gareth had never had. Heaven only knew what his childhood had been like. He had never spoken of it, and Hyacinth was ashamed to realize that she'd never asked.

She'd never even noticed the omission.

Maybe, just maybe, he deserved a little understanding on her part.

He would still have to beg her forgiveness; she wasn't *that* full of kindness and charity.

But she could try to understand, and she could love him, and maybe, if she tried with everything she had, she could fill that void within him.

Whatever it was he needed, maybe she could be it.

And maybe that would be all that mattered.

But in the meantime, Hyacinth was going to have to expend a bit of energy to bring about her happy ending. And she had a feeling that a note wasn't going to be sufficient.

It was time to be brazen, time to be bold.

Time to beard the lion in his den, to—

"I say, Hyacinth," came her mother's voice, "are you quite all right?"

She shook her head, even as she said, "I'm perfectly well. Just thinking like a fool, that's all."

A fool in love.

Chapter 18

Later that afternoon, in the small study in Gareth's very small suite of apartments. Our hero has come to the conclusion that he must take action.

He does not realize that Hyacinth is about to beat him to the punch.

 A grand gesture.

That, Gareth decided, was what he needed. A grand gesture.

Women loved grand gestures, and while Hyacinth was certainly rather unlike any other woman he'd had dealings with, she was still a woman, and she would certainly be at least a little swayed by a grand gesture.

Wouldn't she?

Well, she'd better, Gareth thought grumpily, because he didn't know what else to do.

But the problem with grand gestures was that the grandest ones tended to require money, which was one thing Gareth had in short supply. And the ones that didn't require a great deal of money usually involved some poor sod embarrassing himself in a most public manner—

reciting poetry or singing a ballad, or making some sort of sappy declaration with eight hundred witnesses.

Not, Gareth decided, anything he was likely to do.

But Hyacinth was, as he'd often noted, an uncommon sort of female, which meant that—hopefully—an uncommon sort of gesture would work with her.

He would show her he cared, and she'd forget all this nonsense about his father, and all would be well.

All had to be well.

"Mr. St. Clair, you have a visitor."

He looked up. He'd been seated behind his desk for so long it was a wonder he hadn't grown roots. His valet was standing in the doorway to his office. As Gareth could not afford a butler—and really, who needed one with only four rooms to care for—Phelps often assumed those duties as well.

"Show him in," Gareth said, somewhat absently, sliding some books over the papers currently sitting on his desk.

"Er . . ." *Cough cough. Cough cough cough.*

Gareth looked up. "Is there a problem?"

"Well . . . no . . ." The valet looked pained. Gareth tried to take pity on him. Poor Mr. Phelps hadn't realized that he would occasionally be acting as a butler when he'd interviewed for the position, and clearly he'd never been taught the butlerian skill of keeping one's face devoid of all emotion.

"Mr. Phelps?" Gareth queried.

"He is a she, Mr. St. Clair."

"A hermaphrodite, Mr. Phelps?" Gareth asked, just to see the poor fellow blush.

To his credit, the valet made no reaction save squaring his jaw. "It is Miss Bridgerton."

Gareth jumped to his feet so quickly he smacked both his thighs on the edge of the desk. "Here?" he asked. "Now?"

Phelps nodded, looking just a little bit pleased at his discomfiture. "She gave me her card. She was rather polite about it all. As if it were nothing out of the ordinary."

Gareth's mind spun, trying to figure out why on earth Hyacinth would do something so ill-advised as to call upon him at his home in the middle of the day. Not that the middle of the night would have been better, but still, any number of busybodies might have seen her entering the building.

"Ah, show her in," he said. He couldn't very well turn her out. As it was, he would certainly have to return her to her home himself. He couldn't imagine she'd come with a proper escort. She'd probably brought no one save that peppermint-eating maid of hers, and heaven knew she was no protection on the streets of London.

He crossed his arms as he waited. His rooms were set up in a square, and one could access his study from either the dining room or his bedchamber. Unfortunately, the day maid had chosen this day to provide the dining room floor with some sort of twice-yearly wax that she swore (rather vocally and on her dear mother's grave) would keep the floor clean *and* ward off disease. As a result, the table had been shoved up against the door to the study, which meant that the only way in was through his bedroom.

Gareth groaned and shook his head. The last thing he needed was to picture Hyacinth in his bedroom.

He hoped she felt awkward passing through. It was the least she deserved, coming out here on her own.

"Gareth," she said, appearing in the doorway.

And all his good intentions flew right out the window.

"What the devil are you doing here?" he demanded.

"It's nice to see you, too," she said, with such composure that he felt like a fool.

But still he plodded on. "Any number of people could have seen you. Have you no care for your reputation?"

She shrugged delicately, pulling off her gloves. "I'm engaged to be married. You can't cry off, and I don't intend to, so I doubt I'll be forever ruined if someone catches me."

Gareth tried to ignore the rush of relief he felt at her words. He had, of course, gone to great lengths to ensure that she could not cry off, and she had already said that she would not, but all the same, it was surprisingly good to hear it again.

"Very well," he said slowly, choosing his words with great care. "Why, then, are you here?"

"I am not here to discuss your father," she said briskly, "if that is what worries you."

"I'm not worried," he bit off.

She lifted one brow. Damn, but *why* had he chosen to marry the one woman in the world who could do that? Or at least the one woman of his acquaintance.

"I'm not," he said testily.

She said nothing in direct reply, but she did give him a look that said she didn't believe him for one instant. "I have come," she said, "to discuss the jewels."

"The jewels," he repeated.

"Yes," she replied, still in that prim, businesslike voice of hers. "I hope you have not forgotten about them."

"How could I?" he murmured. She was starting to irritate him, he realized. Or rather, her demeanor was. He was still roiling inside, on edge just from the very sight of her, and she was utterly cool, almost preternaturally composed.

"I hope you still intend to look for them," she said. "We have come too far to give up now."

"Have you any idea where we might begin?" he asked, keeping his voice scrupulously even. "If I recall correctly, we seem to have hit a bit of a brick wall."

She reached into her reticule and pulled out the latest clue from Isabella, which she'd had in her possession ever since they had parted a few days earlier. With careful, steady fingers she unfolded it and smoothed it open on his desk. "I took the liberty of taking this to my brother Colin," she said. She looked up and reminded him, "You had given me your permission to do so."

He gave her a brief nod of agreement.

"As I mentioned, he has traveled extensively on the Continent, and he seems to feel that it is written in a Slavic language. After consulting a map, he guessed that it is Slovene." At his blank stare, she added, "It is what they speak in Slovenia."

Gareth blinked. "Is there such a country?"

For the first time in the interview, Hyacinth smiled. "There is. I must confess, I was unaware of its existence as well. It's more of a region, really. To the north and east of Italy."

"Part of Austria-Hungary, then?"

Hyacinth nodded. "And the Holy Roman Empire before that. Was your grandmother from the north of Italy?"

Gareth suddenly realized that he had no idea. Grandmother Isabella had loved to tell him stories of her childhood in Italy, but they had been tales of food and holidays—the sorts of things a very young boy might find interesting. If she'd mentioned the town of her birth, he had been too young to take note. "I don't know," he said, feeling rather foolish—and in truth, somewhat inconsiderate—for his ignorance. "I suppose she must have been. She wasn't very dark. Her coloring was a bit like mine, actually."

Hyacinth nodded. "I had wondered about that. Neither you nor your father has much of a Mediterranean look about you."

Gareth smiled tightly. He could not speak for the baron, but there was a very good reason why *he* did not look as if he carried any Italian blood.

"Well," Hyacinth said, looking back down at the sheet of paper she had laid on his desk. "If she was from the northeast, it stands to reason that she might have lived near the Slovene border and thus been familiar with the language. Or at least familiar enough to pen two sentences in it."

"I can't imagine that she thought anyone here in England might be able to translate it, though."

"Exactly," she said, making an animated motion of agreement. When it became apparent that Gareth had no idea what she was talking about, she continued with, "If you wanted to make a clue particularly difficult, wouldn't you write it in the most obscure language possible?"

"It's really a pity I don't speak Chinese," he murmured.

She gave him a look—either of impatience or irritation; he wasn't sure which—then continued with, "I am also convinced that this must be the final clue. Anyone who had got this far would be forced to expend quite a lot of energy, and quite possibly expense as well to obtain a translation. Surely she wouldn't force someone to go through the trouble twice."

Gareth looked down at the unfamiliar words, chewing on his lower lip as he pondered this.

"Don't you agree?" Hyacinth pressed.

He looked up, shrugging. "Well, *you* would."

Her mouth fell open. "What do you mean? That's simply not—" She stopped, reflecting on his words. "Very well, I would. But I think we can both agree that, for better or for worse, I am a bit more diabolical than a typical female. Or male, for that matter," she muttered.

Gareth smiled wryly, wondering if he ought to be made more nervous by the phrase, "for better or for worse."

"Do you think your grandmother would be as devious as, er . . ."—she cleared her throat—"I?" Hyacinth seemed to lose a little steam toward the end of the question, and Gareth suddenly saw in her eyes that she was not as collected as she wished for him to believe.

"I don't know," he said quite honestly. "She passed away when I was rather young. My recollections and perceptions are those of a seven-year-old boy."

"Well," she said, tapping her fingers against the desk in a revealingly nervous gesture. "We can certainly begin our search for a speaker of Slovene." She rolled her eyes as she added, somewhat dryly, "There must be one somewhere in London."

"One would think," he murmured, mostly just to egg her on. He shouldn't do it; he should be far wiser by now, but there was something so . . . entertaining about Hyacinth when she was determined.

And as usual, she did not disappoint. "In the meantime," she stated, her voice marvelously matter-of-fact, "I believe we should return to Clair House."

"And search it from top to bottom?" he asked, so politely that it had to be clear that he thought she was mad.

"Of course not," she said with a scowl.

He almost smiled. That was much more like her.

"But it seems to me," she added, "that the jewels must be hidden in her bedchamber."

"And why would you think that?"

"Where else would she put them?"

"Her dressing room," he suggested, tilting his head to the side, "the drawing room, the attic, the butler's closet, the guest bedroom, the *other* guest bedroom—"

"But where," she cut in, looking rather annoyed with his sarcasm, "would make the most sense? Thus far, she has been keeping everything to the areas of the house least visited by your grandfather. Where better than her bedchamber?"

He eyed her thoughtfully and for long enough to make her blush. Finally, he said, "We know he visited her there at least twice."

She blinked. "Twice?"

"My father and my father's younger brother. He died at Trafalgar," he explained, even though she hadn't asked.

"Oh." That seemed to take the winds out of her sails. At least momentarily. "I'm sorry."

Gareth shrugged. "It was a long time ago, but thank you."

She nodded slowly, looking as if she wasn't quite sure what to say now. "Right," she finally said. "Well."

"Right," he echoed.

"Well."

"Well," he said softly.

"Oh, hang it all!" she burst out. "I cannot stand this. I am not *made* to sit idly by and brush things under the rug."

Gareth opened his mouth to speak, not that he had any idea of what to say, but Hyacinth wasn't done.

"I know I should be quiet, and I know I should leave well enough alone, but I can't. I just can't do it." She looked at him, and she looked like she wanted to grab his shoulders and shake. "Do you understand?"

"Not a word," he admitted.

"I have to know!" she cried out. "I have to know why you asked me to marry you."

It was a topic he did not wish to revisit. "I thought you said you didn't come here to discuss my father."

"I lied," she said. "You didn't really believe me, did you?"

"No," he realized. "I don't suppose I did."

"I just—I can't—" She wrung her hands together, looking more pained and tortured than he'd ever seen her. A few strands of her hair had come loose from its pinnings, probably the result of her anxious gestures, and her color was high.

But it was her eyes that looked the most changed. There was a desperation there, a strange discomfort that did not belong.

And he realized that that was the thing about Hyacinth, the distinguishing characteristic that set her so apart from the rest of humanity. She was always at ease in her own skin. She knew who she was, and she liked who she was, and he supposed that was a large part of why he so enjoyed her company.

And he realized that she had—and she was—so many things he'd always wanted.

She knew her place in this world. She knew where she belonged.

She knew who she belonged with.

And he wanted the same. He wanted it with an intensity that cut right down to his soul. It was a strange, almost indescribable jealousy, but it was there. And it seared him.

"If you have any feeling for me whatsoever," she said, "you will understand how bloody difficult this is for me, so for the love of God, Gareth, will you *say something*?"

"I—" He opened his mouth to speak, but the words seemed to strangle him. Why *had* he asked her to marry him? There were a hundred reasons, a thousand. He tried to remember just what it was that had pushed the idea into his mind. It had come to him suddenly—he remembered that. But he didn't recall exactly why, except that it had seemed the right thing to do.

Not because it was expected, not because it was proper, but just because it was right.

And yes, it was true that it had crossed his mind that it would be the ultimate win in this never-ending game with his father, but that wasn't *why* he'd done it.

He'd done it because he'd had to.

Because he couldn't imagine not doing it.

Because he loved her.

He felt himself slide, and thank God the desk was behind him, or he'd have ended up on the floor.

How on earth had this happened? He was in love with Hyacinth Bridgerton.

Surely someone somewhere was laughing about this.

"I'll go," she said, her voice breaking, and it was only when she reached the door that he realized he must have been silent for a full minute.

"No!" he called out, and his voice sounded impossibly hoarse. "Wait!" And then:

"Please."

She stopped, turned. Shut the door.

And he realized that he had to tell her. Not that he loved her—*that* he wasn't quite ready to reveal. But he had to tell her the truth about his birth. He couldn't trick her into marriage.

"Hyacinth, I—"

The words jammed in his throat. He'd never told anyone. Not even his grandmother. No one knew the truth except for him and the baron.

For ten years, Gareth had kept it inside, allowed it to grow and fill him until sometimes it felt like it was all that he was. Nothing but a secret. Nothing but a lie.

"I need to tell you something," he said haltingly, and she must have sensed that this was something out of the ordinary, because she went very still.

And Hyacinth was rarely still.

"I—My father . . ."

It was strange. He'd never thought to say it, had never rehearsed the words. And he didn't know how to put them together, didn't know which sentence to choose.

"He's not my father," he finally blurted out.

Hyacinth blinked. Twice.

"I don't know who my real father is."

Still, she said nothing.

"I expect I never will."

He watched her face, waited for some sort of reaction. She was expressionless, so completely devoid of movement that she didn't look like herself. And then, just when he was certain that he'd lost her forever, her mouth came together in a peevish line, and she said:

"Well. That's a relief, I must say."

His lips parted. "I beg your pardon."

"I wasn't particularly excited about my children carrying Lord St. Clair's blood." She shrugged, lifting her brows in a particularly Hyacinthish expression. "I'm happy for them to have his title—it's a handy thing to possess, after all—but his blood is quite another thing. He's remarkably bad-tempered, did you know that?"

Gareth nodded, a bubble of giddy emotion rising within him. "I'd noticed," he heard himself say.

"I suppose we'll have to keep it a secret," she said, as if she were speaking of nothing more than the idlest of gossip. "Who else knows?"

He blinked, still a little dazed by her matter-of-fact approach to the problem. "Just the baron and me, as far as I'm aware."

"And your real father."

"I hope not," Gareth said, and he realized that it was the first time he'd actually allowed himself to say the words—even, really, to think them.

"He might not have known," Hyacinth said quietly, "or

he might have thought you were better off with the St. Clairs, as a child of nobility."

"I know all that," Gareth said bitterly, "and yet somehow it doesn't make it feel any better."

"Your grandmother might know more."

His eyes flew to her face.

"Isabella," she clarified. "In her diary."

"She wasn't really my grandmother."

"Did she ever act that way? As if you weren't hers?"

He shook his head. "No," he said, losing himself to the memories. "She loved me. I don't know why, but she did."

"It might be," Hyacinth said, her voice catching in the oddest manner, "because you're slightly lovable."

His heart leapt. "Then you don't wish to end the engagement," he said, somewhat cautiously.

She looked at him with an uncommonly direct gaze. "Do you?"

He shook his head.

"Then why," she said, her lips forming the barest of smiles, "would you think that I would?"

"Your family might object."

"Pffft. We're not so high in the instep as that. My brother's wife is the illegitimate daughter of the Earl of Penwood and an actress of God knows what provenance, and any one of us would lay down our lives for her." Her eyes narrowed thoughtfully. "But you are not illegitimate."

He shook his head. "To my father's everlasting despair."

"Well, then," she said, "I don't see a problem. My brother and Sophie like to live quietly in the country, in part because of her past, but we shan't be forced to do the same. Unless of course, you wish to."

"The baron could raise a huge scandal," he warned her.

She smiled. "Are you trying to talk me out of marrying you?"

"I just want you to understand—"

"Because I would hope by now you've learned that it's a tiresome endeavor to attempt to talk me out of anything."

Gareth could only smile at that.

"Your father won't say a word," she stated. "What would be the point? You were born in wedlock, so he can't take away the title, and revealing you as a bastard would only reveal *him* as a cuckold." She waved her hand through the air with great authority. "No man wants that."

His lips curved, and he felt something changing inside of him, as if he were growing lighter, more free. "And you can speak for all men?" he murmured, moving slowly in her direction.

"Would *you* wish to be known as a cuckold?"

He shook his head. "But I don't have to worry about that."

She started to look just a little unnerved—but also excited—as he closed the distance between them. "Not if you keep me happy."

"Why, Hyacinth Bridgerton, is that a threat?"

Her expression turned coy. "Perhaps."

He was only a step away now. "I can see that I have my work cut out for me."

Her chin lifted, and her chest began to rise and fall more rapidly. "I'm not a particularly easy woman."

He found her hand and lifted her fingers to his mouth. "I do enjoy a challenge."

"Then it's a good thing you're—"

He took one of her fingers and slid it into his mouth, and she gasped.

"—marrying me," she somehow finished.

He moved to another finger. "Mmm-hmm."

"I—Ah—I—Ah—"

"You do like to talk," he said with a chuckle.

"What do you—Oh!—"

He smiled to himself as he moved to the inside of her wrist.

"—mean by that?" But there wasn't much punch left in her question. She was quite literally melting against the wall, and he felt like king of the world.

"Oh, nothing much," he murmured, tugging her close so that he could move his lips to the side of her throat. "Just that I'm looking forward to actually marrying you so that you can make as much noise as you'd like."

He couldn't see her face—he was much too busy attending to the neckline of her dress, which clearly had to be brought down—but he knew she blushed. He felt the heat beneath her skin.

"Gareth," she said in feeble protest. "We should stop."

"You don't mean that," he said, sliding his hand under the hem of her skirt once it became clear that the bodice wasn't going to budge.

"No"—she sighed—"not really."

He smiled. "Good."

She let out a moan as his fingers tickled up her leg, and then she must have grasped onto one last shred of sanity, because she said, "But we can't . . . oh."

"No, we can't," he agreed. The desk wouldn't be comfortable, there was no room on the floor, and heaven only knew if Phelps had shut the outer door to his bedroom. He pulled back and gave her a devilish smile. "But we can do other things."

Her eyes opened wide. "What other things?" she asked, sounding delightfully suspicious.

He wound his fingers in hers and then pulled both her hands over her head. "Do you trust me?"

"No," she said, "but I don't care."

Still holding her hands aloft, he leaned her against the door and came in for a kiss. She tasted like tea, and like . . .

Her.

He could count the number of times he'd kissed her on one hand, and yet he still knew, still understood, that this was the essence of her. She was unique in his arms, beneath his kiss, and he knew that no one else would ever do again.

He let go of one of her hands, stroking his way softly down the line of her arm to her shoulder . . . neck . . . jaw. And then his other hand released her and found its way back to the hem of her dress.

She moaned his name, gasping and panting as his fingers moved up her leg.

"Relax," he instructed, his lips hot against her ear.

"I can't."

"You can."

"No," she said, grabbing his face and forcing him to look at her. "I can't."

Gareth laughed aloud, enchanted by her bossiness. "Very well," he said, "don't relax." And then, before she had a chance to respond, he slid his finger past the edge of her underthings and touched her.

"Oh!"

"No relaxing now," he said with a chuckle.

"Gareth," she gasped.

"Oh, Gareth, No Gareth, or More Gareth?" he murmured.

"More," she moaned. "Please."

"I love a woman who knows when to beg," he said, redoubling his efforts.

Her head, which had been thrown back, came down so that she could look him in the eye. "You'll pay for that," she said.

He quirked a brow. "I will?"

She nodded. "Just not now."

He laughed softly. "Fair enough."

He rubbed her gently, using soft friction to bring her to a quivering peak. She was breathing erratically now, her lips parted and her eyes glazed. He loved her face, loved every little curve of it, the way the light hit her cheekbones and the shape of her jaw.

But there was something about it now, when she was lost in her own passion, that took his breath away. She was beautiful—not in a way that would launch a thousand ships, but in a more private fashion.

Her beauty was his and his alone.

And it humbled him.

He leaned down to kiss her, tenderly, with all the love he felt. He wanted to catch her gasp when she climaxed, wanted to feel her breath and her moan with his mouth. His fingers tickled and teased, and she tensed beneath him, her body trapped between his and the wall, grinding against them both.

"Gareth," she gasped, breaking free of the kiss for just long enough to say his name.

"Soon," he promised. He smiled. "Maybe now."

And then, as he captured her for one last kiss, he slid one finger inside of her, even as another continued its caress. He felt her close tight around him, felt her body practically lift off the floor with the force of her passion.

And it was only then that he realized the true measure of his own desire. He was hard and hot and desperate for her, and even so, he'd been so focused on her that he hadn't noticed.

Until now.

He looked at her. She was limp, breathless, and as near to insensible as he'd ever seen her.

Damn.

That was all right, he told himself unconvincingly. They had their whole lives ahead of them. One encounter with a tub of cold water wasn't going to kill him.

"Happy?" he murmured, gazing down at her indulgently.

She nodded, but that was all she managed.

He dropped a kiss on her nose, then remembered the papers he'd left on his desk. They weren't quite complete, but still, it seemed a good time to show them to her.

"I have a present for you," he said.

Her eyes lit up. "You do?"

He nodded. "Just keep in mind that it's the thought that counts."

She smiled, following him to his desk, then taking a seat in the chair in front of it.

Gareth pushed aside some books, then carefully lifted a piece of paper. "It's not done."

"I don't care," she said softly.

But still, he didn't show it to her. "I think it's rather obvious that we are not going to find the jewels," he said.

"No!" she protested. "We can—"

"Shhh. Let me finish."

It went against her every last impulse, but she managed to shut her mouth.

"I am not in possession of a great deal of money," he said.

"That doesn't matter."

He smiled wryly. "I'm glad you feel that way, because while we shan't want for anything, nor will we live like your brothers and sisters."

"I don't need all that," she said quickly. And she didn't. Or at least she hoped she didn't. But she knew, down to the tips of her toes, that she didn't need anything as much as she needed him.

He looked slightly grateful, and also, maybe, just a little bit uncomfortable. "It'll probably be even worse once I inherit the title," he added. "I think the baron is trying to fix it so that he can beggar me from beyond the grave."

"Are you trying to talk me out of marrying you again?"

"Oh, no," he said. "You're most definitely stuck with me now. But I did want you to know that if I could, I would give you the world." He held out the paper. "Starting with this."

She took the sheet into her hands and looked down. It was a drawing, of her.

Her eyes widened with surprise. "Did you do this?" she asked.

He nodded. "I'm not well trained, but I can—"

"It's very good," she said, cutting him off. He would never find his way into history as a famous artist, but the likeness was a good one, and she rather thought he'd captured something in her eyes, something that she'd not seen in any of the portraits of her her family had commissioned.

"I have been thinking about Isabella," he said, leaning against the edge of his desk. "And I remembered a story she told me when I was young. There was a princess, and an evil prince, and"—he smiled ruefully—"a diamond bracelet."

Hyacinth had been watching his face, mesmerized by the warmth in his eyes, but at this she looked quickly back down at the drawing. There, on her wrist, was a diamond bracelet.

"I'm sure it's nothing like what she actually hid," he said, "but it is how I remember her describing it to me, and it is what I would give to you, if only I could."

"Gareth, I—" And she felt tears, welling in her eyes, threatening to spill down her cheeks. "It is the most precious gift I have ever received."

He looked . . . not like he didn't believe her, but rather like he wasn't quite sure that he should. "You don't have to say—"

"It is," she insisted, rising to her feet.

He turned and picked another piece of paper up off the desk. "I drew it here as well," he said, "but larger, so you could see it better."

She took the second piece of paper into her hands and looked down. He'd drawn just the bracelet, as if suspended in air. "It's lovely," she said, touching the image with her fingers.

He gave her a self-deprecating smile. "If it doesn't exist, it should."

She nodded, still examining the drawing. The bracelet was lovely, each link shaped almost like a leaf. It was delicate and whimsical, and Hyacinth ached to place it on her wrist.

But she could never treasure it as much as she did these two drawings. Never.

"I—" She looked up, her lips parting with surprise. She almost said, "I love you."

"I love them," she said instead, but when she looked up at him, she rather fancied that the truth was in her eyes.

I love you.

She smiled and placed her hand over his. She wanted to say it, but she wasn't quite ready. She didn't know why, except that maybe she was afraid to say it first. She, who was afraid of almost nothing, could not quite summon the courage to utter three little words.

It was astounding.

Terrifying.

And she decided to change the mood. "I still want to look for the jewels," she said, clearing her throat until her voice emerged in its customarily efficient manner.

He groaned. "Why won't you give up?"

"Because I . . . Well, because I can't." She clamped her mouth into a frown. "I certainly don't want your father to have them now. Oh." She looked up. "Am I to call him that?"

He shrugged. "I still do. It's a difficult habit to break."

She acknowledged this with a nod. "I don't care if Isabella wasn't really your grandmother. You deserve the bracelet."

He gave her an amused smile. "And why is that?"

That stumped her for a moment. "Because you do," she finally said. "Because someone has to have it, and I don't want it to be him. Because—" She glanced longingly down at the drawing in her hands. "Because this is *gorgeous*."

"Can't we wait to find our Slovenian translator?"

She shook her head, pointing at the note, still lying on the desk. "What if it's not in Slovene?"

"I thought you said it was," he said, clearly exasperated.

"I said my brother *thought* it was," she returned. "Do you know how many languages there are in central Europe?"

He cursed under his breath.

"I know," she said. "It's very frustrating."

He stared at her in disbelief. "That's not why I swore."

"Then why—"

"Because you are going to be the death of me," he ground out.

Hyacinth smiled, pointing her index finger and pressing it right against his chest. "Now you know why I said my family was mad to get me off their hands."

"God help me, I do."

She cocked her head to the side. "Can we go tomorrow?"

"No?"

"The next day?"

"No!"

"Please?" she tried.

He clamped his hands on her shoulders and spun her around until she faced the door. "I'm taking you home," he announced.

She turned, trying to talk over her shoulder. "Pl—"

"No!"

Hyacinth shuffled along, allowing him to push her toward the door. When she could not put it off any longer, she grasped the doorknob, but before she turned it, she twisted back one last time, opened her mouth, and—

"NO!"

"I didn't—"

"Very well," he groaned, practically throwing his arms up in exasperation. "You win."

"Oh, *thank*—"

"But you are not coming."

She froze, her mouth still open and round. "I beg your pardon," she said.

"I will go," he said, looking very much as if he'd rather have all of his teeth pulled. "But you will not."

She stared at him, trying to come up with a way to say, "That's not fair," without sounding juvenile. Deciding that was impossible, she set to work attempting to figure out how to ask how she would know he'd actually gone without sounding as if she didn't trust him.

Botheration, that was a lost cause as well.

So she settled for crossing her arms and skewering him with a glare.

To no effect whatsoever. He just stared down at her and said, "No."

Hyacinth opened her mouth one last time, then gave up, sighed, and said, "Well, I suppose if I could walk all over you, you wouldn't be worth marrying."

He threw back his head and laughed. "You're going to be a fine wife, Hyacinth Bridgerton," he said, nudging her out of the room.

"Hmmph."

He groaned. "Good God, but not if you turn into my grandmother."

"It is my every aspiration," she said archly.

"Pity," he murmured, tugging at her arm so that she came to a halt before they reached his sitting room.

She turned to him, questioning with her eyes.

He curved his lips, all innocence. "Well, I can't do *this* to my grandmother."

"Oh!" she yelped. How had he gotten his hand *there?*

"Or *this.*"

"Gareth!"

"Gareth, yes, or Gareth, no?"

She smiled. She couldn't help it.

"Gareth *more.*"

Chapter 19

The following Tuesday.
Everything important seems to happen on a Tuesday, doesn't it?

"Look what I have!"

Hyacinth grinned as she stood in the doorway of Lady Danbury's drawing room, holding aloft *Miss Davenport and the Dark Marquis.*

"A new book?" Lady D asked from her position across the room. She was seated in her favorite chair, but from the way she held herself, it might as well have been a throne.

"Not just any book," Hyacinth said with a sly smile as she held it forth. "Look."

Lady Danbury took the book in her hands, glanced down, and positively beamed. "We haven't read this one yet," she said. She looked back up at Hyacinth. "I hope it's just as bad as the rest."

"Oh, come now, Lady Danbury," Hyacinth said, taking a seat next to her, "you shouldn't call them bad."

"I didn't say they weren't entertaining," the countess

said, eagerly flipping through the pages. "How many chapters do we have left with dear Miss Butterworth?"

Hyacinth plucked the book in question off a nearby table and opened it to the spot she had marked the previous Tuesday. "Three," she said, flipping back and forth to check.

"Hmmph. I wonder how many cliffs poor Priscilla can hang from in that time."

"Two at least, I should think," Hyacinth murmured. "Provided she isn't struck with the plague."

Lady Danbury attempted to peer at the book over her shoulder. "Do you think it possible? A bit of the bubonic would do wonders for the prose."

Hyacinth chuckled. "Perhaps that should have been the subtitle. *Miss Butterworth and the Mad Baron, or*"—she lowered her voice dramatically—"*A Bit of the Bubonic.*"

"I prefer *Pecked to Death by Pigeons* myself."

"Maybe we *should* write a book," Hyacinth said with a smile, getting ready to launch into chapter eighteen.

Lady Danbury looked as if she wanted to clap Hyacinth on the head. "That is exactly what I've been telling you."

Hyacinth scrunched her nose as she shook her head. "No," she said, "it really wouldn't be much fun past the titles. Do you think anyone would wish to buy a collection of amusing book titles?"

"They would if it had my name on the cover," Lady D said with great authority. "Speaking of which, how is your translation of my grandson's other grandmother's diary coming along?"

Hyacinth's head bobbed slightly as she tried to follow Lady D's convoluted sentence structure. "I'm sorry," she finally said, "how does that have anything to do with people being compelled to purchase a book with your name on the cover?"

Lady Danbury waved her hand forcefully in the air as if Hyacinth's comment were a physical thing she could push away. "You haven't told me anything," she said.

"I'm only a little bit more than halfway through," Hyacinth admitted. "I remember far less Italian than I had thought, and I am finding it a much more difficult task than I had anticipated."

Lady D nodded. "She was a lovely woman."

Hyacinth blinked in surprise. "You knew her? Isabella?"

"Of course I did. Her son married my daughter."

"Oh. Yes," Hyacinth murmured. She didn't know why this hadn't occurred to her before. And she wondered— Did Lady Danbury know anything about the circumstances of Gareth's birth? Gareth had said that she did not, or at least that he had never spoken to her about it. But perhaps each was keeping silent on the assumption that the other did not know.

Hyacinth opened her mouth, then closed it sharply. It was not her place to say anything. It was *not*.

But—

No. She clamped her teeth together, as if that would keep her from blurting anything out. She could not reveal Gareth's secret. She absolutely, positively could not.

"Did you eat something sour?" Lady D asked, without any delicacy whatsoever. "You look rather ill."

"I'm perfectly well," Hyacinth said, pasting a sprightly smile on her face. "I was merely thinking about the diary. I brought it with me, actually. To read in the carriage." She had been working on the translation tirelessly since learning Gareth's secret earlier that week. She wasn't sure if they would ever learn the identity of Gareth's real father, but Isabella's diary seemed to be the best possible place to start the search.

"Did you?" Lady Danbury sat back in her chair, closing her eyes. "Read to me from that instead, why don't you?"

"You don't understand Italian," Hyacinth pointed out.

"I know, but it's a lovely language, so melodious and smooth. And I need to take a nap."

"Are you certain?" Hyacinth asked, reaching into her small satchel for the diary.

"That I need a nap? Yes, more's the pity. It started two years ago. Now I can't exist without one each afternoon."

"Actually, I was referring to the reading of the diary," Hyacinth murmured. "If you wish to fall asleep, there are certainly better methods than my reading to you in Italian."

"Why, Hyacinth," Lady D said, with a noise that sounded suspiciously like a cackle, "are you offering to sing me lullabies?"

Hyacinth rolled her eyes. "You're as bad as a child."

"Whence we came, my dear Miss Bridgerton. Whence we came."

Hyacinth shook her head and found her spot in the diary. She'd left off in the spring of 1793, four years before Gareth's birth. According to what she had read in the carriage on the way over, Gareth's mother was pregnant with what Hyacinth assumed would be Gareth's older brother George. She had suffered two miscarriages before that, which had not endeared her to her husband.

What Hyacinth was finding most interesting about the

tale was the disappointment Isabella expressed about her son. She loved him, yes, but she regretted the degree to which she had allowed her husband to mold him. As a result, Isabella had written, the son was just like the father. He treated his mother with disdain, and his wife fared no better.

Hyacinth was finding the entire tale to be rather sad. She liked Isabella. There was an intelligence and humor to her writing that shone through, even when Hyacinth was not able to translate every word, and Hyacinth liked to think that if they had been of an age, they would have been friends. It saddened her to realize the degree to which Isabella had been stifled and made unhappy by her husband.

And it reinforced her belief that it really did matter who one married. Not for wealth or status, although Hyacinth was not so idealistic that she would pretend those were completely unimportant.

But one only got one life, and, God willing, one husband. And how nice to actually *like* the man to whom one pledged one's troth. Isabella hadn't been beaten or misused, but she had been ignored, and her thoughts and opinions had gone unheard. Her husband sent her off to some remote country house, and he taught his sons by example. Gareth's father treated his wife the exact same way. Hyacinth supposed that Gareth's uncle would have been the same, too, if he had lived long enough to take a wife.

"Are you going to read to me or not?" Lady D asked, somewhat stridently.

Hyacinth looked over at the countess, who had not even bothered to open her eyes for her demand. "Sorry," she said, using her finger to find where she had left off. "I need just a moment to . . . ah, here we are."

Hyacinth cleared her throat and began to read in Italian. "*Si avvicina il giorno in cui nascerà il mio primo nipote. Prego che sia un maschio . . .*"

She translated in her head as she continued to read aloud in Italian:

> *The day draws near in which will be born my first grandchild. I pray that it will be a boy. I would love a little girl—I would probably be allowed to see her and love her more, but it will be better for us all if we have a boy. I am afraid to think how quickly Anne will be forced to endure the attentions of my son if she has a girl.*
>
> *I should love better my own son, but instead I worry about his wife.*

Hyacinth paused, eyeing Lady Danbury for signs that she understood any of the Italian. This was her daughter she was reading about, after all. Hyacinth wondered if the countess had any idea how sad the marriage had been. But Lady D had, remarkably, started to snore.

Hyacinth blinked in surprise—and suspicion. She had never dreamed that Lady Danbury might fall asleep that quickly. She held silent for a few moments, waiting for the countess's eyes to pop open with a loud demand for her to continue.

After a minute, however, Hyacinth was confident that Lady D really had fallen asleep. So she continued reading to herself, laboriously translating each sentence in her head. The next entry was dated a few months later; Isabella expressed her relief that Anne had delivered a boy, who had been christened George. The baron was beside himself with pride, and had even given his wife the gift of a gold bracelet.

Hyacinth flipped a few pages ahead, trying to see how long it would be until Isabella reached 1797, the year of Gareth's birth. One, two, three . . . She counted the pages, passing quickly through the years. Seven, eight, nine . . . Ah, 1796. Gareth had been born in March, so if Isabella had written about his conception, it would be here, not 1797.

Ten pages away, that was all.

And it occurred to her—

Why not skip ahead? There was no law requiring her to read the diary in perfect, chronological order. She could just peek ahead to 1796 and 1797 and see if there was anything relating to Gareth and his parentage. If not, she'd go right back to where she'd left off and start reading anew.

And wasn't it Lady Danbury who'd said that patience most certainly was not a virtue?

Hyacinth glanced ruefully down at 1793, then, holding the five leaves of paper as one, shifted to 1796.

Back . . . forth . . . back . . .

Forth.

She turned to 1796, and planted her left hand down so that she wouldn't turn back again.

Definitely forth.

"*24 June 1796*," she read to herself. "*I arrived at Clair House for a summer visit, only to be informed that my son had already left for London.*"

Hyacinth quickly subtracted months in her head.

Gareth was born in March of 1797. Three months took
her back to December 1796, and another six to—

June.

And Gareth's father was out of town.

Barely able to breathe, Hyacinth read on:

> *Anne seems contented that he is gone, and little*
> *George is such a treasure. Is it so terrible to admit*
> *that I am more happy when Richard isn't here? It is*
> *such a joy to have all the persons I love so close . . .*

Hyacinth scowled as she finished the entry. There was
nothing out of the ordinary there. Nothing about a mysterious stranger, or an improper friend.

She glanced up at Lady Danbury, whose head was now
tilted awkwardly back. Her mouth was hanging a bit
open, too.

Hyacinth turned resolutely back to the diary, turning to
the next entry, dated three months later.

She gasped.

> *Anne is carrying a child. And we all know it cannot*
> *be Richard's. He has been away for two months.*
> *Two months. I am afraid for her. He is furious. But*
> *she will not reveal the truth.*

"Reveal it," Hyacinth ground out. "Reveal it."

"Enh?"

Hyacinth slammed the book shut and looked up. Lady
Danbury was stirring in her seat.

"Why did you stop reading?" Lady D asked groggily.

"I didn't," Hyacinth lied, her fingers holding the diary

so tightly it was a wonder she didn't burn holes through the binding. "You fell asleep."

"Did I?" Lady Danbury murmured. "I must be getting old."

Hyacinth smiled tightly.

"Very well," Lady D said with a wave of her hand. She fidgeted a bit, moving first to the left, then to the right, then back to the left again. "I'm awake now. Let's get back to Miss Butterworth."

Hyacinth was aghast. "*Now?*"

"As opposed to when?"

Hyacinth had no good answer for that. "Very well," she said, with as much patience as she could muster. She forced herself to set the diary down beside her, and she picked up *Miss Butterworth and the Mad Baron* in its stead.

"Ahem." She cleared her throat, turning to the first page of chapter Eighteen. "Ahem."

"Throat bothering you?" Lady Danbury asked. "I still have some tea in the pot."

"It's nothing," Hyacinth said. She exhaled, looked down, and read, with decidedly less animation than was usual, "*The baron was in possession of a secret. Priscilla was quite certain of that. The only question was—would the truth ever be revealed?*"

"Indeed," Hyacinth muttered.

"Enh?"

"I think something important is about to happen," Hyacinth said with a sigh.

"Something important is always about to happen, my dear girl," Lady Danbury said. "And if not, you'd do well to act as if it were. You'll enjoy life better that way."

For Lady Danbury, the comment was uncharacteristically philosophical. Hyacinth paused, considering her words.

"I have no patience with this current fashion for *ennui*," Lady Danbury continued, reaching for her cane and thumping it against the floor. "Ha. When did it become a crime to show an interest in things?"

"I beg your pardon?"

"Just read the book," Lady D said. "I think we're getting to the good part. Finally."

Hyacinth nodded. The problem was, she was getting to the good part of the *other* book. She took a breath, trying to return her attention to *Miss Butterworth*, but the words swam before her eyes. Finally, she looked up at Lady Danbury and said, "I'm sorry, but would you mind terribly if I cut our visit short? I'm not feeling quite the thing."

Lady Danbury stared at her as if she'd just announced that she was carrying Napoleon's love child.

"I would be happy to make it up to you tomorrow," Hyacinth quickly added.

Lady D blinked. "But it's Tuesday."

"I realize that. I—" Hyacinth sighed. "You *are* a creature of habit, aren't you?"

"The hallmark of civilization is routine."

"Yes, I understand, but—"

"But the sign of a truly advanced mind," Lady D cut in, "is the ability to adapt to changing circumstances."

Hyacinth's mouth fell open. Never in her wildest dreams would she have imagined Lady Danbury uttering *that*.

"Go on, dear child," Lady D said, shooing her toward the door. "Do whatever it is that has you so intrigued."

For a moment Hyacinth could do nothing but stare at her. And then, suffused with a feeling that was as lovely as it was warm, she gathered her things, rose to her feet, and crossed the room to Lady Danbury's side.

"You're going to be my grandmother," she said, leaning down and giving her a kiss on the cheek. She'd never assumed such familiarity before, but somehow it felt right.

"You silly child," Lady Danbury said, brushing at her eyes as Hyacinth walked to the door. "In my heart, I've been your grandmother for years. I've just been waiting for you to make it official."

Chapter 20

Later that night. Quite a bit later, actually. Hyacinth's attempts at translation had to be postponed for a lengthy family dinner, followed by an interminable game of charades. Finally, at half eleven, she found the information she was seeking.

Excitement proved stronger than caution . . .

Another ten minutes and Gareth would not have been there to hear the knock. He had pulled on his jumper, a rough, woolen thing that his grandmother would have called dreadfully uncouth but which had the advantage of being black as night. He was just sitting on his sofa to don his most quietly soled boots when he heard it.

A knock. Soft but adamant.

A glance at the clock told him it was almost midnight. Phelps had long since gone to bed, so Gareth went to the door himself, positioning himself near the heavy wood with a, "Yes?"

"It is I," came the insistent reply.

What? No, it couldn't be . . .

He yanked the door open.

"What are you doing here?" he hissed, pulling Hyacinth into the room. She went flying by him, stumbling into a chair as he let go to peer out into the hall. "Didn't you bring someone with you?"

She shook her head. "No time to—"

"Are you mad?" he whispered furiously. "Have you gone stark, raving insane?" He'd thought he'd been angry with her last time she'd done this, running through London on her own after dark. But at least then she'd had some sort of an excuse, having been surprised by his father. This time—*This* time—

He could barely control himself. "I'm going to have to lock you up," he said, more to himself than to her. "That is it. That is the only solution. I am going to have to hold you down and—"

"If you'll just lis—"

"Get in here," he bit off, grabbing her by the arm and pulling her into his bedroom. It was the farthest from Phelps's small quarters off the drawing room. The valet usually slept like the dead, but with Gareth's luck, this would be the night he decided to awaken for a midnight snack.

"Gareth," Hyacinth whispered, scurrying behind him, "I have to tell you—"

He turned on her with furious eyes. "I don't want to hear anything from you that doesn't start with 'I'm a damned fool.' "

She crossed her arms. "Well, I'm certainly not going to say *that*."

He flexed and bent his fingers, the carefully controlled movement the only thing that was keeping him from lunging at her. The world was turning a dangerous shade of red, and all he could think of was the image of her racing across Mayfair, by herself, only to be attacked, mauled—

"I'm going to kill you," he ground out.

Hell, if anyone was going to attack or maul her, it might as well be him.

But she was just shaking her head, not listening to anything he was saying. "Gareth, I have to—"

"No," he said forcefully. "Not a word. Don't say a word. Just sit there—" He blinked, realizing that she was standing, then pointed at the bed. "Sit there," he said, "*quietly* until I figure out what the hell to do with you."

She sat, and for once she didn't look as if she was going to open her mouth to speak. In fact, she looked somewhat smug.

Which made him instantly suspicious. He had no idea how she had figured out that he had chosen that night to return to Clair House for one last search for the jewels. He must have let something slip, alluded to the trip during one of their recent conversations. He would have liked to think that he was more careful than that, but Hyacinth was fiendishly clever, and if anyone could have deduced his intentions, it would be her.

It was a damn fool endeavor in his opinion; he didn't have a clue where the diamonds might be save for Hyacinth's theory about the baroness's bedchamber. But he had promised her he would go, and he must have had a more finely tuned sense of honor than he had thought, because here he was, heading out to Clair House for the third time that month.

He glared at her.

She smiled serenely.

Sending him right over the edge. That was *it*. That was absolutely—

"All right," he said, his voice so low it was almost shaking. "We are going to lay out some rules, right here and right now."

Her spine stiffened. "I beg your pardon."

"When we are married, you will not exit the house without my permission—"

"*Ever?*" she cut in.

"Until you have proven yourself to be a responsible adult," he finished, barely recognizing himself in his own words. But if this was what it took to keep the bloody little fool safe from herself, then so be it.

She let out an impatient breath. "When did you grow so pompous?"

"When I fell in love with you!" he practically roared. Or he would have, if they hadn't been in the middle of a building of apartments, all inhabited by single men who stayed up late and liked to gossip.

"You . . . You . . . You what?"

Her mouth fell open into a fetching little oval, but Gareth was too far gone to appreciate the effect. "I love you, you idiot woman," he said, his arms jerking and flailing like a madman's. It was astonishing, what she had reduced him to. He couldn't remember the last time he'd lost his temper like this, the last time someone had made him so angry that he could barely speak.

Except for her, of course.

He ground his teeth together. "You are the most maddening, frustrating—"

"But—"

"And you *never* know when to stop talking, but God help me, I love you, anyway,—"

"But, Gareth—"

"And if I have to tie you to the damned bed just to keep you safe from yourself, as God is my witness, that is what I'll do."

"But Gareth—"

"Not a word. Not a single bloody word," he said, wagging his finger toward her in an extremely impolite manner. Finally, his hand seemed to freeze, his index finger stuck into a point, and after a few jerky motions, he managed to still himself and drag his hands to his hips.

She was staring at him, her blue eyes large and filled with wonder. Gareth couldn't tear his gaze away as she slowly rose to her feet and closed the distance between them.

"You love me?" she whispered.

"It will be the death of me, I'm sure, but yes." He sighed wearily, exhausted simply by the prospect of it all. "I can't seem to help myself."

"Oh." Her lips quivered, then wobbled, and then somehow she was smiling. "Good."

"Good?" he echoed. "That's all you have to say?"

She stepped forward, touched his cheek. "I love you, too. With all my heart, with everything I am, and everything—"

He'd never know what she'd been about to say. It was lost beneath his kiss.

"Gareth," she gasped, during the bare moment when he paused for breath.

"Not now," he said, his mouth taking hers again. He couldn't stop. He'd told her, and now he had to show her.

He loved her. It was as simple as that.

"But Gareth—"

"Shhh . . ." He held her head in his hands, and he kissed her and kissed her . . . until he made the mistake of freeing her mouth by moving to her throat.

"Gareth, I have to tell you—"

"Not now," he murmured. He had other things in mind.

"But it's very important, and—"

He dragged himself away. "Good God, woman," he grunted. "What *is* it?"

"You have to listen to me," she said, and he felt somewhat vindicated that her breathing was every bit as labored as his. "I know it was mad to come here so late."

"By yourself," he saw fit to add.

"By myself," she granted him, her lips twisting peevishly. "But I swear to you, I wouldn't have done something this foolish if I hadn't needed to speak with you right away."

His mouth tilted wryly. "A note wouldn't have done?"

She shook her head. "Gareth," she said, and her face was so serious it took his breath away, "I know who your father is."

It was as if the floor were slipping away, and yet at the same time, he could not tear his eyes off of hers. He clutched her shoulders, his fingers surely digging too hard into her skin, but he couldn't move. For years to come, if anyone had asked him about that moment, he would have said that she was the only thing holding him upright.

"Who is it?" he asked, almost dreading her reply. His entire adult life he'd wanted this answer, and now that it was here, he could feel nothing but terror.

"It was your father's brother," Hyacinth whispered.

It was as if something had slammed into his chest. "Uncle Edward?"

"Yes," Hyacinth said, her eyes searching his face with a mix of love and concern. "It was in your grandmother's diary. She didn't know at first. No one did. They only knew it couldn't be your fath—er, the baron. He was in London all spring and summer. And your mother . . . wasn't."

"How did she find out?" he whispered. "And was she certain?"

"Isabella figured it out after you were born," Hyacinth said softly. "She said you looked too much like a St. Clair to be a bastard, and Edward had been in residence at Clair House. When your father was gone."

Gareth shook his head, desperately trying to comprehend this. "Did he know?"

"Your father? Or your uncle?"

"My—" He turned, a strange, humorless sound emerging from his throat. "I don't know what to call him. Either of them."

"Your father—Lord St. Clair," she corrected. "He didn't know. Or at least, Isabella didn't think he did. He didn't know that Edward had been at Clair Hall that summer. He was just out of Oxford, and—well, I'm not exactly certain what transpired, but it sounded like he was supposed to go to Scotland with friends. But then he didn't, and so he went to Clair Hall instead. Your grandmother said—" Hyacinth stopped, and her face took on a wide-eyed expression. "Your grandmother," she murmured. "She really *was* your grandmother."

He felt her hand on his shoulder, imploring him to

turn, but somehow he couldn't look at her just then. It was too much. It was all too much.

"Gareth, Isabella *was* your grandmother. She really was."

He closed his eyes, trying to recall Isabella's face. It was hard to do; the memory was so old.

But she had loved him. He remembered that. She had loved him.

And she had known the truth.

Would she have told him? If she had lived to see him an adult, to know the man he had become, would she have told him the truth?

He could never know, but maybe . . . If she had seen how the baron had treated him . . . what they had both become . . .

He liked to think yes.

"Your uncle—" came Hyacinth's voice.

"He knew," Gareth said with low certitude.

"He did? How do you know? Did he say something?"

Gareth shook his head. He didn't know how he knew that Edward had been aware of the truth, but he was certain now that he had. Gareth had been eight when he'd last seen his uncle. Old enough to remember things. Old enough to realize what was important.

And Edward had loved him. Edward had loved him in a way that the baron never had. It was Edward who had taught him to ride, Edward who had given him the gift of a puppy on his seventh birthday.

Edward, who'd known the family well enough to know that the truth would destroy them all. Richard would never forgive Anne for siring a son who was not his, but if he had ever learned that her lover had been his own *brother* . . .

Gareth felt himself sink against the wall, needing support beyond his own two legs. Maybe it was a blessing that it had taken this long for the truth to be revealed.

"Gareth?"

Hyacinth was whispering his name, and he felt her come up next to him, her hand slipping into his with a soft gentleness that made his heart ache.

He didn't know what to think. He didn't know whether he should be angry or relieved. He really was a St. Clair, but after so many years of thinking himself an impostor, it was hard to grasp. And given the behavior of the baron, was that even anything of which to be proud?

He'd lost so much, spent so much time wondering who he was, where he'd come from, and—

"Gareth."

Her voice again, soft, whispering.

She squeezed his hand.

And then suddenly—

He knew.

Not that it didn't all matter, because it did.

But he knew that it didn't matter as much as she did, that the past wasn't as important as the future, and the family he'd lost wasn't nearly as dear to him as the family he would make.

"I love you," he said, his voice finally rising above a whisper. He turned, his heart, his very soul in his eyes. "I love you."

She looked confused by his sudden change in demeanor, but in the end she just smiled—looking for all the world as if she might actually laugh. It was the sort of expression one made when one had too much happiness to keep it all inside.

He wanted to make her look like that every day. Every hour. Every minute.

"I love you, too," she said.

He took her face in his hands and kissed her, once, deeply, on the mouth. "I mean," he said, "I *really* love you."

She quirked a brow. "Is this a contest?"

"It is anything you want," he promised.

She grinned, that enchanting, perfect smile that was so quintessentially hers. "I feel I must warn you, then," she said, cocking her head to the side. "When it comes to contests and games, I always win."

"Always?"

Her eyes grew sly. "Whenever it matters."

He felt himself smile, felt his soul lighten and his worries slip away. "And what, precisely, does that mean?"

"It means," she said, reaching up and undoing the buttons of her coat, "that I really *really* love you."

He backed up, crossing his arms as he gave her an assessing look. "Tell me more."

Her coat fell to the ground. "Is that enough?"

"Oh, not nearly."

She tried to look brazen, but her cheeks were starting to turn pink. "I will need help with the rest," she said, fluttering her lashes.

He was at her side in an instant. "I live to serve you."

"Is that so?" She sounded intrigued by the notion, so dangerously so that Gareth felt compelled to add, "In the bedroom." His fingers found the twin ribbons at her shoulders, and he gave them a tug, causing the bodice of her dress to loosen dangerously.

"More help, milady?" he murmured.

She nodded.

"Perhaps . . ." He looped his fingers around the neckline, preparing to ease it down, but she placed one hand over his. He looked up. She was shaking her head.

"No," she said. "You."

It took him a moment to grasp her meaning, and then a slow smile spread across his face. "But of course, milady," he said, pulling his jumper back over his head. "Anything you say."

"Anything?"

"Right now," he said silkily, "anything."

She smiled. "The buttons."

He moved to the fastenings on his shirt. "As you wish." And in a moment his shirt was on the floor, leaving him naked from the waist up.

He brought his sultry gaze to her face. Her eyes were wide, and her lips parted. He could hear the raspy sound of her breath, in perfect time with the rise and fall of her chest.

She was aroused. Gloriously so, and it was all he could do not to drag her onto the bed then and there.

"Anything else?" he murmured.

Her lips moved, and her eyes flickered toward his breeches. She was too shy, he realized with delight, still too much of an innocent to order him to remove them.

"This?" he asked, hooking his thumb under the waistband.

She nodded.

He peeled off his breeches, his gaze never leaving her face. And he smiled—at the exact moment when her eyes widened.

She wanted to be a sophisticate, but she wasn't. Not yet.

"You're overdressed," he said softly, moving closer, closer, until his face was mere inches from hers. He placed two fingers under her chin and tipped her up, leaning down for a kiss as his other hand found the neckline of her dress and tugged it down.

She fell free, and he moved his hand to the warm skin of her back, pressing her against him until her breasts flattened against his chest. His fingers lightly traced the delicate indentation of her spine, settling at the small of her back, right where her dress rested loosely around her hips.

"I love you," he said, allowing his nose to settle against hers.

"I love you, too."

"I'm so glad," he said, smiling against her ear. "Because if you didn't, this would all be so very awkward."

She laughed, but there was a slightly hesitant quality to it. "Are you saying," she asked, "that all your other women loved you?"

He drew back, taking her face in his hands. "What I am saying," he said, making sure that she was looking deeply into his eyes as he found the words, "is that I never loved them. And I don't know that I could bear it, loving you the way I do, if you didn't return the feeling."

Hyacinth watched his face, losing herself in the deep blue of his eyes. She touched his forehead, then his hair, smoothing one golden lock aside before affectionately tucking it behind his ear.

Part of her wanted to stand like this forever, just looking at his face, memorizing every plane and shadow, from the full curve of his lower lip to the exact arch of his brows. She was going to make her life with this man, give him her love and bear him children, and she was filled with the most wonderful sense of anticipation, as if she were standing at the edge of something, about to embark on a spectacular adventure.

And it all started now.

She tilted her head, leaned in, and raised herself to her toes, just so she could place one kiss on his lips.

"I love you," she said.

"You do, don't you?" he murmured, and she realized that he was just as amazed by this miracle as she was.

"Sometimes I'm going to drive you mad," she warned.

His smile was as lopsided as his shrug. "I'll go to my club."

"And you'll do the same to me," she added.

"You can have tea with your mother." One of his hands found hers as the other moved around her waist, until they were held together almost as in a waltz. "And we'll have the most marvelous time later that night, kissing and begging each other's forgiveness."

"Gareth," she said, wondering if this ought to be a more serious conversation.

"No one said we had to spend every waking moment together," he said, "but at the end of the day"—he leaned down and kissed each of her eyebrows, in turn—"and most of the time during, there is no one I would rather see, no one whose voice I would rather hear, and no one whose mind I would rather explore."

He kissed her then. Once, slowly and deeply. "I love you, Hyacinth Bridgerton. And I always will."

"Oh, Gareth." She would have liked to have said something more eloquent, but his words would have to be enough for the both of them, because in that moment she was overcome, too full of emotion to do anything more than sigh his name.

And when he scooped her into his arms and carried her to his bed, all she could do was say, "Yes."

Her dress fell away before she reached the mattress, and by the time his body covered hers, they were skin against skin. There was something thrilling about being beneath him, feeling his power, his strength. He could dominate her if he so chose, hurt her even, and yet in his arms she became the most priceless of treasures.

His hands roamed her body, searing a path across her skin. Hyacinth felt every touch to the core of her being. He stroked her arm, and she felt it in her belly; he touched her shoulder, and she tingled in her toes.

He kissed her lips, and her heart sang.

He nudged her legs apart, and his body cradled itself next to hers. She could feel him, hard and insistent, but this time there was no fear, no apprehension. Just an overwhelming need to have him, to take him within her and wrap herself around him.

She wanted him. She wanted every inch of him, every bit of himself that he was able to give.

"Please," she begged, straining her hips toward his. "Please."

He didn't say anything, but she could hear his need in the roughness of his breath. He moved closer, positioning himself near her opening, and she arched herself closer to meet him.

She clutched at his shoulders, her fingers biting into his skin. There was something wild within her, something new and hungry. She needed him. She needed this. Now.

"Gareth," she gasped, desperately trying to press herself against him.

He moved a little, changing the angle, and he began to slide in.

It was what she wanted, what she'd expected, but still, the first touch of him was a shock. She stretched, she pulled, and there was even a little bit of pain, but still, it felt good, and it felt right, and she wanted more.

"Hy . . . Hy . . . Hy . . ." he was saying, his breath coming in harsh little bursts as he moved forward, each thrust filling her more completely. And then, finally, he was there, pressed so fully within her that his body met hers.

"Oh my God," she gasped, her head thrown back by the force of it all.

He moved, forward and back, the friction whipping her into insensibility. She reached, she clawed, she grasped— anything to bring him closer, anything to reach the tipping point.

She knew where she was going this time.

"Gareth!" she cried out, the noise captured by his mouth as he swooped in for a kiss.

Something within her began to tighten and coil, twisting and tensing until she was certain she'd shatter. And then, just when she couldn't possibly bear it for one second longer, it all reached its peak, and something burst within her, something amazing and true.

And as she arched, as her body threatened to shatter with the force of it, she felt Gareth grow frenzied and wild, and he buried his face in her neck as he let out a primal shout, pouring himself into her.

For a minute, maybe two, all they could do was

breathe. And then, finally, Gareth rolled off of her, still holding her close as he settled onto his side.

"Oh, my," she said, because it seemed to sum up everything she was feeling. "Oh, my."

"When are we getting married?" he asked, pulling her gently until they were curved like two spoons.

"Six weeks."

"Two," he said. "Whatever you have to tell your mother, I don't care. Get it changed to two, or I'll haul you off to Gretna."

Hyacinth nodded, snuggling herself against him, reveling in the feel of him behind her. "Two," she said, the word practically a sigh. "Maybe even just one."

"Even better," he agreed.

They lay together for several minutes, enjoying the silence, and then Hyacinth twisted in his arms, craning her neck so that she could see his face. "Were you going out to Clair House this evening?"

"You didn't know?"

She shook her head. "I didn't think you were going to go again."

"I promised you I would."

"Well, yes," she said, "but I thought you were lying, just to be nice."

Gareth swore under his breath. "You are going to be the death of me. I can't believe you didn't really mean for me to go."

"Of course I meant for you to go," she said. "I just didn't think you would." And then she sat up, so suddenly that the bed shook. Her eyes widened, and they took on a dangerous glow and sparkle. "Let's go. Tonight."

Easy answer. "No."

"Oh, please. Please. As a wedding gift to me."

"No," he said.

"I understand your reluctance—"

"No," he repeated, trying to ignore the sinking feeling in his stomach. The sinking feeling that he was going to relent. "No, I don't think you do."

"But really," she said, her eyes bright and convincing, "what do we have to lose? We're getting married in two weeks—"

He lifted one brow.

"Next week," she corrected. "Next week, I promise."

He pondered that. It *was* tempting.

"Please," she said. "You know you want to."

"Why," he wondered aloud, "do I feel like I am back at university, with the most degenerate of my friends convincing me that I must drink three more glasses of gin?"

"Why would you wish to be friends with a degenerate?" she asked. Then she smiled with wicked curiosity. "And did you do it?"

Gareth pondered the wisdom of answering that; truly he didn't wish for her to know the worst of his schoolboy excesses. But it would get her off the topic of the jewels, and—

"Let's go," she urged again. "*I* know you want to."

"I know what I want to do," he murmured, curving one hand around her bottom, "and it is not that."

"Don't you want the jewels?" she prodded.

He started to stroke her. "Mmm-hmmm."

"Gareth!" she yelped, trying to squirm away.

"Gareth yes, or Gareth—"

"No," she said firmly, somehow eluding him and wrig

gling to the other side of the bed. "Gareth, *no*. Not until we go to Clair House to look for the jewels."

"Good Lord," he muttered. "It's *Lysistrata*, come home to me in human form."

She tossed a triumphant smile over her shoulder as she pulled on her clothing.

He rose to his feet, knowing he was defeated. And besides, she did have a point. His main worry had been for her reputation; as long as she remained by his side, he was fully confident of his ability to keep her safe. If they were indeed going to marry in a week or two, their antics, if caught, would be brushed aside with a wink and a leer. But still, he felt like he ought to offer up at least a token of resistance, so he said, "Aren't you supposed to be tired after all this bedplay?"

"Positively energized."

He let out a weary breath. "This is the last time," he said sternly.

Her reply was immediate. "I promise."

He pulled on his clothing. "I mean it. If we do not find the jewels tonight, we don't go again until I inherit. Then you may tear the place apart, stone by stone if you like."

"It won't be necessary," she said. "We're going to find them tonight. I can feel it in my bones."

Gareth thought of several retorts, none of which was fit for her ears.

She looked down at herself with a rueful expression. "I'm not really dressed for it," she said, fingering the folds of her skirt. The fabric was dark, but it was not the boy's breeches she'd donned on their last two expeditions.

He didn't even bother to suggest that they postpone

their hunt. There was no point. Not when she was practically glowing with excitement.

And sure enough, she pointed one foot out from beneath the hem of her dress, saying, "But I am wearing my most comfortable footwear, and surely that is the most important thing."

"Surely."

She ignored his peevishness. "Are you ready?"

"As I'll ever be," he said with a patently false smile. But the truth was, she'd planted the seed of excitement within him, and he was already mapping his route in his mind. If he hadn't wanted to go, if he weren't convinced of his ability to keep her safe, he would have lashed her to the bed before allowing her to take one step out into the night.

He took her hand, lifted it to his mouth, kissed her. "Shall we be off?" he asked.

She nodded and tiptoed in front of him, out into the hall. "We're going to find them," she said softly. "I know we will."

Chapter 21

"We're not going to find them."

Hyacinth had her hands planted on her hips as she surveyed the baroness's bedchamber. They had spent fifteen minutes getting to Clair House, five sneaking in through the faulty window and creeping up to the bedchamber, and the last ten searching every last nook and corner.

The jewels were nowhere.

It was not like Hyacinth to admit defeat. In fact, it was so wholly out of character that the words, "We're not going to find them," had come out sounding more surprised than anything else.

It hadn't occurred to her that they might not find the jewels. She'd imagined the scene a hundred times in her head, she'd plotted and planned, she'd thought the entire scheme to death, and not once had she ever pictured herself coming up empty-handed.

She felt as if she'd slammed into a brick wall.

Maybe she had been foolishly optimistic. Maybe she had just been blind. But this time, she'd been wrong.

"Do you give up?" Gareth asked, looking up at her. He was crouching next to the bed, feeling for panels in the wall behind the headboard. And he sounded . . . not pleased, exactly, but rather somewhat *done*, if that made any sense.

He'd known that they weren't going to find anything. Or if he hadn't known it, he had been almost sure of it. And he'd come tonight mostly just to humor her. Hyacinth decided she loved him all the more for that.

But now, his expression, his aspect, everything in his voice seemed to say one thing—*We tried, we lost, can we please just move on*?

There was no satisfied smirk, no "I told you so," just a flat, matter-of-fact stare, with perhaps the barest hint of disappointment, as if a tiny corner of him had been hoping to be proven wrong.

"Hyacinth?" Gareth said, when she didn't reply.

"I . . . Well . . ." She didn't know what to say.

"We haven't much time," he cut in, his face taking on a steely expression. Clearly, her time for reflection was over. He rose to his feet, brushing his hands against each other to rid them of dust. The baroness's bedchamber had been shut off, and it didn't appear to be on a regular cleaning schedule. "Tonight is the baron's monthly meeting with his hound-breeding club."

"Hound-breeding?" Hyacinth echoed. "In London?"

"They meet on the last Tuesday of the month without fail," Gareth explained. "They have been doing it for years. To keep abreast of pertinent knowledge while they're in London."

"Does pertinent knowledge change very often?" Hy

acinth asked. It was just the sort of random tidbit of information that always interested her.

"I have no idea," Gareth replied briskly. "It's probably just an excuse to get together and drink. The meetings always end at eleven, and then they spend about two hours in social discourse. Which means the baron will be home"—he pulled out his pocket watch and swore under his breath—"now."

Hyacinth nodded glumly. "I give up," she said. "I don't think I've ever uttered those words while not under duress, but I give up."

Gareth chucked her softly under her chin. "It's not the end of the world, Hy. And just think, you may resume your mission once the baron finally kicks off, and I inherit the house. Which," he added thoughtfully, "I actually have some right to." He shook his head. "Imagine that."

"Do you think Isabella meant for anyone to find them?" she asked.

"I don't know," Gareth replied. "One would think that if she had, she might have chosen a more accessible language for her final hint than Slovene."

"We should go," Hyacinth said, sighing. "I need to return home in any case. If I'm to pester my mother for a change in the wedding date, I want to do it now, while she's sleepy and easy to sway."

Gareth looked at her over his shoulder as he placed his hand on the doorknob. "You *are* diabolical."

"You didn't believe it before?"

He smiled, then gave her a nod when it was safe to creep out into the hall. Together they moved down the stairs to the drawing room with the faulty window. Swiftly and silently, they slipped outside and hopped down to the alley below.

Gareth walked in front, stopping at the alley's end and stretching one arm behind him to keep Hyacinth at a distance while he peered out onto Dover Street.

"Let's go," he whispered, jerking his head toward the street. They had come over in a hansom cab—Gareth's apartments were not quite close enough to walk—and they'd left it waiting two intersections away. It wasn't really necessary to ride back to Hyacinth's house, which was just on the other side of Mayfair, but Gareth had decided that as long as they had the cab, they might as well make use of it. There was a good spot where they could be let out, right around the corner from Number Five, that was set back in shadows and with very few windows looking out upon it.

"This way," Gareth said, taking Hyacinth's hand and tugging her along. "Come on, we can—"

He stopped, stumbled. Hyacinth had halted in her tracks.

"What is it?" he hissed, turning to look at her.

But she wasn't looking at him. Instead, her eyes were focused on something—someone—to the right.

The baron.

Gareth froze. Lord St. Clair—his father, his uncle, whatever he should call him—was standing at the top of the steps leading to Clair House. His key was in his hand, and he had obviously spotted them just as he was about to enter the building.

"This is interesting," the baron said. His eyes glittered.

Gareth felt his chest puff out, some sort of instinctive

show of bravado as he pushed Hyacinth partly behind him. "Sir," he said. It was all he'd ever called the man, and some habits were hard to break.

"Imagine my curiosity," the baron murmured. "This is the second time I have run across you here in the middle of the night."

Gareth said nothing.

"And now"—Lord St. Clair motioned to Hyacinth—"you have brought your lovely betrothed with you. Unorthodox, I must say. Does her family know she is running about after midnight?"

"What do you want?" Gareth asked in a hard voice.

But the baron only chuckled. "I believe the more pertinent question is what do *you* want? Unless you intend to attempt to convince me that you are just here for the fresh night air."

Gareth stared at him, looking for signs of resemblance. They were all there—the nose, the eyes, the way they held their shoulders. It was why Gareth had never, until that fateful day in the baron's office, thought he might be a bastard. He'd been so baffled as a child; his father had treated him with such contempt. Once he'd grown old enough to understand a bit of what went on between men and women, he had wondered about it—his mother's infidelity would seem a likely explanation for his father's behavior toward him.

But he'd dismissed the notion every time. There was that damned St. Clair nose, right in the middle of his face. And then the baron had looked him in the eye and said that he was not his, that he couldn't be, that the nose was mere coincidence.

Gareth had believed him. The baron was many things,

but he was not stupid, and he certainly knew how to count to nine.

Neither of them had dreamed that the nose might be something more than coincidence, that Gareth might be a St. Clair, after all.

He tried to remember—had the baron loved his brother? Had Richard and Edward St. Clair been close? Gareth couldn't recall them in each other's company, but then again, he'd been banished to the nursery most of the time, anyway.

"Well?" the baron demanded. "What do you have to say for yourself?"

And there it was, on the tip of his tongue. Gareth looked him in the eye—the man who had, for so many years, been the ruling force in his life—and he almost said—*Nothing at all, Uncle Richard.*

It would have been the best kind of direct hit, a complete surprise, designed to stagger and strike.

It would have been worth it just for the shock on the baron's face.

It would have been perfect.

Except that Gareth didn't want to do it. He didn't need to.

And *that* took his breath away.

Before, he would have tried to guess how his father might feel. Would he be relieved to know that the barony would go to a true St. Clair, or would he instead be enraged, devastated by the knowledge that he had been cuckolded by his own brother?

Before, Gareth would have weighed his options, balanced them, then gone with his instincts and tried to deliver the most crushing blow.

But now . . .

He didn't care.

He would never love the man. Hell, he would never even like him. But for the first time in his life, he was reaching a point where it just didn't matter.

And he was stunned by how good that felt.

He took Hyacinth's hand, interlocked their fingers. "We're just out for a stroll," he said smoothly. It was a patently ridiculous statement, but Gareth delivered it with his usual *savoir-faire*, in the same tone that he always used with the baron. "Come along, Miss Bridgerton," he added, turning his body to lead her down the street.

But Hyacinth didn't move. Gareth turned to look at her, and she seemed frozen into place. She looked at him with questioning eyes, and he knew she couldn't believe that he'd held silent.

Gareth looked at her, then he looked at Lord St. Clair, and then he looked within himself. And he realized that while his never-ending war with the baron might not matter, the truth did. Not because it had the power to wound, just because it was the truth, and it had to be told.

It was the secret that had defined both of their lives for so long. And it was time that they were both set free.

"I have to tell you something," Gareth said, looking the baron in the eye. It wasn't easy, being this direct. He had no experience speaking to this man without malice. He felt strange, stripped bare.

Lord St. Clair said nothing, but his expression changed slightly, became more watchful.

"I am in possession of Grandmother St. Clair's diary," Gareth said. At the baron's startled expression, he added,

"Caroline found it among George's effects with a note instructing her to give it to me."

"He did not know that you are not her grandson," the baron said sharply.

Gareth opened his mouth to retort, "*But I was*," but he managed to bite off the comment. He would do this right. He had to do this right. Hyacinth was at his side, and suddenly his angry ways seemed callow, immature. He didn't want her to see him like that. He didn't want to *be* like that.

"Miss Bridgerton has some knowledge of Italian," Gareth continued, keeping his voice even. "She has assisted me in its translation."

The baron looked at Hyacinth, his piercing eyes studying her for a moment before turning back to Gareth.

"Isabella knew who my father was," Gareth said softly. "It was Uncle Edward."

The baron said nothing, not a word. Except for the slight parting of his lips, he was so still that Gareth wondered if he was even breathing.

Had he known? Had he suspected?

As Gareth and Hyacinth stood in silence, the baron turned and looked down the street, his eyes settling on some far-off point. When he turned back, he was as white as a sheet.

He cleared his throat and nodded. Just once, as an acknowledgment. "You should marry that girl," he said, motioning with his head toward Hyacinth. "The Lord knows you're going to need her dowry."

And then he walked up the rest of the steps, let himself into his home, and shut the door.

"That's *all*?" Hyacinth said, after a moment of jus

standing there with her mouth agape. "That's all he's going to *say*?"

Gareth felt himself begin to shake. It was laughter, he realized, almost as an aside. He was laughing.

"He can't do that," Hyacinth protested, her eyes flashing with indignation. "You just revealed the biggest secret of both of your lives, and all he does is—are you *laughing*?"

Gareth shook his head, even though it was clear that he was.

"What's so funny?" Hyacinth asked suspiciously.

And her expression was so . . . *her*. It made him laugh even harder.

"What's so funny?" she asked again, except this time she looked as if she might smile, too. "*Gareth*," she persisted, tugging on his sleeve. "Tell me."

He shrugged helplessly. "I'm happy," he said, and he realized it was true. He'd enjoyed himself in his life, and he'd certainly had many happy moments, but it had been so long since he'd felt this—happiness, complete and whole. He'd almost forgotten the sensation.

She placed her hand abruptly on his brow. "Are you feverish?" she muttered.

"I'm fine." He pulled her into his arms. "I'm better than fine."

"Gareth!" she gasped, ducking away as he swooped down for a kiss. "Are you mad? We're in the middle of Dover Street, and it's—"

He cut her off with a kiss.

"It's the middle of the night," she spluttered.

He grinned devilishly. "But I'm going to marry you next week, remember?"

"Yes, but—"

"Speaking of which," he murmured.

Hyacinth's mouth fell open as he dropped down to one knee. "What are you doing?" she squeaked, frantically looking this way and that. Lord St. Clair was surely peeking out at them, and heaven only knew who else was, too. "Someone will see," she whispered.

He seemed unconcerned. "People will say we're in love."

"I—" Good heavens, but how did a woman argue against that?

"Hyacinth Bridgerton," he said, taking her hand in his, "will you marry me?"

She blinked in confusion. "I already said I would."

"Yes, but as you said, I did not ask you for the right reasons. They were mostly the right reasons, but not all."

"I—I—" She was stumbling on the words, choking on the emotion.

He was staring up at her, his eyes glowing clear and blue in the dim light of the streetlamps. "I am asking you to marry me because I love you," he said, "because I cannot imagine living my life without you. I want to see your face in the morning, and then at night, and a hundred times in between. I want to grow old with you, I want to laugh with you, and I want to sigh to my friends about how managing you are, all the while secretly knowing I am the luckiest man in town."

"What?" she demanded.

He shrugged. "A man's got to keep up appearances. I'd be universally detested if everyone realizes how perfect you are."

"Oh." Again, how could a woman argue with *that*?

And then his eyes grew serious. "I want you to be my family. I want you to be my wife."

She stared down at him. He was gazing at her with such obvious love and devotion, she hardly knew what to do. It seemed to surround her, embrace her, and she knew that *this* was poetry, this was music.

This was love.

He smiled up at her, and all she could do was smile back, dimly aware that her cheeks were growing wet.

"Hyacinth," he said. "Hyacinth."

And she nodded. Or at least she thought she did.

He squeezed her hands as he rose to his feet. "I never thought I'd have to say this to you, of all people, but for God's sake, *say* something, woman!"

"Yes," she said. And she threw herself into his arms. "Yes!"

Epilogue

A few moments to bring us up to date . . .

Four days after the end of our tale, Gareth called upon Lord Wrotham, only to find that the earl in no way felt the betrothal was binding, especially after he related Lady Bridgerton's promise to take one of the younger Wrotham daughters under her wing the following season.

Four days after that, Gareth was informed by Lady Bridgerton, in no uncertain manner, that her youngest child would not be married in haste, and he was forced to wait two months before wedding Hyacinth in an elaborate yet tasteful ceremony at St. George's, in London.

Eleven months after that, Hyacinth gave birth to a healthy baby boy, christened George.

Two years after that, they were blessed with a daughter, christened Isabella.

Four years after that, Lord St. Clair was thrown from his horse during a fox hunt and instantly killed. Gareth assumed the title, and he and Hyacinth moved to their new town residence at Clair House.

That was six years ago. She has been looking for the jewels ever since . . .

* * *

"Haven't you already searched this room?"

Hyacinth looked up from her position on the floor of the baroness's washroom. Gareth was standing in the doorway, gazing down at her with an indulgent expression.

"Not for at least a month," she replied, testing the baseboards for loose sections—as if she hadn't yanked and prodded them countless times before.

"Darling," Gareth said, and she knew from his tone what he was thinking.

She gave him a pointed look. "Don't."

"Darling," he said again.

"No." She turned back to the baseboards. "I don't want to hear it. If it takes until the day I die, I will find these bloody jewels."

"Hyacinth."

She ignored him, pressing along the seam where the baseboard met the floor.

Gareth watched her for several seconds before remarking, "I'm quite certain you've done that before."

She spared him only the briefest of glances before rising to inspect the window frame.

"Hyacinth," he said.

She turned so suddenly that she almost lost her balance. "The note said 'Cleanliness is next to Godliness, and the Kingdom of Heaven is rich indeed.'"

"In Slovene," he said wryly.

"Three Slovenians," she reminded him. "Three Slovenians read the clue, and they all reached the same translation."

And it certainly hadn't been easy to find three Slovenians.

"Hyacinth," Gareth said, as if he hadn't already uttered her name twice . . . and countless times before that, always in the same slightly resigned tone.

"It has to be here," she said. "It has to."

Gareth shrugged. "Very well," he said, "but Isabella has translated a passage from the Italian, and she wishes for you to check her work."

Hyacinth paused, sighed, then lifted her fingers from the windowsill. At the age of eight, her daughter had announced that she wished to learn the language of her namesake, and Hyacinth and Gareth had hired a tutor to offer instruction three mornings each week. Within a year, Isabella's fluency had outstripped her mother's, and Hyacinth was forced to employ the tutor for herself the other two mornings just to keep up.

"Why is it you've never studied Italian?" she asked, as Gareth led her through the bedroom and into the hallway.

"I've no head for languages," he said blithely, "and no need for it, with my two ladies at my side."

Hyacinth rolled her eyes. "I'm not going to tell you any more naughty words," she warned.

He chuckled. "Then I'm not going to slip Signorina Orsini any more pound notes with instructions to *teach* you the naughty words."

Hyacinth turned to him in horror. "You didn't!"

"I did."

Her lips pursed. "And you don't even look the least bit remorseful about it."

"Remorseful?" He chuckled, deep in his throat, and then leaned down to press his lips against her ear. There were a few words of Italian he bothered to commit to memory; he whispered every one of them to her.

"Gareth!" she squeaked.

"Gareth, yes? Or Gareth, no?"

She sighed. She couldn't help it. "Gareth, *more*."

Isabella St. Clair tapped her pencil against the side of her head as she regarded the words she'd recently written. It was a challenge, translating from one language to another. The literal meaning never read quite right, so one had to choose one's idioms with the utmost of care. But this—she glanced over at the open page in Galileo's *Discorso intorno alle cose che stanno, in sù l'acqua, ò che in quella si muovono*—this was perfect.

Perfect perfect perfect.

Her three favorite words.

She glanced toward the door, waiting for her mother to appear. Isabella loved translating scientific texts because her mother always seemed to stumble on the technical words, and it was, of course, always good fun to watch her mum pretend that she actually knew more Italian than her daughter.

Not that Isabella was mean-spirited. She pursed her lips, considering that. She wasn't mean-spirited; the only person she adored more than her mother was her great-grandmother Danbury, who, although confined to a wheeled chair, still managed to wield her cane with almost as much accuracy as her tongue.

Isabella smiled. When she grew up, she wanted to be first exactly like her mother, and then, when she was through with that, just like Great-Grandmama.

She sighed. It would be a marvelous life.

But what was *taking* so long? It had been ages since she'd sent her father down—and it should be added that she loved him with equal fervor; it was just that he was merely a man, and she couldn't very well aspire to grow to be *him*.

She grimaced. Her mother and father were probably giggling and whispering and ducking into a darkened corner. Good heavens. It was downright embarrassing.

Isabella stood, resigning herself to a long wait. She might as well use the washroom. Carefully setting her pencil down, she glanced one last time at the door and crossed the room to the nursery washroom. Tucked high in the eaves of the old mansion, it was, somewhat unexpectedly, her favorite room in the house. Someone in years gone past had obviously taken a liking to the little room, and it had been tiled rather festively in what she could only assume was some sort of Eastern fashion. There were lovely blues and shimmering aquas and yellows that were streaks of pure sunshine.

If it had been big enough for Isabella to drag in a bed and call it her chamber, she would have done. As it was, she thought it was particularly amusing that the loveliest room in the house (in her opinion, at least) was the most humble.

The nursery washroom? Only the servants' quarters were considered of less prestige.

Isabella did her business, tucked the chamber pot back in the corner, and headed back for the door. But before she got there, something caught her eye.

A crack. Between two of the tiles.

"That wasn't there before," Isabella murmured.

She crouched, then finally lowered herself to her bottom so that she could inspect the crack, which ran from the floor to the top of the first tile, about six inches up. It wasn't the sort of thing most people would notice, but Isabella was not most people. She noticed everything.

And this was something new.

Frustrated with her inability to get really close, she shifted to her forearms and knees, then laid her cheek against the floor.

"Hmmm." She poked the tile to the right of the crack, then the left. "Hmmm."

Why would a crack suddenly open up in her bathroom wall? Surely Clair House, which was well over a hundred years old, was done with its shifting and settling. And while she'd heard that there were far distant areas where the earth shifted and shook, it didn't happen anyplace as civilized as *London*.

Had she kicked the wall without thinking? Dropped something?

She poked again. And again.

She drew back her arm, preparing to pound a little harder, but then stopped. Her mother's bathroom was directly below. If she made a terrible racket, Mummy was sure to come up and demand to know what she was doing. And although she'd sent her father down to retrieve her mother eons earlier, it was quite a good bet that Mummy was still in her washroom.

And when Mummy went into her washroom—Well, either she was out in a minute, or she was there for an hour. It was the strangest thing.

So Isabella did not want to make a lot of noise. Surely her parents would frown upon her taking the house apart.

But perhaps a little tap . . .

She did a little nursery rhyme to decide which tile to attack, chose the one to the left, and hit it a little harder. Nothing happened.

She stuck her fingernail at the edge of the crack and dug it in. A tiny piece of plaster lodged under her nail.

"Hmmm." Perhaps she could extend the crack . . .

She glanced over at her vanity table until her eyes fell upon a silver comb. That might work. She grabbed it and carefully positioned the last tooth near the edge of the crack. And then, with precise movements, she drew it back and tapped it against the plaster that ran between the tiles.

The crack snaked upward! Right before her eyes!

She did it again, this time positioning her comb over the left tile. Nothing. She tried it over the right.

And then harder.

Isabella gasped as the crack literally shot through the plaster, until it ran all the way along the top of the tile. And then she did it a few more times until it ran down the other side.

With bated breath, she dug her nails in on either side of the tile and pulled. She shifted it back and forth, shimmying and jimmying, prying with all her might.

And then, with a creak and a groan that reminded her of the way her great-grandmother moved when she managed to hoist herself from her wheeled chair into her bed, the tile gave way.

Isabella set it down carefully, then peered at what was left. Where there should have been nothing but wall, there was a little compartment, just a few inches square. Isabella reached in, pinching her fingers together to make her hand long and skinny.

She felt something soft. Like velvet.

She pulled it out. It was a little bag, held together with a soft, silky cord.

Isabella straightened quickly, crossing her legs so that she was sitting Indian style. She slid one finger inside the bag, widening the mouth, which had been pulled tight.

And then, with her right hand, she upended it, sliding the contents into her left.

"*Oh my G—*"

Isabella quickly swallowed her shriek. A veritable pool of diamonds had showered into her hand.

It was a necklace. And a bracelet. And while she did not think of herself as the sort of girl who lost her mind over baubles and clothes, *OH MY GOD* these were the most beautiful things she had ever seen.

"Isabella?"

Her mother. Oh, no. Oh no oh no oh no.

"Isabella? Where are you?"

"In—" She stopped to clear her throat; her voice had come out like a squeak. "Just in the washroom, Mummy. I'll be out in a moment."

What should she do? What should she do?

Oh, very well, she knew what she should do. But what did she *want* to do?

"Is this your translation here on the table?" came her mother's voice.

"Er, yes!" She coughed. "It's from Galileo. The original is right next to it."

"Oh." Her mother paused. Her voice sounded funny. "Why did you—Never mind."

Isabella looked frantically at the jewels. She had only a moment to decide.

"Isabella!" her mother called. "Did you remember to do your sums this morning? You're starting dancing lessons this afternoon. Did you recall?"

Dancing lessons? Isabella's face twisted, rather as if she'd swallowed lye.

"Monsieur Larouche will be here at two. Promptly. So you will need . . ."

Isabella stared at the diamonds. Hard. So hard that her peripheral vision slipped away, and the noise around her faded into nothing. Gone were the sounds of the street floating through the open window. Gone was her mother's voice, droning on about dancing lessons and the importance of punctuality. Gone was everything but the blood rushing past her ears and the quick, uneven sound of her own breath.

Isabella looked down at the diamonds.

And then she smiled.

And put them back.

Dear Reader,

Have you ever wondered what happened to your favorite characters after you closed the final page? Wanted just a little bit more of a favorite novel? I have, and if the questions from my readers are any indication, I'm not the only one. So after countless requests from Bridgerton fans, I decided to try something a little different, and I wrote a "2nd Epilogue" for each of the novels. These are the stories that come after the stories.

At first, the Bridgerton 2nd Epilogues were available exclusively online; later they were published (along with a novella about Violet Bridgerton) in a collection called **The Bridgertons: Happily Ever After.** Now, for the first time, each 2nd Epilogue is being included with the novel it follows. I hope you enjoy Gareth and Hyacinth as they continue their journey.

Warmly,
Julia Quinn

It's in His Kiss:
The 2nd Epilogue

847, and all has come full circle. Truly.

Immph.

It was official, then.

She had become her mother.

Hyacinth St. Clair fought the urge to bury her
ce in her hands as she sat on the cushioned
ench at Mme. Langlois, Dressmaker, by far the
ost fashionable modiste in all London.

She counted to ten, in three languages, and
en, just for good measure, swallowed and let
it an exhale. Because, really, it would not do to
se her temper in such a public setting.

No matter how desperately she wanted to *throt-*
her daughter.

"Mummy." Isabella poked her head out from
hind the curtain. Hyacinth noted that the word
d been a statement, not a question.

"Yes?" she returned, affixing onto her face an
pression of such placid serenity she might have

qualified for one of those pietà paintings they ha
seen when last they'd traveled to Rome.

"Not the pink."

Hyacinth waved a hand. Anything to refrai
from speaking.

"Not the purple, either."

"I don't believe I suggested purple," Hyacint
murmured.

"The blue's not right, and nor is the red, an
frankly, I just don't understand this insistenc
society seems to have upon white, and well, if
might express my opinion—"

Hyacinth felt herself slump. Who knew motl
erhood could be so tiring? And really, shouldr
she be *used* to this by now?

"—a girl really ought to wear the color that mo
complements her complexion, and not what son
overimportant ninny at Almack's deems fashio
able."

"I agree wholeheartedly," Hyacinth said.

"You do?" Isabella's face lit up, and Hyacintl
breath positively caught, because she looked s
like her own mother in that moment it was almo
eerie.

"Yes," Hyacinth said, "but you're still getting
least one in white."

"But—"

"No buts!"

"But—"

"Isabella."

Isabella muttered something in Italian.

"I heard that," Hyacinth said sharply.

Isabella smiled, a curve of lips so sweet th
only her own mother (certainly *not* her fathe
who freely admitted himself wound around h

nger) would recognize the deviousness under-
eath. "But did you understand it?" she asked,
linking three times in rapid succession.

And because Hyacinth knew that she would be
apped by her lie, she gritted her teeth and told
ie truth. "No."

"I didn't think so," Isabella said. "But if you're
iterested, what I said was—"

"Not—" Hyacinth stopped, forcing her voice to
lower volume; panic at what Isabella might say
ad caused her outburst to come out overly loud.
ie cleared her throat. "Not now. Not here," she
lded meaningfully. Good heavens, her daugh-
r had no sense of propriety. She had such opin-
ns, and while Hyacinth was always in favor of a
male with opinions, she was even more in favor
a female who knew *when* to share such opin-
ns.

Isabella stepped out of her dressing room, clad
a lovely gown of white with sage green trim-
ing that Hyacinth knew she'd turn her nose up
, and sat beside her on the bench. "What are you
hispering about?" she asked.

"I wasn't whispering," Hyacinth said.

"Your lips were moving."

"Were they?"

"They were," Isabella confirmed.

"If you must know, I was sending off an apol-
;y to your grandmother."

"Grandmama Violet?" Isabella asked, looking
ound. "Is she here?"

"No, but I thought she was deserving of my re-
orse, nonetheless."

Isabella blinked and cocked her head to the
le in question. "Why?"

"All those times," Hyacinth said, hating how
tired her voice sounded. "All those times she said
to me, 'I hope you have a child *just like you* . . .'"

"And you do," Isabella said, surprising her with
a light kiss to the cheek. "Isn't it just delightful?"

Hyacinth looked at her daughter. Isabella was
nineteen. She'd made her debut the year before, the
grand success. She was, Hyacinth thought rather
objectively, far prettier than she herself had ever
been. Her hair was a breathtaking strawberry
blond, a throwback to some long-forgotten ances-
tor on heaven knew which side of the family. And
the curls—oh, my, they were the bane of Isabella's existence, but Hyacinth adored them. When
Isabella had been a toddler, they'd bounced in
perfect little ringlets, completely untamable and
always delightful.

And now . . . Sometimes Hyacinth looked at
her and saw the woman she'd become, and she
couldn't even breathe, so powerful was the emotion squeezing across her chest. It was a love she
couldn't have imagined, so fierce and so tender,
and yet at the same time the girl drove her positively batty.

Right now, for example.

Isabella was smiling innocently at her. Too innocently, truth be told, and then she looked down
at the slightly poufy skirt on the dress Hyacinth
loved (and Isabella would hate) and picked absently at the green ribbon trimmings.

"Mummy?" she said.

It was a question this time, not a statement,
which meant that Isabella wanted something
and (for a change) wasn't quite certain how to go
about getting it.

"Do you think this year—"

"No," Hyacinth said. And this time she really did send up a silent apology to her mother. Good heavens, was this what Violet had gone through? *Eight* times?

"You don't even know what I was going to ask."

"Of course I know what you were going to ask. When will you learn that I *always* know?"

"Now that is not true."

"It's more true than it is untrue."

"You can be quite supercilious, did you know that?"

Hyacinth shrugged. "I'm your mother."

Isabella's lips clamped into a line, and Hyacinth enjoyed a full four seconds of peace before she asked, "But this year, do you think we can—"

"We are not traveling."

Isabella's lips parted with surprise. Hyacinth fought the urge to let out a triumphal shout.

"How did you kn—"

Hyacinth patted her daughter's hand. "I told you, I always know. And much as I'm sure we would all enjoy a bit of travel, we will remain in London for the season, and you, my girl, will smile and dance and look for a husband."

Cue the bit about becoming her mother.

Hyacinth sighed. Violet Bridgerton was probably laughing about this, this very minute. In fact, she'd been laughing about it for nineteen years.

"Just like you," Violet liked to say, grinning at Hyacinth as she tousled Isabella's curls. "Just like you."

"Just like you, Mother," Hyacinth murmured with a smile, picturing Violet's face in her mind. "And now I'm just like you."

*An hour or so later. Gareth, too, has grown and
changed, although, we soon shall see, not in
any of the ways that matter . . .*

Gareth St. Clair leaned back in his chair, paus
ing to savor his brandy as he glanced around hi
office. There really was a remarkable sense o
satisfaction in a job well-done and completed o
time. It wasn't a sensation he'd been used to in hi
youth, but it was something he'd come to enjoy o
a near daily basis now.

It had taken several years to restore the St. Clai
fortunes to a respectable level. His father—he'
never quite got 'round to calling him anythin
else—had stopped his systematic plundering an
eased into a vague sort of neglect once he learne
the truth about Gareth's birth. So Gareth sup
posed it could have been a great deal worse.

But when Gareth had assumed the title, h
discovered that he'd inherited debts, mortgage
and houses that had been emptied of almost a
valuables. Hyacinth's dowry, which had increase
with prudent investments upon their marriag
went a long way toward fixing the situation, bu
still, Gareth had had to work harder and wit
more diligence than he'd ever dreamed possib
to wrench his family out of debt.

The funny thing was, he'd enjoyed it.

Who would have thought that he, of all peopl
would find such satisfaction in hard work? H
desk was spotless, his ledgers neat and tidy, an
he could put his fingers on any important doc
ment in under a minute. His accounts alway
summed properly, his properties were thrivin
and his tenants were healthy and prosperous.

He took another sip of his drink, letting the mellow fire roll down his throat. Heaven.

Life was perfect. Truly. Perfect.

George was finishing up at Cambridge, Isabella would surely choose a husband this year, and Hyacinth . . .

He chuckled. Hyacinth was still Hyacinth. She'd become a bit more sedate with age, or maybe it was just that motherhood had smoothed off her rough edges, but she was still the same outspoken, delightful, perfectly wonderful Hyacinth.

She drove him crazy half the time, but it was a nice sort of crazy, and even though he sometimes sighed to his friends and nodded tiredly when they all complained about their wives, secretly he knew he was the luckiest man in London. Hell, England even. The world.

He set his drink down, then tapped his fingers against the elegantly wrapped box sitting on the corner of his desk. He'd purchased it that morning at Mme. LaFleur, the dress shop he knew Hyacinth did not frequent, in order to spare her the embarrassment of having to deal with salespeople who knew every piece of lingerie in her wardrobe.

French silk, Belgian lace.

He smiled. Just a little bit of French silk, trimmed with a minuscule amount of Belgian lace.

It would look heavenly on her.

What there was of it.

He sat back in his chair, savoring the daydream. It was going to be a long, lovely night. Maybe even . . .

His eyebrows rose as he tried to remember his wife's schedule for the day. Maybe even a long, lovely afternoon. When *was* she due home? And would she have either of the children with her?

He closed his eyes, picturing her in various states of undress, followed by various interesting poses, followed by various *fascinating* activities.

He groaned. She was going to have to return home *very* soon, because his imagination was far too active not to be satisfied, and—

"*Gareth!*"

Not the most mellifluous of tones. The lovely erotic haze floating about his head disappeared entirely. Well, almost entirely. Hyacinth might not have looked the least bit inclined for a bit of afternoon sport as she stood in the doorway, her eyes narrowed and jaw clenched, but she was *there*, and that was half the battle.

"Shut the door," he murmured, rising to his feet.

"Do you know what your daughter did?"

"Your daughter, you mean?"

"Our daughter," she ground out. But she shut the door.

"Do I want to know?"

"*Gareth!*"

"Very well," he sighed, followed by a dutiful "What did she do?"

He'd had this conversation before, of course. Countless times. The answer usually had something to do with something involving marriage and Isabella's somewhat unconventional views of the subject. And of course, Hyacinth's frustration with the whole situation.

It rarely varied.

"Well, it wasn't so much what she did," Hyacinth said.

He hid his smile. This was also not unexpected. "It's more what she won't do."

"Jump to your bidding?"

"*Gareth.*"

He halved the distance between them. "Aren't enough?"

"I beg your pardon?"

He reached out, tugged at her hand, pulled her ently against him. "I always jump to your bid-ing," he murmured.

She recognized the look in his eye. "Now?" he twisted around until she could see the closed oor. "Isabella is upstairs."

"She won't hear."

"But she could—"

His lips found her neck. "There's a lock on the oor."

"But she'll know—"

He started working on the buttons of her frock. e was *very* good at buttons. "She's a smart girl," e said, stepping back to enjoy his handiwork as e fabric fell away. He *loved* when his wife didn't ear a chemise.

"Gareth!"

He leaned down and took one rosy-tipped east into his mouth before she could object.

"Oh, Gareth!" And her knees went weak. Just ough for him to scoop her up and take her to e sofa. The one with the extra-deep cushions.

"More?"

"God, yes," she groaned.

He slid his hand under her skirt until he could kle her senseless. "Such token resistance," he urmured. "Admit it. You always want me."

"Twenty years of marriage isn't admissio enough?"

"Twenty-two years, and I want to hear it fror your lips."

She moaned when he slipped a finger insid of her. "Almost always," she conceded. "I almo: always want you."

He sighed for dramatic effect, even as he smile into her neck. "I shall have to work harder, then.

He looked up at her. She was gazing dow at him with an arch expression, clearly over he fleeting attempt at uprightness and respectabilit

"Much harder," she agreed. "And a bit faste too, while you're at it."

He laughed out loud at that.

"Gareth!" Hyacinth might be a wanton in pr vate, but she was always aware of the servants.

"Don't worry," he said with a smile. "I'll be quie I'll be very, very quiet." With one easy movemer he bunched her skirts well above her waist and sl down until his head was between her legs. "It's yo my darling, who will have to control your volume

"Oh. Oh. Oh . . ."

"More?"

"Definitely more."

He licked her then. She tasted like heaven. Ar when she squirmed, it was always a treat.

"Oh my heavens. Oh my . . . Oh my . . ."

He smiled against her, then swirled a circle her until she let out a quiet little shriek. He love doing this to her, loved bringing her, his capat and articulate wife, to senseless abandon.

Twenty-two years. Who would have thoug that after twenty-two years he'd still want th

ne woman, this one woman only, and this one
roman so intensely?

"Oh, Gareth," she was panting. "Oh, Gareth . . .
1ore, Gareth . . ."

He redoubled his efforts. She was close. He
new her so well, knew the curve and shape of her
ody, the way she moved when she was aroused,
1e way she breathed when she wanted him. She
as close.

And then she was gone, arching and gasping
ntil her body went limp.

He chuckled to himself as she batted him away.
1e always did that when she was done, saying
1e couldn't bear one more touch, that she'd surely
e if she wasn't given the chance to float down to
ormalcy.

He moved, curling against her body until he
uld see her face. "That was nice," she said.

He lifted a brow. "Nice?"

"Very nice."

"Nice enough to reciprocate?"

Her lips curved. "Oh, I don't know if it was *that*
ce."

His hand went to his trousers. "I shall have to
fer a repeat engagement, then."

Her lips parted in surprise.

"A variation on a theme, if you will."

She twisted her neck to look down. "What are
u doing?"

He grinned lasciviously. "Enjoying the fruits of
y labors." And then she gasped as he slid inside of
r, and he gasped from the sheer pleasure of it all,
d then he thought how very much he loved her.

And then he thought nothing much at all.

*The following day. We didn't really think
that Hyacinth would give up, did we?*

Late afternoon found Hyacinth back at h
second favorite pastime. Although *favorite* didr
seem quite the right adjective, nor was *pastime* th
correct noun. *Compulsion* probably fit the descri]
tion better, as did *miserable*, or perhaps *unrelentin*
Wretched?

Inevitable.

She sighed. Definitely inevitable. An inevitab
compulsion.

How long had she lived in this house? Fiftee
years?

Fifteen years. Fifteen years and a few montl
atop that, and she was still searching for tho.
bloody jewels.

One would think she'd have given up by no
Certainly, anyone else would have given up l
now. She was, she had to admit, the most ridic
lously stubborn person of her own acquaintanc

Except, perhaps, her own daughter. Hyacin
had never told Isabella about the jewels, if on
because she knew that Isabella would join in tl
search with an unhealthy fervor to rival her ow
She hadn't told her son, George, either, because
would tell Isabella. And Hyacinth would nev
get that girl married off if she thought there wa:
fortune in jewels to be found in her home.

Not that Isabella would want the jewels
fortune's sake. Hyacinth knew her daughter w
enough to realize that in some matters—possil
most—Isabella was exactly like her. And Hy
cinth's search for the jewels had never been abc
the money they might bring. Oh, she freely adn

1 that she and Gareth could use the money (and
uld have done with it even more so a few years
ck). But it wasn't about that. It was the principle.
vas the glory.

It was the desperate need to finally clutch those
ody rocks in her hand and shake them before
r husband's face and say, "See? See? I haven't
en mad all these years!"

Gareth had long since given up on the jewels.
ey probably didn't even exist, he told her. Some-
e had surely found them years earlier. They'd
ed in Clair House for *fifteen years*, for heaven's
ce. If Hyacinth was going to find them, she'd
ve located them by now, so why did she con-
ue to torture herself?

An excellent question.

Hyacinth gritted her teeth together as she
wled across the washroom floor for what was
ely the eight hundredth time in her life. She
ew all that. Lord help her, she knew it, but she
ldn't give up now. If she gave up now, what
. that say about the past fifteen years? Wasted
e? All of it, wasted time?

She couldn't bear the thought.

Plus, she really wasn't the sort to give up, was
? If she did, it would be so completely at odds
h everything she knew about herself. Would
t mean she was getting old?

She wasn't ready to get old. Perhaps that was
curse of being the youngest of eight children.
e was never quite ready to be old.

She leaned down even lower, planting her
ek against the cool tile of the floor so that she
ld peer under the tub. No old lady would do
, would she? No old lady would—

"Ah, there you are, Hyacinth."

It was Gareth, poking his head in. He did n look the least bit surprised to find his wife in su an odd position. But he did say, "It's been seve months since your last search, hasn't it?"

She looked up. "I thought of something."

"Something you hadn't already thought of?"

"Yes," she ground out, lying through her tee

"Checking behind the tile?" he queried polite

"Under the tub," she said reluctantly, movi herself into a seated position.

He blinked, shifting his gaze to the large cla footed tub. "Did you move that?" he asked, voice incredulous.

She nodded. It was amazing the sort of stren; one could summon when properly motivated.

He looked at her, then at the tub, then back aga "No," he said. "It's not possible. You didn't—"

"I did."

"You couldn't—"

"I could," she said, beginning to enjoy hers She didn't get to surprise him these days nearly often as she would have liked. "Just a few inch she admitted.

He looked back over at the tub.

"Maybe just one," she allowed.

For a moment she thought he would sim shrug his shoulders and leave her to her ende ors, but then he surprised her by saying, "Wo you like some help?"

It took her a few seconds to ascertain his me ing. "With the tub?" she asked.

He nodded, crossing the short distance to edge of its basin. "If you can move it an inch

urself," he said, "surely the two of us can triple
it. Or more."

Hyacinth rose to her feet. "I thought you didn't
lieve that the jewels are still here."

"I don't." He planted his hands on his hips as
surveyed the tub, looking for the best grip.
ut you do, and surely this must fall within the
lm of husbandly duties."

"Oh." Hyacinth swallowed, feeling a little guilty
thinking him so unsupportive. "Thank you."

He motioned for her to grab a spot on the op-
site side. "Did you lift?" he asked. "Or shove?"

"Shove. With my shoulder, actually." She
nted to a narrow spot between the tub and the
ll. "I wedged myself in there, then hooked my
ulder right under the lip, and—"

But Gareth was already holding his hand up to
p her. "No more," he said. "Don't tell me. I beg
ou."

"Why not?"

He looked at her for a long moment before an-
ering, "I don't really know. But I don't want the
ails."

"Very well." She went to the spot he'd indicated
d grabbed the lip. "Thank you, anyway."

"It's my—" He paused. "Well, it's not my plea-
e. But it's something."

he smiled to herself. He really was the best of
bands.

hree attempts later, however, it became ap-
ent that they were not going to budge the tub
hat manner. "We're going to have to use the
ge and shove method," Hyacinth announced.
s the only way."

Gareth gave her a resigned nod, and togeth
they squeezed into the narrow space between t
tub and the wall.

"I have to say," he said, bending his knees a
planting the soles of his boots against the wa
"this is all very undignified."

Hyacinth had nothing to say to that, so she j
grunted. He could interpret the noise any way
wished.

"This should really count for something,"
murmured.

"I beg your pardon?"

"This." He motioned with his hand, wh
could have meant just about anything, as :
wasn't quite certain whether he was referring
the wall, the floor, the tub, or some particle of d
floating through the air.

"As gestures go," he continued, "it's not
terribly grand, but I would think, should I e
forget your birthday, for example, that this ou
to go some distance in restoring myself to ye
good graces."

Hyacinth lifted a brow. "You couldn't do t
out of the goodness of your heart?"

He gave her a regal nod. "I could. And in fac
am. But one never knows when one—"

"Oh, for heaven's sake," Hyacinth mutter
"You do live to torture me, don't you?"

"It keeps the mind sharp," he said affably. "V
well. Shall we have at it?"

She nodded.

"On my count," he said, bracing his should
"One, two . . . *three.*"

With a heave and a groan, they both put al
their weight into the task, and the tub slid re

rantly across the floor. The noise was horrible,
 scraping and squeaking, and when Hyacinth
ɔked down she saw unattractive white marks
:ing across the tile. "Oh, dear," she murmured.
Gareth twisted around, his face creasing into
peeved expression when he saw that they'd
ɔved the tub a mere four inches. "I would have
ɔught we'd have made a bit more progress than
it," he said.

"It's heavy," she said, rather unnecessarily.
For a moment he did nothing but blink at the
all sliver of floor they'd uncovered. "What do
u plan to do now?" he asked.

Her mouth twisted slightly in a somewhat
mped expression. "I'm not sure," she admitted.
heck the floor, I imagine."

"You haven't done so already?" And then, when
 didn't answer in, oh, half a second, he added,
 the fifteen years since you moved here?"

"I've *felt* along the floor, of course," she said
ickly, since it was quite obvious that her arm
under the tub. "But it's just not the same as a
ual inspection, and—"

"Good luck," he cut in, rising to his feet.

"You're leaving?"

"Did you wish for me to stay?"

She hadn't expected him to stay, but now that
was here . . . "Yes," she said, surprised by her
n answer. "Why not?"

He smiled at her then, and the expression was
warm, and loving, and best of all, familiar. "I
ld buy you a diamond necklace," he said softly,
ing back down.

She reached out, placed her hand on his. "I
ɔw you could."

They sat in silence for a minute, and then Hy
cinth scooted herself closer to her husband, l
ting out a comfortable exhale as she eased agair
his side, letting her head rest on his shoulder. "I
you know why I love you?" she said softly.

His fingers laced through hers. "Why?"

"You could have bought me a necklace," s
said. "And you could have hidden it." She turn
her head so that she could kiss the curve of
neck. "Just so that I could have found it, you cou
have hidden it. But you didn't."

"I—"

"And don't say you never thought of it," s
said, turning back so that she was once aga
facing the wall, just a few inches away. But l
head was on his shoulder, and he was facing
same wall, and even though they weren't looki
at each other, their hands were still entwined, a
somehow the position was everything a marria
should be.

"Because I know you," she said, feeling a sm
growing inside. "I know you, and you know i
and it's just the loveliest thing."

He squeezed her hand, then kissed the top
her head. "If it's here, you'll find it."

She sighed. "Or die trying."

He chuckled.

"That shouldn't be funny," she informed hir

"But it is."

"I know."

"I love you," he said.

"I know."

And really, what more could she want?

…anwhile six feet away . . .

…abella was quite used to the antics of her par-
…ts. She accepted the fact that they tugged each
…her into dark corners with far more frequency
…n was seemly. She thought nothing of the fact
…t her mother was one of the most outspoken
…men in London or that her father was still so
…ndsome that her own friends sighed and stam-
…red in his presence. In fact, she rather enjoyed
…ng the daughter of such an unconventional
…ple. Oh, on the outside they were all that was
…per, to be sure, with only the nicest sort of rep-
…tion for high-spiritedness.

…But behind the closed doors of Clair House . . .

…bella knew that her friends were not encour-
…d to share their opinions as she was. Most of her
…nds were not even encouraged to have opinions.
…d certainly most young ladies of her acquain-
…ce had not been given the opportunity to study
…dern languages, nor to delay a social debut by
… year in order to travel on the continent.

…o, when all was said and done, Isabella
…ught herself quite fortunate as pertained to
… parents, and if that meant overlooking the oc-
…ional episodes of Not Acting One's Age—well,
…as worth it, and she'd learned to ignore much
…heir behavior.

…But when she'd sought out her mother this
…ernoon—to acquiesce on the matter of the
…ite gown with the dullish green trim, she
…ght add—and instead found her parents on the
…shroom floor pushing a *bathtub* . . .

Well, really, that was a bit much, even for t
St. Clairs.

And who would have faulted her for remaini
to eavesdrop?

Not her mother, Isabella decided as she lean
in. There was no way Hyacinth St. Clair wou
have done the right thing and walked away. O
couldn't live with the woman for nineteen yea
without learning *that*. And as for her father—we
Isabella rather thought he would have stayed
listen as well, especially as they were making
so *easy* for her, facing the wall as they were, w
their backs to the open doorway, indeed w
bathtub between them.

"What do you plan to do now?" her fatl
was asking, his voice laced with that particu
brand of amusement he seemed to reserve for l
mother.

"I don't know," her mother replied, soun
ing uncharacteristically . . . well, not *un*sure, l
certainly not as sure as usual. "Check the floo
imagine."

Check the floor? What on earth were they ta
ing about? Isabella leaned forward for a bet
listen, just in time to hear her father ask, "Y
haven't done so already? In the fifteen years si
you moved here?"

"I've felt along the floor," her mother retort
sounding much more like herself. "But it's not
same as a visual inspection, and—"

"Good luck," her father said, and then— •
no! He was leaving!

Isabella started to scramble, but then someth
must have happened because he sat back do•
She inched back toward the open doorway—

Carefully, carefully now, he could get up at any ~~m~~oment. Holding her breath, she leaned in, unable ~~to~~ take her eyes off of the backs of her parents' heads. "I could buy you a diamond necklace," her father ~~sai~~d.

A diamond necklace?

A diamond . . .

Fifteen years.

Moving a tub?

In a washroom?

Fifteen years.

Her mother had searched for fifteen years.

For a diamond necklace?

A diamond necklace.

A diamond . . .

Oh. Dear. God.

What was she going to do? What was she going ~~to~~ do? She knew what she must do, but good God, ~~how~~ was she supposed to do it?

And what could she say? What could she pos-~~sib~~ly say to—

Forget that for now. Forget it because her mother ~~wa~~s talking again and she was saying, "You could ~~ha~~ve bought me a necklace. And you could have ~~hi~~dden it. Just so that I could have found it, you ~~cou~~ld have hidden it. But you didn't."

There was so much love in her voice it made Isa-~~bel~~la's heart ache. And something about it seemed ~~to~~ sum up everything that her parents were. To ~~the~~mselves, to each other.

~~T~~o their children.

~~A~~nd suddenly the moment was too personal to ~~dwell~~ upon, even for her. She crept from the room, ~~the~~n ran to her own chamber, sagging into a chair ~~the instant~~ as soon as she closed the door.

Because she knew what her mother had be
looking for for so very long.

It was sitting in the bottom drawer of her des
And it was more than a necklace. It was an enti
parure—a necklace, bracelet, and ring, a veritat
shower of diamonds, each stone framed by tv
delicate aquamarines. Isabella had found the
when she was ten, hidden in a small cavity behii
one of the Turkish tiles in the nursery washroo
She *should* have said something about them. S
knew that she should. But she hadn't, and s
wasn't even sure why.

Maybe it was because she had found the
Maybe because she loved having a secret. May
it was because she hadn't thought they belonged
anyone else, or indeed, that anyone even knew
their existence. Certainly she hadn't thought tl
her mother had been searching for fifteen years.

Her mother!

Her mother was the last person anyone wou
imagine was keeping a secret. No one wou
think ill of Isabella for not thinking, when sh
discovered the diamonds— *Oh, surely my mot
must be looking for these and has chosen, for her o
devious reasons, not to tell me about it.*

Truly, when all was said and done, this v
really her mother's fault. If Hyacinth had *told I*
that she was searching for jewels, Isabella wo
immediately have confessed. Or if not imme
ately, then soon enough to satisfy everyone's c
science.

And now, speaking of consciences, hers v
beating a nasty little tattoo in her chest. It wa
most unpleasant—and unfamiliar—feeling.

It wasn't that Isabella was the soul of sw

ss and light, all sugary smiles and pious plati-
des. Heavens, no, she avoided such girls like
e plague. But by the same token, she rarely did
ything that was likely to make her feel guilty
terward, if only because perhaps—and only
rhaps—her notions of propriety and morality
ere ever-so-slightly flexible.

But now she had a lump in the pit of her stom-
h, a lump with peculiar talent for sending bile
her throat. Her hands were shaking, and she
t ill. Not feverish, not even aguey, just ill. With
rself.

Letting out an uneven breath, Isabella rose to her
t and crossed the room to her desk, a delicate
:oco piece her namesake great-grandmother had
ught over from Italy. She'd put the jewels there
ee years back, when she'd finally moved out
the top-floor nursery. She'd discovered a secret
npartment at the back of the bottom drawer. This
dn't particularly surprised her; there seemed to
an uncommon number of secret compartments
the furniture at Clair House, much of which had
n imported from Italy. But it *was* a boon and
her convenient, and so one day, when her family
s off at some *ton* function they had deemed
bella too young to attend, she'd sneaked back
to the nursery, retrieved the jewels from their
ling place behind the tile (which she had rather
ourcefully plastered back up), and moved them
er desk.

They'd remained there ever since, except for
odd occasion when Isabella took them out and
d them on, thinking how nice they would look
h her new gown, but *how* was she to explain
ir existence to her parents?

Now it seemed that no explanation would ha`
been necessary. Or perhaps just a different sort
explanation.

A very different sort.

Settling into the desk chair, Isabella lean`
down and retrieved the jewels from the secr`
compartment. They were still in the same cord`
velvet bag in which she'd found them. She s`
them free, letting them pool luxuriously on t`
desktop. She didn't know much about jewels, b`
surely these had to be of the finest quality. Th`
caught the sunlight with an indescribable mag`
almost as if each stone could somehow captu`
the light and then send it showering off in eve`
direction.

Isabella didn't like to think herself greedy`
materialistic, but in the presence of such treasu`
she understood how diamonds could make a m`
go a little bit mad. Or why women longed so d`
perately for one more piece, one more stone th`
was bigger, more finely cut than the last.

But these did not belong to her. Maybe th`
belonged to no one. But if anyone had a right`
them, it was most definitely her mother. Isabe`
didn't know how or why Hyacinth knew of th`
existence, but that didn't seem to matter. F`
mother had some sort of connection to the jew`
some sort of important knowledge. And if th`
belonged to anyone, they belonged to her.

Reluctantly, Isabella slid them back into the l`
and tightened the gold cord so that none of `
pieces could slip out. She knew what she had`
do now. She knew exactly what she had to do.

But after that . . .

The torture would be in the waiting.

ne year later

had been two months since Hyacinth had last
arched for the jewels, but Gareth was busy with
me sort of estate matter, she had no good books
read, and, well, she just felt . . . itchy.

This happened from time to time. She'd go
onths without searching, weeks and days with-
t even thinking about the diamonds, and then
mething would happen to remind her, to start
r wondering, and there she was again—obsessed
d frustrated, sneaking about the house so that no
e would realize what she was up to.

And the truth was, she was embarrassed. No
atter how one looked at it, she was at least a little
of a fool. Either the jewels were hidden away at
air House and she hadn't found them despite
teen years of searching, or they weren't hidden,
d she'd been chasing a delusion. She couldn't
en imagine how she might explain this to her
ildren, the servants surely thought her more
n a little bit mad (they'd all caught her snoop-
; about a washroom at one point or another),
d Gareth—well, he was sweet and he humored
r, but all the same, Hyacinth kept her activities
herself.

It was just better that way.

She'd chosen the nursery washroom for the af-
noon's search. Not for any particular reason, of
irse, but she'd finished her systematic search
all of the servants' washrooms (always an en-
vor that required some sensitivity and finesse),
d before that she'd done her own washroom,
d so the nursery seemed a good choice. After
s she'd move to some of the second floor wash-

rooms. George had moved into his own lodging and if there really was a merciful God, Isabel would be married before long, and Hyacin would not have to worry about anyone stumbling upon her as she poked, pried, and quite possib pulled the tiles from the walls.

Hyacinth put her hands on her hips and took deep breath as she surveyed the small room. She always liked it. The tiling was, or at least appeared to be, Turkish, and Hyacinth had to think that t Eastern peoples must enjoy far less sedate liv than the British, because the colors never failed put her in a splendid mood—all royal blues an dreamy aquas, with streaks of yellow and orang

Hyacinth had been to the south of Italy once, the beach. It looked exactly like this room, sun and sparkly in ways that the shores of Engla never seemed to achieve.

She squinted at the crown molding, looking cracks or indentations, then dropped to her han and knees for her usual inspection of the low tiles.

She didn't know what she hoped to find, wl might have suddenly made an appearance tl she hadn't detected during the other, oh, at leas dozen previous searches.

But she had to keep going. She had to becau she simply had no choice. There was somethi inside of her that just would not let go. And—

She stopped. Blinked. What was that?

Slowly, because she couldn't quite believe tl she'd found anything new—it had been ove decade since any of her searches had changed any measurable manner—she leaned in.

A crack.

It was small. It was faint. But it was definitely a
rack, running from the floor to the top of the first
le, about six inches up. It wasn't the sort of thing
ost people would notice, but Hyacinth wasn't
ost people, and sad as it sounded, she had prac-
cally made a career of inspecting washrooms.

Frustrated with her inability to get really close,
e shifted to her forearms and knees, then laid
r cheek against the floor. She poked the tile to
e right of the crack, then the left.

Nothing happened.

She stuck her fingernail at the edge of the crack,
d dug it in. A tiny piece of plaster lodged under
r nail.

A strange excitement began to build in her
est, squeezing, fluttering, rendering her almost
capable of drawing breath.

"Calm down," she whispered, even those words
ming out on a shake. She grabbed the little
isel she always took with her on her searches.
's probably nothing. It's probably—"

She jammed the chisel in the crack, surely with
re force than was necessary. And then she
isted. If one of the tiles was loose, the torque
uld cause it to press outward, and—

"Oh!"

The tile quite literally popped out, landing on
floor with a clatter. Behind it was a small cavity.

Hyacinth squeezed her eyes shut. She'd waited
r entire adult life for this moment, and now she
uldn't even bring herself to look. "Please," she
ispered. *"Please."*

She reached in.

"Please. Oh, please."

She touched something. Something soft. Lil velvet.

With shaking fingers she drew it out. It was little bag, held together with a soft, silky cord.

Hyacinth straightened slowly, crossing her le; so that she was sitting Indian style. She slid o finger inside the bag, widening the mouth, whic had been pulled tight.

And then, with her right hand, she upended sliding the contents into her left.

Oh my G—

"Gareth!" she shrieked. "Gareth!"

"I did it," she whispered, gazing down at t pool of jewels now spilling from her left hand. did it."

And then she bellowed it.

"I DID IT!!!!"

She looped the necklace around her neck, st clutching the bracelet and ring in her hand.

"I did it, I did it, I did it." She was singing now, hopping up and down, almost dancir almost crying. "I did it!"

"Hyacinth!" It was Gareth, out of breath fro taking four flights of stairs two steps at a time.

She looked at him, and she could swear s could feel her eyes shining. "I did it!" She laughe almost crazily. "I did it!"

For a moment he could do nothing but sta His face grew slack, and Hyacinth thought might actually lose his footing.

"I did it," she said again. "I did it."

And then he took her hand, took the ring, a slipped it onto her finger. "So you did," he sa leaning down to kiss her knuckles. "So you dic

Meanwhile, one floor down . . .

"*Gareth!*"

Isabella looked up from the book she was reading, glancing toward the ceiling. Her bedchamber was directly below the nursery, rather in line with the washroom, actually.

"*I did it!*"

Isabella turned back to her book.

And she smiled.

Meet the Bridgerton family ...

❧❧

The Bridgertons are by far the most prolific family in the upper echelons of society. Such industriousness on the part of the viscountess and the late viscount is commendable, although one can find only banality in their choice of names for their children. Anthony, Benedict, Colin, Daphne, Eloise, Francesca, Gregory, and Hyacinth (orderliness is, of course, beneficial in all things, but one would think that intelligent parents would be able to keep their children straight without needing to alphabetize their names).

It has been said that Lady Bridgerton's dearest goal is to see all of her offspring happily married, but truly, one can only wonder if this is an impossible feat. Eight children? Eight happy marriages? It boggles the mind.

LADY WHISTLEDOWN'S SOCIETY PAPERS,
SUMMER 1813

The Duke and I

❧❧

WHO: Daphne Bridgerton and the Duke of
         Hastings.
WHAT: A sham courtship.
WHERE: London, of course. Where else could
         one pull off such a thing?
WHY: They each have their reasons, neither
         of which includes falling in love . . .

The Viscount Who Loved Me

The season has opened for the year of 1814, and there is little reason to hope that we will see any noticeable change from 1813. The ranks of society are once again filled with Ambitious Mamas, whose only aim is to see their Darling Daughters married off to Determined Bachelors. Discussion amongst the Mamas fingers Viscount Bridgerton as this year's most eligible catch, and indeed, if the poor man's hair looks ruffled and windblown, it is because he cannot go anywhere without some young miss batting her eyelashes with such vigor and speed as to create a breeze of hurricane force. Perhaps the only young lady not interested in Bridgerton is Miss Katharine Sheffield, and in fact, her demeanor toward the viscount occasionally borders on the hostile.

And that is why, Dear Reader, This Author feels that a match between Bridgerton and Miss Sheffield would be just the thing to enliven an otherwise ordinary season.

LADY WHISTLEDOWN'S SOCIETY PAPERS, 13 APRIL 1814

An Offer From a Gentleman

The 1815 season is well under way, and while one
would think that all talk would be of Wellington and
Waterloo, in truth, there is little change from the conversations of 1814, which centered around that most
eternal of society topics—marriage.

As usual, the matrimonial hopes among the debutante set center upon the Bridgerton family, most
specifically the eldest of the available brothers,
Benedict. He might not possess a title, but his handsome face, pleasing form, and heavy purse appear to
have made up for that lack handily. Indeed, This
Author has heard, on more than one occasion, an
Ambitious Mama saying of her daughter: "She'll
marry a duke . . . or a Bridgerton."

For his part, Mr. Bridgerton seems most uninter-
ested in the young ladies who frequent society events.
He attends almost every party, yet he does nothing
but watch the doors, presumably waiting for some
special person.

Perhaps . . .

A potential bride?

LADY WHISTLEDOWN'S SOCIETY PAPERS, 12 JULY 1815

Romancing Mister Bridgerton

❧❧

April is nearly upon us, and with it a new social season here in London. Ambitious Mamas can be found at dress-shops all across town with their Darling Debutantes, eager to purchase that one magical evening gown that they simply know will mean the difference between marriage and spinsterhood.

As for their prey—the Determined Bachelors—Mr. Colin Bridgerton once again tops the list of desirable husbands, even though he is not yet back from his recent trip abroad. He has no title, that is true, but he is in abundant possession of looks, fortune, and, as anyone who has ever spent even a minute in London knows, charm.

But Mr. Bridgerton has reached the somewhat advanced age of three-and-thirty without ever showing an interest in any particular young lady, and there is little reason to anticipate that 1824 will be any different from 1823 in this respect.

Perhaps the Darling Debutantes—and perhaps more importantly their Ambitious Mamas—would do well to look elsewhere. If Mr. Bridgerton is looking for a wife, he hides that desire well.

On the other hand, is that not just the sort of challenge a debutante likes best?

LADY WHISTLEDOWN'S SOCIETY PAPERS

To Sir Phillip, With Love

. . I know you say I shall someday like boys, but I say never! NEVER!!! With three exclamation points!!!

> —from Eloise Bridgerton to her mother,
> shoved under Violet Bridgerton's door
> during Eloise's eighth year

. . I never dreamed that a season could be so exciting! The men are so handsome and charming. I know I shall fall in love straightaway. How could I not?

> —from Eloise Bridgerton to her brother Colin,
> upon the occasion of her London debut

. . I am quite certain I shall never marry. If there was someone out there for me, don't you think I should have found him by now?

> —from Eloise Bridgerton to her
> dear friend Penelope Featherington,
> during her sixth season as a debutante

. . this is my last chance. I am grabbing destiny with both my hands and throwing caution to the wind. Sir Phillip, please, *please*, be all that I have imagined you to be. Because if you are the man your letters portray you to be, I think I could love you. And if you felt the same . . .

> —from Eloise Bridgerton, jotted on a scrap of paper
> on her way to meet Sir Phillip Crane
> for the very first time

When He Was Wicked

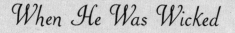

WHAT DOES IT MEAN TO BE WICKED?

*F*or Michael Stirling, it was a hidden love, an insatiable longing for the one woman who could never be his.

WHAT DOES IT MEAN TO BE WANTON?

*F*or Francesca Bridgerton, it started with a single kiss, placed on her lips by the one man she never thought she'd desire.

WHAT HAPPENS WHEN THERE ARE NO MORE SECRETS?

*F*ind out in Julia Quinn's most breathtaking and passionate romance yet . . .

It's In His Kiss

Our Cast of Characters

Hyacinth Bridgerton: The youngest of the famed Bridgerton siblings, she's a little too smart, a little too outspoken, and certainly not your average romance heroine. She's also, much to her dismay, falling in love with . . .

Gareth St. Clair: There are some men in London with wicked reputations, and there are others who are handsome as sin. But Gareth is the only one who manages to combine the two with such devilish success. He'd be a complete rogue, if not for . . .

Lady Danbury: Grandmother to Gareth, mentor to Hyacinth, she has an opinion on everything, especially love and marriage. And she'd like nothing better than to see Gareth and Hyacinth joined in holy matrimony. Luckily, she's to have help from . . .

One meddling mother, one overprotective brother, one very bad string quartet, one (thankfully fictional) mad baron, and of course, let us not forget the shepherdess, the unicorn, and Henry the Eighth.

Join them all in the most memorable love story of the year . . .

On the Way to the Wedding

In which:

Firstly, Gregory Bridgerton falls in love with the wrong woman, and

Secondly, she falls in love with someone else, but

Thirdly, Lucy Abernathy decides to meddle; however,

Fourthly, she falls in love with Gregory, which is highly inconvenient because

Fifthly, she is practically engaged to Lord Haselby, but

Sixthly, Gregory falls in love with Lucy.

Which leaves everyone in a bit of a pickle.

Watch them all find their happy endings in:

The stunning conclusion
to the Bridgerton series
Available now

THE SMYTHE-SMITH QUARTET BY
#1 *NEW YORK TIMES*
BESTSELLING AUTHOR

JUST LIKE HEAVEN
978-0-06-149190-0

ria Smythe-Smith is to play the violin (badly) in the annual
ale performed by the Smythe-Smith quartet. But first she's
nined to marry by the end of the season. When her advances
urned, can Marcus Holroyd, her brother Daniel's best
, swoop in and steal her heart in time for the musicale?

A NIGHT LIKE THIS
978-0-06-207290-0

Wynter is not who she says she is, but she's managing quite
a governess to three highborn young ladies. Daniel Smythe-
might be in mortal danger, but that's not going to stop the
earl from falling in love. And when he spies a mysterious
1 at his family's annual musicale, he vows to pursue her.

THE SUM OF ALL KISSES
978-0-06-207292-4

Prentice has never had patience for dramatic females,
ady Sarah Pleinsworth has never been acquainted with
rds *shy* or *retiring*. Besides, a reckless duel has left Hugh
ruined leg, and now he could never court a woman like
Sarah, much less dream of marrying her.

SECRETS OF SIR RICHARD KENWORTHY
978-0-06-207294-8

hard Kenworthy has less than a month to find a bride, and
e sees Iris Smythe-Smith hiding behind her cello at her
s infamous musicale, he thinks he might have struck gold.
used to blending into the background, so when Richard
courts her, she can't quite believe it's true.

Don't miss the Bridgerton 2nd Epilogues
where you get the story *after* the st...

Because when you're a Bridgerton, Happ...
Ever After is a whole lot of fun.

Available as a collection in
The Bridgertons: Happily Ever After,
wherever books are sold.

Visit **www.juliaquinn.com** for Bridgerton FAQs
and the interactive Bridgerton family tree.

juliaquinn.com

#1 *New York Times* Bestselling Author

Julia Quinn

The Secret Diaries of Miss Miranda Cheev

978-0-06-123083-7

When Miranda Cheever was ten, Nigel Bevelstoke, the
dashing Viscount Turner, kissed her hand and promised h
one day she would be as beautiful as she was already sma
And even at ten, Miranda knew she would love him foreve

The Lost Duke of Wyndham

978-0-06-087610-4

Grace Eversleigh has spent the last five years toiling as the
companion to the dowager Duchess of Wyndham. It is a
thankless job...until Jack Audley, the long-lost son of the
House of Wyndham, lands in her life, all rakish smiles
and debonair charm.

Mr. Cavendish, I Presume

978-0-06-087611-1

A mere six months old when she's contractually engaged
to Thomas Cavendish, the Duke of Wyndham, Amelia
Willoughby has spent her life waiting to be married. But the
worlds are rocked by the arrival of his long-lost cousin, wh
may be the true Duke of Wyndham...and Amelia's intende

What Happens In London

978-0-06-149188-7

When Olivia Bevelstoke is told her new neighbor may hav
killed his fiancée, she doesn't believe it, but, still, how can
help spying on him, just to be sure? She stakes out a spot n
her bedroom window and discovers a most intriguing ma
who is definitely up to something...